ALONE ON THE SHIELD

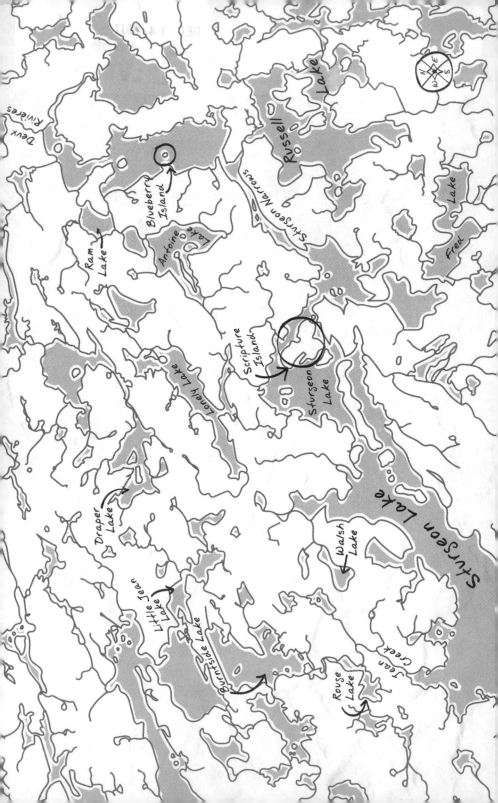

ALONE ON THE SHIELD

A NOVEL

KIRK LANDERS

ACADEMY

CHICAGO

Copyright © 2018 by Kirk Landers
All rights reserved
Published by Academy Chicago Publishers
An imprint of Chicago Review Press Incorporated
814 North Franklin Street
Chicago, Illinois 60610
ISBN 978-1-61373-991-4

Library of Congress Cataloging-in-Publication Data
Names: Landers, Kirk, author.
Title: Alone on the Shield: a novel / Kirk Landers.
Description: Chicago, Illinois: Chicago Review Press, 2018.
Identifiers: LCCN 2017001440 (print) | LCCN 2017022652
    (ebook) | ISBN 9781613739921 (pdf) | ISBN 9781613739945
    (epub) | ISBN 9781613739938 (kindle) | ISBN 9781613739914
    (paperback)
Subjects: LCSH: Man-woman relationships—Canada—Fiction.
    | Baby boom generation—Fiction. | Romance fiction. | BISAC:
    FICTION / General.
Classification: LCC PS3612.A547744 (ebook) | LCC PS3612.
    A547744 A46 2018 (print) | DDC 813/.6–dc23
LC record available at https://lccn. loc.gov/2017001440

Cover design: Joan Sommers
Cover photo: Kennedy707 Photography/Moment Collection/Getty Images
    Royalty-Free
Typesetting: Nord Compo
Map illustration: Lindsey Cleworth Schauer

Printed in the United States of America
5 4 3 2 1

To Catherine, with a C
Saver of lives, soother of souls

For eons, there was only water. Until the volcanoes shot fire from the belly of the earth, stacking rocks on rocks until there was land, then more rocks until there were mountains.

In time, the mountains wore down, turned to dust and sand and dirt in which things would grow.

Then came the ice. And it came again. It scrubbed away the flotsam and jetsam of the ages and epochs and eras and eons and pushed it south to make fertile plains and prairies where things would grow and life would prosper.

All that remained was the ancient bedrock, gashed and scarred as if ravaged by the claws of an apocalyptic bear, and every slash and cut became a bottomless lake filled with water as cold as ice. When it was done, it was a place of terrible beauty protected from hungry life-forms by cruel seasons and an absence of plenty.

It would be called the Canadian Shield and it would be home to the desperate and the pure.

1

Pender couldn't get his mind back into his body. He could see himself in profile, striding through the office bay, but he couldn't feel his feet touching the floor and he couldn't hear anything but the vague whistle in his ears, the tinnitus that had been there from the first week of rifle training long, long ago. The cubicle farm floated in and out of focus, like a dream. His scalp tingled as if his hair was standing on end.

He recognized it. An adrenaline surge, like working a jungle trail in pitch darkness, hoping to hear Charlie before he heard you.

Except this walk was in daylight, in the full upright position, and when he got to the end of the hall, he was going to get shot. Not with a bullet. With a termination notice.

The most worthless, miserable, stupidest empty suit in the Global Media executive corps was finally getting his chance to fire Pender.

Charles Jamison Blue pretended to scrutinize something on his computer when his assistant announced Pender's arrival. He signaled with one hand that he was busy, like a lord instructing a peasant to remain standing and try not to stink.

Pender waved back like a guy who couldn't give a shit and took a chair at Charles Jamison Blue's conference table. From the table you were supposed to gaze in wonder at his wall of honors, which included his degrees and awards and, in the center of it all, a framed photo of Blue shaking hands with President Reagan. But Pender didn't look at the wall of honor. He looked out the window. This year, 2008, had been rough. The divorce. The economy going up in smoke. Two wars being waged. The publishing business in a death spiral. The world in chaos.

"Have a seat, Pender," Blue murmured as he punched his keyboard. He waited a moment before turning to face Pender. It was one of his games. Pender was supposed to think Blue didn't see him sit without permission. In Vietnam you'd just shove a frag up the ass of an idiot like Blue and be done with it, but here in civilization you had to let them run things, even when they ran them into the ground. Everything Blue knew about publishing was on a spreadsheet, and his only deeply held belief was that making his budget numbers every quarter would keep him highly paid and employable, which was all that mattered. Ass-kissing frauds like Blue were devouring American businesses from within, like giant tapeworms passing through an organism without vision or thought, just a relentless appetite.

Blue finally turned to Pender and smiled widely. He was wearing a hundred-dollar pinstripe shirt and his Ivy League tie, a striper in the colors that other Ivy Leaguers would recognize, a sartorial version of the secret handshake for the snobbery elite. His Savile Row suit coat hung like a precious tapestry on the back of his door. Pender laughed. Despite a thousand dollars' worth of clothing and a two-hundred-thousand-dollar education, Blue was just a fat, paste-eating kid who had become a fat, incompetent man.

"I'm sure you know why we're here." Blue said it like a teacher preparing to discipline a miscreant pupil.

"I do. No need for speeches. Just give me the paperwork." Pender said it without looking at Blue. The man's arrogance and stupidity had always brought out the worst in Pender, and today there was a volcano brewing in Pender's head. Today, his worst wouldn't just be an insulting remark or an untimely smirk. Today, what he'd really like to do is push Blue's sneering face through the glass top of his completely empty desk.

"It didn't have to be like this, Pender."

"I agree. You could have gone into some other field, and all these magazines would still be healthy."

"I didn't cause the recession. And I tried to save you from yourself."

Pender shook his head. "For five years you've been cutting pages and cutting people and raising rates. What did you think was going to happen?"

"Just following company policy. If you'd done the same thing we might still have a place for you."

Pender focused on Blue's immaculate desk to keep his anger at bay. He had defied Blue's brainless edicts from the start, often going over his head in the company to do so, more often just ignoring him. It kept the magazine strong, which made their relationship even worse.

"Anyway," Pender said, "who tells me about health insurance and severance pay?"

"You can pick up a severance packet in HR when you leave. We'll mail you whatever else. Don't expect much in severance, though."

"Twenty-five years doesn't get much love anymore, huh?"

"The old days are long gone, Pender. You never understood that."

"I understood more than you think. What I misunderstood was, I thought it was about profits. It's not. It's about something even baser, though I'm still not sure what that is."

Blue struck his Ivy League MBA pose, straightening his back, sucking in his gut a little, holding his head erect so he could look down his nose at Pender like a learned scholar patiently coaxing intelligence from a naive student. "It *is* about profit, but not the glacial growth you old guys look for. These magazines? Yesterday's news. They'll never operate at more than a ten or fifteen percent margin ever again. Time to move to some other field. Information technology. Digital communications. It's a new world, and you aren't part of it."

Pender stirred. "I find honor in that."

"Honor!" Blue said the word with contempt. "Business isn't about honor. It's about winners and losers. You're a loser."

He stood. It was an imperious gesture to a subordinate that the meeting was over. Pender slouched in his chair and crossed one leg over the other.

"So, are you going to the bathroom or have I been fired?" Pender asked.

"Nothing left but the handshake," said Blue. He tried to keep his voice nonchalant, but Pender's act was irritating him.

Pender uncoiled his six-foot frame and stood in front of Blue. Neither of them offered a handshake or tried to hide the contempt he had for the other. "I wish I could say it was a pleasure working with you," said Blue. "But it wasn't. You are an arrogant, egotistical, self-righteous editor, and you've been earning this termination from the time I met you."

"Well, thank you," said Pender. "I can only hope I irritated you as much as you have me. It's a lot to hope for, but I do."

"There you go again. Do you even understand what you've done to yourself? Your wife left you. You've got no job. You're sixty years old in an economy where forty is ancient. You'll never work in magazine publishing again. You won't be trotting off to Paris to speak. No more interviews on CNN. You've won your last award. You've chaired your last meeting. All that's left of your life is an empty house. Get it, Pender? You're dead."

Blue put his hands on his hips and rolled on the balls of his feet, a corporate warrior's victory dance. Pender stared at him with an expression that began as curiosity and morphed into an intensity that made the executive uncomfortable. That was the very moment that it came crashing into Pender's head with a force that pushed out all other thought. That was when he realized everything he had done, everything he had believed in, everything he had wished for had been truly and completely corrupted in the space of his adult life. This company was a lie. America was a lie. He was a lie. The truth was Charles Jamison Blue, standing in front of him like a braying jackass. Rage clouded Pender's vision.

"You can pick up your separation kit in HR," Blue said. "Go on, now. We're done here."

As the last syllable evaporated into the ether, months of suppressed rage burst from Pender's mind to his fist and he hit the man in his plentiful gut. It was a short, wicked left hook, thrown with the unleashed fury of an enraged genie escaping at last from a bottle. Pender's fist drove deep into Blue's diaphragm, forcing the air from his lungs. The starched impresario gasped and doubled over. Tears came to his eyes. He fell ass-first onto his chair, his lips forming a fish face as he tried to feed air into his lungs. When he could finally breathe, Blue wept tears of frustration and anger.

Pender watched, mesmerized. He couldn't believe what he had done. He was astonished to see a grown man cry from a single punch. He could still feel his fist driving into the fat man's middle, could feel the flesh give way like it was made of pillows and water balloons. Dimly he understood this was certainly the end of his career. This was the end of everything.

He tried to get his mind and body working again, tried to shake off the numbing reality of the situation, tried to think of something positive that could come of this.

"At least I'll never have to take shit from a brainless twit like you." He was looking at Blue, but he was saying it mostly to himself. It wasn't much of a reward for the sacrifice of a career of journalistic achievement and industry celebrity. *Menu* was a perennial award winner in the business magazine industry, and Pender, its celebrated chief editor, had become an industry icon, one of the most sought-after speakers for events in the restaurant and hospitality business, and a go-to expert for general media reporters working on stories in the field. He had seen the world from first-class airline seats and five-star hotels, interviewed the greatest chefs on every continent, been quoted by television and newspaper reporters. And now, it was over. Just like that.

Pender straightened up and left Blue's office. He picked up a few personal belongings in his own office and left the building without stopping at HR. Strong winds caught the exit door and banged it shut behind him as if a giant iron gate had closed. Pender imagined a massive deadbolt sliding into place, banning him to a raw wasteland where he would wander alone for the rest of his days.

"I bet you're glad this is our last appointment, eh, Doc?"

Pender smiled as he said it, but there was a sardonic veneer to his tone, like always. The wiry middle-aged man across the coffee table from him shifted uncomfortably.

"I'm not a doctor. I'm a licensed social worker. Why should I be glad this is our last appointment?" The therapist stayed with the standard script, which bugged Pender. Answer questions with questions, say nothing definitive, bill an hour for forty minutes of work. Accomplish absolutely goddamn nothing.

"You always seem relieved to see me go." Pender didn't look angry when he said it, but there was always that door, waiting to swing open.

"I had hoped we would have made more progress by this point," the therapist admitted.

"You're too modest. It's been a couple months and I haven't hit anyone. It's a miracle. I've been rehabilitated."

"I don't appreciate your sarcasm. You have an anger problem. You're here because you hit your boss. You said yourself you're so angry you have trouble sleeping at night."

"Actually, it was my boss's boss, and he wasn't a real person so much as a horse's ass who thinks it's cool to shit and eat from the same hole."

The counselor winced. "No matter what you think of someone, you can't go around hitting them."

"That's my point," said Pender. "I don't hit people anymore. Even people like Little Boy Blue who really should get popped now and then. I've just said no. You've cured me. Thank you. Thank you."

The therapist sighed. "Your sarcasm isn't constructive. If my report says you're a danger to others, you could face serious charges. You have a lot to lose."

"Come on, we both know that's not true." Pender paused and looked about the small office, the stuffed book shelves, the placid wall art, the soft light fading to shadows at the perimeter. The therapist waited for him to speak, all technique, all the time. It pissed him off.

"We're just here so the company can say they did something if Blue decides to sue," Pender said. "You agreed to eight sessions with me because it's easy money. Eight sessions isn't enough to establish how regular my bowel movements are, let alone how psychotic I may or may not be. I'm here because I have nothing better to do."

"You may face assault and battery charges," said the therapist.

Pender smiled his sarcastic smile again. "Maybe I pay a fine, do community service, apologize. C'mon, it wasn't the crime of the century. The crime of the century was what Chuckie and the other stiffs did to that company."

"Wise up. If they press charges, you won't ever get another job in your chosen field."

"I'm not going to get another job in my field anyway. That's one thing Blue had right. I'm sixty years old and the magazine industry is dead. It's 2008. The financial crisis? Maybe you've heard about it? No one hires experience anymore. It's all about saving money. But don't worry, I'm not going to hit anyone. I shouldn't have hit Blue, as much as he deserved it. As good as it felt. I shouldn't have. I knew it right away."

"Yet you still got into a set-to with those canoeists." The counselor leafed through his notes. "Yes, just before our first session. You were in a canoe race and they bumped into you. You tracked them down and . . . same thing, yes? You smashed their paddles and begged them to hit you. It's a pattern."

"They didn't just bump into me. They capsized me and left me upside down in the river. They laughed about it. Isn't that in your notes? What kind of notes do you take? To qualify as a rational man in your estimation, must I accept their assault and suck on it?"

"There were alternatives to violence. You could've registered a complaint with the police or with the race managers."

"Come on. I say this, they say that, the cops don't know who's telling the truth. The punks walk away laughing. My way, they'll think twice before they ram another canoeist. Society is better for what I did."

"Mr. Pender, it seems that whatever you do is fine. It's the world that's wrong."

"How am I wrong here? Someone bullies you and you have to take it? So Blue can taunt me to my face and get away with it because if I respond, I'm wrong? Do I complain to HR? The company just fired me. HR doesn't care unless I have grounds for a lawsuit. So I'm supposed to just take it, like a good little office boy, and he does it again to the next guy?"

Pender took a breath and tried to relax.

"Same with the goddamn canoeists. They knocked me over and laughed about it because they've always gotten away with it, thanks to people like you. The only thing that's illegal in our society is standing up for yourself when these petty little shits work the cracks in the system."

"How long have you felt like this?"

"Since I came home from Vietnam to a country run by a bunch of phony, draft-dodging cowards." Pender shook his head. "Goddamn. I thought everyone was there, but most people were back here, getting the good jobs, partying, getting laid."

"That's a long time to carry a grudge."

Pender shrugged. "Most of the time you bury it. Just put it in a dark corner of your mind and get on with things."

"What's different now?"

Pender thought awhile and smiled ironically. "The anger's all that's left. All the things I focused on all these years are gone. My career. My wife. My daughter's on her own. I have money in the bank, but in every other way, I'm bankrupt."

Bewilderment swept over Pender's face. "Where did it go?"

The therapist's eyebrows arched in question. "You have money and freedom. How bad can it be?"

"I'm sixty years old, and I don't have a reason to get up in the morning. And when I get up, I have no place to go."

"Have you considered taking up a hobby or volunteering? Or maybe traveling?"

Pender shrugged. "I'm planning a trip. But it's not like I have a place I'd rather be. It's that I can't stand it where I am."

The therapist stared at him for a long moment. "Where are you going?" he said finally.

"I'm heading up to Ontario. I'm going to spend a month or so in a canoe wilderness called Quetico."

"And after that?"

"Who knows?" said Pender. "I won't be coming back here. Maybe I'll take a train to Prince Edward Island, poke around 'til I get bored or someone runs me out of town. I could go on to Paris. I think I'd look good in a beret, sipping coffee at a sidewalk table, maybe faking like I'm an artist up on Montmartre. What do you think?"

"Canoeing by yourself sounds dangerous. Aren't there bears and wolves up there?"

"You never see the wolves, and the bears are mostly shy, like big dogs. I've been soloing up there for years. This is just a longer stretch than usual. I'll have one break in the monotony. I'll be meeting an old girlfriend for a few days. I haven't seen her in forty years."

"A romantic liaison?"

"No. I'm looking in on some old friends on this trip. When I found out Annette was up in Atikokan, I added her to the list. She agreed, so we're meeting at her favorite island."

"Forty years is a long time," said the therapist. "I'm surprised you still remembered her."

Pender glanced away, focusing on a book-lined wall. "I did my best to forget her, but there were a lot of dark nights in Vietnam, sitting in the rain, getting your mind off the bugs and the jungle rot. You had to see with your eyes and hear with your ears, but you needed to do something with your mind so you wouldn't go crazy. My mind kept coming back to her."

"What happened between you?"

Pender thought for a moment. "Ah, stupid mistake. Not the only one in my life. It'll be nice to see her."

"Does she know about your anger issues?"

"Sure. We've been exchanging e-mails for a while, and I don't keep secrets. But she knows I'm no threat to her."

"Why is that?"

"She's not a bully."

The therapist's timer chimed softly, signaling the end of the session.

"Mr. Pender," said the therapist, "whatever you think of me or my motives for seeing you, I assure you that you are in need of further therapy. Eight sessions aren't enough to get into your issues, but if you were staying with me, we'd explore the possibility that you are suffering from the delayed onset of posttraumatic stress disorder."

"My war was four decades ago."

"Don't kid yourself. It happens. And beyond that, war isn't the only condition that can cause PTSD. Whatever the cause, you have deep-seated anger issues. You have a tendency to blow up at others, and I worry that you may be a danger to yourself. You need counseling."

"I don't believe in God, and I don't believe in head-shrinking. How about you tell the company I'm not going to hurt anyone, and I'll make my way swiftly out of the country."

The therapist shook his head. "I'll tell your former employer we've gone as far as we can and that I've recommended further therapy and you have resolved to avoid physical confrontations in the future."

The therapist considered him for a moment, like he had more to say. Pender waited.

"You can't walk away from everything," the therapist said finally. "It's all part of you. You need to stay connected."

"To what?"

"Your daughter, for example. You should reach out to her."

"She barely knows I exist. She'll be fine with me disappearing. It'll save her the Christmas card and birthday phone call."

"From what you've told me, I'd say she may be trying to get your attention. It happens that way sometimes with kids and parents. She may want you to show you love her. If you can't see her before you go, at least write to her. Help her understand why you're doing what you're doing."

Pender stared at the therapist, silent, like he'd just seen the earth move and was trying to understand it.

"Mr. Pender?" the therapist asked gently.

Pender focused on him and smiled self-consciously. "Sorry. You're right. Maybe I'll keep a journal for her. I'll tell her about Quetico and why wilderness matters. And I'll tell her who I am, really."

"I hope she reads it."

Pender shrugged indifferently. His moment of introspection had passed. "Maybe she will, maybe she won't. I'll write it and take what comes."

"Good luck, Mr. Pender. I hope you find some kind of inner peace someday."

Pender stood and offered a handshake to the therapist. "I wonder who I'd be if I had inner peace."

Pender drove directly to his shell of an apartment. His footsteps raised echoes as he entered the barren dwelling. It was his divorce abode, a temporary residence to give him shelter while he decided where to live next. The living room contained an old couch, a table and a chair, and, incongruously, a sleek solo canoe, a wilderness tripper in uncoated Kevlar, light and fast, more than seventeen feet long, and bearing the scratches and scars of repeated encounters with rocky shores and submerged shoals. His sleeping bag and pad lay in the middle of the bedroom floor, along with a duffel bag and two large voyageur packs filled with all his earthly possessions except the scarred laptop on the table.

He sat at the table and stared into space. He tried to visualize his life from now on, but the only thing left other than the routine minutiae was the trip to Quetico. At least that event would be different this time. No deadlines. And a date with his college girlfriend. It had seemed like such a great idea when they set it up, but as he pondered it now, he knew it would be another disappointment. They had nothing in common but a forty-year-old memory and a passion for paddling alone into the Quetico wilderness. Still, it wasn't like he had anything else to do.

He fired up the computer, logged on to his e-mail account, and wrote a message to Annette Blain, the former Annette DuBose, the first love of his life who turned out to own a business on the edge of Quetico, the second love of his life.

"Leaving in the morning. See you on the island August 10. —Pender."

He shut down the computer and surveyed the stark confines around him. It was so like the prison of his life. He sighed. Empty. Meaningless. How could the future be any worse?

2

Annette crossed her arms as soon as he started talking. The man had manic eyes, and his body was as tense as a drawn hunting bow.

"I want to make you rich," he said. He smiled wide, lips thin and tight. There was no sincerity in his words and something more like menace in his body language. This was a canned sales pitch that worked with people who could be overpowered by his dominance. Like a television preacher who could convert the weak into paying parishioners, and who ignored everyone else because the converts were all that mattered.

Annette crossed her legs and raised her eyebrows skeptically.

"I'm going to make you a great offer for your cabins. More than you ever dreamed you'd get."

"They're not for sale," said Annette. "I would have saved us both some time if I'd known that's what you wanted."

"Hear me out, Ms. Blain," he said. Smooth, unruffled, like he knew she was going to say that. "This is perfect for both of us. I need an office for my fly-in cabin business, and I need

a place to put up clients before and after their trips. This is
the perfect place." He said it like she was supposed to clap
and be glad. She didn't and she wasn't.

The man got more intense, leaning across the table a little.
"You don't need the cabins anymore. You run the biggest
outfitting business in northwest Ontario. You've arrived! Sell
the cabins to me, and you can live in town and concentrate
on the canoe business. And you'll have hundreds of thousands
of dollars in the bank just waiting for when you want to head
for Florida."

"Florida is my idea of hell," said Annette. "The cabins aren't
for sale."

"You don't want to be rich?" The man tried to grin, but
his face formed something more like a leering grimace.

"How rich were you going to make me, Mr. . . ." Annette's
question tapered off as she tried to remember his name.

"Williams. Dwight Williams." He wasn't perturbed at all
and didn't pause even to take a breath. "I have a cashier's
check right here for three hundred thousand Canadian dollars."

"I'm supposed to jump up and down at that price?" Annette
was deliberately incredulous.

"That's a fair offer!" Williams insisted.

"I could get that just by making a phone call, probably a
lot more."

"Not with the recession in the U.S.," said Williams. "I did
my research. Three hundred thousand is what the place is
worth. It's ten times what you paid for it."

Annette stood. "When I choose to sell, it will be for more
than three hundred thousand. If I get rich from selling, it
won't be because of the buyer; it will be because of what
I've created. The cabins aren't for sale."

Williams leaned across the table, his face inches from hers, flushed with anger. "Name your price," he hissed. It was a challenge.

Annette stood her ground and locked eyes with him. "The cabins aren't for sale. Our business is done."

"You're selling to the Gilberts, aren't you?" He said it like an accusation, like a man who found out his wife was cheating on him.

"My cabins are my business. Please leave."

"You don't understand. I need this property." His voice was loud now, his face red. "I'm trying to be nice about it."

"You have failed, Mr. Williams. Leave. Leave now."

As Annette spoke, her daughter stepped into the kitchen, a shotgun in hand.

"What are you going to do with that, Missy?" Williams laughed. "You gonna shoot me?"

"She won't have to," said Annette. "You're leaving right now." Her voice was calm.

Williams looked from one woman to the other and shrugged. "Didn't mean to ruffle feathers, ladies. Just trying to make a deal."

Annette gestured to the door and followed him out.

"There are three hotels in town that would be glad to have your clients' business," said Annette. "And there are several storefronts available for your office. But I'd advise you to sell your cabins and do something else, somewhere else. Your act won't play here."

"Oh really?" Sarcasm dripped from Williams's voice.

Annette nodded. "Don't be fooled by how friendly everyone is. You get in their faces and you'll have real trouble. I'm the only person in Atikokan who'd let you walk out of here with your balls still attached to your body."

Williams smiled, like he wasn't impressed, and got in his car. "I'll keep it in mind," he said, and then drove off, his tires spitting gravel and dirt in his wake.

Christy was just getting off the phone when Annette walked back to the door.

"Sorry about the noise, Christy. Were you going to shoot him?"

"I could shoot a bear, but I'm not sure I could have shot that man."

"I'm glad you didn't. Next time just call a neighbor."

"I called the Gilberts. I just called back and told them the crisis had passed. They want to hear about it tonight. You guys have a meeting?"

Annette nodded. The Gilberts were going to offer to buy her out. What was it about the financial crisis that made her modest enterprise so interesting all of a sudden?

———

Annette and Dan Gilbert sipped cold beers at one of the tables in the trip planning room at Canadian Shield Outfitters.

It had been a long day for both of them, the midsummer rush—everyone trying to get in their canoe trips or fishing excursions before school started. The building was her favorite indoor place in Atikokan, with rough-hewn pine walls studded with a taxidermist's zoo of Canadian Shield fish and mammals. The lower reaches of one wall displayed topographical maps for the 1,837 square miles of Quetico Provincial Park, while topo maps for the even vaster White Otter Wilderness Area lined another. The building had the feel of a trapper's cabin, dim, cozy, lightly scented with the lingering aroma of

the morning's coffee. In winter, the potbelly stove added a
hint of wood smoke and heat that drew people together to
tell stories.

Dan's father and a partner built the place in 1970, the
same year Annette and her husband moved to Atikokan. They
were draft resisters, ready to start a new life in a wilderness
still unsullied by ruthless capitalists and in a country that
lived peacefully in the shadow of the U.S. As successful and
busy as they were, the Gilberts always had time to answer
questions for the young American expats trying to make a
go of it on the Shield.

They talked about families first, especially Annette's
younger daughter, who had endured a sudden divorce and
moved back to Atikokan in the dead of winter with a three-
year-old daughter in tow.

"She's getting her feet back under herself," said Annette.
"But she didn't see it coming."

They let the conversation lapse into silence. It was one of
the things she loved about Atikokan. People didn't feel like
they had to fill every minute with talk.

"How does she like our little arrangement?" Dan was starting to get to the point of the meeting. Annette had been
managing CSO's canoe business since May. It was an intri-
cate arrangement: she also managed her own canoe outfitting
business, keeping the brands separate, but running all the
customers out of the CSO facility. And her daughter took
over the management of Annette's cabins.

"She loves it. She can take care of the cabins and see to
her daughter at the same time. And Christy likes having her
own show to run."

"Think she'll stay?" Dan asked.

Annette sighed. "I don't know. I don't even know what to hope for. I love having her here. Our arrangement with you has been good for both of us. But she's still young and she's always been a romantic and there are so few eligible men here . . ."

Dan nodded in understanding. Atikokan was a hardscrabble town in the middle of the vast Canadian Shield, a wilderness of ancient rocks, bottomless lakes, and sprawling forests interrupted only by bogs and the remnants of surface mines and a few narrow ribbons of roadway. Its population was barely three thousand and falling, and it was the largest community for a hundred miles.

"I guess you know why I'm asking . . ."

Annette sighed again. "Yes. And, yes, I like our arrangement. I have more income than I ever had before and Christy has a great situation, but I don't see this as a long-term arrangement. It's hard to explain to my clients why they're getting outfitted at Canadian Shield. I tell them that I'm running both canoe businesses and they accept it. But over time I'll lose my business identity, and it'll be hard when we separate the businesses again. So I'm hoping you're going to tell me you've found someone to run the canoe business. I promise I won't cry my eyes out."

Dan rubbed his chin and offered a wry smile. "Well, we hope we have someone."

He sat forward, elbows on the table. "Here's the thing. Dad wants to ease off and have me run the business. I can't do the cabins and the airplanes and the canoe outfitting myself, and the people we've interviewed . . . well, the ones who had the qualifications all had baggage. One is a drunk, one I'm pretty sure is a thief, and the others are people who change jobs every couple years for whatever reason. And none of them want to manage the canoe business—they want the cabins, because that's where the money is.

"Our canoe business isn't growing but turns a nice profit. We want to keep it going and we think it can grow a little if the person running it is passionate about the business."

Dan Gilbert locked eyes with Annette.

"So, we'd really like to work out a long-term arrangement with you to run it. You're smart, you're honest, customers like you. You love the business. You've guided. You know Quetico and White Otter like your backyard. That's what it takes to make the business go, that and promoting it in the winter. There's enough money to keep us both happy, especially when we combine your outfitting business with ours. Can we talk about it?"

Dan had his father's charm, and his engaging directness. Annette had known him all his life. He and Christy even dated at times during high school, though the school was so small, that was almost inevitable. Annette couldn't help but smile.

"I owe you and your family a lot," she said to him. "And you know I love you guys. But if I go to work for you, I lose my independence. And I've had some bad experiences with that."

"You mean Rob?" Dan asked, referencing Annette's ex-husband.

"It's Robert now," she corrected. "He's a tenured professor. And he's an American. You can't call him a three-letter word."

"Does he still think we have snakes here?" Dan chuckled.

Annette smiled. Her ex-husband had found life on the Canadian Shield far more challenging than the Shangri-la they had anticipated in 1970 when they sought shelter from the Vietnam War.

"I don't know," she said. "It was the mosquitoes that drove him away, though. Poor guy. That first winter almost killed him. Twenty hours of darkness, minus thirty for a week, frozen pipes. Using the outhouse when 'freezing your ass off' wasn't just an expression. Spring was better until the first big bug hatch. He looked like a teenager with acne he had so many red welts on his skin.

"That's what sent him off to grad school," Annette recalled. "I don't know what I would have done if we didn't have the cabins then."

"You did a great job with them," said Dan.

Annette smiled. She had turned the rickety cabins into a profitable enterprise with guile and grit—helped by a steady influx of customers sent her way by Dan's father, who recommended Annette's cabins to clients needing a place to stay the night before they launched into the wilderness.

"About our arrangement," Dan said, changing the subject.

"Yes. That." Annette smiled.

"We could buy you out, the outfitting business and the cabins. There'd be enough money to give you some financial security, and we'd pay you a good salary to stay on. Christy too."

"Thanks, Dan. But I can't give up my independence."

"You're not lumping us in with that Williams fellow, are you?"

Annette laughed. "Never! Where did that, that man come from, anyway?"

"He used to manage fly-in cabins for a business out of Fort Frances," said Dan. "Did Christy really haul out a shotgun?"

"He's a very unpleasant man."

"He left a trail of people saying that. Glad you're not doing business with him. I don't think he'd be a good addition to the community."

Dan shifted in his chair. "What if we did it as an acquisition and you got shares in Canadian Shield Ventures? You'd be a minority shareholder, but you'd have a vote. We'd merge the canoe businesses, have Christy manage the drive-in cabins as long as she wanted to, and you could sell her your shares when you retire. It could work out for everyone."

Annette sat back in her chair, silent for a moment. She hadn't anticipated that offer. "You know what? I'll think about it . . . but only because it's you asking. If it was anyone else, this would've ended a while ago." She smiled a little, deep in thought. "It scarred me, you know. Being alone in the wilderness with two babies. I had to borrow money from my parents. I didn't really think I'd make it, but I couldn't think of anything else to do. I don't ever want to be dependent on anyone again."

"I understand," said Dan, "Think about the merger idea. You wouldn't be completely independent anymore, but you'd own a piece of the whole thing canoes, cabins, planes, the lodge . . ."

Annette nodded yes. "By the way," she said. "Don't forget I'm taking next week for my Quetico holiday."

"Got you covered. Where are you going?"

"My secret island."

Dan smiled. Everyone in the outfitting business had their favorite Quetico hideaways, and they often compared notes. But Annette had one favorite place that she kept a secret.

"Believe it or not, I have a date." She smiled and blushed lightly. "Not bad for a grandma, eh?"

"Not bad for anyone," said Dan. "Are we going to meet this guy?"

"Probably not. He's starting in the Boundary Waters on the Minnesota side. In fact, he's launching this week sometime. He thinks he's going to spend a month in the Boundary Waters and Quetico. I just hope he lasts long enough to meet me."

"Solo trips sound good 'til you do them," said Dan. "A lot of people give it up after a few days."

"Pender says he's soloed up here for twenty years or so. In fact, he knows you and your dad. He's used Canadian Shield Outfitters for some of his trips."

"Pender? I remember him. Gabe Pender, right?"

Annette nodded yes.

"Quiet guy, always in good shape," Dan recalled. "Good paddler. He did long trips. He had us fly him to the far corners of the park, and he'd paddle out." Canadian Shield Ventures, the parent company of CSO, included an air service with three floatplanes to get clients to their wilderness cabins and, on occasion, to drop canoeists at designated areas on the fringes of Quetico.

"When you could get him to talk, he told good stories," Dan said. "One I remember, he had a young bear that kept coming into his camp. He'd chase it away, but it kept coming back. Finally, he hid in the bushes and ambushed the poor thing when it came back. Jumped out of the scrub screaming and banging a couple of pans together. Scared the pee out of it, I guess. I don't know many people who'd bully a bear. I guess I'd bet he shows up."

"That sounds like something the young Gabe Pender might have tried," said Annette.

"I got the sense he was well off. Never worried about what things cost. Once he told me he came up here when his wife and daughter did vacations in Paris, Rio, Rome, places like that. I asked him why he didn't join them, and he said those were business destinations for him. Quetico was where he found peace."

Dan looked at Annette and got that twinkle in his eye again. "How do you know him?"

"We dated in college."

"No kidding! I keep forgetting you started out in life as a Yank."

"My misspent youth."

"So, you were dating people, including Pender, then Rob came along and swept you off your feet . . .?"

"No. Pender and I were pretty serious, but the war got in the way."

"He was for it, you were against?"

"I was against it. He wasn't for or against it. He said war wasn't a moral decision for him, it was a practical one. Your country calls, you go. Drove me crazy."

"Doesn't sound like you were oil and water."

"It got personal. It shouldn't have, but we were young and strong-willed. Do you ever know more about the world than when you're a twenty-one-year-old college senior? So here we are. I'm the queen of the Quetico wilderness, and he's a rich American who's going to spend a month in my backyard."

"When was the last time you saw him?" Dan asked.

"Forty years ago," said Annette. "We've been e-mailing back and forth for a few months. Meeting seemed like it might be fun."

They made small talk for a few more minutes, and then Annette stood to leave.

"Think about our offer," said Dan. "We can work on the numbers, but you'd end up with a nest egg for your retirement."

Annette smiled and made her goodbye, but Dan's thought echoed in her mind the rest of the night. Retirement. She was getting up in years, a woman alone in a hard world. What would she do when she couldn't carry a canoe and a pack on the long, rugged portage trails that connected the lakes and rivers of the Canadian Shield, when she couldn't paddle a ten-hour day, couldn't guide? How would she live? Where?

3

Pender started feeling better about everything as soon as he headed north. Not giddy or elated but like things were finally starting to happen. After a winter of planning and a spring of training for long, hard paddles and steep, treacherous portages, he was finally moving.

He would slowly wend his way north to Ely, Minnesota, in the ancient Blazer he bought to replace the BMW. He wanted something that he could abandon when he got to Ely. When he went into the wilderness this time, there would be no strings attached. When he entered the Boundary Waters, he'd leave his old life. He'd paddle across the border into Quetico and explore until he ran out of food or got bored. When he came out of the park, he'd start his new life, whatever that might be.

It sounded better than it felt. He felt like a man with no place to go, no close ties to anyone, no reason for being.

Pender stopped for dinner in Eau Claire, Wisconsin, the first day out. It was a steak and walleye place he had often patronized on his trips home from Quetico, family-owned, quiet, illuminated by the gentle glow of large aquariums filled with northwoods game fish. It was a casual, relaxing night in the eatery. His meal went down well. He felt mellow for the first time in months. He decided to stay the night and savor the moment.

"Any vacancies next door?" he asked the waiter.

"You bet," the man said. "Want me to reserve you a room?"

Pender nodded and ordered a second beer. It went down in tiny sips, cold and smooth, laced with soulful hops. He shifted his languid gaze between the setting sun outside and the bright fish tanks inside, finding between them a moment of inner peace marked by glimpses of happy moments from days gone by.

He woke the next morning with no agenda. There was no place he had to be, nothing he had to do. He was no longer a clocks and calendars kind of person. At breakfast he heard two fishermen talking about the Chippewa Flowage just down the highway. The name stirred memories. He'd often thought about stopping on the way to or from Quetico to paddle and fish Wisconsin's great rivers, the Chippewa especially.

And further back in time, Chippewa Falls was a name that evoked images of the old Wisconsin, laid-back, green and lush, friendly. Pender's mind filled with a memory from that time.

Spring 1975.

"Jesus, Pender! We're late! Get John! We're really, really late!" Pender had never seen Peg so panic-stricken. "The wedding's at 4, not 4:30!" She stared at the card that had been on their refrigerator for a month and on the motel room dresser for two days. Their best friends' wedding. Evelyn and John tying the knot. Pender, John's best man. Pender wanted with all his heart to look at the card and find that, no, the wedding was at 4:30

like they'd been thinking all day. But Peg never got stuff like that wrong, and it pissed her off when he doubted her.

They shook John from his nap, threw on their formal clothing, and dashed to church in Pender's car, a gas-guzzling Camaro with a roaring V-8 engine that shook the pines as they shot through the hills and careened through curves, Peg praying out loud that they wouldn't hit a deer, John praying Evelyn would still be at the church when they arrived, Pender wishing to Christ he'd read shit like that card once in a while instead of trusting his memory, which sucked.

They skidded to a stop in front of the little church snuggled in the woods, a cloud of dust settling to the earth in their wake. Evelyn stood at the front door looking down at them, a princess bride with a white smile and blonde hair, wearing her mother's wedding dress.

"You better get him here on time, Pender!" she called. "This is shotgun country."

"You have a shotgun?" Pender yelled back as they scrambled up the steps.

"No, honey," she said. "I have big tits and a lot of ex-boyfriends who have shotguns." It was a joke, and they laughed with her. She was the kind of woman who could say things like that and you'd laugh with her.

Pender drove out toward the river, found a cheap motel, and spent the next couple days paddling the Chippewa. He'd get out early and fish, stop around nine for granola and coffee, then paddle upstream. He'd stop somewhere in the early afternoon to read and nap and laze in the sun. In the late afternoon he started drifting with the current back to his put-in place.

His leisure thoughts bounced from one thing to the next: his fall from grace in the publishing world, his failed marriage, what it would be like to see Annette again. When he thought about the proximity of Chippewa Falls, he thought about Evelyn.

"Want to know a secret?" Evelyn's eyes were too bright, her smile too wide. They had all consumed too much wine, and Pender could see Evelyn was at that dangerous stage of giddy inebriation where things got said that shouldn't be said.

"Maybe not, Ev."

She stood closer to him, looking up, flashing her toothpaste-commercial smile, her hands on her hips in a stance that was both defiant and seductive.

"I'm going to tell you anyway. I used to think if it didn't work out between John and me, you know, I'd like to be with you."

"I'm glad things worked out between you two. You were made for each other."

"I still think about you." She waited for him to respond, but Pender couldn't think of anything to say.

"I'm flattered," he said finally.

Peg and John returned to the bar, saving him from further floundering. Pender and Evelyn never spoke of that moment again.

That was back when friends were about laughter and discovering new things, Pender thought as he drove back to the motel. Before friends became business. Before life became full-time serious. He couldn't remember a particular point in time when it changed, but it did. Everything changed. Him, Peg, John, Evelyn. They all stopped loving each other and went their separate ways.

Pender sat in his sterile motel room thinking about where to eat. The silence was interrupted only by tires crunching over gravel as cars came and went outside. In between cars, there was just the ever-present tinnitus ringing in his ears. It should have been relaxing, but it was more like a song about loneliness. Pender made himself focus on where to eat. He detested chains and fast-food places but didn't know many alternatives in Chippewa Falls. Just one, really. He sighed. What the hell. He'd never pass this way again. He fired up the ancient Blazer and pointed it in the direction of the north-woods diner that had been in Evelyn's family for fifty years. He didn't think she'd be there. Hoped she wouldn't be there. But he had to stop in. This was the last time he'd ever come this way, the last contact with his youth.

The Chippewa Diner was the kind of place that made Pender love crossing the border into Wisconsin back in the sixties and seventies. It had anything you wanted, fresh and fried. The smell of cooking oil and French fries thick in the air. Friendly waitresses, friendly short-order cooks. Lively conversations all over the room, none of them serious. The Wisconsin of that era had been a great place to be a tourist or a kid. Or both. No one had airs. You were always welcome.

What a difference time can make, thought Pender as he entered the place. From the outside it looked more weather-beaten than it had back when the world was young. Inside, the aromas of fried foods and the buzz of conversation still filled the air, but it felt different. A sign above the cash register read, THIS IS A CHRISTIAN RESTAURANT. "Christian" was underlined. The wall art included a portrait of Jesus, light skinned and immaculately groomed, and photos of people at a church.

A teenage girl greeted Pender. She was maybe seventeen, too much eye makeup, a barbed wire tattoo around her ankle. Neither friendly nor unfriendly, she just told him to follow her. As he sat, she said something that started with "Today's special" and continued in a staccato burst of unintelligible consonants separated by indistinguishable vowels. Small-town Wisconsin had caught up to the big city, thought Pender. Maybe broiled food would be next.

The menu on his table shared its holder with a brochure for a church. Probably the one whose parishioners graced the walls, he figured. He scanned the menu. Standard diner fare, everything homemade.

Pender ordered and took a long look around. A dinner crowd of couples and families, all ages. Everyone seemed to know each other.

He spotted Evelyn. She stood at the cash register, ringing up payments, helping the waitresses seat customers and shuttle food. She had put on a few pounds, but she was still a looker. Her Scandinavian blonde hair was still light, though age had taken some of its brightness. Her strong facial features still made her a handsome woman, her eyes a shade of blue so bright he could see it from thirty feet away.

Watching her work, Pender figured the cook must be her husband. The one who came after John. They chatted sometimes, not about orders. Evelyn wouldn't have a lover. Had to be her husband.

Pender's mind wandered back in time again, to when it came apart for Evelyn and John. When the babysitter from across the street got their daughter naked and fondled her, when the law said it was powerless to act because there were no physical signs of molestation and no witnesses. When sex became a filthy, dirty thing to Evelyn. When she found she couldn't stand men anymore, at least, not the men she knew.

Pender gave the molester a blanket party one night, a night when John and Evelyn were at a social function with lots of witnesses. He roughed up the kid a little, no broken bones, and left him tied up and gagged at his own back door. The family got the message. Packed up and moved out lickety-split.

It helped John but not Evelyn. Nothing helped Evelyn until she found Jesus. Jesus gave her direction but couldn't restore her faith in humanity. She homeschooled the kids to protect their purity, then put them in Christian schools. Did church stuff daily. Made John quit drinking. Made John take up the Bible. Told John nothing he could do would ever make her want to have sex with him again.

And asked Pender to never again come to their home, not unless he accepted Jesus as his lord and savior. This from a woman who just a moment ago was one of his closest friends, who was once on the brink of telling him she wanted to sleep with him.

He lost them both. Evelyn divorced John and moved back to Wisconsin. He and John managed to keep up a friendship for a few more years, then an acquaintanceship, then nothing. They stayed in touch long enough for John to share the news that Evelyn had remarried. John said he hoped the guy wasn't expecting to get laid.

Toward the end of his meal, Evelyn noticed him from her command perch. Her face went through the stages of recognition: Do I know him? Yes I do. What's *he* doing here? After Pender's table had been cleared and his coffee served, she sat down across from him, her face humorless.

"Are you Gabe Pender?" she asked. No smile.

"Hi, Evelyn. It's been a long time."

"Must be twenty-five years."

"I hope they've been good ones for you," said Pender.

"Very good." Evelyn looked away, then back at him. "How's Peg?"

"Peg is pretty much the king of the universe right now. Company president. Rich. Powerful. Looks younger than she did when she was thirty-five. Has men lining up to ask her out."

Evelyn cocked her head. "You're . . ."

"Yeah, divorced. Just this year. It turns out, you're never too old."

Evelyn didn't smile. In fact, her face seemed grimmer somehow.

"Have you found God yet, Gabe?"

"No," sighed Pender. "All I've found is a great spiritual wasteland."

"You need to accept Jesus Christ as your personal savior." She rattled off the words like a familiar script, her face still a stern mask.

"It's just not in me." Pender tried to say it in a way that wouldn't offend.

"It's in all of us. Just open your heart to the Lord."

"I'll keep trying," Pender said.

"What brings you here?" Her tone was cold again. Suspicious.

"Just passing through on my way north. Every time I come through the area I think about you. And John. And Peg and I. How it was." As Pender talked, Evelyn's face turned sour.

"I know," he said. "We've all moved on from there. But it was a happy time. I just stopped in for one final salute to happy times." He raised his coffee cup to her and sipped from it.

Evelyn gave him a cold stare, shaking her head from side to side. "I don't remember anything happy about those times. We were stupid and irresponsible. When I think of how I was then, I shudder."

Pender shrugged. "When I think of how you were then, I see someone who was happy and living life to the fullest. That's how I see all of us back then."

"We were ruled by our vices. Smoking, drinking, lust. It was evil. That's why all the bad things happened to us . . . the divorces, my baby . . . all of it."

"Do you think I'm evil, Evelyn?"

She nodded yes, slowly but emphatically.

Pender stared, mesmerized by the woman in front of him and the memory of how she used to be. He tried to break the tension. "I guess you'll want me to pay in cash then."

Her face wore the coldness of a vengeful prophet. "I want you not to come back."

Pender looked her in the eye for a moment, saw no trace of humanity. "Okay," he said with a sadness that started deep in his core. He rose and said goodbye softly, hoping maybe she'd change her mind, let the person she used to be come forth, at least for a moment. But her grim countenance never changed. He reached into his pocket for cash, left a tip on the table and twelve dollars with his receipt by the cash register. When he reached the door, he glanced back. Evelyn was still sitting at the table, staring at the far wall. She looked like a statue hammered from stone by an angry artist.

As he walked to his car, Pender got that feeling again, the one where he was maybe dead, where he couldn't feel his body anymore and was seeing everything from someplace else.

The people from the happy moments in his life were gone, turned to dust by the ravages of life. This was worse than losing Peg. She at least had a life. Evelyn, once so full of life, was just going through the motions now. Her human goodness was long dead. He wished he could cry, could somehow wash away the morose currents that were sweeping him to a far-off sea.

4

"I have things set up so I can get away next week. If you'd like a little company."

Annette blinked, caught off guard, momentarily at a loss for words.

"Bill," she said, "this is personal time for me."

"We haven't been seeing much of each other. I thought you might like a little company out there."

Annette didn't want to state the obvious, didn't want to hurt his feelings. He was a nice man, a lonely man trying to rekindle something that was over months ago and shouldn't have happened in the first place.

"I'm not lonely out there," she told him. "I feel peace. I love the silence. I love the space. But, this isn't my usual solo trip. I'm meeting an old college boyfriend in the park."

Bill's face flushed and his jaw tensed. "I can't believe it. After all we've meant to each other. Why didn't you tell me?"

"Because it's not your business. Our affair was over months ago. We never should have gotten involved in the first place. May is one of my best friends. So are you. Let's keep it there."

"You know she can't . . ." Bill didn't finish the sentence.

"I know. But that doesn't give us the right to sneak around behind her back. She'd be devastated if she found out."

"It's not hurting her!" he exclaimed. "I'm still there for her. I don't let her want for anything."

"I know," said Annette. "You're a good man. The best. I just can't do it anymore. Period. It's over. I hope we can still be friends, but we will never be lovers again."

Bill's anger melted into a sadness so profound Annette wanted to hug him. He looked like a child who had just lost a parent. She understood the feeling. The Canadian Shield was the most beautiful place on earth, except when your life was out of balance. Then it was a desolate, empty land where aching loneliness stalked you through endless days in summer and endless nights in winter.

"Okay," he said. He choked a little, then hurried from her sight so she wouldn't see him lose control.

The metallic sound of the door latch clicking into place echoed in her mind, a door closing on the brief experiment with romance in her second life. It was the beginning of another period of aloneness. She still had Christy and Rebecca, but they would be moving on sooner or later. It would happen fast. A man would come along, a spark would ignite, Christy would have to take a chance that it was the real thing, and she'd be off to Toronto or Winnipeg or one of the cities to the south. And Annette would be left to face the endless dark winters alone. Again.

———————

"How did he take it?" There was genuine surprise on Christy's face as she asked the question. She was a tall, strong woman, like her mother, with large, soft eyes that spoke of compassion and a face that seemed to radiate gentle humor.

"Not well," Annette sighed. When Christy returned home an adult woman, one of Annette's first resolutions was to keep no secrets, even the embarrassing stuff. That included her affair with Bill and her correspondence with Pender.

"It's not easy to accept what's left," Annette said. "I understand how he feels."

"Why did you do it then? It's not like anyone was getting hurt."

Annette shook her head. "That's what I used to tell myself. But that was never the real question. I was betraying a friend. And I was doing something that made me feel guilty. It had to stop."

"Was it because you're meeting that guy in the park?"

Annette had thought about that before. "Maybe. I hope not, but maybe," she said.

"Why?" asked Christy. "It's not any of his business who you're sleeping with."

Annette smiled at her daughter. Christy's support was one of the few luxuries in her life. "No, none of his business at all. But I think what happened was, when we started e-mailing and decided to meet, it made me think back to those times when we were so young and life was waiting for us and I was sort of piecing together the things I believed in. When I looked at myself through that young woman's eyes, I liked a lot of what I saw—you and Rebecca, Annie, this business. But I didn't like seeing me having an affair with a married man. It wasn't right, and it was . . . desperate."

They were quiet for a while, lost in their own thoughts as they folded linens and towels for the cabins.

"I saw your little confrontation with the guy in number three this morning," said Annette.

Christy smiled slyly. "Oh, that."

"What happened?"

"Just what you think happened," said Christy. "He came in while I was making the bed. I started to leave so he could have some privacy, and he tried to kiss me. He followed me out and I smacked him."

"You sure did. I could hear it from here. What did you say to him?"

"I told him if he touched my body again, I'd rip the flesh off his face."

"My goodness. What a violent thought."

"It worked."

"I guess it did," said Annette. "I thought he was going to cry."

"What would you have done if he kept trying to force himself on me?" asked Christy.

Annette laughed. "I would have run down there and ripped the flesh off his face."

After another silence, Christy stopped her labors to take a sip of coffee. She glanced at her mother, still folding towels. "Are you sure about meeting that guy alone in the park?"

"Gabe Pender?" replied Annette. "Why not?"

"Well, he sounds kind of violent. And you'd be out there all by yourself."

Annette stopped folding. "The Gabe Pender I knew had trouble with authority. If you told him he had to do something, he'd rebel. If you gave him his space, he gave you yours."

"So you don't think he's dangerous?"

"No. In his e-mails he sounds a lot like the guy I knew in college."

"You haven't seen him in forty years. He could be psychotic. He could be a rapist or a dope addict."

"Do you think we change so much between twenty-one and sixty?"

"He's divorced. Do you know why his wife left him? Maybe he beat her."

"I know what he said. He said they just drifted apart. Different interests, different values."

"What wife beater ever said the marriage ended because he liked to beat the crap out of women?"

Annette sighed. "I just can't picture Gabe Pender hitting a woman."

"He hit his boss, didn't he? And he accosted those guys in the canoe race."

"I can see him hitting his boss, especially if the guy was as much of a jerk as Pender said he was. And I've thought about the thing with the canoeists. You know, if they knocked someone over in one of our races, chances are they'd need medical attention at the ER. Pender just broke their paddles."

"I bet he wanted to break their noses."

"He probably did."

Christy stared at her mother. "You two didn't just date in college, did you?" She said it suspiciously, more statement than question.

"What else do you think we did?" Annette responded flippantly.

"I mean, he wasn't just another guy you dated. He was special."

"I guess he was, in a way."

Christy cocked her head and smiled. "Come on," she said.

"He *was* special. Of the men I knew in college, your father and Pender are the only ones I remember." Annette glanced away, deep in thought. "We argued a lot. Sometimes he'd argue the other side even when he agreed with me. He could be really frustrating, but it was always interesting with him."

"He sounds like one of those people who likes to hear themselves talk." Christy wrinkled her nose when she said it.

"No. That was your dad. Pender liked to engage me in debate. He was showing off, but he respected my intellect, too. Sounds passé to you now, but back then a lot of men didn't like women who had opinions and smarts. He did. That's why it was so exciting being with him. One reason."

"Were you involved with him sexually?"

Annette frowned, trying to decide how much she should share with her daughter. "Yes," she said, finally.

"And?"

"And we enjoyed each other. And that's as far as I'm going with this."

Christy laughed. "I believe you're actually blushing!"

"Believe what you want."

"Still," said Christy, "I'd feel a lot better if someone was going with you. Just in case. I can get away for a few days, just to make sure he's okay . . ."

"That's sweet of you, honey," said Annette. "But no. I'm going alone. I can handle whatever comes along. Goodness knows I've dealt with men when I had to."

"What if he, you know, wants to have sex?"

Annette laughed. "Christy," she exclaimed, "I'm sixty years old. So is he. If he wants to have sex and has the erection to prove it, let's just accept it for the miracle it is."

"Does that mean you'd say yes?"

"That means I'd make up my mind when it happens, which it won't."

As they labored in silence, Annette's mind filled with college memories.

"You got the same grade I did and you don't have a single footnote!" She wasn't just angry, she was pissed. She didn't like him anyway. He argued every point in every discussion, always had a different point of view on every book and character. He didn't socialize with anyone. And he got an A on a paper that contained no research.

"Footnotes aren't important. They just mean, instead of thinking for yourself, you copied down what a bunch of self-important assholes said about something."

She flushed and fumed. It would have felt good to slap him. So disrespectful. And yet, as she locked eyes with him, he wasn't sneering. He didn't seem disrespectful.

"You're too smart to settle for being a parrot," he said.

"How do you know?"

He blushed and fidgeted. All her anger and resentment evaporated as she realized he couldn't find words. He was interested in her, and he was vulnerable. The two thoughts came to her simultaneously and rocked her. She blinked. He was kind of handsome. His face was expressive. There was fire in his eyes.

"It's obvious." He was still beet red.

She didn't know what to say. She'd know what to say if she just wanted to leave him there, but that's not what she wanted. The silence got uncomfortable. He shuffled his feet and locked eyes with her again.

"Could we have coffee sometime?"

So began the most intense love affair of her life.

5

Sleep came in tortured bits for Pender, a continuing replay of his encounter with Evelyn. He woke every time he looked into her dead eyes, a queasy feeling in his stomach, his mind filled with fear and mourning. Lives that started with such joy and promise shouldn't have turned out this way.

An hour before sunrise, he gave up trying to sleep and started north. As he drove through the black void of predawn, he felt like he was living an eerie nightmare in which everything in his life had been destroyed in the blink of an eye. He survived the toxic episode only to find himself a solitary man surrounded by a phantom race of people who looked real but who were indifferent to everyone and everything.

If he could relive those years, would he? The more Pender thought about it, the more he thought, no. It had been so pointless. It would have been better if he had died in Vietnam so that someone else could live instead, maybe one of the people whose loved ones left notes and teddy bears for them at the memorial. Someone whose life would have been more cherished than his.

When daylight came, he tried to decide whether to keep heading north, out of the state, or spend a couple of days on Wisconsin's Lake Superior shore. When he was planning this part of the trip, he liked the idea of taking in the arty, weather-beaten towns along the coast, enjoying the cafés, the galleries, the rugged Lake Superior coastline. And he could look in on his best friend and most valued colleague, Patrick O'Quinn, for a final farewell.

But Evelyn's ghost was chasing him from the state like a vengeful ghoul. If he stayed in Wisconsin even an extra hour or two, the cancer that was eating the easygoing vacationland of his youth would consume him, too.

He was still equivocating as he neared the city of Superior and the sign for Highway 13 came into view. It was the road that followed the Lake Superior shore along the peninsula, to Cornucopia, Bayfield, the Apostle Islands, and Ashland. He stopped on the shoulder of the road and thought it over for a moment. As much as he wanted to escape the nightmare, he hated to give in to his fears. And he couldn't shake the thought that he would never see O'Quinn again.

Like a dread-filled grunt taking the point on a patrol in hostile territory, he headed up the peninsula on 13. It was too early to go to Quetico. There were farewells to be made, doors to close.

Patrick O'Quinn's tiny village consisted of maybe a dozen buildings strung along Highway 13. The community center-piece was a natural bay that housed a marina and walking paths. A sign at the edge of town set the population at ninety-eight, most of whom lived on the back roads in the sprawling pine forests. Only a few houses were located along the commercial drag. Pender found a coffee shop. He ordered coffee and asked for a phone book. The proprietor laughed, said he hadn't seen one in years, asked who Pender was looking for.

"A guy named Patrick O'Quinn. Photographer—"

"Wears a beret," the proprietor cut in.

Pender nodded. Smiled. That stupid hat probably got him a ton of abuse in the northern reaches of Wisconsin. The Tennessee of the North he had called it back in the days of their youth when they traveled the state looking for stories, stopping to fish.

The proprietor directed him to a flat above an art gallery. Figured.

Pender didn't have a cell phone, and there weren't any pay phones in town, so he drank coffee, read a newspaper, and strolled the harbor until nine o'clock, then went calling.

His knock on the second-floor door brought a cautious peek through a narrow opening, a chain holding the door partially closed. The partial face on the other side belonged to a woman with gray-blue eyes, medium height.

"Yes?" Her voice was hesitant, suspicious. Jesus, Pender thought, this isn't exactly Bedford-Stuyvesant.

"Hi. I'm looking for Patrick O'Quinn?"

"What do you want with him?"

"I wanted to say hello. We're old friends. We used to work together."

"Who are you?"

"Pender."

Her face wrinkled in thought, as if the name was familiar but she couldn't place it. "Do you have a first name?"

"Yeah, but no one ever uses it."

"Wait a moment." She closed and locked the door. He could hear her feet padding away. A few minutes later she was back, the door opened a crack, chain still in place.

"Come back in an hour. He'll see you then."

Pender said okay, but she was already closing the door. Not the warmest welcome an old friend ever got. He wondered about the woman, why she was so suspicious. He shrugged. Not the first time someone disliked him on sight, maybe not the last either, though time was getting short for that particular ritual.

He stopped at the first-floor landing to check the name on the mailbox. Minton and O'Quinn. The Minton was typed, O'Quinn was a handwritten addition. Pender wandered the waterfront again, found a sit-down restaurant, had a hot breakfast, chatted up the waitress and another patron, and then walked back to the Minton and O'Quinn household.

This time the lady opened the door all the way. She was slight of build, fiftyish, attractive. Short hair, straight with blonde streaks, those complex gray-blue eyes. The summer sun had given her fair skin a tawny tan, and the Lake Superior winds left her with faint red highlights on her cheekbones. Ms. Minton was the most attractive of the O'Quinn ladies Pender had met. Nice that some good things come later in life, he thought.

"I'm Carrie," she said, leading him into the living room of a spacious flat. She stopped, extended a hand for a handshake.

"Pat's been sick," she said. A nice voice, hushed, like in a hospital or church. "It's cancer. Pancreatic. He's been through chemo. They don't think he's going to make it. He's worried you won't recognize him. It's been tough." She tried to say the words without emotion, rattle them off like a schoolkid reciting memorized lines, but it was there, the little crack between syllables, the descending intonations at the end of phrases, the sad eyes just above the brave smile.

"Shit," said Pender. He shook his head slowly.

"No argument here," she said, and led him down a hallway to the bedroom where O'Quinn waited.

O'Quinn greeted him as soon as he entered the bedroom. "You sure have a great sense of timing." His humor helped take the edge off Pender's shock at the sight of him. Deathly pale. Emaciated. A desiccated shadow of the man Pender had known. A skeleton with skin and odd tufts of hair and a dying ember of life.

"Well, if you'd write once in a while, I could have been up here a long time ago. Jesus, Patrick, you look like shit."

"Yeah, but I look better than I feel." He smiled, too weak to laugh.

"So this is where you disappeared to?" Pender took in the room, the pictures on the wall, the view of the morning sky from the windows.

"My own little paradise." He paused and closed his eyes.

"He owns the shop downstairs," explained Carrie.

"Best two years of my life," said O'Quinn. "Except for the last few months, of course." He closed his eyes again and drifted off.

"He sells the works of local artists and his own photography."

"Let me guess," said Pender. "He pays the artists a bigger commission than the other guys and doesn't take enough profit."

"He pays a nice commission and makes enough money to pay the bills and keep the doors open," she responded.

"That's my Patrick." Pender turned to Carrie. "I've missed him. I understand why he took off, but I missed him."

"He talks about you, about your work together. What kind of editor you were. He loves you."

"He's the best photographer I ever knew. He could get journalism and art in the same shot, you know? I remember a cover he did for my construction magazine way back when. He'd already shot a hundred frames or so, and it started raining. Most people would pack up and get out. He already had the setup shot—clean machines, posed bosses. Why risk your equipment, right? But the construction crew kept working in the rain, which became a total deluge. It grabbed Pat. He got out there with them and shot for an hour in a monsoon rain. He came away with the most dramatic construction photos anyone ever saw, mud streaming out of the loader bucket, rain splashing off the hard hats, workers up to their calves in muck, their clothes stuck to their skins. Smiling like a bunch of kids at the beach. Greatest construction shot ever. Defined construction work like nothing else I ever saw. He won a national award for it."

Carrie nodded, eyes watery. She took Pender's hand and led him back to the living room, stopped in front of a picture on the wall. It was the shot Pender had just described. The walls of the room were festooned with other dramatic photos—sports, nature, cars, architecture, food.

"If there was a God," said Pender, "the motherfuckers who destroyed these magazines would be dead and Pat's life would just be starting."

Carrie cried. Pender put his arms around her. She buried her forehead in his chest and sobbed silently.

When she recovered they went back to O'Quinn's room.

"Trying to steal my girl?" he asked as they sat down.

"I'd only embarrass myself," said Pender. "Never had much luck with women, though I was finally able to make Peg happy."

"Buy her a nice polo pony? A yacht?"

"Naw," drawled Pender. "I signed her divorce papers."

"No kidding," said O'Quinn, smiling. "Why in the hell would she want a divorce? You getting it on with the maid?"

"No. The maid wasn't interested in me either. No, what broke poor Peg's heart was me getting old and dull. Did I tell you I also got fired?"

"You? You got fired? I can't believe it. You're an institution!" O'Quinn's face was animated in disbelief.

"Not much use for institutions in the brave new world of corporate publishing I'm afraid. They're letting the air out of the magazines because they want to write them off. Your publishing hero Charles Jamison Blue thought the strategy was brilliant."

"That empty suit is still around?"

"In all his glory."

"Did he tell you to your face or send you a memo?"

"He couldn't wait to give me the news himself. He really enjoyed it, right up to the time I popped him. Left hook to the gut. It was an immature and beastly action on my part."

O'Quinn's smile consumed his emaciated face. "Goddamn but I'd have loved to see that! Tell me about it, every detail. This might be the last best story of the rest of my life."

Pender took him through the whole sequence of events, including his anger management sessions.

"But it must have felt good going down, eh?" said O'Quinn. "I used to dream of doing something like that to those Ivy League idiots."

"You're one of the few people who could understand how good it felt," said Pender. "It was like finding Jesus."

They sat quietly for a while, lost in thought.

"It's been building in me, Patrick," said Pender, finally. "I feel this rage all the time, deep inside. I try to control it, but sometimes the mad genie just roars out of the bottle. Everything that's happened since Vietnam has been a lie. And the bastards who are spinning the lie are getting rich and they're laughing at us and they don't care where the lie ends as long as it ends with them being rich. I watch these stupid CEOs who don't know shit about the businesses they're in run their companies into the ground and make millions doing it. And the phony chicken hawks who wave flags from their cars but wouldn't serve on a bet. It pisses me off. It's like people like you and I have wasted our lives being puppets in their game."

Pender paused in thought. "So, yeah, it felt . . . great." He looked at Carrie. "I'm not as psychotic as I sound, honest. I hadn't had a fight since I got out of the army. But that little lapse . . . it was like scooping a fingerful of frosting from a cake you can't afford to buy. Watching that pompous bastard turn blue trying to get his breath, seeing him sit his fat ass on the chair and cry. Goddamn, it was better than an orgasm. At this stage of my life, anyway."

"Better than a job?" O'Quinn asked.

"Yeah, Pat," said Pender. "No one was going to hire me anyway, but even if someone was interested, there isn't much left. No one's focused on greatness anymore, not even growth. The whole industry is about cost cutting. It's like running a baseball team by managing the scoreboard."

As Pender vented some more, O'Quinn gently nodded off again. Pender and Carrie strolled to the coffee shop, then toured O'Quinn's art gallery. Between bits of artist biographies and local notes, Carrie answered Pender's questions about her and O'Quinn.

Carrie was fifty-three. She was a Berkeley girl, an art major, and a counterculturist, too late for the revolution but full of fire and passion. After she graduated she tried teaching in Mendocino, but her passion was art, not dealing with kids who wanted to be doing something else. So she became a painter of expressionistic canvases and a waitress. She made more money waitressing. She tried marriage, but it was too confining. When Mendocino got too yuppified, she moved on to Sonoma County and, when the BMWs invaded, she migrated to the Lake Superior shore of Wisconsin.

"I do okay here," she said. "I got a deal as a sales clerk in Patrick's shop long before he got here. I got paid and I got to have my work on display and I got a great deal on the apartment. And this is a great area. The few jerks we get are gone by the time the cold weather sets in."

Pender stopped in front of one of Carrie's canvases, an explosion of blues and whites with dashes of warm colors and multicolored streaks. "Sailboats?" he asked.

"Good one! Yes. It's a sailboat race on Lake Superior."

"Yeah, I can feel the speed."

"You're saying all the right things. Want to buy it?"

"I'd love to," Pender said. "But I don't have walls anymore."

Carrie glanced at him quizzically.

"No more house, no apartment. No address. That's my home." He gestured to his vehicle outside. "And in a week or so, I won't even have the truck."

"Where are you going?" Carrie asked.

"The Boundary Waters, Quetico."

"For forever?"

"For as long as it lasts."

"What then?"

Pender shrugged. "Haven't gotten that far. What about you?" he asked. "Do you still work here?"

"Yes. My hours are way down because I'm taking care of Pat, but yes, I still work here. He's leaving the place to me, so he's been teaching me how to run the business."

"So you're staying? When he . . ."

"Yes. When he passes, I'll stay. Everything I love is here. Him. The shop. The lake. The people around here. Even the godforsaken winters. As inhumanly cold as it gets, it's incredibly majestic."

"I envy you," Pender said.

"Me?"

"I envy you having a place you love and people you love."

When they went back up to the apartment, O'Quinn was awake, waiting for them. He asked about Pender's plans after Quetico.

"I always wanted to see the Maritimes," Pender said. "Whenever *National Geographic* ran a spread on them I thought, damn, that should have been you and me doing that, the words and pictures. Wouldn't that have been the life?"

They recollected their misadventures as a failed freelance team in their post-Vietnam days.

When O'Quinn needed to rest, Pender strolled through the town and along the lakefront, memories of his postwar days suddenly fresh in his mind. He had been steered into a singles complex by a friend, the fourth roommate in a bachelor townhouse. Two hip, urbane up-and-comers who sidestepped the draft, launched promising careers, and were popular with women. And two others who weren't any of those things. O'Quinn and Pender. Veterans of an unpopular war. Crap jobs. Socially challenged.

They both wanted to be freelancers, to experience variety and independence in their work. To pursue adventure. Do work for *National Geo* and the bigs of magazinedom, collaborate on books.

They pursued the dream for almost two years. O'Quinn worked nights as a janitor to pay his bills, Pender edited press releases for a local shopper. They spent weekends trying to hustle stories. Between them, they barely eked out enough money to pay their rent and groceries and keep one of their junk cars running. In the second winter of their enterprise, Pender's car died. They shared O'Quinn's ancient heap until one morning, as Pender depressed the clutch to shift gears, the floor of the vehicle gave way, forming a sort of scoop that funneled new-fallen snow into the cockpit.

The man at the welding shop laughed, said the steel it would take to make the repair was probably worth more than the car. He had a point.

Pender tapped his savings to get a used car so they could pursue new jobs. By spring Pender was working for a trade magazine and O'Quinn caught on as a staff photographer with a suburban paper, then a daily in central Illinois. Pender graduated to a senior staff position on a construction title, then *Menu*, the company's flagship magazine. O'Quinn came back to Chicago as a freelancer, busy with newspaper assignments, weddings, and in-home portraits.

Pender assigned work to O'Quinn as he rose in the ranks, especially when he became editor in chief of *Menu*. So they stayed in touch with business lunches through marriages, children, braces, college. O'Quinn's divorce.

O'Quinn's divorce was an especially malicious event. He was shocked when she served the papers, more shocked when he realized how well planned it all was. The youngest son had just gone off to college, and Pat's replacement was packed and ready to move in the day the divorce was finalized.

Not long after that he got tired of the routine of his business, told Pender and a few others he was going to do something different, somewhere different. And then one day he just disappeared.

Pender located him in the winter of his own discontent when an Internet search turned up his name and his business on the Wisconsin shores of Lake Superior.

What a long, strange journey, he thought.

They dined together that night. As Carrie cleared the table and started dishes, O'Quinn started to fade again.

"Patrick," said Pender. "Before you nod off . . . I'm leaving early tomorrow. Real early. I don't sleep much anymore, you know? So I wanted to say goodbye. And, don't get mad, but I have to ask this or it's going to haunt me forever. I have some money. More than I need. Can I help with anything? Medical bills, the mortgage, whatever . . ."

O'Quinn smiled drowsily. "I always wanted to have a rich friend," he said. "But no, we're good. Thanks. How'd you get so rich, anyway?"

"I married well," said Pender. O'Quinn cocked an eye in question.

"Peg insisted we buy that place on the river right after the hundred-year flood," explained Pender. "We got it for a song because it had flooded. Then it just kept appreciating, especially after the flood abatement projects were completed. And we kept doing well ourselves. So we had a lot of marital assets to split up, including a two-million-dollar house."

"She split it with you?" O'Quinn could hardly imagine such largesse.

"She did. What she lacks in personal warmth she makes up for in a strong sense of fair play. Who knew?"

When O'Quinn nodded off, Pender prepared to leave. He gave Carrie a slip of paper with his financial manager's name on it. "You can reach me through this guy if you or Pat need anything. Or if Pat makes a miracle recovery . . ." His voice trailed off for a moment. "You know, Pat and I always talked about paddling the Mississippi together . . ." Pender sobbed. Carrie put her arms around him and cried.

"God, I can't believe we didn't do that. What a waste!"

She hugged harder. "Let it go, sweetie. If you live right, there's always something left undone."

Pender nodded. "And you let me know if you need any help . . . financial or whatever."

She nodded. They hugged a final time, and Pender left. Another farewell completed. Another door closed. A lonely universe waiting for him.

6

Rob showed up at Quetico Outpost during one of the busiest weeks of the season, the second Mrs. Blain in tow.

They just popped in on their way to Toronto, to see Rob's daughter and first grandchild. For Christy's sake, Annette tried not to resent the intrusion, but it wasn't easy. The new wife, Janice, was only a few years older than Christy and bubbled over with girlie enthusiasm for everything. Her effervescence was punctuated by stylish fashions—she wore a designer suit in the wilderness—and breasts bigger than watermelons.

"Thing is," Rob was saying, Janice gushing a wet red lipstick smile at her as he talked, "The White Otter is full tonight, and we were wondering if you had a cabin available . . ."

In that moment, the truth about her ex-husband loomed before her in a tableau with the stark reality of a political cartoon. Until that moment, she had defined him by his intellect, his passionate speech, his good looks, and by his flaws—his penchant for skirt chasing, his inability to adapt to life on the Canadian Shield. But as he stood beside his child bride and panhandled for a free room from his ex-wife, she realized that he was defined by shallowness and insensitivity. The realization didn't make her mad. It made her sad.

"Check with Christy on that," she said. "She's running the cabins this summer. She'll know if we have something open."

"How's she doing?" Rob tried to get a conversation going, to feel better about the situation he had created. If he hadn't become a political science professor, he would have been a used car salesman or maybe a politician.

"She's great." Annette gestured to the office. "She's in there. So is your granddaughter. If you're lucky you might get to change a dirty diaper." Annette suppressed a chuckle. Rob had been terrified of shit-filled diapers at first sight. Indeed, he had to force himself to even hold his infant daughters, what with the puke and pee and poop they emitted.

The only thing worse than stinky kids was the vast, silent wilderness, with its dark, howling winters, summers of ferocious insects, and total absence of culture. No high-powered political movements, no poetry readings. He lasted two years in the Canadian Eden he had picked for his asylum. After two years he decided it was time to get a master's degree in Toronto, eleven hundred miles away. After that, he came back for a month or so in the summers—enough to get Annette pregnant twice. The master's segued into a PhD, then to a faculty position. When the U.S. offered a conditional amnesty for draft dodgers, Rob worked fast to nail down a professorship in Minnesota and moved south with the alacrity of a migrating duck. His objections to America's foreign policies had been long since forgotten, along with his marriage vows.

The irony didn't escape Annette. Canada had been his idea, but it was her country. She wasn't going back.

Christy had a cabin for them, of course, and Annette invited them for dinner so that her daughter and granddaughter could share a little more time with them. As they sat, Rob asked if they had any wine. He wanted to propose a toast. Not enough to bring the wine, of course.

Annette opened a bottle of British Columbia red, not allowing herself to be offended at her ex-husband's attitude. When the wine was poured, Rob toasted his first grandchild with so much gusto you'd have thought the child had just emerged from the womb. Annette dutifully raised her glass, sipped, and began eating.

Rob prattled about university life, the book he was working on, the articles he had published. Annette was silently astonished that the man could possibly think this tripe was of interest to the people he had left behind many years ago.

When he finally paused to take a bite of food, she asked Janice what she did.

"I'm an interior designer," she said, blinking her eyes like a movie star in front of bright camera lights. "I do mostly commercial, but I've been getting some big residential jobs lately."

"Tell them about the Gatsby house," said Rob.

Janice smiled indulgently. "Busby, honey. Gatsby was a book. I think." She laughed at her own joke.

"The Busby house is an ultramodern mansion, just fantastic. Eight bedrooms, ten bathrooms, a ballroom, tennis courts . . ."

Annette zoned out as Janice rattled off the conspicuous excesses of the house and detailed the colors and fabrics that she used to frost the patrician cake. Thank God she had escaped that drivel, she thought. Better a week of minus thirty cold than a day of festooning the wealthy in a gilded embryo.

"That's very impressive," Annette said when the woman finished. "It sounds like your career is really taking off."

"Yes," Janice said, wrinkling her little nose with practiced cuteness. "But not for long. We're trying to get pregnant, and I want to stay home with the baby for a few years."

Out of the corner of her vision, Annette could see Christy freeze, her fork halfway to her mouth, staring in shock at Janice.

"Well," said Annette. "I hope Rob does as well by you as he did by me in that department. There may be better husbands, but I can't imagine better kids."

Janice stared at Annette, wanting to say something, unable to summon words. Rob had turned scarlet and was staring at his plate. Christy was politely trying to suppress a grin.

"I'd like to propose a toast," said Annette, raising her glass high. "To fertile ovaries, men with high sperm counts, and kids we can love forever. The older I get the more I realize the rest of it is just the flotsam and jetsam of life."

After dinner, when Rob and his wife departed for their cabin, Annette worked on the computer, updating the Quick Books for the canoe outfitting partnership while Christy put her daughter to bed. The house fell silent until Christy returned to the living room.

"He's weak. He's just a weak man." Christy's words filled the hushed room like rolling thunder. Annette stopped her work.

"Who are you talking about?"

"Dad," said Christy. "But it applies to Aaron, too. It makes me wonder if there are any strong men anymore."

"I couldn't say for sure," said Annette. "It seems like there are quite a few around here, but most of them are married. And who knows what goes on behind closed doors."

The room went silent again as both women mulled their thoughts.

"The other thing, . . . you always have to remember that we're all weak in some way."

"How are you weak?" Christy asked.

Annette shared a bemused smile. "Chocolate. This place. Wanting to get laid now and then. I think we could put together a list, not that I care to."

"How is this place a weakness?"

"Oh, you know," Annette sighed. "As long as I'm here I can never have romance in my life, and I'd like that. I never thought about it before, but after Gabe started writing, it came back, the wanting to love someone that way. There aren't any eligible men here. I suppose there aren't many for a woman my age anywhere else either. But I couldn't live anywhere else now anyway."

"What about Gabe? What if he's the one?"

Annette stood and stretched. "He's not. Our time came and went a long time ago." She said it and she meant it, but as she pictured his face in her mind a small smile played at her lips.

"So why are you seeing him?"

"It will be fun. And interesting. He's still a good-looking guy, he's smart, and he knows things I don't know. Just talking to him used to be fun, and, judging from his e-mails, it probably still is."

Christy sat next to Annette. "You know, what you were saying about never finding romance here? I wonder if that's me, too."

"I wonder, too," said Annette, putting an arm around her daughter. "It might be different for you. You're younger and there are a few young single men around here and we get customers coming through. So maybe something good will happen. But it might not. You might need to think about relocating at some point. I'd miss you like crazy, you and

Rebecca. But it would be worse to have you stay here for me and miss out on real intimacy and a real partner."

Annette poured the last dregs of the dinner wine into a wineglass, and the two women stood on the patio, sharing the wine, looking out on the lake as the sun cast long shadows from the far horizon. The air was settling into the usual evening calm, the lake's surface like glass.

"When I see the lake like that, I always think of our first canoe trip with you," said Annette. "You were just a few months old and Rob thought I was crazy, but I wanted you to grow up with this place in your blood. So we went. Just four days. We paddled from Beaverhouse to Batchewaung. It was bright and sunny when we put in, but we didn't even get off Quetico Lake before the rain started. It rained for forty-eight hours. We were worried to death about you, but you did just fine and so did your sister. Then, on the third day, the rain stopped, and when we paddled into Batch, the park turned into paradise. The sun was shining, no wind. Not a sound. Not a whisper. Midafternoon and the lake was like a mirror. You could see the clouds in the water so clearly you couldn't tell where the water ended and the sky started. It was like the canoe was floating in the clouds. It was one of the most amazing moments in my life."

"What did Dad think of it?" Christy asked.

"He said it was like nature was reading a poem to us," said Annette.

"He said that?"

"Yes. Believe it or not, he once was someone who believed in good causes and had a strong aesthetic sense."

"It's not easy to picture."

"Don't be too hard on the old boy, Christy. We all do the best we can."

7

The kid rolled into the hotel parking lot in Pender's SUV promptly at six. Pender's canoe was already secured on the roof rack. He threw his packs in back, and they set out for the put-in.

Pender was quiet.

"You sure about the vehicle?"

"Yeah," said Pender.

"I'll sign it back to you any time." He had an earnestness about him that Pender liked.

"Don't worry. It's yours. Appreciate the planning info. It was a good trade."

"There's a big weather system rolling in," the kid said.

"Oh?" said Pender. Not that interested.

"You sure you want to go out now?"

Pender looked at him and took a minute to focus. "I've been wet before." He shrugged.

"It's the wind. It's gonna blow. And you're starting in a wetland. If you have to camp there, could be ugly. And if you keep going, you'll have to deal with the wind on the lakes."

Pender shrugged again.

"I wouldn't say anything except you hired me to help you trip plan."

"You earned every nickel. And every mile you get out of this vehicle."

"You know what you're doing," said the kid. "But I have to say it—don't get caught out in big water when this thing hits."

Pender nodded. Silence.

"I was thinking about your trip last night, the part about your date." The teenager glanced at him. "That's really cool. Where are you going to meet?"

"Where would you meet an old girlfriend in Quetico?" Pender asked.

The young man thought for a minute. "I think I'd pick one of the clear-water lakes with pine forests. Maybe Shelley or Keats. What about you?"

"I might go for Badwater Lake. It half kills you just getting there, so it seems like paradise when you can finally camp. But the lady picked the lake."

"So where are you going?"

"I'm sworn to secrecy."

"C'mon, it's not like I'm going to rat you out to Homeland Security."

"I know," Pender laughed. "But it was important to the lady so I promised."

"Do you always keep your promises?"

"I try."

The kid nodded.

"I can tell you this much," said Pender. "We're meeting on an island in a lake I've never seen. I've been past it but never portaged in. She says that happens a lot. That's why it's such a great place. We'll have lunch. After that, who knows? Maybe we'll hate each other and go our separate ways."

"You might hate each other?"

"Well, sure. We haven't spoken in forty years. The last thing she said to me was . . ." Pender's voice trailed off. "Well, we fought a lot then." He shrugged.

The kid shook his head. "So you're meeting someone you dated in college?" Pender nodded. "And you haven't seen her since?" He nodded again. "And you have no idea what she looks like?"

"I've seen a picture of her. I'd know her from a bear or even your mother."

"You know my mother?"

Pender gave the teen a sour smile. "Very funny."

"She paddles solo in Quetico?" There was incredulity in the young man's voice. "I've never heard of a woman doing a solo trip in the Boundary Waters or Quetico. Heck, guys going out alone are pretty rare."

"She's not your average woman," said Pender. "She's been soloing for years. She guides. She has her own outfitting business on the Canadian side."

The teen shook his head in wonder. "Hell of a blind date."

A moment later, he glanced at Pender again. "Why not just go to her place? Why start here?"

Pender sighed, looked out the window. "I need it to be a journey."

The kid pondered that thought for a moment. "What if something happens to you? You crash your boat or get laid up somewhere. She won't know."

Pender shrugged. "The vagaries of life." As he said it, he could hear his old platoon sergeant. *Do everything you're taught, and you might make it home alive. Then again, no matter how good you are, if there's a bullet with your name on it . . .* The sergeant shrugged. The vagaries of life.

They drove north and west until the kid slowed abruptly and turned off the road, eased through a narrow break in the brush, and stopped in a small parking area.

They hauled Pender's gear a half mile to the launch site. The trail was wide and clear, like a path in Central Park, nothing like the rough cobs Pender would be traversing in Quetico.

The trail ended in a small clearing at a river bank. The kid watched Pender walk straight to the water and deftly drop his canoe in the shallows. The canoe was a long, sleek solo-tripping canoe with the scarred hull of a wilderness boat—a serious boat for a serious canoeist. It had seen a lot of rocks and beaches and been pushed over a lot of snags and beaver houses. Pender shrugged off his pack and placed it in the front of the canoe. The kid handed him the second pack, which he placed behind the seat. He removed one of the paddles lashed to the thwarts, and he was ready to go.

Well done, the kid thought. He hauled the canoe and the food pack on one trip, like a guide would, but didn't go macho, carrying too much, moving too fast. Pull a muscle out here, and your fun time turns to agony. Break a leg or ankle, and you're in real trouble.

Pender paused beside the canoe, gazing at the northern reaches of the river. The waters were dark and still. The overcast morning sky was being consumed by a bank of low, black clouds approaching like a wall of despair.

"Weather's coming," the kid said, raising his voice enough to be heard.

Pender nodded. He floated the canoe in the shallows to check her trim, inching packs to and fro to even the load.

"You sure you want to put in now?" the kid asked again.

"Yeah. What the hell?" said Pender.

"Okay then," he said. "But be careful out there, hey."

"Thanks." Pender shook the kid's hand, stepped into his canoe, and began his last voyage in the Boundary Waters Canoe Area.

Black vapors hung in angry coils from the dark sky, so low it seemed like you could touch them. The air was still and filled with tension, like a fuse had been lit and everything—the birds, the bears, the insects, the wind itself—was waiting for the violent explosion.

And yet, it was relaxing. Pender was finally alone. Not another human in sight, not a sound, not even a loon or a raven. He breathed deeply and let his mind focus on the silence and stillness, felt the air flow by his skin as the canoe glided forward like a phantom.

For the first time in months, Pender felt a sense of peace. True, a storm was rolling in, but that was just rain and wind. He was out of the shit storms of a jaded civilization. He was clean and free.

He headed north in a creek-like passage through a reedy bog and a weed-choked stream, then into wetlands dotted by clumps of evergreen trees. He paddled easily, enjoying the weightless sensation of the canoe floating on a light current, low in the river, out of the wind. He had to get out several times to tow the boat through shallows and twice more to hoist it over downed timber.

Once, as he strained to pull the canoe through a stretch of low water and deep silt, he looked up to see a moose cow and her calf gazing at him, maybe fifty feet away. They were

chewing green shoots and stopped to stare, as if incredulous
that some life-form would be doing what he was doing.

Pender laughed. It *was* crazy. His shirt was soaked with
sweat, his quick-dry pants were covered with stinky black
silt up to his thighs, he had another hour or two of this in
front of him and a nasty storm getting ready to make his life
miserable. And yet, it was liberating. Food would taste better,
sleep would be deeper, his days fuller.

Light rain started as he entered the first lake. It was less
than a mile long, and he crossed it in minutes, glad to be
paddling in deep water again. He could see colorful tents
marking four camps on the little lake as he passed. It was like
a subdivision, something to get through as fast as possible.
Pender could only be happy in emptiness.

Two miles and two short portages later, the storm hit with
all its fury just as he entered the last lake before the border
lakes. In minutes the breeze became a wind out of the southwest, then swirled and shifted suddenly, coming from the
north, then picked up intensity. Waves formed quickly—a
chop, then breaking waves, then whitecaps and deep troughs.
At another time in his life, he would have headed for shelter.
It was the wise thing to do. But not this year. To hell with
the storm. His whole life was a storm. He pressed on.

He steered his boat into the waves and paddled hard to
maintain forward motion and keep the canoe hitting the waves
straight on. If he got sideways to waves that big, he would
capsize in the blink of an eye. Even if he managed not to
drown, he'd lose a lot of gear—maybe all of it—and his trip
would be over.

The wind built to stiff gusts, some coming at a different
angle from the waves. The quartering winds tried to push the
nose of the canoe on an angle to the waves, with a capsize

certain to follow. So Pender fought the wind and waves as if his life depended on it, fought to keep the bow pointing into the waves, paddling ten, twenty, even thirty consecutive strokes on one side of the canoe to maintain his angle.

Then rain came in pelts. The wind and surf were too dangerous for him to pause even for a few seconds to don his rain gear. Mistake number one, he thought. He should have put on the rain gear before he got in open water. There couldn't be a mistake number two.

He gritted his teeth and paddled furiously. He willed himself to reach the lee of a peninsula a kilometer ahead. He focused on the waves, blocked out the pain and exhaustion. Ignored the fear and the nightmares about drowning.

It took another twenty minutes to reach the calm waters of the peninsula's lee side. He stopped in the shallows, donned his raincoat, took a long drink of water, and eyed the banks of the peninsula's shore. He could sit out the storm in the protected water there. He could see a tent on the peninsula and another farther down the shore. The lake was pockmarked with campsites.

"Hell no." He said it even though he had no audience. He wouldn't base camp with a bunch of picnickers. He was a wilderness tripper, and he'd settle for nothing less.

He checked his map and compass and paddled back into the tempest. It took another twenty minutes to reach the choppy waters of the lake's partially sheltered north shore. Shielded from the wind, he portaged past a fast-moving creek and then paddled to the portage trail that led to the border lake.

The launch area into the border lake was partially sheltered from the wind. A large landmass a few hundred meters northeast of the put-in made it seem as though Pender was launching into another small lake, but he was entering the southern end of the sprawling Lac La Croix, a twisting mass of islands and inlets and peninsulas forming roughly twenty miles of liquid border between Minnesota and Ontario. As soon as he passed that landmass he would be in unprotected water again, fighting for his life.

After a short rest, Pender floated into the bay, hugging the shore to take advantage of the sheltered water while he could. At the end of the landmass he looked north and saw whitecaps and deep troughs and wind whistling spray into the air. It would have been scary if he thought about it, but he didn't.

Pender paddled into the mayhem, and his world became impossible. Wild winds whipped the lake into a cauldron of boiling waves and drove the rain horizontally into his face. The canoe bounced and lurched crazily as he thrashed to keep it upright. The wind and waves nearly turned him over several times, but he saved himself each time, reaching out in wide sweeping brace strokes to keep the hull from rolling and to keep the bow heading into the waves.

Despite his boatmanship, he was losing the battle. Water splashed over the bow with each wave, and each time he braced he took water over the gunnels. Water already sloshed in the bottom of the boat. The extra weight made the boat hard to handle. He was close to swamping.

He fought his way to the shoreline and hugged it as he continued north. He remembered the kid's notations on the map indicating there was a campsite on that shore and another on an island a half kilometer farther north. As he drew near the first campsite, his hopes for shelter were dashed by the sight of two canoes on the shore, hulls up. Above the water-line, on a ten-foot rise, two tents shook in the wind and four men huddled under a canopy that slanted into the weather, sheltering them from the gale. They saw him just as he started to move on. Two came down to the shore to hail him, beer cans in hand.

"Come on up, bud," one of them yelled. A heavy, burly guy with a pink complexion. "Plenty of room!" Pender could barely hear him in the roar of the wind.

"Plenty of beer!" said the other guy, like he had found the secret to eternal happiness. He was heavy, balding, with several days' beard. He held his beer can aloft as if celebrating.

Pender expressed his regrets with a shaking head and paddled on.

"It's too dangerous!" shouted the first guy.

But his words were lost in the wind. Pender wasn't in the mood for company, especially not beer-swilling fishermen. He'd seen an ice chest by their tents. An ice chest! It infuriated him. The beer cans, too. Cans and bottles were illegal in the pristine Boundary Waters/Quetico wilderness and an insult to anyone who loved the place. It would be better to die than spend time with assholes like that.

He thrashed against the elements for another five hundred meters to the other campsite. It was a dismal little spot on a low island, the land rising a few feet above shallows filled with reeds and low-lying scrub. It was the kind of site in the kind of place that desperate paddlers settled for when weather or darkness or sheer exhaustion demanded an immediate stop in their journeys. That was him. He was tired and hungry and, despite his exertions, becoming more chilled by the minute . . . a warning that hypothermia was lurking.

Pender didn't bother with the established campsite near the water. He moved into the pines and found a small wind-protected area formed by a rock structure about four feet

high. The ground was lumpy, hard, and slanted—horrible for
sleeping—but it was well drained and protected from falling
trees, and if the wind didn't shift, he'd be able to cook on his
gas stove. That was as good as he would do today.

He ate a meal of salami, soup, nuts, and raisins in the tent
amid a steady driving wind, intermittent rains, and nightmare
skies. He started writing in the journal to his daughter. He
scrawled, "Dear Margaret," then stopped. What do you say
to someone you loved more than life itself for twenty years
and now don't know?

He wrote about her birth and early childhood because
that's what he was thinking about. He could see her in his
mind, so unbelievably tiny, so vulnerable. It had seemed
impossible she could survive, and he couldn't imagine himself sleeping soundly ever again for all the worrying he did.
Jesus, had that been him?

Eventually he drifted off to sleep, sitting up, his back
against the food pack, his butt cushioned on his flotation
vest. Keeping the food pack inside the tent was a calculated
risk, but the wind was too fierce to hang a pack this day, and
Pender was in a meaner mood than any Quetico black bear.

He awakened a little after 11 PM, startled by the sense that
something had changed. The wind and rain had stopped, and
there was a vague, distant noise in the stillness. He emerged
from the tent into the light of a billion stars and a large
glowing moon. Light so bright he could see his shadow. And
spectacular. He held his breath in awe as he surveyed a night
sky exploding in a luminescence greater than all the combined
fireworks displays in history.

Slowly, he became aware of the distant noise. It was the
pulsing bass of rock and roll. Tinny guitar notes. Cymbals.

The drunken laughter of the beer-swilling fishermen camped on the near point.

He tried to resist the anger, but he couldn't. He tried to block out the faint noise, but it was all he could hear. He tried not to think about elegant acts of retribution, but they filled his mind like a movie he couldn't stop watching.

He tried to resist hating the drunken louts partying like they were in a bar, but the frustrations of dealing with people fascinated with the stink of their own shit flowed from every pore of his body until he all could hear was the voices rolling across the dark lake.

He tried to sleep again, succeeding only in dozing off for brief naps, fantasizing about appropriate acts of wilderness justice for the goons who would treat this pristine place like a country bar. At 2:30 AM the voices were gone, but sleep was impossible. Under the blazing night sky he struck camp. When he was done, he lay down on his raincoat and gazed at the heavens for a long while, light from a billion stars reminding him how insignificant he was and how briefly he would be part of the cosmos.

How ironic, he thought, that most of humanity can no longer see the heavens displayed like this because we have blinded ourselves with the ambient lighting of civilization.

That irony stirred him to action. He loaded his canoe and paddled toward the fishermen's campsite. The nearer he got, the more it felt like being on an ambush patrol many years ago. Stealth. Silence. Adrenaline building. The world around him in sharp focus.

He stopped just short of the shore and walked the boat to the beach area. He moved to the fishermen's canoes, as silent as a shadow, carried them to the beach, and placed them next to his canoe. He worked his way up to the campsite, pausing with each step to avoid the noise of a dislodged rock or snapping twig or tripping over an unseen guy line.

The campsite had log benches erected in a square with the fire ring forming the fourth side. Packs were bunched against the benches. Tarps covered a kitchen area. He could see the beer chest, its white top glowing in the night light. The boom box sat next to it.

He picked up the boom box and made his way back to the canoes, moving like a ghost.

He put the boom box in his canoe and used nylon cord to connect the fishermen's canoes to each other, then to his boat, like a three-canoe train. He eased all three canoes into the water and paddled away. The fishermen's camp remained dark and silent, the only noise the dripping of water from his paddle as he brought it forward at the end of each stroke.

He stopped in a shallow bay, just out of sight from the fishermen's camp. He untied the line to the first canoe and lashed it to the boom box, then lowered the device into the water, feeding line hand-over-hand until it touched bottom. He left the fishermen's canoes in their hidden mooring and began paddling in an easterly direction, picking his way through the islands and reefs. He would stay in the border lakes, paddling south and east for a day or two, then move into Quetico and work his way slowly east and north.

As he paddled, Pender wondered if the morning winds would blow the canoes into the view of the fishermen. He wondered if they'd have the guts to swim for the boats. Only a few hundred meters or so but in sixty-degree water, it would be no cakewalk. He shrugged. It didn't matter to him. The boats would be found soon enough, and whoever found them would find the owners. They'd be out of commission for a day at most. They'd be mad, of course. Those kind always are. They might even try to find him. A recon guy would figure him for a tripper, maybe check the portages going east and south, try to get lucky.

He thought about that as he paddled in the eerie light of a star-filled sky and thought even more about what kind of person thinks he's going to get chased in a wilderness by the victims of a mostly harmless prank.

At the first dim light of morning, he portaged into the next lake. By the time the sun peeked above the tree line to the east, Pender was halfway to his next portage. He would be miles from the scene of his crime before noon. And in a day or two he would disappear into the labyrinthine wilds of Quetico, where he would be invisible, nothing more than a molecule in an eighteen-hundred-square mile maze of lakes and rivers and forests.

8

The Stuarts and their dog burst into the Canadian Shield Outfitters building at 6:30 in the morning, a high-energy power couple, freshly showered and groomed, clad in fine L.L. Bean outdoor clothing, and eager to take on the world.

Mr. Stuart was in his forties, a tall, fleshy man in good shape. He walked with the decisiveness of a commanding general and oozed self-importance. Even if Annette hadn't read their file, she would have known he was the owner of a large company in the U.S.

Mrs. Stuart was nearly as tall as Annette, athletic, and very toned. A fitness fanatic. She was in her late thirties, maybe even forty, elegantly beautiful in a day-spa kind of way, with highlighted hair, a nice tan, and skin as perfect as a cover girl's. Annette felt a pang of something like jealousy. Mrs. Stuart looked a lot like the elegant women in the photos of Gabe Pender's restaurant industry events. There were endless pages of them on the Internet, the events and the glamor people and Pender. So many she wondered why he would have any lingering interest in her.

Mrs. Stuart tried to control the dog, a manic cross between a Labrador and a standard poodle that had not stopped moving since they entered the place. When he caught sight of the animals mounted on the walls, he pranced and bucked for the chance to give chase.

Annette smiled and introduced herself. "I've prepared your trip plan, and I'll be taking you through your gear and your trip plan this morning," she said. Mrs. Stuart smiled slightly as they shook hands; her husband stared at Annette for a moment before accepting her outstretched hand.

He flushed angrily. "I thought I was dealing with Guy and Dan Gilbert."

As in man-to-man, executive-to-executive, realized Annette.

"I've been running the canoe outfitting business since spring," said Annette. "Don't worry, I've been guiding in Quetico for twenty-five years. I know your route very well . . ."

As she said it, Stuart's face flushed again. She started to wonder why, and then she knew. How macho could his Quetico expedition be if a woman had already done it?

"But I took the liberty of consulting with Dan, too, so you get the benefit of a lot of experience." She made it sound like they didn't do that for everyone.

"Sure, sure," said Stuart. "All the same, I'd like to see Guy or Dan. Can you call one of them?"

Annette refused to be offended. "Sorry, Guy is out of town, and Dan is doing a fly-in party right now. He'll be back around ten, if you want to wait. Otherwise, you're in good hands. Really."

"We can't wait that long. Goddamn it, this is no way to run a business. I have half a mind to just blow the whole thing off. Who's taking us to French Lake?"

"I'll be taking you." Annette focused on the paperwork in her hands. She didn't need to see the man's disappointment at the knowledge his conquest of nature was starting with a woman driver.

The dog was panting and straining against its leash. Mrs. Stuart was struggling to hold him in check. Stuart glanced at the dog, then at Annette. "Okay, let's get going."

"We have a few things to do here, first," said Annette. "I want to show you your maps and talk you through the route. Then we need to go through your packs so you know where everything is. I'll show you how to set up the tent and light the stove."

"No need," said Stuart. "I'm sure we can figure it out."

Annette frowned. The worst complaints Quetico outfitters received came from novices like the Stuarts who thought backpacking in the mountains prepared them for canoe camping in the Canadian Shield.

"I just want to get going," he said. "We've safaried in Africa, backpacked the Rockies, kayaked in Greenland, all that stuff. I know how to pitch a tent and light a stove. We're good to go." He gestured impatiently with one hand, a hurry-up motion coming from an important man accustomed to giving orders and having people snap-to immediately.

Annette held her tongue. People like Stuart usually didn't come to the Quetico side of the border, but this one had something to prove, something the Boundary Waters wasn't big enough to handle. He wanted to do a long trip, cross Quetico. He came to Canadian Shield Outfitters because of CSO's fly-in/paddle-out trip. Very macho. The client is flown into a lake on one of Quetico's borders, then paddles out. Or, in his case, vice versa. He and his wife would be paddling from the northeast corner of Quetico through the heart of the park to the Minnesota border, then east to the southeast corner of Quetico, where a CSO floatplane would air-lift them back to Atikokan.

"Okay," said Annette. "But we have to do a trip plan review. It's the law. I can't put you in the park without making sure you know your route and what to do in an emergency." It wasn't Ontario law, but it was her law and that was close enough.

He sighed like an important man having to put up with a petty bureaucrat. "Okay," he said. "Lexie, take that mutt outside. This'll just take a minute."

Annette suggested they both sit in for the trip plan review, but Stuart waved her off. "I take care of this stuff," he said.

"But if you have an accident—"

"Then we both die." He cut her off, finished the sentence, and turned his back on her all in one quick moment. Mrs. Stuart left the building in silent strides, her body tense, the dog hopping and circling her, wrapping her in the leash.

"Your charts are in here," Annette told him, heading for the trip planning room. Stuart ignored her for several long moments, taking time to gaze at the array of stuffed wildlife on the walls of the main room. Making sure she knew who was in charge. When he finally joined her, she started taking him through his route, pointing out landmarks for portages, places to fish for different species, locations of primitive campsites. As she started on the second day, he cut her off again.

"I don't need this, Miss. I've studied these maps already, and I talked to Dan. Lexie and I have read books about this place. We're ready."

Annette stared at him for a moment. "If you get ten days of good weather, this might be as easy as you think it's going to be. But we almost never get ten consecutive days of good weather. Chances are you're going to get wind and rain some of the time, and things can get very difficult. It'll just take a few minutes."

"We'll be fine."

Annette shrugged. She packaged their charts in waterproof plastic and loaded them and their gear in a CSO van. Stuart sat in front. His wife settled into the back seat with the dog, trying to control his hyperactive whining and jumping.

"How long have you had the dog?" Annette asked.

"Got him last winter when we decided to do this trip." The man said it like it was a grand proclamation. "Lexie was worried about the bears. Problem solved. He'll make enough noise to discourage any bear."

Annette tried to hide her smile. Quetico's black bears tended to be shy creatures, keeping their distance from canoe trippers. The worst of them were more nuisances than dangerous, unless you got between a sow and her cub.

"Have you boat-trained the dog?" she asked. A big hyper dog in a trip-laden canoe could be a much bigger danger than bears.

"Yeah. They're born to it." The man waved his hand dismissively. "We had him out a couple times, made him sit. He was fine."

"Did you have him lying on packs?" A seventy-pound dog lying on top of a voyageur pack raised the canoe's center of gravity substantially. If the dog stood and tried to move around, the results could be catastrophic.

"He'll be fine." Stuart smiled.

"Do me a favor," said Annette. "Make it a point to wear your flotation vests today."

"We know what we're doing, Miss." Stuart looked out the window, away from Annette.

"Humor me. Just for today," said Annette. "More than a few dog trips start out wet." Stuart smiled and agreed without a shred of sincerity.

As Annette steered the van through the curves and hills of Highway 11 on her way back to Atikokan, her thoughts returned to Lexie Stuart. She had looked so imperious when she walked in the door—beautiful, rich, and glamorous. Annette had assumed Mrs. Stuart was a powerful woman in her own right, maybe the owner of her own company or the president of someone else's. Someone used to giving orders. Someone who had an active sex life, maybe with her husband, maybe with someone else.

And yet she obeyed her husband with the silent acquiescence of a housemaid. Annette tried to understand how that could be, but she couldn't. No one had ever treated her that way, not even Rob. Not even the youthful Pender.

Which got her thinking about the photos on the *Menu* website, the ones showing Pender posing with famous chefs and restaurateurs, with beautiful talk-show personalities, speaking to large groups of sumptuously dressed power people. He had lived the life of the American ideal. Rich. Well known, if not famous. Connected to the glitterati. He was still an attractive man and probably well off. He could have his pick of countless women, all of them younger and more attractive than her.

What kind of man leaves that behind to spend a month in the wilderness and rendezvous with a grandmother with weather-beaten skin and the wardrobe of a coal miner? The more she thought about it, the more she figured he must not be interested in sex anymore. Maybe the divorce did it. Or just age. It happened. A whole industry had evolved to help mature men get boners at the right time. She snickered at the thought.

Maybe the rendezvous really would be just a picnic and a handshake, two old friends getting caught up. When she told Christy that's how it would be, that's what she expected. But in the dark, lonely moments of the Canadian night, she sometimes dreamed that it would be like old times. They'd meet. They'd touch. The electricity would flow again. She'd feel those feelings, like when they were kids in college. As she dreamed it, she felt it, and the sensation was so intense she sometimes had to get up and walk it off, let the chill of the night divert her thoughts back to the here and now, create space from the impossible fantasy. She was a sixty-year-old grandmother, far past the age of torrid sex and steamy love affairs.

9

Pender paddled easily all day, hugging the Canadian side of the border lakes, basking in the beauty of a perfect day in Eden. He kept focused on the here and now, the waterfowl bobbing on the water, the bow of his canoe slicing through the water, the forest next to him, jack pines giving way to spruce, birch to red pines, to species he couldn't identify.

When he stopped to make coffee, he thought about the fat fishermen and wondered if they had found their canoes yet. He could picture them, hopping mad, wanting blood, threatening to come after him. He laughed at the thought. His leisurely pace was probably faster than they could sprint, and they wouldn't have any idea what direction he was traveling. Maybe next year they'd go to a fishing lodge or some kind of shit-kicker convention where they belonged.

In midafternoon he cast a lure out and trolled it behind the canoe, fishing for dinner as he went. Forty minutes later he boated a meal-sized northern pike on the edge of a reef, filleted it on a rocky islet, and then looked for a place to camp.

He favored the Quetico side of the border lakes because it was less used and Canada didn't require trippers to camp in designated campsites. It would be easy to disappear in Quetico, and that's what he wanted—a total departure from the grid.

He found an obscure island covered with pines that was perfect for his needs. Its lake-facing shore rose steeply to fifty-foot bluffs, making canoe access almost impossible. He paddled to the other side, which was separated from the mainland by a narrow channel clogged with reeds and brush, making access difficult for canoeists. There was no established campsite on the island or the mainland, so there would be no neighbors and no ranger patrols stopping by. Pender picked his way through the vegetation and rocky rubble to shore and hauled his gear well into the tree line, out of sight from the channel. There was just enough flat land for a campsite, and it was perfectly secluded, shielded from the main body of the lake by the tall mound that consumed the rest of the island. He built a fire ring in a small opening in the trees, cleared rocks and pinecones from a space where his tent would go, and collected dead wood for his fire.

He cooked his meal while the sun was still bright so the flames wouldn't give away his presence, and he kept the fire small, almost smokeless. He hiked up the mound behind his campsite to eat, perched on a rock overlooking the lake, taking care to stay in the shadows so no roving ranger would see him and come by to check his permit. He didn't have one. He was off the grid. He believed in paying for permits to support the wilderness, had always done it, and he'd make this trip right someday, too. But for right now, this trip was different. This was about escape, a big *up yours* to everyone who ever drew lines or made rules or told you to just wait your goddamn turn. He needed to disappear from that world and melt into this one the way a wolf could, just slip into the green and vanish like a dream at sunrise.

Pender ate slowly and got outside himself mentally, focusing on the world around him. An eagle floated high overhead in search of fish. Two canoes moved slowly in opposing directions on the big lake, maybe fishing, maybe just enjoying an early-evening paddle. A scrawny squirrel stared at him from ten feet away, and he stared back, thinking the squirrel probably never saw a human being before, because, really, who but Pender would ever camp here?

When the meal was over, the dishes washed, and the campfire ashes dispersed, he set up his tent and wrote in his journal. He told his daughter about his trip, described the lake he was on, what he'd been thinking about, how he hoped she was well. As the early-evening calm swept over the woods and water, he moved back up the bluff and found a comfortable perch overlooking the lake. He relaxed and let his senses take in the gentle transition from evening to night in a world as quiet as a whisper.

An hour before dark, he noticed two men in a canoe moving rapidly south. They were big men, and they paddled hard and fast. He thought they were looking for a campsite because they stopped at the two established campsites Pender could see. At the first one, they hailed the camp from the water and two campers came down to the beach. After a short exchange Pender couldn't hear, the canoeists paddled directly to the second site. Again they sat offshore and hailed the site, but this time, no one returned their greeting. Instead of taking the campsite, though, they paddled farther south, moving fast. Pender was puzzled. If they weren't looking for a campsite, what were they doing?

Then it hit him with a jolt. They were looking for *some-one*. He felt a shock through his entire body. He knew who they were, even though it wasn't possible. It was the fishermen. Two of the four. He had managed to piss off two beer-swilling, fat-gut fishermen who could paddle like the wind and were mad enough to strangle a bear.

It couldn't be. No one was crazy enough to search for someone in a canoe in this wilderness. It was impossible. There were maybe two dozen different ways he could have gone between their camp and here. It was impossible they'd come this way. But deep inside, Pender knew it was them. Jesus, what were the odds?

He took a breath, told himself to think like a recon man. They had played the odds that he'd stay on the border lakes, and they'd guessed right about which direction he went when he got to the border. That wasn't so remarkable. Tomorrow would be much more difficult for them. They'd have to guess if he stayed on the border, slipped back into the Boundary Waters, or paddled into Quetico. There were so many trip options for him the only way they could trail him would be asking other canoe parties if they'd seen him. His disadvantage was being a solo canoeist. There weren't many. Fewer still in a seventeen-and-a-half-foot uncoated Kevlar boat. But if no one saw him, the trail would run cold tomorrow.

He broke camp in the dark the next morning. Before he got under way, he stared into the blackness to the south, where the fat boys had gone, searching for lights or any sign of a canoe, listening for any sound. Nothing. He paddled in the opposite direction for an hour in darkness and the dimmest light of early morning, avoiding the logical portages into the Quetico hinterlands, heading instead for a long, hard trail no rational canoeist would use.

Shortly after first light, he located the portage trail at the northern extremity of a deep bay, but his hope for a surreptitious entry into Quetico was smashed. Just a few steps from the trail was a tent with a canoe out front. Two men making breakfast saw him and waved.

Bad luck, he thought. If the fat boys asked here, they'd be on his trail again. But then again, the fat boys would be nuts to burn an hour to check out this deep bay. The odds were much better that they were tired of looking for him. They'd have jobs to get back to, families waiting.

Pender took the precaution of stashing the gear for his second trip back in the trees, out of sight from the bay. He loaded a pack and the canoe and started down the trail. It was a grueling hike with a mix of steep grades and muddy flats, but Pender enjoyed the workout, knowing no one else would be dumb enough to use this trail.

As he struggled through his second trip, he encountered two paddlers going the opposite way. Young guys. Late teens, early twenties maybe. They exchanged greetings. One called out, "Hey, nice boat. I bet that thing flies, eh?"

Pender smiled, nodded, and kept moving, but the damage was done. Another canoe party had seen him and they saw his canoe and they saw where he was going.

When he got to the other side, a third member of the group was just hoisting a pack on his shoulders.

"Nice boat." He wanted to start a conversation.

"Thanks," said Pender, placing his canoe in the water, then loading both packs, trying to keep moving.

"Traveling by yourself?"

"Yup."

"Doesn't that get lonely?"

"Nah."

"Where you headed?"

"Lac La Croix." There was logic to Pender's lie. A loop from here back to Lac La Croix was a good trip plan for a strong paddler. If the fat boys talked to this group, they'd leave this lake in the wrong direction and never see or hear of Pender again.

He stepped into the canoe and paddled into a lake he'd never seen before, leaving in his wake three more people who knew he entered the lake that morning. He still wasn't worried that the fat boys would find him, but he'd survived Vietnam thanks to luck and caution, and he'd play it safe for a couple days, just in case, keep moving, avoid popular lakes, camp in hidden sites.

He paddled and portaged north and east, covering more lakes that he'd never seen before, encountering no one. He was getting into Quetico's least-seen parts.

Each morning he woke before sunrise, struck camp in the dark, pushed off as the sky lightened. Paddled long and hard as if he was racing, portaged hard and fast, for no other reason than to feel the exhaustion. To create physical pain that got his mind off everything else. To be exhausted enough to sleep through the night and not think about his train wreck of a life.

He took his breakfasts on the water as he watched the sun rise above tree-studded bluffs, listened to the gulls and loons. He made coffee at a morning portage. Lunches came at the end of midday portages, a quick sandwich and a handful of peanuts on the beach, washed down with cold lake water. Dinner was fish cooked over a campfire to conserve his freeze-dried rations and stove fuel.

Pender considered himself a poor fisherman at best, but even he could catch a meal-sized northern or bass in Quetico. He started looking for promising structures around four o'clock each day—rocky reefs, steep-drop cliffs, deep weeds, and creek mouths. He'd invest a half dozen casts in each, and then move on, trolling a lure to the next spot. He'd catch his fish and fillet it on a nearby rock structure, leaving the remains for the gulls and scavengers. Then he'd look for a campsite at least a kilometer away from where he cleaned the fish. He'd prepare his meal before setting up camp, partly to enjoy the freshest fish in the world, partly so that if a bear lured in by his cooking aromas refused to leave, he could depart with little trouble. It had never happened to him, but an old guide had told him about the technique and he adopted it for himself ever since. The guide told him that sometimes you had to pitch your tent in the dark, so Pender had practiced pitching his tent at night in the backyard of his fashionable suburban home. His wife and daughter thought maybe he was losing his mind, but he insisted that being the only person on the block who could pitch a tent in the dark would bring great status to the family. He was the only one who thought that was funny.

He lost himself in the rhythms of the days. The silence. The hard work. The tired muscles. Falling asleep to the weeping calls of the loons and breezes whispering in the conifers. The days became a blur. Rain, sun, fog. The quiescence of the mornings, the afternoon breezes. The portages in smears of green and granite. Blue-water lakes, coffee-colored bogs. Clouds. Mist. Sun.

He tried to focus on the moment. Staying on his bearing mark. Regulating his paddling cadence. Carving his strokes to correct for wind and waves. Scanning for movement, for the chance to see a moose or bear or wolf. He tried to keep his idle time to a minimum and use it to plan the next day.

Tried not to think about his life. The disaster of his life.

Each night as he ate in the glow of dying campfire embers and washed dishes in the light of a headlamp, he allowed himself to think about Annette. He tried to think about her with detached passion, to keep his expectations low. This was not a time in his life for optimism. But the thing was, he had never forgotten her. Of all the people in his life, there had probably never been a week that he hadn't thought about her at least once. Her voice. Her smile. Her beauty. The goodness of her that he could feel, even when they were arguing madly. Which was often.

"I hope you get drafted and you go to Vietnam and you get shot and you die there!"

God, the greatest breakup line ever. He had thought about it just about every day he was in the army. Freezing his ass off in basic training. Boiling in the putrid heat in advanced infantry training. And especially in Vietnam. Swatting mosquitoes, sitting in the rain all night waiting for Charlie to walk into an ambush, drinking warm beer in camp, mounting a prostitute on R&R. It was always there. The woman he couldn't get out of his mind wanted him dead. Even when he could realize she didn't mean it, it hurt.

Forty years later, sitting in the middle of an empty wilderness, trying to deal with the end of his life, he still remembered what she had said, her voice when she said it, her precise diction that added such elegance to everything she said.

"I hope you get drafted and you go to Vietnam and you get shot and you die there!"

He wondered what she looked like now. The small photo of her in the brochure revealed a slim build and strong facial structure, but that was it. She'd have some lines and wrinkles. God knows he did. He wasn't expecting a college beauty.

Didn't want one. His ex was a glamour girl, and look how that turned out. It would be enough if Annette was just a nice person. No shattered ego, no seething anger about life's unfairness. The opposite of him.

But he told himself to expect the worst because that's how these things always turned out. It would be fun for a day or two. Talk about old times, conjure sweet reminiscences of that brief moment of innocence they shared. Get caught up on the last forty years. Where were you when this happened or that? When did you think of me? What did you think? Your kids. Your business. Your life 'til now. What's next?

Then it would get real. Life's disappointments. Arguments, maybe, like old times, over conflicting priorities. She had given up everything to live a principled life. She was a good-hearted Canadian, and she'd made something of herself. He had moved from one moral shit storm to the next—war, corporate war, and the accumulation of wealth. She would find it hard to respect him. He couldn't blame her, but he was done with the judgments of others. Two, maybe three days on the island, he told himself. Then he'd move deeper into Quetico, where only the lost souls go, hoping a compass and a map and the haunting isolation of a beautiful void would somehow bring meaning to their lives. He would bushwhack into no-name lakes, slog into remote bogs, scramble up heights no man had seen in a hundred years, just for the sheer hell of doing it. He would seek out Quetico's most impossible portages and follow them to lakes of oblivion. And when he got tired of it all or when he ran out of food or when the cold weather came, he'd come out of the wilderness and take a train somewhere far away.

10

"The Copellas are due in three days," Annette told Christy. They were reviewing the notes she had compiled in preparation for her trip. "They're not the greatest paddlers, so I want you to take care of their trip plan and take them to the launch yourself."

Christy nodded.

"If there's any wind, you be down here with binoculars and watch them cross the lake," Annette said.

"Okay, Mom!"

"And have your canoe with you, just in case they need a rescue."

"Stop it! I know how to take care of customers."

"I just want to make sure you don't have Eric or one of the other summer people handle it." She shrugged. "They're nice people, and they deserve our best."

Christy watched her mother organize gear in the small outbuilding they used for their outfitting business. Their canoe customers left from Canadian Shield Outfitters, but they carried Quetico Outpost gear, carefully packed by Annette and Christy the night before. Annette was distracted tonight, too caught up in her own thoughts, smiling too wide at quips that weren't that good, her face too animated when she spoke.

"Are you nervous?" Christy asked.

"What, that you'll run off with Eric when I'm gone?" She straightened from her labors, and the two exchanged glances.

"You know what I mean," Christy said. "It's, you know, exciting. Exotic, sort of."

"You mean it's weird. I think that's what I like about it. At my age, you don't get to do too many weird things with men anymore." She put her hands on her hips and looked at her daughter thoughtfully.

"What if he tries to force himself on you?"

Annette laughed. "He's sixty. I'm sixty. He wouldn't force himself on me. He'd ask me to join him in prayer for an erection that lasts long enough to get the deed done."

Christy was long past blushing at her mother's earthy declarations about sex. "Nice try, but you're nervous about something. I can see it."

"Oh, it's just, I'd like this to be fun, but I have a feeling it's going to be sad and depressing in the end. Gabe's had so many things go wrong in his life, and there are so many signs of anger. I just have a feeling I won't like him."

"Why?"

"Your skin isn't the only thing that gets wrinkled and weathered with age," Annette said. "Your soul does too. Things that were cute when you were young get sharp edges later in life. Like your dad's womanizing. Like me having an affair with a married man.

"Even though we argued all the time, Gabe had a kind of purity about him. Deep down inside, he was an idealist. I'd think of him from time to time, even after I married your father. Especially after I married your father. I never regretted doing what I did because I got you and Anne out of it. But Gabe became kind of a symbol of how good a man can be."

"But you argued all the time?" Christy's face was a study in confusion.

"Yes. It's hard to explain. We were both full of self-importance and energy and all the arrogance of youth. There was plenty to dislike. But deep down inside, I always knew he was someone who put other things above his own satisfaction. He cared about the people around him, his society, his culture. If he's become a broken, bitter old man who bitches about everything, that would make the world just a little lonelier."

Annette loaded her food pack while Christy loaded the gear pack that would carry her tent, sleeping bag, and clothing. After a few minutes of silence, Christy stopped and looked at her mother. "How did it get started with you and him? Must have been before Dad . . ."

Annette paused, not sure she wanted to answer her daughter's question.

"Your dad and I were an on-again, off-again item in college," she started, picking her words carefully. "Gabe and I were in the same literature class. I didn't like him at first. He'd always take a contrary point of view in class discussions. And he didn't dress right. He wasn't a prep and he wasn't a hippie and he didn't care."

"You were like that?" Christy was in disbelief.

"Everybody's like that in college. So were you. Anyway, I noticed he kept getting As on papers even though he didn't do any research. I told him what I thought about that, and we had our first argument. But it got us talking to each other, and, somewhere in there, I just fell for him."

"That doesn't make any sense." Christy smiled when she said it, like she understood anyway.

"He was his own man, and I thought that was intoxicating."

They worked in silence for a while, Annette's thoughts flashing back to that time, so long ago.

September 1967.

She was Rob's girl. Rob the Throb. Handsome, smart, smooth. Headed for law school. President of the student council. Cocky, but in a charming way that made him easy to like.

They were an item. There had been a few missteps. He had a few dalliances with other coeds. But they worked through it. They planned to marry when they graduated. She would join him at whatever law school he ended up choosing. Harvard, he hoped, but Yale would do. A career in politics maybe.

It was the politics that drew him, then her, into the movement. He had idealistic objections to the war anyway, but if he wanted to stay out front of the student body even at a conservative Midwestern school, he had to be actively antiwar. So they evolved. From slacks and skirts to patched-up blue jeans. From close-cropped razor cut and puffy bouffant to long, shaggy locks accented with beads, head bands, and accoutrements du jour.

She became aware that it was as much a uniform as skirts and blouses had been, that they were as conformist in their nonconformity as they had been in their conformity days. That's when she started to notice Pender. Mostly because he pissed her off. It was his unspoken arrogance. He was a Greek, first of all, and didn't seem to care that it was uncool. And he never spoke to anyone except the prof. He came to their Modern American Authors class dressed like a postbeatnik prep or something. Loafers, no socks. Jeans, no holes, but old. Button-down shirt, but worn under a cut-off sweatshirt that started the week with a fraternity symbol showing and ended the week inside out.

Annette didn't like his clothes and didn't like his attitude, and she especially didn't like his activity in class. He volunteered answers to the professor's questions. He liked to participate in discussions. It was the only time he talked, and he could get very animated. It was irritating, for some reason. And the prof liked him. It was obvious. Some of his points were wildly divergent from the professor's teachings, but they were clever and energetically defended and the prof liked that.

Why she disliked him but didn't mind the several intellectuals who, with Pender, dominated discussions, she couldn't say. But she couldn't stand him. So much so that one day she finally vented to him. They had gotten graded papers back and she saw his grade, an A–, and the title of his paper, "Who's Got a Match in 'Lie Down in Darkness'?" Clearly his paper bore no resemblance to the painstakingly researched, heavily footnoted work that had earned her another A.

She tapped him on the shoulder. "May I see your paper?" she asked.

After a slight pause—he seemed surprised that she talked to him—he handed it to her.

"Would you like to see mine?" she asked. He accepted it but flipped through it quickly. She scanned his almost as fast. Not a single footnote. Instead of quoting heralded literary critics, he constructed his own criticism, which was much different from the mainstream interpretation of the book's main characters. The arrogant shit!

After class she gave his paper back to him. "Where do you get this stuff?" she asked angrily. "I can't believe you get such good grades for so little research!"

Real anger flashed in his eyes. "What's so brilliant about parroting stuff someone else wrote?" he answered.

"That was the assignment." She couldn't hide her anger. "To analyze the plot and characters based on our reading of the book and at least three critics. It really irks me that I spent hours in the library reading the critics and you blow it off and get almost the same grade."

"And I don't see how you deserve a better grade for not having an original thought," he responded. "I don't give a damn what some so-called critic thinks. Literature is about what the reader thinks."

His answer bugged her all weekend. She hadn't thought of education as a forum for creative thinking, except in courses explicitly designed for creativity, like art or creative writing. She was amazed that he could get by doing that. She tried to chalk it up to favoritism by the prof—a man giving another man a break in a male-dominated world. But, of course, she got a better grade for following the traditional path and doing it well.

After that he would say hello to her when they saw each other before class. A noncommittal, soft-smile hello. She returned the greeting with equal equanimity. He still aggravated her. Maybe even more because she noticed he was sort of attractive. She couldn't quite say why. He had moody brown eyes that flashed with passion. Solid chin. Athletic build. He was no Rob, but she kept thinking about him, wondering why she thought about him when she didn't like him.

Later, after a really obnoxious class session in which he had taken on the prof and two of the scholars in the class in a debate over symbolism in Old Man and the Sea, *he ended up walking beside her on their way out of the building. His adrenaline was still pumping and it bugged her. He said something to her and she answered. He began chatting away about something—she was too nettled to pay attention. At the bottom of the stairs outside the building, they paused and faced each other.*

"Why are you in a fraternity?" she blurted out. She couldn't believe she had said it when she heard her voice make the sounds. It wasn't like her at all, but she was irritated beyond reason with him.

He blinked at first and hesitated. "Oh, you mean, why aren't I like you freethinkers? Because when I got here, every asshole I met told me only assholes go Greek." He started to walk away, offended, then stopped. "How 'independent' do you think you are? You all wear prefaded bell-bottom jeans and the beads and the hair and everything. It's a goddamn uniform, and if I have to wear a uniform to fuck a girl like you, I'll go without."

"You don't have to be gross about it," she huffed. And left.

Now she really couldn't get him out of her mind. She thought about him when she researched papers in the library. She thought about him when she dressed and when she looked at how Rob and other men were dressed. She thought about him when she and Rob made love. She replayed the confrontation endlessly, initially to confirm that his response was as uncalled for as it was obscene, later to see how she might have come across as arrogant. By Friday she had condemned herself for being an arrogant bitch and sought him out after class to apologize.

"You were right to be angry with me. I was rude. I'm sorry." She braced for a sarcastic response, but he just stared at her. The silence grew. She felt herself squirming, not sure what it meant, finally deciding he was just staring her down. A statement all by itself. You're not worthy of words.

"Okay," she said summarily. "See you around." She started to go. He touched her shoulder.

"I just didn't know what to say."

That stopped her cold. He was sincere, and he seemed to be struggling to say more. She realized he was tongue-tied. Mr. Ego. How about that? She waited.

"I dream about you," he said. He blushed crimson and turned and left before she could move a muscle. As she watched him leave, her mind filled with the vision of his face when he said he dreamed about her. It was the most romantic thing anyone had ever said to her. The most romantic thing she could imagine.

She sought him out after that. They started taking coffee together after Modern American Authors, then lunch on Tuesdays and Thursdays. In November they were in a one-act student play together. By Thanksgiving it was all she could do to keep her hands off him.

Christy made each of them a cup of Quetico Outpost tea, their own concoction of powdered tea and apple cider and cinnamon, served scalding hot. They took their tea on the patio behind the house, gazing past the cabins to the lake. The sun was behind the horizon, their world becoming dim and quiet. Annette inhaled deeply. Twilight was one of the perfect moments on the Canadian Shield. You could still see the lakes and the trees, and you could already see stars, and all the world was wrapped in quiet. The silence was a lullaby and the view was eternity. How could anyone walk away from that?

"If you don't like him, just come home," Christy said. "You have me and Rebecca and a lot of friends here. Your world doesn't revolve around him."

Annette kissed her daughter on the cheek and smiled. "You're right," she said.

11

"Well, shit."

After crashing blindly through dense forest for an eternity, Pender stumbled into the open and teetered on the edge of a small bog. Probably a lake twenty years ago, now a murky swamp choked with plant life and oozing black water as viscous as oil.

He sighed. The best part of this little side trip had been the getting here. A mile with no trail, crashing through the bush, navigating by dead reckoning with a compass. Not an outing for the faint hearted. Following compass headings in dense brush and forest, with the land constantly falling away or rising, was as much art as science.

He hoisted the heavy food pack on his shoulders and started the long trek back. It would have been easier if he'd left the food pack with the canoe and his other gear, but he didn't want to risk losing his food to a marauding bear.

As he dodged and grunted through the thick foliage and steep bluffs, he let his mind roam. Annette's image floated forth from his memories, back when it started between them.

Sitting on the steps of the library, still arguing about the papers they were working on for Modern American Authors. It was cold. The kind of cold that brought color to the face of a pretty girl, let you see the vapors of your breath mingle with hers. Cold enough that it felt good to sit with their bodies touching because it was warm.

"Why do you argue all the time?" She was smiling, but she was serious, too.

"It brings out the best in you."

"By making me angry?"

"No." Pender blew on his hands to warm them in the chill. "By bringing out the real you. Making you stick up for yourself."

"Instead of what?"

"Sticking with the script. Saying what you're supposed to say. There's a lot more to you than those 'make love not war' stiffs."

"Those are my friends. We share an ideal."

"No, you have the ideals. They recite the lines like parrots and wait for their hit on the roach. You have honesty and depth."

"That's the nicest thing you've ever said to me."

It had never occurred to him that such a beautiful woman cared what he thought. It put her in a different context. Suddenly it was personal, and it overpowered him. His heart raced. His mouth went dry.

"What are you thinking?" There was doubt in her voice, like she wasn't sure what he'd say. Her, the most beautiful girl on campus.

The only thing he could think of was how lovely she was and how soft her lips must be and that if she were his girlfriend, he'd be with her every minute, not like that jackass she was seeing now.

"What?" she said again. "Are you making fun of me?"

He shook his head no. Words wouldn't come to him.

She read him. Against all odds, she read him and just like that leaned over and kissed him, soft and long. He could feel her skin, her breath, her body pivoting to his. They sprawled on the steps of the library, locked in embrace. He inhaled her scent—fresh air, faint lilacs, something else, velvety and distant.

They embraced passionately until other students started teasing them. They stood, smiled at each other a little sheepishly, and began walking. Annette abruptly stopped and turned in front of Pender.

"Was that real or are you just trying to get in my pants?"

"It was real."

"I bet. You probably bed a different girl every week."

"Not even every year."

"Right."

"I'll wake up tomorrow still remembering what you smell like and what your body feels like, and I'll go crazy thinking that you're waking up with Senator Peabody or whatever your boyfriend's name is. So, yeah, it's real."

She put her fingers on his lips. "Rob and I broke up a couple weeks ago."

"You dumped Boy Wonder?"

"He dumped me." She smiled, maybe covering the hurt. "Lots of girls are interested in him. I think he needs to take a taste test."

"He doesn't deserve you."

"He's got his faults, but his work is important. And people look up to him."

"Yeah, people looked up to Hitler and Stalin, too. You're too good for him."

"Too good for the most popular guy on campus?"

"Yeah. Way too good. Too beautiful. Too smart. Too . . ." He searched for a word. "Too deep."

"You know all this about me after one kiss?"

"No, after a month of wondering why the hell it hurt so much that you didn't like me."

So began their affair.

Pender's recollections were shattered as the baseball-sized stones under his right foot gave way. He fell hard, before he knew he was falling, and hit on his back and tailbone and slid down the steep slope. The pack saved his head from banging against the rocks, but his back and tailbone were shot with pain.

He lay still for a moment, assessing the damage. His back throbbed, but he could move his fingers and toes and head. He unfastened the pack and wriggled out of the shoulder harness. More agony gripped his lower back. He had to hold his breath to withstand the shock. He calmed his body so he could breathe. When he was ready, he took a deep breath, held it, and forced himself into a sitting position. He could feel something like a red-hot poker being shoved down his spine. It made him gasp. When the worst passed, he pivoted onto his knees, holding his breath, clinching his teeth to work through the pain.

He tried to stand, cried out, and bent forward, hands on thighs, to arrest the fire shooting through his back and down his right leg. Standing brought tears to his eyes, but he willed himself to remain upright. When the initial shock receded, he tried to stretch his lower back. First he did toe-touches, then tried to swivel his hips slowly to each side, then lay down awkwardly on his back and pulled his knees to his chest. Each change of position brought agony and curses, but he pushed on.

Ten minutes later, Pender rolled onto his knees and used a sapling to lift himself to a standing position. The pain was almost tolerable once he was erect, but each change of position brought body-freezing tentacles of anguish. Holding the sapling, he tested his ability to take steps. When he thought he could walk, he eyed the food pack. He thought if he could get it on his back without passing out, he could make it the rest of the way.

He positioned the pack on a gentle slope and sat in front of it, yelping and seeing stars as he swiveled into place. He looped his arms into the harness, and when he felt he could handle the pain, he struggled to his feet. Lightning bolts shot through his back with an intensity that made him hold his breath. It passed, but he knew his first step downhill would be excruciating. He focused on the next step, then the next, swinging his hands from tree to tree as he slowly shuffled down the slope. He scaled down one slope and up the next one. By the time he got back to his gear, the piercing fire in his lower spine that made him curse and tear up had given way to a throbbing ache.

Pender had hidden the rest of his gear just inside the tree line to avoid attention from rangers or passing trippers. As he reached it, his peripheral vision picked up movement on the lake. He slid behind cover and watched a canoe moving north at a rapid clip. He blinked. The paddlers looked a lot like the fat fishermen, big and strong and fast.

Jesus, he thought, could it be? How in the hell would they figure him for this lake? There were dozens of other possibilities. Maybe a hundred. And how could they have this much time? It wasn't like he'd stolen the family fortune or something.

As they disappeared in the northern reaches of the lake, he wondered what he should do. He needed to paddle for the rest of the day to make his rendezvous with Annette on time, but he wasn't sure he could paddle at all. Even if he could, in his damaged condition, if the fat boys saw him, they would overtake him easily, and he was in no shape to defend himself.

He pulled his gear farther back into the tree line and looked for a place to camp.

———————

Annette paddled the solo canoe with easy efficiency, spacing short, smooth paddle strokes to get the maximum glide from her boat. By lunchtime she had already covered ten miles of open water and portaged into the first of a chain of small lakes. She paused to update her trip planning book occasionally, noting the condition of established campsites and portage trails along the way.

As Annette's mind wandered from thought to thought, she imagined running into the arrogant Stuart party; they had come this way a few days earlier. She imagined finding them in trouble and having to blow off Pender to get them to safety.

She pushed the thought from her mind.

At the far end of the lake, she scanned the shoreline for signs of a creek, found it, a dark opening in the tree line flanked by a large sloping rock on one side and a pine forest on the other.

As she approached the take-out, a huge bull moose lumbered out of the brush into the shallows and stared at her. Annette stopped her canoe abruptly, keeping a respectful distance from him. He was all of six feet tall at the shoulder, and his antlers reached close to ten feet high. He weighed more than a half ton, and he was the king of the northwoods. Only a fool would challenge him.

The moose plunged his head into the water and emerged with a mouthful of shoots. He eyed her casually as he chewed, no fear in his gaze, not even wariness. After another mouthful, he moseyed off, slower than slow motion, and faded into the woods like a ghost—one moment a lumbering giant, the next, a memory.

Annette paused a beat to savor the encounter. As often as she had come upon moose and bear and otter and the other creatures of the Canadian Shield, it never got old. The encounter jogged her memory of another meeting, one she'd never forget. It had come deep in the park on a solo trip just like this one. She had passed close to a wooded island just a few feet from the mainland and looked up to see a mother wolf staring at her while her cubs rolled on the ground behind her, playing, oblivious to the human interloper. Mama Wolf had been on full alert, her ears up, her eyes never moving from Annette. But she was curious, too. She probably had never seen a human so close before. Annette had stopped and stared, letting her mind take in the details of the wolf, her bright eyes, her elegant coat, clean with just a few fringes of molted hair from the summer shedding, long legs, strong body.

"You are so beautiful." Annette had spoken softly to the wolf, hoping to extend the moment. She kept speaking, putting into words the beauty she saw, how cute the cubs were, how much she hoped they would all survive the winter.

It had lasted for just a minute. Then the wolf had gathered her cubs and trotted them down the shore, across the channel to the mainland, and disappeared into the forest.

Annette had dreamed of that encounter many times in the intervening years, and the familiar memory got her through the short portage into the next lake. She handled the weight of her pack and canoe with the ease of a young man in good shape. Only a few other local women could haul such a big load such a long distance, and they were in their twenties or thirties. When it came to paddling and portaging, Annette was in a granny class all by herself.

12

Searing pain woke Pender constantly through the night, making him wish for once that he was in an established campsite with a nice, level tent area, no roots or boulders. Instead, he was sleeping rough, his tent on a grade, the ground beneath him rocky and irregular. Each time he woke he grimaced and groaned and stared into the darkness, trying not to despair, resolving to rest until morning if he could, reminding himself that he'd done this for days on end in Vietnam, in rain and bugs, with people trying to kill him. Eventually, he'd fade into a half sleep, then awaken when some jerk or motion of his body sent shooting pain from his back down his right leg to his shin.

Around 4:30 he gave up. The muscles in his lower back were locked in spasms. He had to grit his teeth and hold his breath to roll off his back. Stars popped in his vision. He lay on his side, teeth clenched, eating the pain, wondering what his spine looked like. Slipped disc? Fracture? Could he survive this?

The impulse to sob passed. He took in a lungful of air, held his breath, gritted his teeth, and tried to get out of the sleeping bag, tried to fight through the scalding pain. Stopped when he got to all fours, took another breath, pulled the sleeping bag off. Cried out. Groaned. Ground his teeth. Opened the tent door and fly, ate the pain. Rolled out the door, ate the pain. Used a tree to help himself onto his feet, stood stooped over with his hands on his knees, holding his breath to withstand the pain.

It was pitch-black outside, signaling an overcast sky, and Pender could smell rain. Perfect. He willed himself to straighten into a standing position. Flashbulbs popped in his vision. He felt faint, held the tree, let it pass.

He forced himself to move around, to increase blood flow to his convulsing muscles and stretch and warm them. As he stretched and walked, he scanned the darkness on the lake, looking for any trace of light coming from the north, where the fat boys headed last night, listening in the still air for any sound of movement. Nothing.

He opened his food pack and pulled out coffee-making paraphernalia. The movements made him wince and gasp, but the pain was eroding a little. He found his first aid kit and downed four tablets of ibuprofen, then set up his stove to boil water, keeping it behind a log so the flame would be virtually invisible from the north, where the fat boys might be lurking. He sat on a small boulder and leaned against a tree trunk, sipping hot coffee, waiting for daylight. He wondered if he could get himself out of here, and he wondered how in the hell the fat boys had tracked him to this lake system.

They had to be asking everyone they encountered if they had seen a solo tripper in a Kevlar canoe. There probably wouldn't be more than two trippers in the whole park who fit that description, and probably just him. That could have gotten them close, and they maybe guessed that he'd be on this lake system. If you had the gumption to get into it, it was a spectacular series of long, narrow lakes lying end to end for miles, connected by a creek.

Pender thought about the fat boys. He wondered what drove them, why they'd go to such lengths over nothing more than a practical joke. They were headed in the right direction, but they were still looking for a needle in a haystack. After today, finding him would be impossible. Today, he'd be leaving this chain to move west, to meet Annette, and when he left this chain, the fat boys would never find him.

If his body would let him.

He pushed the doubt from his mind with scorn. He would paddle today. He'd make miles. He'd bury whatever pain came with it. Nothing would stop him.

When the bravado wore off, Pender wondered if he had done permanent injury to his spine. He wondered if he had the strength to portage. The steep bluffs were hard enough in good health; with a severely damaged back they might be impossible.

Pender even wondered if he could still paddle. It was possible he was trapped here, in the middle of an eighteen-hundred-square-mile wilderness, scores of miles and dozens of portages from the nearest road. It was possible he might not even be able to get off this lake.

He wondered if he had the strength to deal with a storm. Probably not. He could envision one blowing in as he crossed open water, could feel the boat turning sideways to the wind and surf, him powerless to correct the motion. He could feel the boat going over, could feel the icy water envelop him like embalming fluid.

"Shit!"

He swore out loud, stopping his imagination. Outraged by his own self-pity. I'm not afraid to die! The thought scorched his mind. I'm the meanest motherfucker in the valley.

He used the tree to help him stand, groaning and cursing. He repeated the procedure over and over again as he struck camp. He shoved off just as the first beams of daylight revealed the slate-gray sky of an overcast day.

A November sky, thought Pender. A death sky.

———————

Annette traversed a long, narrow, reef-strewn lake into a small bay that ended in a rocky pinch point formed by a low island that nearly touched both shores of the lake.

She made her way to a primitive campsite on the western extremity of the island. She preferred it to more comfortable sites for its privacy and its coarse sand beach, great for bathing.

She set up camp, and got ready to bathe while the sun was still warm. She stripped on the beach and waded out to a flat rock in two feet of water. She used the rock as a shelf for her soap and shampoo and washed her hair and body—quickly. Even after decades of wilderness tripping, the bone-numbing cold of the Quetico waters took her breath away.

Afterward, she lay on the rock, faceup, soaking in the perfect solitude. The late afternoon sun caressed her skin with soft warmth. The air barely moved. She could hear the singsong trill of birds in the distance. She closed her eyes dreamily, almost sleeping. Her mind drifted back to the university. To 1968.

"Do you believe in anything?" she asked.

Pender started to answer, a little flushed with anger, stopped, thought. *"Maybe not."*

"So you'd be fine with going to war and killing people?"

"If I had to, I guess."

"That wouldn't bother you? Killing someone's father or brother?"

"I think I'd be more concerned about them killing me."

"That's really shallow."

"Why do you get to pass judgment? You don't get drafted. You can afford to philosophize. You have nothing to lose. And don't get me started on your hippie-dippy friends with their phony compassion. They don't give a shit about anything but themselves."

"They're dedicated to peace and making the world a better place. What are you dedicated to?"

"They're dedicated to smoking dope and getting laid after the next rally. I'd like to get laid too, but I'm not going to stand there with a goddamn candle in my hand and sing protest songs to do it."

"What do you stand for, Pender?"

"I stand for graduating before my money runs out."

"And then?"

"Then I deal with whatever's on the other side."

"If you get drafted?"

"I go."

Her ruminations were interrupted by the whack of a paddle hitting a gunnel. She sat up and looked toward the main bay. Two canoes with four men were passing through, heading southwest, trying to make the next lake before dark. They didn't see her. They were paddling hard, looking straight ahead, seasoned trippers moving fast late in the day.

When they passed, she waded ashore and dressed. The sun was low, creating long shadows. She assembled her fishing pole and began casting in the shadowy waters.

After a half hour with no strikes, she launched her canoe and worked the drop-offs around the island. Eventually she picked up a meal-sized walleye in the deep channel between the island and the mainland.

She filleted and skinned it on a rock formation a half mile from her campsite, leaving the entrails for the gulls circling above. As she prepared to launch her canoe, Annette sensed another presence nearby. It startled her, and she whirled to scan the near shore. A big yellow dog stared at her, still as a statue, his body tense.

It looked like a pet, but no pet should be there. No one else was camping on the lake. Her mind whirled with possibilities. Most likely the dog had been lost by a canoe party. It happened once in a while. Or it could be with an owner who went hiking up the ridge and didn't make it back.

Annette paddled slowly toward the dog, not sure if it was friendly. As she drew near, the dog's tail started to wag and it barked excitedly, then jumped up and down and barked louder. She could see he was male, and he seemed friendly. In fact, he seemed deliriously happy at the prospect of human companionship. The dog splashed into the water and swam for her canoe.

To Annette's shock and horror, the dog tried to scramble aboard the boat, nearly capsizing her. "No!" she yelled, prodding him with her paddle. But the dog tried again. This time she shrieked "No!" and thumped him on the head with her paddle blade.

The dog desisted but followed her into the shallows, and when his feet made ground, he leaped into the canoe. His weight grounded the boat in a few inches of water. Annette jumped out and ordered the animal out. The dog leaped from the canoe and then leaped on her, his front paws striking her in the chest. She fell butt-first like she'd been shot, and the dog was on her instantly, tail wagging, tongue out, panting dog breath into her face.

"Get off me!" She tried to scream it, but it came out as more of a grunt. She shoved the dog away and struggled to her feet. Her lower body was soaked. The dog danced and splashed gaily as she watched, hands on hips.

Annette reached for the canoe to prevent it from floating out into the lake. The dog leaped into the boat, sitting as it rocked, tail wagging, tongue hanging happily from the side of his mouth. He looked inebriated.

"Get out!" she ordered, gesturing with her hand. The dog started to respond, then sat again. He was not going to be left here by himself.

Annette reached out to him. As he licked her hand, she grasped his collar and pulled him out of the boat. The dog followed her obediently. On the rocky shore, she gave him a cursory inspection. No ID tags, just a U.S. rabies tag. He looked like the Stuarts' dog, but she hadn't seen much of him at the CSO building. Seemed healthy. Matted coat. Lonely. Friendly. And no force on earth was going to keep him from going with her.

She called into the dense woods that started just a few feet from the water and rose up a steep incline for fifty feet. "Hello? Anybody here? Is this your dog?"

She yelled several times, but knew it was a waste of time. There was no canoe on the beach but hers. She was the only human for miles. She looked at the dog again. "I guess we're stuck with each other," she said. The dog sat, looking her in the eye, wagging his tail.

Annette put the dog in the canoe behind her seat and attempted to launch. After just a few paddling strokes, the dog thrust his nose beneath the canoe seat, found her fish filets, and snatched them, foil and all. He stood triumphantly and began to circle to lie down and eat his prize. The boat capsized before Annette could brace. She saved the fishing gear, but the filets were gone. The dog was happily chewing the last of them when she pulled the canoe ashore. She swung a paddle at him, missing him by a wide margin. The dog wagged his tail as if it was a game.

She dumped the water out of the boat and launched again, this time putting the dog in front. Each time he made a movement—any movement—she rapped him on the head with her paddle and yelled, "Stay." It wasn't a hard blow. She didn't want to hurt him, and she especially didn't want to break the paddle. It was just hard enough to make a bonking noise that had unsettled every dog she'd ever boat-trained. The third time she corrected him, she yelled, "Stay, you son of a bitch."

That worked. The big yellow dog lay flat in the boat, sighed, and calmed down. This dog responds to obscenities, Annette thought, just like human males. She concluded he must have been abandoned or maybe wandered off from camp and got lost. Or maybe he capsized his master's boat one time too many.

While the dog was still calm, she went back to the area where she had caught the walleye and caught two more. She guessed the dog hadn't eaten in a while, so one fish was for him. She decided to clean the fish in camp and paddle out to the rocks with the waste material later, by herself.

The dog seemed to know what camp was about. He barked and raced around the area for several minutes while Annette brought the canoe ashore. As she prepared the food, he stayed at her side, watching every move, drooling like a big yellow waterfall.

Annette placed the fish in a pan on the rocks of her fire pit as she set to building a fire. When the dog made a move for the fish, she raised her arms like the boogeyman and screamed, "No!" He dashed back several feet, sat, and wagged his tail, his face a picture of innocence.

"You bastard!" she added, making her voice sound angry.

Sure enough, his tail stopped wagging, he retreated several more feet and lay down, chin on the ground, eyes pleading.

"Right, Fido. You're real innocent," she said to him. He wagged his tail hopefully and moved to her side. "You scarf one more fish, and I'll drown your miserable hide."

He looked her in the eye and wagged his tail. As Annette cooked the meal, the dog curled up at her feet, but he came to full attention when she was ready to eat. She put his fish fillets on a small aluminum plate and placed it near her perch by the fire. He devoured the food before she could even begin her own meal and sat himself in front of her, staring, his eyes following every movement of her fork.

"What's your name?" she asked as she ate. "If we're going to travel together, we ought to know each other's names. I'm Annette. I'm a wild woman, in the outdoors sense of the word. I haven't had a dog since, oh gosh, ten or fifteen years I guess.

"Now, you need a name, and since you aren't giving me one, I'll make one up. Just a temporary thing, okay? 'Til we find your owner. How about 'Yeller'? Like Old Yeller."

She shook her head.

"No. You need a more original name. Gabe Pender wouldn't give you someone else's name, would he?"

The dog looked her in the eye again and wagged his tail, curiosity and anticipation on his face.

"Here's a good name for you. How about Asshole?" The dog's tail whacked against the ground. "No. It would be hard to explain to someone who heard me call you. Or to your owner, if he cares."

She thought about it more as she ate.

"Chaos," she said, breaking the silence. The dog startled at the sound of her voice, stared at her. "That's your name. Chaos. Boy, what a perfect name. A yellow storm named Chaos.

"Okay, Chaos. Here's the deal. Don't steal my food and don't capsize my boat, and everything else will be fine. If you don't want to come with me, you don't have to. If you want to, though, be there when I shove off. I'm not waiting for you."

After she washed dishes, Annette paddled out to the far rocks to dump the fish entrails for the scavengers. Chaos jumped in the canoe before she did. She started to make him get out, thought the better of it, positioned him in front, where she could watch him, and set out again.

Later, back in camp, he sat next to her on a boulder over-looking the lake as she sipped tea and watched the day fade to night. He leaned against her. She leaned against him. It was relaxing. His warmth felt good in the chill of the night. They stayed like that until all light was gone, listening to the soft sounds of water lapping at the shore, seeing the first stars blink on in the heavens. Annette sighed and let a tumble of images pour through her inner vision. Christy smiling at her as she left. Her granddaughter peeking up at her from her bed. Paddling in a pristine Quetico rock garden years ago, towering boulders rising above her. She saw her home. Her parents. College. The young Gabe Pender. Pleasant memories from near and far. Sweet, wistful visions from a life that still seemed short.

As Annette kneeled at the water's edge to rinse her cup, two loons began an exchange of mournful wails, one on her lake, the other on the next lake west. Rising from the dark of night in a vast, empty wilderness, their calls sang of love and a misty sadness, of loneliness and the memory of intimacy. Their night music was a serenade to the bittersweet nature of life, she thought. You start your life as a collector of precious moments and end it clinging to them. No matter how much you love the people you love, we all end up on different lakes, calling to each other in the night.

When she opened the tent, Chaos shot in. She thought about pulling him out. She had never let dogs sleep in her house, or her tent. But she relented. He was a pretty good guy, and he was scared and lonely. She knew what that was like. It would be nice to snuggle with a kindred spirit tonight.

13

Pender felt like he'd been shot and the bullet was lodged in his vertebrae, and every time he moved, the bullet ground against the bone and tried to sever the large nerve inside, tried to paralyze him. He knew it wasn't a bullet, but the pain was exhausting and the fear that he might inflict permanent damage on his spinal cord lurked like a sneering doubt in the shadows of his mind. He paddled warily under a pewter-gray sky so ominous he could taste metal in his mouth. He kept a close watch to the north for signs of a canoe and hugged the shore in case he had to make for cover. He didn't expect the fat boys to double back, but you never knew.

He experimented with his paddle stroke, trying to find a combination of reach and rhythm that would propel him without making his back worse. He settled on short strokes, with very little reach forward and none to the rear. He eliminated J-strokes, the paddle motion used to keep the canoe tracking straight. Pender's J-stroke included a slight twist in his torso that produced pain. Not crippling pain, warning pain. Warning that if he J-stroked for a couple of hours, he'd be crippled by nightfall.

He paddled through a few minutes of misty precipitation, but the gray sky never erupted. The still morning air gave way to light breezes out of the southwest, pushing him on his way. He labored to his first portage. His map promised a short, rough trail following the banks of a creek. No precarious climbs, not much up and down.

Pender sloshed through calf-deep water to shore and unloaded his gear. The pain had been manageable. Movement had kept his back muscles warm and out of spasm. He hadn't had to bend much to unload the boat. He took a moment to change from sandals into boots to make the hike to the next lake as easy as possible.

He shouldered the food pack and grabbed paddles and life jacket for the first carry. It went quickly and easily, as did the second trip.

By the time he launched into the next lake, he actually felt better. The walking had been a good break from paddling. Bending still produced pain, but it was manageable.

Pender paddled into a deep, narrow chasm, its walls towering above him in steep green slopes and jagged cliffs. The waterway was called a lake on the map, but it was a creek system, so narrow in places that his paddle sounds echoed from the walls. For a little more than an hour, he soaked in the stunning beauty of Quetico and forgot about his pain, his lost life, and the impossibility of his situation. As he traversed the narrowest part of the cavern, a bald eagle floated overhead, searching for fish, passing so close to Pender he could see the precise line where its white feathers gave way to the tawny brown feathers of its main body.

He had wanted to paddle this water for as long as he had been coming to Quetico, this eerily narrow, freakishly deep passage gouged from ancient rocks by forces of nature beyond the imaginations of most humans. He wanted to fish there, to experience fighting a big northern lurking in the icy depths of a narrow, bottomless creek. But he resisted the temptation to dig out his fishing gear. He had to make time or he would miss Annette. He would let her down. That was playing on his mind more and more. He would have just made it to the island in time if he hadn't gotten hurt; now he was in trouble. Everything was slower for him—paddling, portaging, breaking camp. He was in danger of missing Annette, and there was nothing worse than the shame that came with breaking a promise. Even though they probably wouldn't even like each other, he couldn't let her down.

He promised himself he'd come back to this place as he pushed on as hard as he could. He'd camp here and fish here. He'd lie in his canoe and watch the eagle float overhead. He'd climb to the top of the cliffs. He'd paddle into the boggy reaches of the lake, maybe fish for bass, look for moose. Breathe.

Pender increased his paddling cadence as much as he dared. At the northeast end of the lake, a small bay to the right held the portage into the next lake in the creek system. That was where the fat boys would be looking for him. But Pender veered left, heading into an obscure narrow inlet lined by steep cliffs on one side and rolling slopes on the other. The inlet was virtually invisible from the main lake, looking like just another gap in the shoreline. It led to a portage trail into a different creek system—a lot less attractive than the one he was leaving, but faster to Annette's island.

When he finally found the portage trail, he knew it was going to be a bitch. The trail was actually a rock-ribbed water path that drained runoff from the heights above. It dropped more than a hundred feet at an angle severe enough to look like a small waterfall when the heavens opened up. The sight would inspire wonderment—unless you had to climb it with a hundred pounds of gear on your shoulders, in which case the emotion would be more like dread.

He tried not to think about how hard the portage was going to be. He tried to just keep himself on automatic pilot. He had to make time. He had to protect his aching body. He lashed the paddles and life jacket to the food pack, hoisted it on his shoulders, and slipped through the forest opening to the rocky trail that seemed to climb vertically to the sky.

As much as he had trained for this trip, by the time he reached the top of the climb he was puffing for air and his back ached. Sweat streamed off his head and body. His legs felt watery, his head light. He wanted to take a minute to catch his breath, but he pushed on, knowing if he took a break, it would become a habit and he'd never get to Annette's island on time.

The landscape flattened out, and the forest gave way to large openings of boggy terrain—some of it solid with grassy covering, some of it a floating island formed by tangles of roots and detritus with grasses and scrub growing on it. In places, the ground sagged under Pender's weight, and water seeped into the void left by his boots. Twice his boot crashed through the surface and he sank into the muck up to his knee as stabbing pain shot through his back and bitter curses poured through his clenched teeth.

By the time he reached the end of the trail, his back throbbed. He was tired and soaking wet with perspiration. His boots were full of dark water. He had several new mosquito bites. He ignored the discomfort, put it in a closet in his mind, and closed the door to it, focused on what he needed to do. Like Vietnam. He peeled off the pack and went back for the rest of his gear. When he reached the quaking bog where he had crashed through the surface on the first trip, he took time to mark a detour with branches and small rocks.

The second carry started with disaster. He slipped on the first ascent and slid several feet down the precipice on his knees and shins. The front of the canoe banged hard against the rocks above, jarring his neck and shoulders where the portage yoke rested. His boots caught on embedded rocks just in time to keep him from tumbling into a pitched roll down the slope and maybe breaking his neck with the portage yoke. As it was, his pants were torn and he had raw strawberries on both shins and knees. More scars for the collection.

When he crested the steep slope, Pender was a wreck, and he still had many miles to go if he was to get to Annette's island on time. He used his anxiety to propel him forward through the pain and misery, even as another part of his consciousness wondered if Annette would be laughing if she saw how badly he had botched this portage, how stupidly he had allowed himself to fall when he hurt himself in the first place. She would have a hard time taking him seriously, he thought. He was having a bit of a hard time with that, too.

Annette and Chaos woke to skies draped in dark, low-hanging clouds like a funeral, the air still and the waters eerily calm. Annette took her time, making a hot breakfast and sipping coffee, waiting to see if a storm would blow in. She fried eggs and ham over a camp stove, fed Chaos the remains of her breakfast, and then washed the dishes. The sky was still gloomy, but there were no other signs of a storm. She struck camp, loaded the canoe, and tried to get Chaos ready for paddling. It was a delicate exercise. He had to ride atop a pack, which would raise the canoe's center of gravity and put them at risk of capsizing if he moved around too much.

She tried having him jump on the pack in front of her after she was seated and could brace the boat. He jumped aboard but wanted to circle before lying down, then lay with his weight off center. His weight and position made the boat list dangerously to one side.

Annette ordered him off the boat with words and a hand gesture. He jumped off. She got out of the canoe and ordered him on again, patting her hand on the pack. He jumped back on and started his circling routine again. "No!" she commanded. She grasped him by the collar and forced him to lie down, then pushed him until he was centered. Each time he tried to stand or move, she corrected him by pulling him down and nudging him back into place.

When he was stable, she got into the canoe herself . . . and he stood and circled to face her. She got out of the canoe and went through it all again. After another fifteen minutes of trial and error, she set off for the portage to the west. In the twenty minutes it took to get to there, Chaos started to rise several times. Each time, she bumped his head with her paddle blade and yelled "No!" before he got out of the prone position. His last attempt to get up came as they neared shore for the portage. She corrected him, then stopped the canoe several feet from shore and waited. He started to rise again, and she corrected him again. After a minute of stillness, she got out of the canoe in knee-deep water. As he started to rise, she corrected him again.

"You're going to have to do this on command, old friend," she said. "So we're going to make every take-out and put-in a learning exercise."

When she got to the bow of the canoe, she said, "Go ahead," and gestured to shore. Chaos sprang from his down position into the water and splashed ashore with the unrestrained glee of a child in a chocolate factory.

As Annette hauled her gear, Chaos ran riotously along the trail and crashed into the brush to follow animal scents. But when she began loading the canoe, the dog clung closely to her.

"Guess you don't want to miss another boat, huh?" She said it with a smile but with a tinge of sadness, too. He was a good guy. He didn't deserve to be left behind.

Annette crossed the next lake in a light sprinkle and still winds. She looked for signs of the trippers who had passed her camp the night before, but they were long gone.

Her next carry was what she called a "separation portage" when she plotted trips for customers. The trail was nearly a mile long and semirugged, with lots of rolling terrain. Many canoeists avoided such tests. There were scores of beautiful lakes that could be accessed via shorter, easier trails. So long, difficult portages created separation from human traffic. Your reward for taking the long haul was days of travel in an empty wilderness.

Despite her strength and conditioning, Annette was breathing hard and perspiring when she completed the first carry. Her legs felt like rubber and her shoulders ached from the pads of the canoe yolk pressing down on them for more than thirty minutes. Still, she paused only to drink deeply from her water bottle, then hustled back to get the rest of her gear. Resting would just add time and pain to the process. She kept moving and focused her mind on other things.

So she thought about what Pender would think of her if he could see her now. A Chicago lady would call her pace

"power walking," she thought. A Chicago lady would be wearing designer gym clothes, and her body would be model trim.
Pender wouldn't see her until she had showered, had her hair
done at some posh salon, put on a designer dress and heels,
did her face with makeup that was just right for the season,
lipstick in this season's shade.

What would he think of his old flame now, a wilderness
woman? How long since she had worn heels? Twenty years?
Thirty? Had she ever worn them in Canada? What about
makeup? She couldn't remember a time she'd worn makeup
since she immigrated to Canada. She had a couple of dresses
and she wore them on special occasions, but she could barely
remember what they felt like.

By the time Pender saw her, she'd have three days of
wilderness exertions clinging to her, that outdoorsy fragrance
that comes from sweat and rain and all-the-time fresh air,
from chill nights and warm days and cooking over a wood
fire, from baths in water so cold it made your skin purple.
Maybe he'd like that, though. He loved Quetico. How prissy
could he be? Maybe he'd prefer rugged outdoor grannies to
young debutantes with big silicone breasts and short skirts.

And maybe pigs would fly.

Annette's conversations with herself did nothing good for
her self-esteem, but the carry was over before she really knew
it, before she had resolved anything.

Chaos had reveled in the long double portage, racing back
and forth from one end to the other, racking up miles of exercise. He was more than ready to clamber aboard the canoe
again and laze in the gray sun that was just beginning to burn
through the morning overcast. The moment Annette gestured
for him to jump on the front pack, he sprang lightly to his

spot, circled once and flopped down—perfectly centered. Annette smiled, impressed. "Well done, Mr. Chaos," she said.

They were making good time and Chaos was steady in the boat, so Annette shifted to a relaxed pace. It was a big lake, stretching about five kilometers east to west with a large bay on its west end and a smaller bay south of that. It was a deep, cold-water lake popular with lake trout fishermen in the spring but less visited in the summer.

She made notes on her map about the condition of the campsites, then rigged her fishing pole with a heavy, deep-running silver spoon and spent twenty minutes jigging for lake trout in one of the deepest parts of the lake. They were deep in August, fifty feet, a hundred feet, or even deeper, and much harder to find and catch than bass or walleye. But this was a rare opportunity to fish for summer trout from a canoe: calm winds, overcast skies, cool water. Any kind of wind made deep-water fishing from a canoe more difficult than it was worth.

As Annette cast the heavy rig and let it flash and tumble into the depths, she looked about. From the middle of the lake, the shoreline looked flat and featureless, even though most of the shore was lined with steep bluffs that would make her next portage a good physical test. That was the thing about summer trout fishing: aesthetically, it sucked. You're in the middle of a big lake. You're fishing blindly in deep, deep water. You can't do much to get the fish to bite—just lift up the line and let the lure drop and flutter, hoping the flash will make some hungry trout strike, and keep doing it for as long as your mind can stand it.

It's just that she had a taste for trout, and if she got lucky, she could get one big enough to feed both of them.

As she jigged, she wondered what Pender was doing and where he was. She figured he was in the central region of the park by now, moving west to their meeting place. He'd be on one of the small lakes there. He told her he preferred small lakes, clear water, and pine forests. Then again, when they compared trip notes, it was clear he had plenty of experience in the bogs and the spruce and birch forests. It would be like preferring a Mercedes and settling for a BMW, Annette thought. She had no use for luxury cars, but she tried to frame his life against the culture of conspicuous consumption that was the hallmark of the America she had left behind.

If he was fishing right now, it would probably be for bass. He said he only fished for food and went for the easiest prey because he wasn't much good at it. In August that would be smallmouth bass. Warm water and sunlight made walleye fishing more challenging, trout fishing was ridiculous, and no one fished for northerns—you just caught them when you were fishing for something else.

She wondered if Pender shaved and bathed regularly in the bush, or if he went feral like some trippers. She wondered, with a start, if he was even in the park, if he was really coming to the island, or if he had opted for some other entertainment at the last minute and exercised his male option to do it and not say a word.

Which was when her pole gradually bowed over and the reel started to whine as it let out line. Annette checked to see if she was drifting, trying to ascertain if she had a fish or a snag deep down below. No wind, hardly even a breeze. It was probably a fish. She kept the line taut and let the drag setting on the reel do its job. The fish could pull off line but only at the expense of a lot of energy. When it paused to rest, she would reel it in. She had no idea how big the fish was. At seventy feet of depth, a goldfish would feel like a whale.

Fifteen minutes later, she saw the fish for the first time— a fairly large lake trout. Ten feet from the boat, it went on another run, stripping line off the reel like a salt-water game fish. Annette kept the pole tip up to maintain tension in the line and waited for the run to end, then reeled in the fish again. After two more shorter runs, the fish was played out. She brought it in to the side of the canoe for the hard part—getting it in the boat without getting cut on the hook or its teeth. The spoon was clearly visible in the corner of the trout's mouth. She knelt on the bottom of the boat to keep the canoe's center of gravity low and then reached under her seat to grasp an orange plastic device with pliers-like jaws for handling toothy fish. She used it to grasp the fish's lower jaw and plucked it from the water, bracing herself to hang on as the trout flipped powerfully. When it tired, she removed the lure and threaded a stringer through its mouth and gill plate. Maybe eighteen inches, she thought. A feast for two.

As she tied the stringer to the back of her seat, she noticed Chaos for the first time since the fish hit. He had turned completely to face her—probably while she was boating the fish. His ears were perked and his tail up and wagging, but he was still in a prone position and centered.

"Oh my, Chaos," she said to him as she patted his head, "That must have been an excruciating temptation! Good boy!"

She rinsed off her hands, dried them in the air, and paddled to their last portage of the day. When Chaos tried to rise and turn again—he liked to look forward—she verbally corrected him and readied the paddle for a whack. He obeyed the verbal command.

The trail started with a challenging climb, but otherwise it was
an easy hike and less than a quarter mile in length. Annette
hauled the canoe and gear pack on the first trip, the fish
stringer lashed to the back of the pack. She made the first
trip as rapidly as possible and put the fish in shallow water,
tied to the canoe, hoping no eagle or bear or otter happened
along before she got back with the rest of her gear.

She was just finishing her second carry when Chaos erupted
in a barking frenzy. He was ahead of her, out of her sight,
probably in the launch area. The feverish pitch of his barking
alarmed her. He wasn't chasing squirrels. He was trying to
scare someone or something. A bear? A couple of innocent
paddlers coming the other way? As she broke into a slow
jog, Annette half hoped it was a bear. Together they could
shoo off a black bear without much problem. But a couple of
paddlers, minding their own business, minds focused only on
the portage ahead of them, getting scared by a half-crazy dog
coming out of nowhere? That could be trouble. Complaint
to the park rangers kind of trouble. Bad enough for a regular
paddler but really hard to explain for an outfitter.

She emerged from the forest to the beach area and froze,
trying to comprehend the strange tableau in front of her. Her
gear lay to one side of the beach where she left it. Chaos was
midway between the tree line and the water, still barking, the
hackles raised on his back as if he was confronting a grizzly
bear. On the beach were the Stuarts—of course, it would have
to be customers, the nastiest customers in months. They had
landed their canoe and off-loaded some gear. Mrs. Stuart was
halfway between the boat and the dog, kneeling, gesturing to

Chaos to come to her. Her husband stood at water's edge, watching, hands on hips, clenched teeth, a sneer on his face.

"Stop it!" Annette commanded Chaos as she came alongside him. His panicky barking ebbed. She repeated the command, and he gave a couple of intermittent yips and then went quiet. He looked at her and wagged his tail uncertainly. He was ill at ease in the presence of the Stuarts.

Mrs. Stuart stood silently, still looking at the dog. Her husband flashed a humorless grin.

"That's my goddamn dog you have there, Miss."

"How long since you've seen him?" Annette asked.

"Three days. Not that it's any of your business. Just hand him over." Stuart extended his hand and gestured for Annette to bring him the dog. Like a lord commanding a servant.

"Why did you abandon him?" Annette held her ground, and the dog stayed with her.

"That's none of your business!" The man started to lurch toward her, angry like a bull. In the moment it took him to step forward, Annette dropped the paddles and fishing pole in her hands, unfastened the belt on her pack, and dropped it on the ground behind her. Before he took a second step, she had snatched one of the paddles and brandished it in two hands like a martial arts combatant with a parrying stick. It was reflexive.

Mrs. Stuart jumped between them, facing her husband. Her health-club body was tense. Annette could just see Mr. Stuart's angry red face over her shoulder. She could feel his rage.

"Stop! Stop it right there, George!" Mrs. Stuart said. Her tone was sharp, authoritative. He stopped. His face flushed crimson. Two women giving him lip. But he stayed where he was. He could brush his wife aside if he wanted. He could overwhelm both of them. He was a big man. But his wife's tone was a warning that there would be repercussions if he did. So he stayed where he was.

Mrs. Stuart turned to Annette. "The dog kept jumping off the canoe, and he capsized us twice. We lost a lot of gear and a lot of food. George screamed at him and kicked him and wanted to drown him, but he got free and ran off. Abandoning him seemed like his best chance at survival." She shrugged apologetically.

Annette stared at the woman for a moment. She hadn't expected the lady to speak, hadn't heard her say more than a few words when they were getting ready for the trip. Wouldn't have guessed she had the strength to stand up to her husband. And another part of Annette's mind was conscious of how beautiful this middle-aged woman was, even in the bush without makeup and a hairdresser. Smooth complexion, pretty coloring. Was this what she gave up to be a woman of the Ontario wilderness? And Pender. There must be dozens of women like this in Pender's circles. Even the married ones, some of them, the ones with husbands like Stuart, would be interested in a man like him. When Pender met her he would see a withered shadow of the schoolgirl he once knew, a wilderness granny. Someone you have lunch with, pay the tab and forget about.

"Why do you want him now?" Annette posed the question to George Stuart. His sneer had given way to a lemon-sucking contortion of lips, eyes, and jaws.

"Because he's mine!" he bellowed. "I paid good money for him. He's mine."

"But you don't even like him," his wife said.

"I hate him! But he's mine. And if I want to drown him or kick him to death, that's my prerogative."

"Not here," said Annette. "In Ontario we have laws against animal abuse." She didn't know if that was true or not, but it should be true. She'd make it true. She'd deal with the consequences later.

"So you're stealing my dog?"

"If your dog wants to go with you, I won't stop him," said Annette. "But he doesn't look like he wants to go with you, and I'm not going to make him."

"So you're stealing my dog. I'll press charges. You can count on it."

"Stop it, George!" his wife said.

"Keep out of this. You've said enough already."

Mrs. Stuart stood her ground. "If you press charges, I'll give them a statement about what you did to this dog and how this lady saved his life. Now let's get this godforsaken trip over with!"

She looked at Annette and shrugged. "We're going back. We're low on food, we lost the stove, we don't have stakes for the tent. We're in bad shape. We need to cancel the floatplane and pay for the lost gear."

Annette nodded sympathetically. "I'm sorry it turned out so bad for you."

She looked at the two of them for a moment. "I have a deal for you. I'll cover the cost of the lost gear in return for the dog."

Stuart started to object, but his wife interceded. "Done!" She turned to him, a grim expression on her face. "Well?"

He flashed an angry grimace and turned away from her, an alpha male's way of giving up without giving in.

"Okay," said Annette. "Now, get your map. I'll show you a faster way to get out of here." She sketched a route on their topo map to a closer take-out spot, wrote the Canadian Shield

Outfitters phone number on the map, and explained how to use the phone at the take-out.

"Cancel your floatplane as soon as you get in so you get your deposit back," she told Mrs. Stuart, "and don't forget to tell them about our deal on the gear. They'll believe you."

As the Stuarts repacked their canoe, Annette and Lexie exchanged a few pleasantries in passing, enough to make Annette think the lady might be a decent person, despite the roaring jerk she was married to. When George went into the woods to pee, Annette smiled at the woman and said, "This is a special place for the right people. You ought to get together with an adventurous girlfriend or two and come up here for a ladies-only trip."

"You'd take us after all this?" The woman gestured with her hand at the dog and the woods where her husband had gone.

"Hey, I've been married. I'd never hold a woman's husband against her." They laughed. "You seem like a good person. And if you want your dog back, I'd surrender him to you."

"He's better off with you," Mrs. Stuart said, her eyes misty.

They shook hands, just as Stuart emerged from the forest, still glowering. "Let's go," he said, gesturing to his wife, ignoring Annette altogether.

Annette watched them leave. She wondered if Mrs. Stuart would really consider coming up here on her own someday. Not likely. But she would have fun if she did. What the heck. Just having a week away from Mr. Hotshot would have to be a great vacation.

14

Annette waited until the Stuarts were out of sight and then launched her canoe into the crystalline blue waters of the big lake. It was one of the great jewels of Quetico, a long, winding bottomless lake that stretched more than twenty miles across the northwest quadrant of the park. Paddlers experienced it like a series of small lakes connected by narrow passages, each as varied as if they had portaged through a series of four or five lakes.

Annette glided into the big water, turning south as she emerged from the portage bay. An hour later she stopped for lunch on a rocky beach. While Chaos romped and swam, she filleted the trout and left the entrails and skin on a high rock that jutted into the lake. Gulls were circling in the sky before she finished washing the knife and her dishes. Every trace of the fish parts left on the rock would be gone within an hour after they left.

The gentle breezes of morning gave way to mild afternoon winds out of the southwest as Annette entered the lake's popular Narrows, a five-kilometer stretch where the shores pinched in to widths of less than fifty yards in places. The area was easily accessible from several popular entries into Quetico and featured good bass and walleye fishing, idyllic campsites perched atop the forested rocks on each shore, and protection from prevailing winds. It was one of the most popular destinations in the park.

As she pressed on, she considered how much farther to go. If the weather held and she worked at it, she could get within two hours or so of the island today. On the other hand, if she arrived too early in the morning, she'd already be there when Pender came along and that might look a little anxious, a granny trying too hard. Which was uncomfortably close to the truth, the more she thought about it.

No, she'd paddle on a while longer but camp early. The Sturgeon Narrows gave way to two kilometers of open water, then the lake narrowed, widened, and narrowed again. She stopped in the midafternoon, taking a campsite perched like an eagle's aerie above a boulder-strewn stretch of waterway that separated the mainland from a sheer-sided island by maybe fifty feet. Getting her gear up to the campsite was a vigorous workout, but the view was worth it. Chaos romped in the forest while Annette set up her camp and gathered wood for an evening fire.

As she laid out neat stacks of kindling, starter tinder, and bigger pieces of wood sawed to length, she wondered where Pender was and what he was doing. An image came into her mind: What if he happened along tonight, trying to make time, running out of daylight, saw her fire? She imagined him hailing the campsite from down below, asking if he might pitch a tent somewhere, use her fire for a quick meal. Him coming up the slope, the two of them slowly recognizing each other, him kissing her like when they were kids . . .

Chaos charged out of the woods and ran a circle around her, tongue out, tail wagging. He sat next to the fire pit, tail still wagging, looking her in the eye, his body tense with anticipation.

"You like it here, I guess," said Annette. She straightened from her labors and went to her food pack to set up her kitchen. The dog fell in beside her, step for step, still looking her in the eye, tongue still out, wet with saliva now.

"Oh, you like it here because you're hungry, right?"

As she knelt to set up the stove on the rocks of the fire pit, Chaos snuggled next to her, expertly pushing his cold, wet nose under her arm, then tilting his face upward to lick her.

"Stop that, you rogue!" she laughed and pushed his face away from hers. "No French kissing on the first date." He wagged his tail. "Or the second. Or any time with dogs, okay? Get it?" He wagged his tail as if in agreement, but she didn't take him seriously.

Pender was nowhere near Annette at that moment. He was more than a day behind her, camped on a swampy little lake where his body gave out in the early afternoon. Healthy, he would have pressed on for hours, wouldn't have stopped until he knew he could get to Annette's island the next day.

But he wasn't healthy. Seven hours of paddling and portaging had left him in anguish. His back ached and sent out shooting pains when he moved too far or too fast. It affected everything he did, attacking his will like a ruthless enemy wielding a white-hot knife. The route that followed his difficult portage that morning had looked easy on the topo map, but it played much harder. By the time he launched into this

dark, swampy lake, he had nothing left. It was all he could do
to load his canoe and begin scouring the shoreline for a place
to camp. There were no established campsites on this lake.
This was the kind of lake where only the desperate camped,
the ones who ran out of daylight or energy or luck when they
got here. Like Pender.

All he really wanted was solid ground a few feet above lake
level. An open area where he could set up his tent would be
nice. He'd cook over the gas stove again, no problem.

He settled for a point that sat three or four feet above
water level and sloped gently upward for twenty yards or
so, then gave way to a bog in an advanced state of atrophy.
The point was covered with grasses and scrub, and held some
late-season mosquitoes. He found a small flat area covered
by grassy growth but free of woody brush. He pitched his
tent in the knee-deep grass, hoping the soft vegetation might
cushion his sleep. After that, he sank two sticks in the soft
earth and put his boots on them to start drying out. Then
he sat on a rock and slowly stretched his taut back muscles,
arching, bending forward, turning gently from side to side.
He lay on his back and pulled his knees to his chest, then
repeated everything, over and over. It hurt like hell at first,
but after he worked it for twenty minutes or so, his back
loosened and the aching ebbed to a tolerable level.

He picked his way through the scrub and grass to explore
what the point had to offer, which was pretty much nothing.
It was a featureless, bland piece of real estate, one end dipped
in a dreary lake with stained water, the other leading to a few
sparse trees and acres of reeds and low-lying bog vegetation.

He found a rock that had two flat sides to cook on and set
it up beside his sitting rock. As he boiled water for his freeze-
dried dinner, he scribbled an emotional note to Annette in

his journal and another to his daughter . . . in case he didn't make it out alive. As he wrote, he realized how depressed he was, contemplating death when really, it was just discomfort he was suffering from. And he realized how important the rendezvous with Annette had become to him.

As I ponder my bleak circumstances, I realize that meeting you on the island is what I've been living for all these months, he wrote. *I have nothing else, no other plan. I'm going to arrive late, but I hope you wait for me.*

He ate in silence, gazing at the gloomy lake and the featureless scrub. He had camped in ugly places before, but this was the ugliest. He had contemplated his life under dark skies many times, but this was the darkest. He knew the sun would rise again, the clouds would move on, life would continue. But he didn't try to deny the melancholy of the moment. What would it be like, he thought, to die here? How would it feel? Would he be angry that his life expired in such a dreary place? Especially knowing that if he had stayed on the other route he could die on a spectacular blue-water lake, in a campsite with a lovely view, tucked in among the red pines, with the breezes sifting like silk through long needles, loons calling to one another.

This would be a lonely place to die, your last view of the planet limited to the grass and scrub scratching your face as you lay on the ground, a grim sky overhead, damp air pushing the spindly stalks in rustling waves.

Would the wolves find him first, or would it be other scavengers? He had often thought he'd like to leave his body to Quetico's wolves when his time came. He had heard them many times in his travels in the park, but like many trippers, he'd never seen one in the wild. He had always identified with them somehow. They lived alone when times were good. They dealt with the solitude, fended for themselves. Then they packed up when times were tough. They worked together to take down game too large for them to handle by themselves. They functioned as a team, these solitary creatures, until the seasons let them function alone.

It would be an honor to be consumed by wolves, Pender thought. So much better than rotting away in a box.

Annette woke to a clear sky and the knowledge that, if the weather held, she had an easy day ahead of her. Not even twenty kilometers to the island, less than twelve miles. A full spectrum of Quetico paddling: big water, a gentle creek, small lakes, short portages, beautiful scenery. An easy day to make good time and enjoy the most beautiful place on earth.

She spent twenty minutes casting a lure into the narrows as dawn broke. She didn't catch anything, but that was okay with her. She treated herself to another hot breakfast. There was such a thing as too much fish.

She cooked pancakes and shared them with Chaos, knowing he'd burn off the calories easily on this day of many short portages and settling in a base camp with lots of room for running and exploration.

After washing her dishes, she paused for a luxurious moment to sit on the rocks overlooking the water and the island across the narrows. Chaos came to sit beside her, thrusting his head under her arm, making her pet him. She wondered what Pender would think of the dog. He might not like dogs. He might be allergic to them.

She wondered if he would show up. She thought he would. As a young man, he had taken his promises seriously. She wondered again what he would think when he saw her. Would he see the schoolgirl? The wrinkled granny? The loneliness? The lost dreams? Would he pity her? Think of the sexy young women back in Chicago?

Her eyes moistened. How silly to be so gloomy, she thought. It's lunch with an old friend, not the continuation of a love affair. It will be good to talk to him, to hear his story. What it was like to be a big name in the restaurant business. To live in a million-dollar North Shore estate. To drive exotic cars, hobnob with women in designer clothes, talk to famous chefs.

As her mind wandered, a canoe came into view, coming from the south. When the paddler stopped below her perch, Annette could see he was a park ranger.

"Hello," he called from below. He was a younger man, not more than thirty, nice looking, with that unassuming air that many men in rural Ontario had.

Annette returned his greeting and waved.

"Have you seen a solo canoeist in the last day or two?" the ranger asked. "Wenonah in Kevlar yellow? Middle-aged white male, maybe older?"

"No," said Annette. In the back of her mind she wondered what Pender was paddling. Good God! Could he be in trouble with the law?

"Do I need to be concerned?" she asked.

"I don't think so," said the ranger. "Apparently he harassed some fishermen in the Boundary Waters, then ducked into Quetico. We're just doing a courtesy check, but I don't think there's much chance we'll see him."

"What should I do if I see such a person?" Annette asked with a quizzical smile. What indeed?

The ranger shrugged. "I don't know, really. Probably just avoid him." He tipped his hat, wished Annette well, then continued north on the big lake. Annette wondered if he would encounter Pender. Pender would probably be paddling on this lake today. He could even be camped on the island across the way, but on the opposite side from her. Or he could be a few kilometers to the north or south. She wondered if he was the culprit they were after. It seemed possible. He'd taken revenge on the canoe racers who dumped him and smacked his boss hard enough to make him cry. He wasn't someone who rolled with the punches, at least not right now.

She wondered what it would have taken for Pender to harass a couple of fishermen. Christy would wonder if he had turned into a homicidal maniac who attacked people like pit bulls attack dogs, just for the sport of it. But she knew he wasn't. He wrote with the sensitivity of the young Pender she had known in college, and, while that Pender could drive anyone into a blind snit with his obstinacy, he was a poet and a lover at heart.

She wondered if he'd get apprehended and hauled out by the rangers before he got to their rendezvous. It would be heartbreaking, but somehow she didn't think it would happen. For all his anger and vulnerability, he had an aura about him. Always had. He always landed on his feet.

She smiled to herself as she began breaking camp. What chance did a Quetico ranger have of nabbing Pender? And even if he did, the ranger would probably like him and forget about the whole thing. This was Canada, after all.

15

Annette luxuriated in another day of calm breezes, this one with partly sunny skies to lift the spirits. She deftly navigated island-studded archipelagos and vast open spaces of water, watched hawks and eagles float on currents high above as they hunted for fish, searched the shallows hoping to glimpse a moose. She reached the southern end of the big lake by noon, entering a bizarre Canadian Shield playground of dozens of islands and dozens more reefs and shoals fanning out around a huge peninsula whose rugged shoreline included countless bays and inlets and points.

She navigated west into a narrowing channel that would eventually become a creek. She stopped at an island to take lunch and give Chaos a chance to run off steam. He charged around the small island for several minutes and then plunged into the water to chase seagulls perched on a rocky outcropping fifty feet away. He sent them squawking into the air and celebrated by plunging back into the water to return to the island. After twenty minutes of madcap running and swimming, he lay beside Annette and panted while she ate.

Annette was deep in thought. She was looking at what seemed like a small lake, a kilometer long, a kilometer wide, but she knew it was a Canadian Shield illusion. When she paddled west, the seeming continuous shore on her right would open to a bay. When she entered the bay, she would see a narrow opening to the west. When she paddled through that opening, she would enter a short channel that led to what seemed like another small lake. That lake would seem to end in a reedy bog, but she would paddle through it to find a tiny, narrow creek that she would follow through a succession of small lakes until she finally portaged into her lake.

The impossibility of navigating this place without a map had always made her wonder how the first people here did it. The First Nation people would have had only crude map-making skills and equally crude canoes as they tried to find their way through this archipelago and the many others in Quetico, archipelagos that were deliriously confusing even with a map and compass. How long before they knew this was a creek? What caused someone to figure it out? Why would a hunter or trapper come into this system instead of using the river to the south?

She and Chaos negotiated the creek system without inci-dent. It was still early afternoon when they reached a small lake. Its main body extended west-southwest, ending in a low, narrow inlet that led to a popular portage trail that connected trippers to a chain of lakes that offered beautiful journeys for the fit and adventurous.

But Annette followed the north shore of the small lake into its lesser bay and then to a short, obscure portage that led into her favorite lake, her special place. As she approached the portage take-out, she saw a canoe and a pack on the shore. For a moment, her heart skipped a beat. Could it be Pender?

She had a flashing vision of them passing on the portage trail, recognizing each other. Him saying, "Are you . . .?" A smile playing softly on his face as recognition set in. Him pulling off his pack, embracing her in a tender hug, forty years later.

Two men emerged into the portage area, stopping her dream. One waved while the other shrugged on the pack and picked up paddles and disappeared down the portage trail. The waver easily lifted the canoe onto his shoulders and followed.

They were trippers, probably moving on through her lake on their way north. Few people ever stopped on her lake. In fact, few people even passed through it. That was part of what made it so special. That and its walled shoreline, rising steeply in great smears of green forest and earth-hued cliffs from blue water so crystal clear you could see a pike in twenty-foot depths. It also had intimacy. Even though it was a fairly large lake, it was fractured into small parts and dotted with islands, so every place you went, it felt like a small, hidden lake, and every moment seemed coddled and personal.

The trippers were out of sight by the time Annette finished the short portage. She boarded Chaos and floated slowly along a narrow channel through a canyon of granite and jack pines.

At the end of the channel, she paused for a deep breath and took in the sights. She was in a small body of water, maybe a kilometer square, that hid passages to four other bodies of water of equal or larger size. It was her Eden—a place of fused colors and soft light, pure water, and rarified air. Just sitting here was rejuvenating, taking in the air and the colors, sipping water dipped from the lake. It had been that way from the very first time she happened into this lake, on a somber late-September outing into an empty park. It was a time of chill air and changing leaves and a deep quiet as migratory birds began heading south. She had been a young woman in a marital netherworld then. Two young children, a struggling business, a husband almost permanently gone, not interested in northwest Ontario, not interested in the wilderness, only mildly interested in his children and not at all in her.

She knew the marriage was over but didn't know what to do about it. Her mother drove fourteen hours to come talk to her and stayed for more than a week so Annette could paddle into the wilderness to clear her head.

Much of what she saw on that trip and all that she thought was filtered through a veil of sorrow. She was mourning her children's loss of a father and her loss of a husband and especially the end of their innocence—a magical time so intense and deep, when they had been so committed to each other, when they would have sacrificed anything for each other, when no matter what they had, it was enough because they were together.

She cried because she knew that kind of love could never happen to her again. She was in a new stage of life. She needed to prepare her daughters for life and somehow preserve their ability to love like that someday, if only for a short time. For she knew now, knew for certain, that love like that doesn't last. It can't. It fades or morphs into something else—a different love, and a new one if you're lucky.

And if you're not lucky, it just dies and you have to start over again.

Annette had spent a day in the cold rain and a night below freezing just before she paddled into her lake the first time. She had been out for several days, making up her trip as she went along, trying to decide whether or not to move back to the U.S., live with her parents until she got a job. Get the kids into a good school, prepare them for great careers, success, maybe wealth. Atikokan seemed so barren for them, a tiny, hardscrabble town with endless winters, a high school located nearly a hundred miles from the next-closest school.

But something in her gut was holding her back, and she didn't know what it was until she paddled through that very same canyon a quarter century ago. The day had started cloudy and cold, but as she paddled through the canyon, sunlight seeped through cracks and crevices in the diminishing cloud cover, and when she sat at this very spot in the first bay, the sun poured out of the sky, touching the rocks and the trees and the pristine water with the kind of luminescence ancient painters used for religious art.

And for Annette, it was a religious experience. It was the moment she discovered what she believed in. She believed in this place, its beauty and grandeur, its innocence and solitude. She believed in Canada. She believed this place and her children were the things in life that touched her soul and that her children and this place belonged together.

She camped in an established campsite that first time, but while exploring the lake, she stopped at an island that seemed almost impervious to canoeists, with vertical rock wall shores rising from the water like the walls of a citadel. The single dent in this natural fortress was a narrow beach of sorts, strewn with boulders and rocks and ending with a sheer rock cliff. The cliff had calved many times over the millennia, each event producing hundreds of boulders, large and small, that the ices and winds and rains and floods of thousands of years had pushed and pummeled all over the lake. What was left was a grotto guarded by a treacherous shoal of boulders extending fifty feet out from the shore.

For no particular reason, Annette decided to lunch there. She eased her canoe through the boulder garden but could

only get within ten feet of shore. She secured her boat, then
boulder hopped to shore. She picked her way through the
rubble to the base of the cliff and saw red-leafed scrub trees in
one corner of the grotto and wondered how on earth enough
soil could have accumulated there to support leafy growth.

When she was close enough to touch the leaves, she saw
another one of Quetico's miracles. The soil that sustained the
scrub trickled down from the heights above, curling around
the towering rock facade like a spiral staircase.

Annette ascended the hidden trail to a forested plateau
high above the lake, found a stand of old-growth red pines
on the southwest shore. There were several places to pitch a
tent, and the bluff overlooking the lake was solid rock, perfect
for a fire ring. She moved in that afternoon, carefully jumping
from boulder to boulder with her packs and canoe.

It was a magnificent perch from which to experience
Quetico, like an eagle's nest, looking down on blue waters
and vast forests as far as the eye could see. It was hidden and
private. It was secret and personal. She sat on a rock wall fifty
feet above the lake that afternoon and let the majesty of the
Canadian Shield infuse her body and spirit. She thought this
must be what musical people feel in a concert hall when the
sounds of Mozart fill the air and overwhelm the soul. She
lost all sense of herself that afternoon. There was only the
forest and the water and the bogs and hills, the pine-scented
breezes, the call of the eagle, the rocks, the vast sky, and the
colors. The great silence—she was part of it, and it was her.
That was the very time and place where Annette understood
that this was not a place she could leave. Quetico was part
of her soul. Her children would be educated in the ways of
the world, but they would also know about natural things,
they would know the wilderness, and they would learn about

self-reliance. They could pick up atom splitting and brain surgery somewhere else along the way.

Annette stayed in Atikokan, of course, and got to the lake every year or two after that, always making small improvements in her private campsite. She kept the fire pit out of sight and placed her tent well back in the woods so it wasn't visible from the lake. She found a better approach to the shore through the boulder garden, one not requiring her to boulder hop with gear.

She never found a single trace of another human being on the island, not even a charred rock. The only other people in the world who knew where it was were her daughters—and now Pender.

As she approached the island, her heart beat harder. She wondered if he was there already, his gear up on the bluff, his tent set up, maybe a pot of water boiling. But when she made shore, there was no trace of him, no footprints, no canoe left on the rocks, no gear in sight. She tried not to be disappointed. It was still early in the day, and who knew where Pender was coming from? But it would have been nice to be greeted by a warm smile from long ago.

———

Pender's spirits were buoyed by the clear morning sky and its promise of fair weather, even though his body ached after a long night sleeping on a lumpy ground in cool, damp air. As he grunted and groaned through his morning ministrations, Pender decided that his injury was a ruptured disc, not something dire. He laughed silently at himself: the diagnosis of a great restaurant editor. How could it be wrong? At least his sense of humor was coming back.

He boiled water for coffee as he tore down his tent and packed his gear. He had his coffee and granola as the eastern sky lit up, and was underway minutes later, with miles to go before he would sleep.

As his body warmed and his muscles loosened, he upped his cadence and lengthened his stroke. He would never make it to the island today. It was forty or fifty kilometers away—twenty-five to thirty miles—with fifteen or twenty portages and God knew how many beaver houses and blowdowns to surmount in the creek system he was on. He hoped his body would last for twelve hours of hard paddling and crossing mostly flat, short portages. That would get him to the island by noon tomorrow.

Surely she'd give him a half-day benefit of the doubt. He tried to think of reasons she wouldn't. Maybe she had to get back for business reasons. Or maybe it would just anger her, him being late, being a warmonger Yankee capitalist and late to boot. But she didn't seem hostile in their e-mails. In fact, she sounded mellow.

As he paddled and portaged, Pender thought about her e-mails—about how she described her kids, especially the daughter living with her now, and her grandchild. And how easily she wrote about being abandoned by her husband. Pender shook his head as he pulled on the paddle. What a mind fuck. You give up your country to start a new life with this pseudo-idealistic windbag, and he's gone after one winter. And he's the first one to go back to the U.S. when amnesty comes, leaving you behind for better money and a younger piece of ass.

Pender couldn't fathom how Annette dealt with that so matter-of-factly. If it were him, he'd be deciding between beating the man to death or cutting off his balls. Of course,

Pender had to admit, he wasn't exactly a model of rational thinking these days. But still, even in a contemplative mood, just shooting the bastard wasn't adequate punishment.

His thoughts moved to people he had known in business. His replay of the final drama with group vice president Charles Jamison Blue got him through a particularly nasty bit of creek littered with logs and boulders and beaver houses that required pull-overs and walk-arounds, wading in cold water and slipping on wet surfaces.

His mental focus helped his body withstand a withering pace, and by midafternoon he portaged into the big lake that marked the home stretch to Annette's island. His remarkable progress came at a price. His body ached again. He was hungry and so tired he was starting to feel faint.

He pushed on for a few more kilometers, taking care to hug the shoreline in case the fat boys were looking for him. If they were going back to the U.S. from the Falls Route, they'd use this lake to get there.

Eventually he entered a narrow strait formed by a large island about fifty yards off the mainland shore. There was an empty campsite on a bluff overlooking the strait, and his body told his mind to take it. He landed at a well-worn beach, loaded himself with a pack, paddles, and his water jug, and headed for the trail leading to the campsite above. On his second stride he stepped in a pile of dog poop and cursed.

Pender found neatly stacked and sorted materials for a fire by the fire ring, a welcome gift from a thoughtful camper.

He decided not to have a campfire, though. Physically, he was too sore and too tired to go fishing, so the only cooking for tonight's dinner would be boiling water to rehydrate something. Plus, the fire ring was very visible from the lake. He didn't want to risk having the fat boys find him or having a ranger come calling, since he was without a permit. All of his encounters with rangers in Quetico had been on popular lakes like this one, and most people moving from one end of this lake to the other would come through this narrows, would come right by this campsite.

He boiled water over his gas stove back in the tree line, out of sight from the lake. He ate reconstituted stew from the package it came in and sipped hot chicken broth while sitting on a log that gave him a view of the waterway and the island. As he wrote a journal entry for his daughter, he checked periodically for paddlers on the water, but there were none. It was late in the day. Most people would be in camp now.

Later, as he rinsed his dishes in the dim light of evening, he stood at water's edge and watched a lone canoe meander along an island a kilometer southwest of him. It wasn't the fat boys or a ranger. It was two people out for an evening paddle, their canoe riding high in the water without the weight of their gear aboard. He thought they might be husband and wife or boyfriend and girlfriend, and that made him think of Annette. He wondered how she was handling his absence. He could see her face in his mind, how it would look sad. He could see loneliness in her eyes. He told her he was sorry, and, for the millionth time that day, he hoped she would give him another day to get there.

16

Annette finished the afternoon by taking Chaos fishing in the lake's northwestern bay. She worked weeds and structure in fifteen- and twenty-foot depths, releasing several small fish before taking two nice-sized walleye . . . a little more than she needed, just in case Pender showed up. If not, Chaos would handle the leftovers with relish.

She returned to camp, hoping Pender had floated in while she was gone, disappointed to find he had not.

She cooked, ate, and cleaned dishes in a somber mood but lightened up when Chaos sat beside her on the rock overlooking the lake below. He pushed his head under her arm. She scratched his ears. He rolled onto his side. She petted his chest and shoulder. He rolled onto his back, looked at her with his tongue rolling out one side of his mouth, grinning. If dogs could grin. She laughed, rubbing his chest.

As the sun softened on the western horizon, Annette rummaged through her food pack until she found a flexible plastic container filled with red wine. It was how you brought wine into a park that didn't allow glasses or cans, but it was even better than a bottle since you could squeeze out the air each

time you closed it. Wine lasted for a week without developing off flavors. She had brought two bottles of wine, each in
its own plastic bladder, thinking it would be nice to sip wine
with an old friend from long ago. Not knowing how long they
would share a campfire, or how much they'd drink.

She was going to save the wine until Pender got there,
but now, facing the possibility he wouldn't show up at all
and with a gorgeous sunset coming up in a few minutes, she
resolved to go crazy. She poured a few ounces of wine into
her cup and went back out to her promontory to watch day
turn to night and snuggle with Chaos.

Inevitably, her thoughts turned to Pender. She pictured
him lying flat on a trail somewhere, a broken leg, trying to
drag his canoe behind him as he crawled across the raspy
surface of the trail, a pack on his back, a line from the bow
of the canoe tied to his good leg. She tried to figure if it
would be better to have the other pack in the front or the
back of the boat.

That gave way to a new image of him sitting in a fancy
restaurant with a thirtyish woman with full lips and perfect
skin and seductive cleavage. Talking about great food and
wines. She'd look like a bumpkin by comparison, Annette
thought—and her choice in wine would prove it.

She didn't really believe the broken leg image or the social-
ite image, but he wasn't here. It didn't really matter why he
didn't show up. The thing was, he didn't. That's how her life
was when it came to men. It always ended in disappointment.
She allowed herself to shed a few tears. She'd move on from
this, like always, but it would have been so nice. To feel a
lover's body against yours just once more. To snuggle through
a chilly night in Quetico. In her dreams, she had occasionally let herself imagine what it would be like to be held all

night long by a lover in the endless Ontario winter, to plan a special dinner, to go to the store together.

It had been so long . . .

Annette dreamt of sad things that night. Disappointments. Loneliness. Sorrow. The first Christmas with just the kids, no husband, no family. The first Christmas when even the kids were gone. The deaths of her parents.

She wept in her sleep the way she would never cry in her waking hours, wept soft and wet without inhibition. Pushed away Chaos when he nuzzled her but put her arm around him as she went back to sleep.

At first light, Chaos wriggled free and tried to lick the salt from her face. His wet tongue and dog breath shocked Annette to wakefulness with a jolt. She made a sputtering noise as she tried to clear saliva from her mouth and used her hands to rub it from the rest of her face.

"That's disgusting, you dirty mongrel!" She said it mostly in jest, but Chaos retreated to the far corner of the tent. "Don't be such a sniveling coward. You're supposed to expect some abuse from your mistress. Especially if you're going to go around sticking your tongue in her face and up her nose. Pervert."

She laughed. Chaos put on his smiling face, ears raised, tail thumping on the ground. They crawled from the tent, and Annette got a fire going. She made coffee and sipped it as she pondered breakfast. She had packed in fresh eggs and bacon for today's breakfast, thinking it would be a way to celebrate Pender and her meeting again after forty years. Would it still be good tomorrow? Maybe. Would Pender be here tomorrow? As she considered it, she thought, probably not. He's been in the park for a week or more. If he were going to be here, he would have been on time or early.

The realization took away her hunger, but the coffee tasted good. After a second cup, she cleaned her dishes, extinguished the fire, and gathered firewood to replace what she had used.

She stood on the promontory and scanned the lake, deciding what to do with her day. She should break camp and head for home. It would be a relief to Christy to have her there, and it would help preserve some self-esteem after having been stood up for a date that had been months in the planning.

But she knew one day wasn't long enough to wait. Not in a place this remote. There could be a hundred different reasons why he was late, and many of them were unpleasant to contemplate. She decided to give it one more day. She packed a snack and her fishing gear and took Chaos for a paddle around the lake. She would try to score a walleye for Chaos and check the condition of the established campsite on the lake. She tried to convince herself it would be fun. Not likely. But it would be something to do.

Pender woke with a start, the dream so vivid he could still see Annette's face in his waking vision. It was etched in outrage and hurt, her voice angry. *You didn't show up. You didn't even call! What kind of a human being are you? What do you believe in, Pender? Do you believe in anything?*

He sat bolt upright. "Jesus!" he exclaimed. It startled him anew, the sound of his own voice. He tried to check his watch, but it was inky black in the tent. He groped for his headlamp, felt the stiffness in his back, and realized for the first time that he could move. He was stiff and sore, but he was able to sit up and turn to either side without crying in pain. He found the light. It was 3:30. Too early. There would be no light for another hour and a half.

He tried to sleep. Couldn't. Rolled onto his back and tried to imagine meeting Annette. Sometimes she was angry. Sometimes hurt. Even when she was angry she was crying inside, Pender could feel it. And he suddenly understood that when she said what she had said all those years ago, she was crying inside. *I hope you get drafted and you go to Vietnam and you get shot and you die there.*

It was a love song, a sad one. All those years ago. Jesus, what a waste of two lives. And then came the thought. What if it all happens again for her but not for me? If she's interested and I'm not? Knowing that something had died inside him over the years. His emotional range seemed to stretch from indifference to anger, but mostly indifference. Could he love anyone ever again? It seemed impossible.

At 4:00 he quit trying to sleep. Got up, struck camp, moved his gear down to the lake, and packed his canoe. At 4:30 he launched. It was still pitch-black, and paddling in the dark was risky. The big lake had a lot of structure that was hard to identify in the dark, but he couldn't wait anymore. He navigated by compass and paddled at a moderate speed, hoping if he hit a submerged rock, his canoe might survive the shock.

A half hour later, light seeped over the horizon and Pender was still upright. When he could make out the shadowy forms of rocks and reefs, he upped his speed to a racing pace, digging maniacally into the cold waters, hauling back on the paddle as if running for his life, spurred on by a desperate feeling that he was letting Annette down. He flew across the water, taking advantage of calm winds, flat waters, and a body that was working efficiently. He reached the end of the big lake before 7 AM, took breakfast on a rocky outcropping, and headed for the creek system that led to Annette's lake.

———————

If he hadn't stopped for breakfast, the fat boys wouldn't have seen him. They were crossing the south end of the big lake, heading for the river that would take them back to the Boundary Waters, when one of them spotted a solo canoe heading into the creek to the north. The boat was a good distance off. Even with binoculars, they couldn't tell for sure if it was their guy. As the canoe disappeared in the islands and landmasses, they debated whether or not to give chase. It would take them hours to catch up to the paddler and more hours to get back to where they were now. They would lose another day, probably two, and they had already spent a week chasing the guy.

The stern paddler was done. "Come on, man," he said. "This is stupid. I want to go home. We don't even know if that's our guy. He could be at home. And I need to get home myself. I've got a wife and family, a job."

"I want that motherfucker!" said Gus. "No way that sneaky son of a bitch gets away with what he did to us. One more day. That's all I ask. We'll catch up to him this morning. There's a bunch of portages on that creek. We'll make up a lot of time because he has to double portage. Come on. One more day. How about it?"

Bill gazed long and hard at his friend. This had started out as something else. Yeah, they were pissed, but it was the challenge—could anyone track down a canoeist in a sprawling wilderness with hundreds of lakes and rivers, a place so desolate dozens of lakes didn't even have names? It seemed impossible, but if anyone could do it, they could. And it would be fun.

Somewhere along the way, the thrill of the hunt had given way to a taste for revenge in Gus's mind. That happened with Gus sometimes. They had known each other all their lives, went to the same schools, played the same sports, double dated, stood up at each other's weddings. Most of the time he was a fun-loving, generous guy, everything you could want in a friend. But he had this other side. The obsessive side. He had been a terror on the football field, a savage blocker, a guy who got in such a mental zone for games he was scary. He once got a penalty for blocking a defensive end fifteen yards downfield, ten of them after the whistle had blown. Sometimes he just fixated on something and there was nothing anyone could do. Bill wearily assented. "Let's get it over with."

————————

Annette spent the morning trying not to think about Pender, trying not to worry about him, trying not to feel sorry for herself. If she thought about it, she mostly came back to feeling sorry for herself, a grandmother whose time had passed. She tried not to recall her youth, when boys pursued her, her young womanhood, when polyamorous males and even some females in the movement made passes at her. She tried not to recall when they moved to Atikokan, how male heads turned when she walked down the aisle of a store, the miners, the loggers, the merchants.

And now, when it would be so nice to be wanted, to talk, reminisce, to feel the presence of a kindred spirit, it was just too late. She was a graying, sagging, dimming version of the woman who turned heads. There would be no more lovers for her. Her life would be about her kids, her grandkids, and maybe a couple of friends.

At least she had family, she thought. She was so lucky to have that.

To focus on other things, she toured the northeast segment of her lake, paddling lackadaisically in fine weather, covering the five kilometers to the north end in an hour, then following the shoreline east. It was too early to fish, so she nosed her canoe into shore at a portage site. It was the "other" way into her lake, the northern entry. She had come in from the south.

She told herself she was walking the portage trail for Chaos's sake, so her buddy could get in some running. And Chaos leaped at the opportunity. But in the corner of her consciousness, Annette was hoping Pender would be coming the other way on the trail. They'd see each other, smile, hug strong and warm. She'd help him with the carry. He'd meet Chaos and they'd like each other. They'd paddle to the island, make lunch, lean against each other as they ate, looking out on the lake, talking dreamily about whatever came to mind. The princess fantasy of her childhood, adapted for old age.

It was a bland, boggy trail of medium length, not especially pretty. The last part of the trek was wet, with lengths of saplings lodged side by side like corduroy providing passage over areas of floating bog that wouldn't support the weight of an adult. She paused to repair sections where the thin pine logs had been dislodged, hoping she would rise and see Pender coming up the trail.

But each time she rose to a silent wilderness, alone.

She made herself go to the end of the trail and look out on the tiny lake to the east. There was not a canoe in sight, no campfire smoke, just a pair of mergansers floating offshore. The waterfowl disappeared beneath the water as Chaos charged onto the beach next to her. He stank with black mud and reeked of bog stink, a not-quite-fetid odor that came from the rotting vegetation and black water that created the dark mass of the bog.

"Oh, Chaos," she said with a sigh and a smile. "You are hopeless."

The dog looked at her, tail wagging, tongue lolling to one side. His canine smile. Having the time of his life. Thank goodness one of us is, she thought.

She turned and hiked back to her lake. She rinsed the muck out of Chaos's coat. Then they paddled quietly back toward her island. As they approached it, Annette glanced at her watch. It was too early for lunch, and she couldn't bear the thought of sitting around camp with nothing to do. She would paddle on. She thought about heading to a small, isolated lake where she often fished for walleye and bass but decided to save that option for the afternoon. She wasn't kidding herself, she was staying another night. What was one more day of heartbreak compared to the rest of your life not knowing if he showed up?

She decided to have a look at the other portage. Chaos would get some more exercise, and she would have something to do that kept her out of her depressingly lonely camp.

17

Pender had lost all memory of his pursuers. His entire focus was getting into Annette's lake before lunch. He thought there was a good chance she wouldn't give up on him before lunch. If it was him, he'd at least stay for one more meal, see what happened.

He barely noticed the unfolding landscape of the creek system, even though it was the kind of environment he loved, steep banks and forest giving way to watery bogs and marshes, beaver houses pockmarking the stream. He saw these things, but he didn't absorb them. He looked only for the landmarks that helped him navigate, an island that kept him on a western heading, a tall tree on a high bluff in the distance that gave him a northwest heading. His months of training let him sustain a withering pace without flagging. He almost ran through the short portages that connected the floatable sections of the creek, and he shot through the water portion of the route like a man possessed.

It was by accident that he saw the fat boys. Paddling west out of the last creek portage, he mistook a shallow bay for the large bay he was looking for. When he realized his mistake, he paddled back to the creek. Movement in the east caught his eye. He could see two people in the portage area he had just left, not even a kilometer away.

Alarms went off in his mind. He wanted to believe it was just a couple of trippers. This route saw a little traffic every year, mostly trippers on a route that bypassed Annette's lake in favor of a chain of small lakes that hopscotched west, then north. But Pender's instincts burned with certainty and dread. It was the fat boys. Son of a bitch. Five days later, they find a needle in the haystack. What was it with those guys?

Pender hastily moved out of their line of sight, entering a two-bay lake and sliding a few feet south to put a landmass between him and the canoeists. He studied his map quickly. The route to Annette's lake was through the northern bay of the lake, but if those were the fat boys back there and they saw him heading into that water, they would know where he was going. There would be no escape then. They'd catch him at the portage trail for sure.

In the south bay, where he sat now, he was about a kilometer away from the portage into the more popular small-lake route. If those canoeists were just regular trippers, they'd head for that portage. If it was the fat boys, they'd figure him for that portage too. Pender paddled through a tiny gap in the shore, just a few feet wide, that led to into a marshy pond. In the pond he would be invisible to the canoeists traveling west, but he would be able to see them as they passed.

As he waited for them, Pender thought about his next move. If they were just trippers, he would proceed with haste. If it was the fat boys, his safest option was to wait them out, stay right in the pond, pull everything into the bush, out of sight, and deal with it all tomorrow. But Annette might be gone by then.

He would have to go for the other bay. The question was when to make his move. He could wait until they portaged into the next lake. That seemed like the smart bet until he thought about how smart they were. They wouldn't find any sign of him at the portage, and they'd look for other possibilities.

He would have to bolt for the north bay as soon as they passed his position. It was risky. If one of them turned to look behind their boat, they'd see him and come on the fly. And those guys could really fly, he thought. Jesus, they overtook him when he was paddling at a racing pace!

Pender visualized sliding out of the pond after they passed and disappearing into the other bay before they reached their portage area. By the time the fat boys looked around, he'd be in a place they'd never look. He and Annette would have a good lunch, get acquainted, and talk over old times. It would be nice, at least for a little while, and in a day or two or three, he'd move on, north and east, probably, and forget all about the fat boys who paddled like the wind.

When they passed the pond, he saw it was them. Two burly guys moving like a racing team, not carrying much gear, the hull riding high in the water despite the proportions of the paddlers.

After they passed, he paddled out of the pond and burned hard for the north bay. But it didn't work out the way he envisioned it. The stern paddler somehow sensed movement to the rear and used his paddle like a tiller to quickly turn the canoe. Both men saw Pender at the same time.

Pender was tracking the fat boys' movement and saw them turn, saw them thrash their paddles in the water to come after him. His mind erupted in fear and expletives. He streaked for the north bay and his portage, trying to plan an escape as he ripped paddle strokes. He thought if he got there with enough lead time, say, fifteen minutes, he could throw one pack into the bush, single portage into Annette's lake, then look for a place to hide. He tried to convince himself it could work, but it couldn't. The fat boys would find him if it came down to just one lake with only two ways in and out. Plus, he didn't have a fifteen-minute lead. He'd be lucky to land five minutes ahead of them. He wondered if he could talk them down but realized they'd tracked him for a week in one of the most rugged wildernesses in North America. They'd want blood.

He paddled flat out until he was a hundred feet from shore. He had to slow down to dodge submerged rocks. That would be the perfect end, he thought, gutting his canoe just as two angry rednecks the size of NFL linemen were bearing down on him. As he lowered his cadence, it occurred to him that the few moments of rest might help him deal with the fat boys. Two huge, crazy maniacs who had been chasing him for days, who had impossibly found him in a vast wilderness.

Pender still didn't have a plan when he reached shore, but he had priorities. He'd get his boat and gear onshore. If they were going to take anything from him, they'd have to go through him first. Of course, that's what they wanted to do, but Pender didn't want some kind of stalemate that ended with them taking his food pack and his canoe. He'd rather die first.

He also started working on his attitude. He had to change his focus from running to attacking. You can't fight scared. You have to be the meanest motherfucker in the valley. Be violent. Be cruel. Leave your mark.

When his canoe crunched ashore, he leaped out like a cat, dragged it onto shore, grabbed one pack in each hand, and ran them to the mouth of the portage trail at the edge of the clearing. He ran back for the canoe, dragging it at a trotting pace to the packs, ignoring the scratching sounds of the hull scraping over rocks. He glanced to the lake. The fat boys were so close he could see their red faces and clenched jaws.

He snatched his backup paddle from the canoe, wielding it like a pugil stick. He glanced back at the water. The fat boys were almost to shore, and the closer they got, the stronger and meaner they appeared. The paddle felt light and flimsy. He threw it to one side and foraged in his gear pack, felt the stiffness in his back, ignored it. The fat boys' canoe crunched into the shallows, and the guy in the bow was just getting out. The power paddler.

Pender thrust his hand down one side of the pack and finally felt the handle of his hatchet. He yanked. It moved a few inches and then hooked on something. He looked to the beach. The bow paddler had pulled the canoe ashore, the stern guy was getting out. Pender yanked again. Nothing. Again. Nothing. He looked to the beach. They were coming for him like two mammoth clouds in a world-ending thunderstorm. They were huge and they were fast, and he was going to absorb a terrible beating. He yanked on the hatchet again.

This time it came free.

Pender held the hatchet in his right hand and moved toward the approaching fat boys, trying to surprise them, stop their initiative. He crouched a little, trying to work the stiffness out of his back and look lethal.

The stern paddler stopped short when he saw the hatchet. It still had the leather casing over the hatchet head, but something about Pender told him he knew how to use it. The bow paddler, Gus, kept coming.

"Be ready to die, motherfucker!" screamed Pender. He ripped the cover from his hatchet blade. The guy was as big as a mountain and moved like an athlete.

"Fuck you, asshole!" bellowed Gus. His lips curled back in a battle scream, and he charged Pender like a messenger of death.

Pender dipped to one side, scooped up a rock, and flung it at the man. Gus ducked instinctively but kept coming, just a few feet away. Pender set his feet and feinted with his hatchet hand. It was just enough that Gus flinched a little and reached out with his hands defensively, but he kept coming.

When Gus was there, right there, ready to crush him, Pender dodged to one side, dropped to his knees and swept the hatchet in a murderous arc, knee high. The blunt end of the tool caught a piece of Gus's shin, and the hasp of the hatchet caught the rest. Between the velocity of the swing and the speed of the lunging attacker, the trauma of the impact dropped the huge man as if he'd been shot dead.

Gus wasn't dead, but he was in awful pain, screaming, so overwhelmed by pain he couldn't form words, couldn't curse, could only bellow and howl at the top of his lungs.

Bill started to charge. Pender raised one hand and drew back the hatchet with the other.

"Think about it!" he shouted over Gus's screams. "I'll do what I have to." Bill was massive himself. Pender would have to disable him or be overwhelmed.

Bill looked at his friend. "You broke his fucking leg, you moron!"

"Maybe, maybe not. But if you come for me, I'll have to bust you up. I'll have no choice."

They glared at each other amid Gus's screams. Stalemate.

Gus's bellowing eventually subsided into grunts and groans of agony. Bill went to his side, ran his hands down the damaged shin bone.

"I can't feel a break," he said. He rolled the man's pant leg up to the knee. "I don't see a break. Not that that means anything." Blood was starting to flow, and a huge black bruise was forming. The sight of it repulsed Bill. He looked away, then to Pender.

"What kind of a shit-eating bastard are you anyway? You low-life motherfucker! We try to help you, we offer hospitality, we do this for a stranger, and what do you do? You try to ruin our trip. You trash our stereo, and you steal our canoes. You fuck us over, and all you know about us is that we tried to help you when you were in harm's way. What kind of a miserable rat bastard are you?"

Pender stared at the man, then at his injured friend, then back at the man. "If you leave now, your friend will still be able to paddle and maybe walk. You can make it home."

"Don't worry, asshole. We're going. Just as soon as Gus is able. But you're still a motherfucker and shit for brains."

Pender shrugged, watched, went back to his pack, and pulled out a T-shirt. He took it to the water, soaked it, brought it back to the injured paddler. "Put this on the bruise. It'll help control the swelling and maybe numb some of the pain."

"Oh thanks, motherfucker," said Bill sarcastically. "Like this is going to make everything all better and get you into heaven, right? No way. I still want to know what made you do that. What a bullshit thing to do to people who tried to help you!"

Pender stared at him for several counts, long enough that Bill thought he might have pissed off the guy.

"I shouldn't have taken your canoes. I'm sorry."

"So why did you?"

"You wouldn't understand."

"Try me."

Pender paused. "You dishonored this place." It sounded stupid when he said it out loud, and Bill stared at him in disbelief.

"I don't believe it," Bill said. He unleashed a chain of curses.

Pender shrugged. How can you explain peace to someone who's never known war?

"That's it? Really?"

Pender nodded his head yes, a little sheepishly.

"You ruin our vacation because we drank beer and played music in the park?" Bill's voice was filled with disbelief.

"I thought someone should teach you a lesson," said Pender.

"Why didn't you just ask us to stop?"

"Why would I? If you cared about this place and the other people in it, you wouldn't have been doing what you were doing."

"You're a chicken-shit motherfucker," said Bill.

Gus worked his way into a sitting position, his groans giving way to intermittent grunts. He looked up at Pender once, then away.

"You ready to travel?" Pender asked.

"Don't worry about it," Bill said. "We'll go when we're ready to go."

"I'll help you get him to the boat."

"No. Go on. Get out of here."

"I can't really do that until you leave, know what I mean?"

"You afraid we'll do to you what you did to us?"

"Exactly."

"We aren't like that. We aren't like you."

"Right. You guys chase me all over Quetico and charge me on a beach, two against one, because you want to have a Bible meeting?"

"Crazy nut-job," Gus said, finally able to speak. "Fucking coward. Using a lethal weapon against an unarmed man."

Pender laughed.

"That's funny?" Bill said it, mad. Gus was flushed with anger, too.

"Two guys against one? Two guys going, what, two-seventy each, in their thirties. You calling me a bully?"

Gus started to respond, but Bill cut him off. "He's a crack-pot. Let's get out of here." He helped Gus to his feet. As they hobbled to their canoe, Gus threw Pender's T-shirt on the beach.

Pender watched them paddle away. They were very good paddlers. Very good. He wondered if they might have been friends if they'd met under other circumstances. Maybe. Unless it was a war and they were on the other side, trying to kill him. He'd have had to use the sharp end of the hatchet.

Life can be a mind fuck if you think about it, he sighed. He turned away from the lake and grabbed a pack, ready to finally portage into Annette's lake. He could still make lunch.

When Annette landed at the portage area, Chaos bolted after some waterfowl in the shallows, splashing into the water. She strolled up the trail. He'd probably still be swimming when she got back.

As she walked, she marveled at the irony that her lake and her private campsite were suddenly barren and lonely for her. This had always been her refuge, a place she often visited alone. Amazing, she thought, what new expectations can do to your perspective and your life.

Her contemplations ended as blood-curdling shrieks filled the air, coming from the other side of the portage. Human voices making inhuman noises, like a horror movie. Her mind seized as she tried to fathom how to respond. She was an independent woman of the wilderness, a guide, a leader. But this sounded violent. A bear attack? A murder? She felt weak and vulnerable, wanted to run, but kept thinking, what if someone was hurt? She had to see if she could help.

She trotted as fast as she could along the trail. The screams grew louder as she neared the beach. She could make out male voices and terrible obscenities. It sounded like war, violent and bloody. A few steps from the beach, she slowed to a creep, crouched behind the brush, inching forward to see what was happening.

Peeking out from the foliage, she saw three men in confrontation. One had his back to her and stood a few feet in front of a canoe, two packs, and two paddles; he held a hatchet in one hand. The other two were near the water, one sitting and groaning in great pain, holding his leg, which was red with blood and black with bruising, the other kneeling next to him, concerned. She wondered if the man with the hatchet had broken the injured man's leg. She wondered if the man with the hatchet was Pender. The other two weren't. They were too big, too heavy, and too young. The man with his back to her was trim, athletic. She couldn't tell his age. But if anyone was going to get into a fight twenty miles from the next human being, it would be Pender.

And that's when she remembered. The ranger, looking for a solo canoeist who had done something to some fishermen. Could it be?

The man with his back to her said something she couldn't make out, his voice soft and projected away from her, and the concerned man responded scornfully. "Don't worry about it. We'll go when we're ready to go." Loud. Angry.

The man she couldn't see said something else she couldn't hear, but his tone and his gesture made it seem like he was offering to help.

"No. Go on. Get out of here," said the concerned guy. His friend glared at the man she couldn't see, gritting his teeth in pain, hatred written on his face.

She was trying to figure out why the guys on the ground were giving the orders. She edged closer to the confrontation but stayed camouflaged in the bushes.

"I can't really do that until you leave, know what I mean?" She could hear the man, even though she still couldn't see his face.

"You afraid we'll do to you what you did to us?"

"Exactly."

"We aren't like that. We aren't like you."

"Right. You guys chase me all over Quetico and charge me on a beach, two against one, because you want to have a Bible meeting?"

It had to be Pender. It was the sort of thing Pender would say. Sarcastic, cutting.

The injured man spoke for the first time. "Crazy nut-job," Gus said, finally able to speak. "Fucking coward. Using a lethal weapon against an unarmed man."

The man with the hatchet made an indistinct noise and shook his head.

"That's funny?" the other man asked.

"Two guys against one? Two guys going, what, two-seventy each, in their late thirties. You calling me a bully?"

It sounded like Pender.

The concerned guy cut off his friend's response. "He's a crackpot. Let's get out of here." He helped his friend to his feet, and they hobbled to the canoe, throwing something behind them. They got aboard and paddled away. The man on the beach watched them until they were well on their way, and then turned to the portage trail.

It was Pender. Sunburnt, a little bent, some gray hair peeking out from his bush hat, but the rest was familiar. The structured face, athletic body, the way he moved with a limber nonchalance that spoke of arrogance, somehow. As if the person in the body had never worried about anything. As if all things came easily to him. Including violence, apparently. What had just happened here? What kind of man was he?

It was too late to back out now. Annette stood up to show herself to him. At that moment, Chaos came roaring out of the brush, saw Pender, skidded to a stop in shock, and began barking crazily. Pender stared at the dog in disbelief, then at Annette just as incredulously, as if he was trying to fit these two images into his reality.

As Chaos continued yapping, Pender forced a smile and nodded to Annette. She gave a hesitant wave and nod back, and he started to approach her. Chaos inserted himself between them and growled. Pender winged a kick at him, not a serious kick so much as a dismissive one, like the dog was about as intimidating as a croaking frog. The dog dodged the kick and cowered as Pender snarled an obscenity at him. Quiet descended on the shore. Pender stopped in front of Annette.

"Annette?" He asked it, trying to accompany the question with a friendly smile, not easy after the encounter with the fat boys and her dog.

"Pender." She said it like a statement of fact. She tried to smile back, but there was more doubt than mirth in her expression.

"What happened here?" she asked. "Did you have a fight with those two men?"

"Well, kind of. It's a long story."

"I'll bet. I've never heard of trippers in the park getting into a fight. More than thirty years I've been here, and I've never heard of a fight in Quetico."

Silence. Pender couldn't think of what to say. He was trying to process everything. The situation. His crazy day. His week. His life. What it must look like to Annette. And he was trying to do all this as he appraised her physically. A sixties folk singer with gray hair, he thought. Still lean and fit, some softness at the jawline, but strong features. Beautiful. Hot, in a back-to-nature kind of way. And angry. Just like old times.

"Are we in danger, Gabe? Chaos and I?"

Pender started to speak, then halted, digested what she said. "Chaos? That's his name? Wow. That works." He stopped again, composed himself. "No, you're not in danger, of course not. It's not what you think—"

"Then could you drop the hatchet, please? Or put it away?" She nodded to the tool still in his hand.

He looked at the hatchet, back at her, blushed. "Sure. Sorry."

He laid the hatchet on his pack. "I'm sorry we got off on the wrong foot here. Those two guys . . . we had a run-in a week or so ago . . ." His voice trailed off.

"A week ago? Have they been following you all that time? Did you know a park ranger was looking for a solo canoe-ist who did something to some fishermen in the Boundary Waters? Was that you? What did you do?"

Pender gazed at her thoughtfully. This wasn't going well. Not at all. Jesus, she was going to tell him to go to hell before they even talked about the weather or their kids. Jesus. He shook his head. Life could be such a mind fuck.

"There were four of them camping and fishing on a border lake, U.S. side. They had a big cooler of beer, in cans of course. And that irked me. When I see metal in these campsites I want to, to . . ." He was going to say "kick ass" but realized how violent that sounded. He shrugged. "You know, convince people they shouldn't do that."

Annette had a dubious look on her face.

"Actually, I wanted to let them know in no uncertain terms how much it pissed me off that they'd desecrate this place like that."

"You did something to them because they had cans in the park?" Annette asked, incredulous.

"They were also playing music on a boom box. Loud. Loud enough to keep me awake on the other side of the lake. That made me crazy. So what I did was, I waited until they went to sleep and then I swiped their canoes and their boom box and I used the boom box to anchor their canoes about a half klick away. I couldn't do anything about the cans."

"You stole their canoes?"

"No, I moved them. To a place they couldn't see, but not that far away."

"Did it occur to you that you were putting their lives in danger?"

"No," said Pender, getting testy at her attitude. "It occurred to me that they needed to know other people in this wilderness give a shit about it and won't let a bunch of redneck assholes abuse it. And I think they got the message."

"They followed you for days. What message do you think they got?"

"I think they found out this place is full of left-wing, tree-hugging communists and even the old ones are not worth tangling with. I did that fat son of a bitch a favor. I only hit him once and only with the flat side of the ax, and only on the leg. I didn't even break his leg!"

"Oh, the humanitarian of the year! I can't believe you just said that!" said Annette, her face flushing. "Do you hear yourself? Do you even realize what you're saying? You're a good guy because you didn't kill someone with a hatchet? If you're not an ax murderer, you're okay?"

He flushed deep red and started to answer but stopped when the sense of her last words computed in his mind. He tried not to laugh, tried to stay mad, but he couldn't muffle the snicker. The harder he tried not to, the louder it got.

"I'm sorry," he said. "I'm not laughing at you. It just sounded funny. You can laugh, too, if you want."

Annette smiled a tight smile. "Good one, Pender."

"I'm glad we got that out of the way. We did, didn't we?"

Annette shook her head. She slung his food pack on her shoulders and picked up his paddles. "Lunchtime. Let's sort this out over a meal."

With that, she headed down the trail, Chaos running after her. Pender watched her go, admired her easy gait, how strong she was, but feminine too. And she already hated him. He paused for a moment, trying to let his mind process all the things that had happened in the past fifteen minutes. Jesus. He packed up his hatchet, shouldered the other pack and his canoe, and followed Annette to her lake.

18

Annette dropped Pender's paddles on the beach, threw his pack in her canoe, collected Chaos, and launched before Pender finished the portage. She didn't look back. She was fifty yards away by the time Pender took his first stroke. She paddled leisurely in a canoe with less hull speed than his, but he still had to paddle like a racer to close the gap between them, and even then it took most of a kilometer to draw abreast of her. He was impressed. She had perfect paddle stroke form, far more efficient than him, and faster. It would be nice if she'd take it easy when they paddled together.

The dog started to stand as Pender came aside, and Annette tapped him with a light but curiously loud thump to the head with her paddle. The dog lay down obediently but kept his head up, looking over the gunnel at Pender.

"I see you use the kindness method of dog training," Pender called.

"What do you do? Shoot them? Kick them?" Annette refused to look at him. She had seen his pictures on the Internet, and the glimpse of him on the beach confirmed that he was a graying version of the college boy she had known.

A little more flesh on the face, the lines and creases of age. Slim. Handsome in a weather-beaten kind of way. But too violent to get involved with.

He started to respond, then shut up. He smiled and nodded. He tried to make the smile seem good-natured. "Good one," he said.

They paddled in silence, Pender glancing over to her frequently, Annette staring straight ahead. She was trying not to feel sorry for herself, trying not to write off this encounter despite overwhelming evidence that Pender was a testosterone-driven jackass. He kept hoping she'd look at him, establish eye contact, open up to conversation.

"We could talk, you know," he called to her. "It's not like there's anyone else to talk to."

She continued paddling, eyes straight ahead.

"Come on," he said. "You can't hate me already. We just met. If you give me a chance, in a couple of days you'll know me well enough to really hate me." He stared at her and thought he saw a suppressed smile. He wanted to say something funny about the dog, but they were reaching the rocky shoals of Annette's island.

Annette floated into the take-out area, Pender holding just offshore because the take-out area was too small for two boats to land at the same time. Annette stepped out of her canoe into a foot of water and plucked Pender's pack from her boat. She slung it over one shoulder and then lifted her canoe over the other shoulder and carried it to a nest-like opening in the shore brush, laying it in place, hull up. She hiked up the steep incline to her camp, never looking back at Pender. He watched her ascend the trail. She really was pissed at him.

The dog watched Pender land, but only because he was taking a dump near the trailhead. Pender shook his head. An angry wilderness mama and her shit machine. What a date. And he wondered, as he climbed the trail to her camp, if the pile of poop he stepped in the night before came from her dog.

Annette placed Pender's pack in her kitchen area, a space created by three log benches forming a rectangle with the fire ring as the fourth side. She had built up the fire ring over the years. The fire pit itself was built atop several layers of rocks to prevent root fires, and she had created counter space on each side of it by placing large, flat rocks on top of walls of smaller ones.

Her food pack sat next to another flat rock that formed a tabletop a few feet in front of the fire pit. She sat on a log in front of the table and began sorting through her food pack.

When Pender entered the camp, Chaos bounded toward him, then skidded to a stop as if remembering his willingness to kick a dog. Chaos eyed him warily, but Annette didn't look up from her work or acknowledge his presence. He carried his gear pack to the tenting area, parked it next to Annette's, and mentally noted where he'd pitch his tent.

He meandered up to the kitchen.

Annette was making sandwiches in stony silence, fuming that she had relegated herself to kitchen duty for a violent slob who didn't have the decency to show up on time.

"I'm making lunch, but I'm not your mother, okay? You can do the dishes." She didn't look up when she said it, didn't look at Pender at all.

"Fine," he said. "I'll cook dinner. And do the dishes. I'm not your father, but I think you knew that."

Annette remained silent. She finished the sandwiches and made two cups of soup. "I've got enough fresh food for breakfast and lunch tomorrow. Then that's it," she said. She didn't ask him if he had any fresh food. He wouldn't. He had been in the park for more than a week.

She handed him a plastic cup of soup and his sandwich on a paper towel.

"Somehow I didn't think I'd be welcome tomorrow," he said as he sat on one of the logs.

"I'm thinking about it." Her voice was cold, but she finally looked at him. "Come on," she said. And she led the way to her overlook on the high bluff. She sat on a small boulder and began eating, ignoring Pender. He sat stiffly on the ground near her. They ate in silence, gazing out on the lake and the forests beyond. The brightness of the midday sun made the lake a pale blue color and bleached the shores into faded pastels of green and yellow. A pair of loons floated near shore, the only things moving in an idyllic landscape. As they ate, the only sound came from a light breeze rustling through the pine needles.

Chaos joined them, lying next to Annette, keeping her between him and Pender.

"Nice dog," said Pender.

She nodded.

"How old is he?"

She shrugged. "I don't know."

"Okay. How long have you had him?"

"A few days. I found him on the way here."

Pender waited for her to tell the story, but she went silent.

"Did you find him in the park?" he asked

She nodded.

"Does that happen a lot? Finding dogs in the park?"

"No," said Annette. "He had been abandoned."

"Really? Couldn't he have just wandered off? It's hard to imagine someone abandoning a dog out here."

"He was definitely abandoned."

Pender gradually worked the story of the Stuarts out of her.

"If that guy had charged you, would you have hit him with the paddle?" he asked.

She nodded yes.

He thought about that. "How is that different than me taking down Mr. Football back there?" he asked.

"How is it similar?" Annette hissed her answer. "I didn't antagonize that man. I saved a dog."

"I defended myself, just like you would have."

"You hit that poor man with a hatchet, Pender! You could have killed him."

"You're kidding now, right?" He peered at her face, looking for a tell-tale smile. It wasn't there. Just an angry grimace. "I hit him with the flat side of the hatchet. I didn't use the blade. I could have. I chose not to."

Her face tensed in frustration. "It started with you antagonizing those men, stealing their property. What gives you the right?"

"It started with them playing loud rock and roll in the wilderness. It started with them hauling a case or two of beer in cans into the park. Wouldn't that piss you off?"

"Of course it would. But I wouldn't go steal their property."

"What would you do?"

"I'd tell them they were breaking park rules and being discourteous to others."

"That's what I told them," said Pender. "I just used actions instead of words."

Annette walked back to the fire ring, Chaos at her side. Pender followed, finishing his meal as he walked.

"We need to be able to disagree," he said when he caught up.

"I'm a Canadian. We can disagree without destroying each other. Try it. Maybe you can learn something new, though I doubt it."

Pender couldn't think of anything to say. He picked up the lunch dishes and cleaning materials and made his way down to the beach. He eased his canoe through the shoals and washed dishes about a hundred feet from the island.

When he got back to camp, Annette was sitting on one of the log benches, waiting for him. "You need to understand that what you did to those men is as upsetting to me as what they did was upsetting to you. If you can't understand that, there's really no point in staying here."

"I understand," Pender said, drying the dishes.

She waited for him to say more, but he didn't. "You seem like a violent, angry man," she said. "I don't feel safe around you."

He straightened from his labors, and they locked eyes. He shook his head sadly from side to side. "Okay. I'll go. But if I was what you think I am, it would have been a lot easier to kill that man or break his leg so bad he'd never walk right again."

Annette seethed. "That's right. You had all that training. A hundred ways to kill a person. Thank you for your restraint. You're such a good person."

Pender stood still, immobilized by her anger. "I thought you were someone else," he said finally. He walked toward his gear.

She followed him. "You thought *I* was someone else?" Scorn dripped from her voice. "I thought you were human. I thought you might have a conscience and care about people other than yourself."

He shouldered his gear pack. "Sorry to disappoint," he said, and headed for the trail down to the beach.

Annette rushed in front of him, making him stop, her jaws clenched in anger. "You owe me an apology."

"What?" Pender was shocked. He fumbled for a moment. "Apologize for what? Because I was a day late? I'm sorry. I had an accident that slowed me down."

"Because you came in like a brute, like a . . . crazy man."

Pender started to answer in anger, stopped himself, and took a moment to regain his composure. "I apologize for appearing that way," he said. "That's not who I am." As he stepped around her, he added, "As for the cruelty, I could never rival you in that particular arena."

She stopped him again, planting herself in front of him, one hand held to his chest. "What's that supposed to mean?" she asked.

"Think about it," he said. He tried to walk around her, but she stepped in front of him again.

"No. You tell me about it. Do you have the guts to tell me to my face?"

He started to speak and stopped. "No," he said finally.

"You owe me that much. I used my whole summer vacation to see you. You can at least tell me how I'm such a bad person, because, to tell you the truth, before you got here I thought I was okay."

He nodded his head like he was saying yes. "You don't remember what you said to me when we broke up?" His eyebrows were raised in question and he searched her eyes for recognition.

She puzzled for a moment. "Nothing specific. I remember I was really frustrated." She looked at him. "What did I say?"

Pender shook his head again, side to side, a disgusted look on his face. "At least when I hurt someone, I have the decency to remember what I did. No wonder you're so goddamn righteous."

"What did I say?" Annette blocked him again so he couldn't move past her. "Please. I want to know."

"You said, 'I hope you get drafted and you go to Vietnam and you get shot and die there.' Your exact words. It's like you carved them into my brain. Absolutely the best fuck-you line ever. I'll never forget it. Congratulations."

Horror swept over Annette's face. "Did I really say that? Could I have said that?"

"You know you did," said Pender. "I can see it on your face."

He started to move, but she stopped him, gently this time. "You're right. I said it. And it was a terrible thing to say. I said it in anger. I apologize. I'm sorry. Really. I'm very sorry."

"Apology accepted." He stepped around her. "Thanks for lunch." He started down the trail to the beach.

She followed him. "Gabe, stop. Let's start over again, okay? Let's spend the afternoon paddling around the lake and have a nice dinner tonight."

He paused. "God, I hate to waste a great exit line like that."

Annette blinked, trying to understand what he said. She broke into a smile, finally. "You never were one for straight answers," she said.

They returned to camp and tried to start a conversation, but it was awkward. Annette ended the fumbling with a simple declaration: "Let's go fishing."

They paddled side by side this time, Annette directing them into the northeast bay, where she had paddled that morning. They tried to fish a little, but when the afternoon breezes picked up, the canoes blew quickly downwind, sometimes banging into one another.

"Next time we should lash our boats together," said Annette. Pender nodded. He didn't know what she was talking about—he was strictly a solo guy—but he was glad she was thinking there'd be another time.

They trolled lures for a while, producing a few small fish that they released. Later in the afternoon, they eased into the best walleye waters, a pinch point where the opposing shores of the lake jutted to within a hundred yards or so of each other. They were sheltered from the winds there. Annette talked to Pender as she positioned them between the points.

"There's a reef beneath us," she said. "It's about fifty feet deep in the middle, and it rises gradually to the points we can see. It holds walleye spring through fall. In the spring, they'll be closer to shore, in ten or fifteen feet of water. This late in the summer, you start looking for them in twenty feet and we keep going deeper until we find them. Of course, this is Quetico. They might be in five feet or fifty feet, and we'll never know why." She shrugged as she said it and glanced at Pender. He was staring at her, a small smile on his face.

"What?" she asked.

"You're almost feral," he said. "It's amazing. I'm trying to make that fit with my memory of you. Sophisticated girl from a good family, perfect manners, so . . . beautiful and so comfortable in polite society . . . I'm trying to look at that girl and see this woman."

"And?"

"And I can't do it."

"Well," she said, "I think of you then and now and I see the same person. The college boy, the man, they both have a way of pissing me off like nobody else I know."

"I didn't mean it as an insult. You've changed a lot. I like what I see."

"After two hours you've got me figured out, huh?" There was an edge to her voice.

He realized she thought he was patronizing her. He tried to think of reassuring words, but everything he thought of sounded worse. He shrugged. "Sorry. I didn't mean it that way."

Their conversation was cut short by a school of feeding walleye. In short order, they landed a half dozen fish, keeping three, releasing the others. Pender rigged the keepers on a makeshift stringer and towed them behind his canoe. They spent the next two hours touring that part of the lake, Annette telling Pender about various landmarks and the flora and geography of the place.

They stopped to clean the fish on a rock outcropping, Annette deferring to Pender to see how much skill he had. He had an odd procedure. He started by turning away from her on the rock and hunching for a moment, his head down, the fish in front of him, out of her view. After a few seconds, he straightened up and stabbed each fish in the head, then filleted and skinned them. Annette hadn't seen anyone kill the fish first in years; she thought she was the only one, and she never confessed her practice to anyone other than her daughters.

Pender was reasonably efficient, she noted. His filets came off the bones with little waste; his skinning technique was messier, but the filets were clean. "Well done," she said when he was finished.

"Thanks. I've never done it with an audience before."

They got back in the canoes and headed back to the island.

"Pender?" Annette said on the way, "What were you doing before you killed the fish?"

He shrugged like he had no idea what she was talking about.

"It looked like you were praying," she said. "Have you found religion in your old age?"

"Uh, no. Not praying," he said. "Still an atheist."

"What then?"

He looked embarrassed and didn't answer right away.

"Come on, you can tell me."

"It's a little thing I do. Stupid. I tell the fish I'm sorry for killing them, and, uh, thank them sort of."

Annette suppressed a laugh.

"I know. It's stupid. Go ahead and laugh out loud."

"It's not stupid. It's touching, really. Who knew you had First Nation instincts? You don't seem like the type."

"What type am I?"

"I don't know yet. You're still working up from ax murderer." She laughed as she said it, some pent-up emotion coming out with the humor. Pender smiled. They got to the island as the early-evening sun began casting deep shadows on the campsite.

"I won't hold you to cooking tonight," Annette said as they ascended to the camp.

"You can't stop me now," said Pender. "I've been talking fish recipes with America's greatest chefs for months, and I've been hauling the seasonings for a week."

They made small talk while they worked on the meal. Working together seemed to make conversation come easier, and soon they were chatting like old friends. Annette made the fire and took charge of rehydrating the vegetables and dicing the last of her potatoes while Pender rubbed the filets with herbs and spices and prepared the frying pan. He set aside a large portion for Chaos, who became more interested in him when he started handling the food.

They talked about food, Annette asking him about different regional cuisines, his favorite chefs, and *Menu*'s original recipe awards. Pender was surprised she knew so much about him.

"I Googled your name and got dozens of pages of listings," said Annette. "Speeches, photos, master of ceremonies. It seems like you're a star in a glamorous field."

Pender sighed. "I had a moment in the spotlight. I got to see a lot of places and meet a lot of people, and I had a great time doing it. But it's over now and, to tell you the truth, that's okay with me. It's not bad having my feet on the ground."

"What does that mean?"

"Just that, I think some of us let what we do for a living define us, and when we do well at it, we start thinking we're something more than everyone else. Like, I *deserve* to fly first class, and the people in coach don't. And when you start thinking like that, pretty soon nothing is enough. No meal is quite good enough, no conversation is stimulating enough, every article and project seems like something you've already done. I was well into the 'Is this all there is?' phase of life."

As she listened, Annette was thinking that Pender sounded like the college boy she knew, grown up, a little world-weary, but authentic.

"You're pretty deep for an ax murderer," she said.

"I get that a lot," he replied.

The conversation drifted to the art of fire starting and cooking over campfires, then to Annette's daughters and granddaughter.

After bending to place the fish over the fire, Pender winced as he straightened to a standing position. "Are you okay?" asked Annette.

"Yeah," he said. "I'm getting better every day. I took a tumble a few days ago and really did a number on my back. I was pretty gimpy for a couple days, but I'm good now."

Annette made him describe what happened and how it affected him. "Is that why you were late getting here?" she asked.

"In a way," he said. "But really, I was late because I was afraid to be early. I should have planned to get here a day early. It would have been easy. But I thought waiting here for a day by myself would drive me even crazier, wondering if you'd show up, what you'd be like." He shrugged self-consciously.

She smiled. "I know what you mean. I got so restless I left a day early and came out of French Lake, just to be doing something so I wouldn't constantly be thinking about this. And I didn't want to be the first one here because of just what you said. And we were both right—I've been going stir-crazy knocking around this place. Thank goodness for Chaos."

Lying near them, the dog's ears picked up at the mention of his name.

"Which gets us back to your little drama with Mr. Chaos. Just out of curiosity, what were you going to do with the paddle if he rushed you?" Pender asked.

"I don't know," said Annette. "Try to stick him in the face with it, I guess."

"That would work." Pender smiled wryly. "I'm more of a hatchet man myself, but if you thrust the paddle like they teach in bayonet training, you could stop someone in their tracks, especially if you nailed them in the nose or throat.

Thing is, it's easy to parry something like that unless you're quick and you surprise them."

"You learned a lot in the army, sounds like." She said it with a mix of sadness and accusation.

"They drill some things into your head so well you never forget them." Pender assumed a military command voice and proclaimed, "There's only two kinds of bayonet fighters, Bravo—the quick and the dead." He smiled self-consciously. "It's like you learning how to make fires and find fish. I learned what I had to learn to survive."

"Did you ever wish you weren't there, killing people?"

"I don't think there was ever a time when I didn't wish I could be somewhere else, getting laid, living easy, all that." Pender looked up from the skillet, made eye contact with Annette. "But it wasn't the killing. It was everything. The hardship. Fear. Being treated like a fucking serf by morons who had the power of God over me and were too stupid to know what stupid was. Being hated by people like you back home. Being bored out of my skull except when I was scared out of my wits."

He stared at her for a moment, trying to will himself to shut up, but he couldn't.

"You know, we were doing something we didn't want to do, and everybody hated us for it. Even our own side. The officers hated you because you were a low-life enlisted man. The NCOs hated you because they were lifers and you were a transient who hated their army and thought they were stupid. Back home, the doves hated you because you were a baby-killing maniac, and the hawks because you were a drug addict and a loser."

"At least you had each other," Annette offered. "Band of brothers and all that."

"No," said Pender. "We were all temps. We were on different timetables, so you only knew a guy for a short time before he moved on. Or got shot."

"You're angry about it."

"I'm fucking seething. I've been seething for forty years."

"What would make it better?" She tried not to sound like a mom when she said it.

Pender laughed, a bitter, ironic laugh. "Amnesia. All those 'make love not war' people who were so idealistic in 1969? Most of them are small-government neocons today. They went from free love to free war. They got really brave when the draft went away. And really stingy when it was their money in the pot. If I could forget all that, I'd still have a country and maybe a life. But I can't forget."

He removed the food from the fire, trying to shed the anger.

"Which is how I came to fuck with four fat fishermen for being loud and obnoxious, though truthfully, if I had known how well they paddled and how strong they were, I think I would have kept my indignation to myself."

Pender smiled self-consciously as they took their plates to Annette's promontory to eat.

"I'm sorry for that rant," he said. "It's been building up for a long time, and I haven't talked to anyone in quite a while. Anyone."

"No apology needed," said Annette. "I'm just kind of stunned. I always pictured you as a sort of high-flying deacon of capitalism—eating at fancy places, making big money, living in a sumptuous house. I never thought the war would hit you and stick like that."

"It's a kind of cancer. There are worse kinds."

They ate quietly on the high rocks overlooking Annette's lake. They did dishes together, wading out to a flat rock in knee-deep water. Annette washing, Pender drying and stacking the dishes on the rock. Then they sipped wine by the campfire, swapping dog stories and kid stories until the sun set and Quetico was left in the dark shadows of late evening.

"Do you do night paddles?" asked Annette.

"Not for a long time, but let me set up my tent and we'll go."

"Why set up another tent? Mine's big enough for the three of us. Just throw your bag in there and whatever else and we'll take off."

He hesitated.

"I'm not offering sex," she said. "It just makes no sense to have two tents when there's plenty of room in one."

"Okay," he said, finally. "Good."

Annette hiked down to the canoes while Pender set up his gear. She tried not to be bothered by him saying "Good" when she made the sex thing clear. It wasn't that she wanted to have sex. It was that he obviously didn't find her attractive. She tried to rationalize his reaction; she was, after all, sixty years old. If he wanted sex, he'd have stayed home and played with the bunnies in his photos.

By the time Pender got down to the lake, Annette had already launched both canoes and strapped them together in shallow water just offshore. Chaos sat in Annette's canoe, tail wagging, tongue lolling, waiting.

"How did you do that?" he asked, impressed. Mostly he wondered how she did it so fast. He inspected her work in the dim light of the moon and the first stars.

Two poles, each about five feet long and as thick as a fist, lay across the canoes, one in front, the other in back. They were lashed to each canoe's crossbeam supports with bungee cords, essentially converting the canoes into the twin hulls of a catamaran.

"It's not very strong," said Annette, "But it'll get the job done for tonight." She stepped into her canoe, carefully letting the water drip from each sandal before putting her foot in the boat. Pender did the same. There was something behind his seat. As he reached for it, Annette said, "That's a poncho I carry for whatever. I thought it would make a good pillow for you if you want to lie in the canoe and look at stars."

"Really?" said Pender.

"Well, it takes some agility. And you probably wouldn't want to fall asleep in that position. But yeah, when you get that rare clear night out here, lying down in the middle of the lake and looking at the sky is like seeing creation. I never realized how many stars we had in the sky until I did that."

"Billions," said Pender as they paddled slowly out to deep water. "Maybe hundreds of billions. I read somewhere that astronomers say there are billions of galaxies, or maybe that was solar systems. Either way, it really blows the notion of an interactive god watching over us right out of the water."

"Not for me," said Annette. "When I see all those stars and think about all those galaxies and planets and all of that coming from one big bang that started everything, it makes me realize there is a greater power."

Pender laughed softly. They had debated God in college. It was like old times.

"Okay," he said, "but why would whoever touched off the big bang be hovering around churches and bedrooms on one stinking little planet to hear what each cosmic nit wants for

Christmas or listen to someone beg for help to win a football
game?"

"You're such a cheerful son of a bitch, Pender," said
Annette. "Anyone ever tell you that?"

"Alas, yes. I don't usually talk so much, though. It's been
close to a week since I talked to another person, so I kind of
lost control of my mouth there. Sorry."

"Don't apologize. I always loved your bullshit. It was one
of the things I missed about you."

"You missed me? When?"

Annette stopped paddling and turned to Pender, paused,
put her hand on his wrist. "Let's not get into that right now.
Let's take in the stars." She squeezed his wrist affectionately.

They drifted like weightless leaves floating on water as
serene as a baby's lullaby. As the moon rose higher in the
sky, they lay face up in their canoes and watched millions
of stars come to life, like lights coming on in a giant arena.

"Can you believe this?" Annette asked, her voice strangely
muffled as it came from the bottom of her canoe.

"It's amazing," answered Pender.

"As long as I've lived here, the night skies just take my
breath away. How could you go back to Chicago all those
years after seeing this?"

"Well, I didn't see this very often. I usually had overcast
skies at night, and I slept through most of the clear sky nights.
I sure as hell don't have that problem anymore."

"You have trouble sleeping?" Annette asked.

"Mostly I have trouble staying asleep, but I have trouble
getting to sleep, too. Other than that, no problem."

"You make a joke out of everything. I'm starting to remember that about you."

"And you take everything seriously," said Pender. He paused for a beat, thinking. "You were always very thoughtful, but you hardly ever got mad. Except with me."

"It's true. You had a way of irritating me and fascinating me at the same time. I guess it was an opposites attract thing."

Their conversation waned as they soaked in the night lights. After a long silence, Annette scuffled about in her canoe to sit herself upright again. Pender followed suit. "Ready to go back in?" she asked.

"Yeah. But first, I don't think we were opposites. I think we were very similar people, just living in parallel universes."

"Eh?" A bemused smile played at Annette's lips. Pender could see her face clearly in the light pouring from the sky.

"You were in the antiwar movement and I wasn't, and you think that's what defined us, but it wasn't. What defined us was we both felt a sense of responsibility. I was taught that service to my country is a sacred duty. Country first, then family, then self. I had an obligation to fulfill and I fulfilled it. That's what defined me."

Annette pondered this for a while. "Okay, what defined me?"

"A sense of duty. Giving up everything to go to Canada with that shit-for-brains husband you took. And staying loyal to him even when he betrayed you . . ." Pender's voice tapered off for a moment. "And you didn't just hide here. You came to be a part of the place."

"I take it you mean that as a compliment. I'll try to control my beating heart."

"Don't try to kid me. You feel it too. It's what bonds us. We sacrificed. We fulfilled our responsibilities even when those around us didn't. And after forty years, we're in the same place. We're on an island in the wilderness. All those people who were so righteous about this cause or that one, all the philosophies, all the fad beliefs, all the phony bullshit of a lifetime, it's all over there on the mainland somewhere, rotting away, becoming fertilizer for the next wave of bullshit. And we're here on an island in the wilderness because we lived the same life in parallel universes and forty years later we have more in common with each other than we do with any of the causes or people or institutions we passed along the way."

"You make it sound like a nightmare."

"You worry too much."

They smiled and began the slow paddle back to the island, quiet, Annette still worried about Pender's anguish.

It was nearly 3 AM when they got back to camp and stumbled through the shadows to Annette's tent, so tired that even Chaos was dragging.

"Do you need privacy to change?" Pender asked as Annette unzipped the entry to the tent.

"Will the sight of me in a bra and panties drive you to acts of depravity?"

He started to answer, then stopped. "You put that in a way there's no right answer. Let's just say I understand you are not inviting me in for sex. Despite all evidence to the contrary, I'm somewhat civilized and fully housebroken."

"I bet if someone made you just answer yes or no to a question, it would drive you stark raving mad," Annette snickered as she entered the tent and flipped on a small battery-powered lantern hanging from the top of the tent.

Pender followed and set to inflating his sleeping pad and setting up his sleeping bag even as Chaos tried to lie on them. Out of the corner of his eye, he caught a glimpse of her just as she was getting ready to put on her sleeping clothes. Even in a quick glance in the vague light of the lantern, even trying not to invade her privacy, trying not to see her as a woman, Pender saw the plump fullness of her breasts, the curve of her waist, the feminine roundness of her hips and butt. The sight aroused him. He tried to erase the vision from his mind. It wasn't fair to invade her privacy like that, he thought. But it was nice to be so fully aroused again. It had been a long time.

Pender slipped into a pair of swimming trunks, then reached up bare chested to snap off the lantern. Annette watched, lying on her side, noting his well-defined abs. "You've taken good care of your body," she said.

"So have you."

"No, I really mean it. You look good."

"I really mean it too."

"You don't have to patronize me. I'm not some Rush Street bimbo."

"Well, how about that. I didn't think this was Rush Street. How about just accepting what I say at face value. Have I ever lied to you? When did I ever patronize you?"

After a moment of silence, Annette answered sheepishly. "Okay. Sorry. But I'm, you know, a grandma. Gray hair. Wrinkles."

"You're still beautiful," he said quietly. "Seriously beautiful."

"Thanks," she said. She waited to see if he'd make a pass, thinking a kiss would be nice, see where it leads. But he didn't.

"Thanks for giving me a chance today," he said.

"Don't mention it," said Annette.

"Goodnight."

"Goodnight."

"Goodnight, Chaos, you dog-breath cur."

19

They slept well into the morning, even Pender. He stirred awake and checked his watch around 8:30, and Chaos nudged him impatiently. He let Chaos out, and followed him out of the tent quietly, muffling an involuntary grunt as the first movements of the day set off the pain in his stiff back. He couldn't resist a glance at Annette before he closed the tent. She was deep in sleep, her face a study in peace and beauty. He sighed. She still did it to him, after all these years.

He was bare-chested and barefoot, wearing just a pair of swimming trunks, and the air was cold. Last night's clear skies had given way to partial cloudiness, with darker clouds visible to the west. He waddled tenderly across the rocks and sticks and pine cones to his pack, slid on a fleece sweater, and swapped his swimming trunks for underwear, quick-dry pants, and hiking boots. He got a wood fire going, put water on to boil, and pulled his coffee-making kit and a pancake breakfast from his pack. He had packaged the meal himself, adding small containers of margarine, jelly, and pure maple syrup to the pouch. Luxury.

The fire cracked and snapped in the chill morning air. The sight of flames and the smell of burning pine was invigorating. Pender sat in front of the fire and soaked in the warmth, gazed out on the Canadian Shield vista before him, took a few deep breaths. Chaos came to sit beside him, nudging his head under Pender's arm like they were old buddies. Pender petted him, scratched behind his ears. Chaos luxuriated in the scratching, his face forming a canine smile. Pender gave him a full ear massage, both ears. It made them friends for life.

When the water came to boil, Pender poured a cupful through a filter filled with finely ground coffee. As it dripped slowly into the cup, he scribbled a note to his daughter in his journal, about seeing the universe last night. Annette emerged from the tent just as he finished. He put the journal aside and served her the first cup of coffee and set up to make the second.

"You two make a lot of noise in the morning," she said, her voice still sleepy. She glanced at his journal, then at him, her eyes blinking from the daylight, her hair cascading down around her face and shoulders in sexy tangles. She was wearing quick-dry pants and a T-shirt, standard tripper clothing, but the pants clung to her bottom in a way that Pender noticed, and her T-shirt was snug enough that he could tell she wasn't wearing a bra. Pender stared at her nipples for a moment, arousal trumping manners. He caught himself, raised his eyes to meet hers, blushing. She caught him at it and blushed, too, liking that he looked at her that way. At twenty-one it might have put her off, a man openly sizing her up sexually. At sixty, his lust made her just a little giddy.

"I hope you like coffee," he said, offering her the cup.

She took it, smiling, still sleepy. "I love coffee." She inhaled its aroma. "Mmmm. This is really good. Something tells me this isn't instant."

"No. Coffee is one of my last vices. Wine, too."

"What about sex?" She smiled coyly at him.

"Sex has never been one of my wilderness vices," he stammered. He was trying to be funny, but he was aroused and felt like he shouldn't be, and words weren't coming easily. "I could pack in coffee and wine, but, you know, a willing woman . . ." His ability to speak left him. He stared at her, her eyes, her cleavage, her eyes.

Annette put down her coffee and stood in front of him, their faces close enough they could feel each other's breath on their skin. She put her hand on his penis. It was rigidly erect. She murmured suggestively and looked him in the eye, a small smile on her face. She moved her hand up and down on his erection. She placed one of his hands on her breast and rubbed against him, breathing softly, putting her lips to his, and kissed him long and soft and slow. They embraced, their bodies flush against each other from lips to knees.

"Gabe Pender," she whispered in his ear, "Where have you been all these years?"

They dropped to their knees, groping and clinging, helped each other get naked, clung to each other in the morning chill. Pender gently lowered their conjoined bodies to the ground.

————————

"You must think I'm a nymphomaniac." Annette smiled self-consciously as they uncoiled from a postcoital embrace. They rose slowly, Pender grunting a little from his back pain.

They sat side by side on one of the log benches, fending off Chaos, who wanted to sniff their crotches.

"That's not what I think," said Pender.

Annette waited for him to explain. "And?" she said.

"And . . . I wasn't thinking like that. I'm sixty years old, and I've been making love like a teenager for half the morning. I'm sitting here wondering how I could let forty years with you get away from me."

"So you're saying you could have gotten the sex anywhere but you wish we'd been married all these years?" She laughed as she said it, but the vulnerable part of her was afraid it was true.

"No. I'm not saying anything like that. You're the hottest woman I've been with since the last time I was with you—"

"Good answer," she interrupted.

"—but part of me is mourning that I lost all that time with you. Fucking Vietnam. Corporate bullshit. A two-million-dollar-house with all the warmth of an igloo. White-on-white-in-white, for Christ's sake."

He went quiet again, head in hands. She put an arm around him and hugged. "Lou Rawls Live," she said.

"Huh?"

"White-on-white-in-white. It's from Lou Rawls's monologue on the *Live!* album. 'Street Corner Hustler's Blues.' It was your favorite record. We played it all the time. I've thought about that album so much I actually bought it. 'The Shadow of Your Smile.' I can sing that with him, word for word."

Annette began humming, then sang soulfully off-key, sweet and sad until she broke into tears. She threw her arms around Pender and squeezed with all her strength. Her body racked with sobs, she felt his tears mingle with hers. They embraced as if their lives were ending.

"I sang that song all the time," she whispered in his ear. "And I always thought of you. You colored all my dreams. I never stopped loving you."

"Me too," said Pender. "I sang it and I always thought of you."

"Why did we do that to ourselves?" Annette asked.

Pender shook his head sadly. "Yeah."

Annette's last ration of bacon just started sizzling on the fire when the misting rains began, fine and warm, falling from clouds drifting low and lazy over the Canadian Shield. It could be over in fifteen minutes, or it could be a precursor to a more serious rainfall.

"Maybe we should set up the stove under a tarp," said Annette.

"Ah, let's live dangerously," said Pender. He ran to the tent, grabbed the poncho he had used for a pillow the night before, and returned. He spread the poncho behind his back and lifted his arms as if trying to impersonate a bat. He stretched and shifted until one arm sheltered Annette and the other shielded the fire.

"I always wanted to be your protector," he joked.

"What were you writing when I got up?" she asked.

He blushed. "Oh. Uh, I'm keeping a journal.

"That's nice." She said it in a way that let him know she'd like to hear more about it.

"My anger management counselor said I should reconcile with my daughter and suggested I write to her."

"So you're writing a journal for her?"

"Yeah. Don't read it. You'll lose all respect for me."

"Why?"

"It's a feelings thing. She'll laugh her butt off reading it. But I feel better for having tried."

Annette touched him. "I'm sorry things are so difficult between you two."

"Thanks," he said. He looked away, then back at her. "There are a few entries written to you. If I die before I wake some morning, read 'em, laugh, and use them to start your next fire."

Annette laughed softly. "I'd never do that."

"You have my permission."

They ate side by side on one of the logs, the poncho draped over their heads. As they finished, the rain began in earnest.

"You take the poncho and do the dishes," said Annette. "I'll put up a tarp."

By the time Pender came back up to the camp, Annette had fashioned a lean-to from the tarp and positioned the packs to form a wall of sorts at the low end. They huddled under the crude shelter, using the packs as backrests, and talked through the morning squall.

"What happened to you after graduation?" Pender asked.

"You know what happened to me," Annette replied, frowning at him. "Rob and I got active in the peace movement. The revolution, right? We organized protests at different places around the country. Until his draft notice came. Then we came up here."

"But right after graduation, what did you do?"

"The day after graduation we packed my car and headed to Chicago for an organizational meeting. Three days later we went to Madison. I think it was Ohio after that, or maybe

Indiana. It's kind of a blur. I remember four or five days in San Francisco, but mostly we were in the Midwest. Why?"

Pender shrugged. "I spent about three days trying to work up the courage to call you. Your roommate said you were gone, left no phone number. Your parents said the same thing. I always wondered if I had called right away if things might have been different."

"No," said Annette. "I was committed. Like a nun in a convent. I was devoted to peace and love, to ending the murder and mayhem in Vietnam. Rob was one of the high priests of the movement, so it just kind of happened."

"So you went back to Rob the Throb because he was the booming voice of morality in our times?"

"You're still a sarcastic son of a bitch. And snotty. Very snotty. Yes, I went back to Rob because we were committed to the same things and he made it known he was interested in me."

"Interested in you. That sounds so . . . what? . . . . debutante's ball."

"He wanted to get laid and so did I, okay? And I admired him and we liked each other and we did good work together."

"Did you really think all the people coming to your rallies and protests cared about the war?"

"Of course. Why else would they be there?"

"That's where the party was."

"You know this? How many protests and rallies did you attend?"

"Not one. Not a single one."

"You might have learned something if you had."

Pender turned his head to look directly at her. "Now you're being grandiose. There was no discovery at those things. No one ever brought up a new set of facts or a new philosophy.

Your movement never got beyond 'Make love, not war' intellectually. People just came out to be part of something. Smoke some dope, sing some songs, and get laid."

"We helped raise the conscience of the nation," said Annette. "It was important work. Not everyone bought into it, but lots did and we accomplished something important."

Pender snorted. "The conscience of the nation lasted about as long as a politician's promise. As soon as the draft went away, no one cared about the morality of wars and killing anymore. They just wanted to watch it on TV, and they wanted it to be over quickly."

Annette shook her head in resignation. They weren't ever going to agree on the war. They fell silent for a while.

"Did you get into drugs?" Pender asked.

"More than I should have," said Annette. "Marijuana, of course. In San Francisco we dropped acid. At Woodstock we did acid and speed, a little hashish. I gave it up after that."

"Why?"

"It was getting out of control. We were sleeping around. People were starting to shoot heroin. It was getting dark."

They were silent again for several minutes.

"What about you? What was your drug of choice?"

"Me?" Pender smiled his wry smile. "Nada. Nothing. I didn't do drugs. Not even marijuana. I drank some bourbon, had some Asian beer on R&R, but mostly I stayed straight."

Annette poked him in the ribs with her elbow. "I don't believe you, not even for a minute."

He smiled again. "It's true, though."

"Why? I heard soldiers were always high, the drugs were great and cheap . . ."

"Lots of reasons," said Pender. "I thought it was stupid, getting fucked up when people are trying to kill you. Getting fucked up to get accepted by the druggies. A bunch of losers. Mostly I just wanted to survive. That meant having my senses intact and going home without a drug habit." He shrugged.

"My, my. You were a dull boy."

"Yeah. Compared to big, brave Rob, I was a paste-eating bitch hiding in the school library."

The rain intensified, driving them into the tent, where they struggled to get comfortable. Annette's tent was designed for sleeping, not lounging. There was enough headroom to sit up but no chairs or backrests. They lay on their backs and talked awhile, then drowsed off, then woke and sat up, back-to-back, leaning on each other. Chaos took the opportunity to lie next to them.

"Pender?"

"Yes, dear."

"Were you thrilled when you shot someone? Or did you feel remorse?"

"My war wasn't anywhere near that personal. Most of the firefights I was in were at night. You just saw the muzzle flashes and the tracer rounds. You shot back at the muzzle flashes. Unless it was really hot, in which case you kept your head down, under cover, and just sprayed blindly in their direction, hoping to get lucky, trying to scare them into staying in place."

Annette was silent for a while. "But you did body counts, right? The news was always about body counts."

"Yeah. When we could."

"And how did you feel when you saw the dead?"

"I was a little queasy the first time, but you get over it. You would, too, if that's what you were doing all the time."

"I don't think so, Pender. I think it would make me sick and crazy. It didn't bother you?"

"I'd rather have played poker with them or toured Saigon whorehouses or learned how they grew rice, but we weren't meeting under those circumstances. For them to go home, they had to kill me. For me to go home, I had to kill them. We all did what we had to do."

"You didn't feel remorse when you saw the dead bodies?"

"Mostly I didn't feel anything at all, but when I felt something, I felt powerful. Like I had just bought another day on this earth."

"You never looked at a body and thought, 'That could be me'?"

"I always thought that could be me. I was always glad it wasn't. And I always prayed that if I was going to catch a bullet, it would kill me, then and there. The thing that scared the living shit out of me was getting paralyzed or losing my legs or arms."

"You prayed?"

"Not to God. I just prayed. To fate, I guess. I knew there wasn't a God when I was five, and everything I've seen since then has proven it."

"I thought there were no atheists in foxholes."

"We didn't have foxholes."

"Were there a lot of atheists?"

"I don't know. A lot of the kids were religious when they got there, kissing their crosses and saying prayers and stuff. I think some of them got over it, and some of them went home in body bags. I suppose the ones who went home alive figured it worked, that God looked over them and fucked the other guy. Why would you worship someone like that?"

Annette pondered his answers.

"So you have no conscience about killing people, no God, no higher moral calling?"

"I didn't have a conscience about killing people in a war. But I don't go around killing people. I don't own a gun. I haven't shot one since I came home. I haven't had a fight, other than popping that one arrogant, stupid, corporate bureaucrat last winter."

"What about those canoe racers?"

"It wasn't a fight. I just messed with them. I shouldn't have, but to be honest, I still like the memory of it. I think it'll be a long time before those two motherfuckers knock over another racer and laugh about it. That's the sort of thing a good God would appreciate."

"What about the guys who followed you here?"

"They followed me. I just defended myself."

Annette shook her head. Pender could feel her do it. "What?" he said.

"I was thinking of inviting you to my home when we leave here. But I'm afraid you might have a lot of violence still waiting to get out. Who are you?"

Pender shook his head. "How many firearms do you own?"

"I own a rifle and a shotgun for dealing with bears and wolves. And I've only shot the ones that wouldn't go away."

"Still," said Pender, "peace lovers, two guns. Warmongers, none. And I've never had a fight with a Canadian."

"That's not very convincing."

Pender shrugged.

"You don't care, do you? Jesus, I'm thinking of sharing my home and family, and I'm thinking it's this big deal because this is all I have. And you're thinking, what? How boring that would be? How you want to get going so you can, what?

Beat someone with your hatchet? Get back to Chicago and bed some young bimbo? God, Pender, you're such a shit."

"What?" he was stunned. He swiveled to face her. "I wasn't thinking any of those things. I was defending myself against your accusations. I don't think I'm violent . . ." His voice trailed off. "Despite the mountain of evidence to the contrary."

After a moment, Annette giggled. Pender laughed softly.

"Okay, I guess I have some issues."

"Have you always been this way?"

"No. It just seems to be oozing out of me now. I think I've been angry since you broke up with me, and it just kept building. Going to Vietnam and getting nothing but shit for it. Did you know about that? If a guy had a GI haircut, most of the women in America wouldn't talk to him. Coming home was worse than going to war. Trying to get a job, but the draft dodgers had all the jobs. They were home getting experience while I was shitting in the jungle and swatting mosquitoes."

He dropped his head and closed his eyes for a moment.

"I remember thinking when Jane Fonda went to North Vietnam, everyone hates us, including all the good-looking women, led by Jane Fonda. You think I'm being funny, but I'm not. That's how it felt."

Annette leaned her head to rest on his shoulder and put her hand on his. Pender felt her and liked that she did that, but he couldn't stop.

"Then we do away with the draft, and all the draft dodgers get very brave and want to fight wars. I get into corporate life, and it's all phony. The guys at the top didn't give a shit about the business, just how much money they made, how big their office was, making sure they were in line for the next big promotion. I made those fuckers look good by doing what needed to be done, and they hated me for not doing what they said to do."

"Were you trying to be an executive?" Annette asked it doubtfully. Pender didn't seem the type.

"No. No, I just wanted to be left alone. Let our magazine team do what we need to do and don't even pretend you understand it. Just keep the fuck out of the way and count the money when it comes in."

He took a deep breath.

"Same in 'Nam. The stupidity could just take your breath away. One time the base commander took away our bullets. It was New Year's, and he was afraid we'd shoot tracers to celebrate. So our whole camp was defended by a few guys with two clips of ammo each. In a goddamn war zone!"

Annette squeezed his hand, not sure what to say.

"It gave me an edge," said Pender. "The people I met in business didn't know what a shit storm was and wouldn't walk through one on a bet. I knew I was tougher and meaner than them."

He smiled.

"The anger's been inside me for a long time. I think busting that thumb-sucking twit Chuckie Blue in the gut was sort of the cork coming out of the champagne bottle. It felt good. But that was just the first bubble coming out. There were lots more. The corporate bubble. The war bubble. The draft-dodging, neocon, coward bubble. The Jane Fonda bubble . . ."

He lapsed into silence.

When she couldn't take the tension anymore, she nudged him in the ribs. "So, I guess the question is, how much do you like champagne?"

20

By midmorning the rains passed, giving way to a classic Quetico summer day with vaguely overcast skies, gentle winds, and mild air temperatures.

Annette rigged the canoes together again, and the three of them paddled into the west bay to fish. She positioned them on a reef that often held walleye and smallmouth bass.

"Get to it, Yank," she said. "I'll hold us in place, and you have yourself some tourist fun. Cast off the bow and let it drop to twenty, twenty-five feet."

Pender stood in one canoe and cast while Annette sat in the other and used an assortment of paddle strokes to hold the craft above the structure. She did it effortlessly, as a skilled equestrian might ride a horse or a professional point guard might dribble a basketball.

The fishing was slow. Pender cast out a plastic grub on a lead-headed jig and retrieved it slowly, letting the jig drop and flutter every few turns of the reel. Songbirds twittered a melodic singsong in the distance. A breeze ruffled the water surface. Rays of sun spiked through the clouds. Pender glanced around between casts. Chaos was sprawled on his back in the front of Annette's canoe, his legs skyward as if posing for a Snoopy cartoon. Annette peered toward a far shore with an unfocused gaze. He thought she might be bored.

"Why did you marry him? Rob?"

Annette came out of her reverie and thought for a moment. "I don't know—why did you marry your wife?"

"No fair. I asked first."

"Well, that's my answer. Why does anyone marry anyone?"

"I married Peg because the sex was good and she didn't really need me. It took me a long time to figure that out, but it's true. I was faithful and I did all the stuff I was supposed to do, but I needed some distance in my marriage. Peg was smart and fun and sexy and completely shut off from deep emotional entanglements. We were perfect for each other. Until we weren't."

Annette watched Pender cast and retrieve in silence.

"I think it was momentum for me," she said finally. "I had convinced myself that Rob was one of the gods of the great social revolution. I thought we would create a better society based on love, and Rob and I would be at the center of it. When we started, I thought he was like JFK or Martin Luther King, a man with greatness about him."

She paused and looked at Pender self-consciously. "No wisecracks?"

He glanced at her. "None."

"I thought you despised Rob."

"This isn't about him."

"Even before we came up here, I could already see some cracks in his veneer. He liked sleeping with other women, he was vain, and he got jealous of other people who got more podium time or more publicity. He'd get furious sometimes, swear he was going to do something else. Then some big shot in the movement would come around, and he'd be all over the guy about how much he wanted to work with him, all the things he could do. He wanted fame and power so bad he was willing to humiliate himself to get it."

"The universal politician," said Pender.

Annette shot him a small smile. "I'd be embarrassed for him, but he never seemed to get what a fool he was making of himself. Still, we were in it together, and when his draft notice came, I couldn't leave him. Not then. It would have been abandonment. He wanted to come to Canada. I suggested Toronto or Ottawa, real cities, close enough to see our families once in a while. Or Vancouver if we wanted to make a clean break. But he wanted the wilderness. He'd been reading back-to-nature stuff. It was very big back then. You know, live off the land, be self reliant, get away from chemicals and pollution."

She took a deep breath and watched him cast. He glanced at her. "And?" he said.

"So we end up in a place with no soil and a ninety-day growing season that started with the hatching of the most voracious mosquitoes in North America. There was hunting and fishing, of course, but Rob didn't like being cold or hot or dirty. He couldn't stand the stink of a skinned deer or even cleaning fish. He hated the place. I thought we'd move to Toronto, especially when he decided to get his master's. But he made excuses why it would be better if he went alone and came back on breaks and long weekends. He was done with me—I knew that. But we played the game for a while. I had the girls. He finished one degree, started the PhD, got an assistantship. He made a lame offer for us to join him then, but it was over. I had lost all respect for him. And besides, I had something here. I had found out a lot about myself. I

could run a business. I could fish. I could shoot a bear if I
had to. I could paddle a canoe. I was already a damn good
guide. I had really good friends. I was part of a community.
It wasn't fame and fortune, but it was me. It wasn't me being
someone's wife or daughter. I had tapped into who I really
was. So I stayed. And eventually we called it quits."

Quiet overtook the boat. Pender kept casting and retrieving.

"Didn't it get you when he went back to the U.S.? When
you told me about that, I wanted to kick his ass into next
year."

"That's not how I deal with life. As for how I felt, well,
I wasn't surprised. Any idealism he had harbored, it died a
long time ago. Probably before we moved to Ontario. His
ethics were situational at best. When he went back to the
U.S. I guess my main thought was, that's where he belongs."

"I agree with you there," said Pender. "That's what the
whole show is about down there. I got mine and fuck you."

Pender reeled in a small walleye and released it.

"You sound so easygoing about Rob. Didn't you get mad?
Don't you think back and wish you had it to do over again?
Something?"

"I guess I did get mad, but mostly I was just sad. All my
dreams died when he went to Toronto. That's when it was
over. He wasn't the man I thought he was. By the time we
divorced, I had bigger things on my mind than him. I was
alone in the wilderness with two babies and a half dozen cabins and a huge old black bear that kept raiding my garbage."

Pender finished a retrieve and turned to look at her, eyebrows raised.

"I couldn't do anything about Rob, but the bear was scar-
ing me to death. One night I dreamed that it ate my babies.

I went into town the next day and asked the police what could be done. Basically they told me they'd swing by now and then, and if it was there, they'd shoot it for me, but if I really wanted to get rid of it, I should shoot it myself. So I bought a shotgun and a box of slugs they use to shoot bears with and I hired one of the First Nation guides to teach me how to shoot the gun and how to shoot a bear. And a few days later, old black bear waddles into my property, busts open the cover on the garbage, and starts foraging, and I walk out there and shoot the old coot in the back of the head. Rob? I didn't miss him much. I had things to do."

Pender raised his hands as if surrendering. "You don't have to shoot me. I'll stay out of the garbage."

"I wish I could believe that," said Annette.

Pender retrieved a cast in silence.

"Yes," she said, breaking the quiet. "I thought about it once, what would I do if I had it all to do over again? I'd have to do it all the same way. I couldn't trade my kids and grandbaby for a better husband and different kids. I wouldn't trade them for anything."

Pender nodded as he reeled in the line. "I can understand that," he said. She was silent. He glanced at her. She was lost in thought. And beautiful. Something about her posture rang all the old bells.

"Rob was a disappointment," she said, finally, "but he got me where I needed to go and he went away when I needed space to grow. So everything worked out just right. No regrets."

"So when you said you thought about me, that was what? Just idle daydreaming?" Pender asked.

Annette made eye contact with him. "No. That was an ache. I knew you were my big mistake. I didn't think about it much when we were busy, but up here, in the long winters, alone, a lot of time to myself, I thought about you a lot."

"But you have no regrets?"

"It's like you say. Sometimes there's no right answer. Would we have been happier together? Would we have had kids and grandkids I love just as much? Yes. But I had kids with Rob and I love them and I wouldn't give them up for a do-over with you. Not for anything."

Pender was still chewing on her answer when the walleye started biting.

The fishing expedition ended quickly. Pender took meal-sized fish on three consecutive casts. He put them on a stringer, and they started drifting with the breeze, paddling just enough to keep off reefs and away from shore. When they reached the east end of the bay, Annette asked him if he'd like to do some sport fishing.

"Thanks, but no," he said. "I fish for food. I feel kind of guilty when I mess up some fish's day just to haul him in and release him. No matter what you do, some of those guys die."

"You are a strange man," Annette mused. "Hard on people, soft on fish." She thought for a moment. "It's too early to go back to camp. How about helping me clean up the campsite on this lake?"

Pender nodded his assent.

Though lightly used, the established campsite on the lake had seen some abuse. The fire ring had half-burned trail food containers and bag ties in it. Charred wood littered the cooking area. The latrine area had been dug up and picked over by an animal, leaving pockets of undegraded toilet paper peeking out of the green foliage. But the centerpiece of Annette's attention was an elaborate hut-like structure built from woven tree branches to store packs.

"Wow," said Pender, examining the craftsmanship. "Someone's really into wilderness crafts. I wonder how long it took to make this?"

Annette pursed her lips. "It has to come down," she said. "The park doesn't allow this kind of stuff, and for good reason."

"What's the reason? I think it's inspirational."

"It encourages people to abuse the ecosystem. Those branches didn't come from dead fall. Someone took them off live trees. And even beyond environment damage, if everyone does this, pretty soon you don't have a wilderness anymore. You have one of those ugly parks you Americans like. Swings and water slides and those hideous RVs."

"*We* Americans?" Pender questioned. "Don't you ever think of yourself as an American anymore?"

"Not ever," said Annette. "I'm a Canadian. I don't even know what the U.S. is anymore, and I'm a Canadian because I love being in a country that appreciates the natural state of things. I love being part of a country that puts more value in each other's welfare than getting rich."

Pender nodded. "No argument here. I just think I'd always think of myself as an immigrant, you know? Canadian by way of the U.S."

"So you're going back when this trip is over?"

"No. Maybe someday, but not any time soon. It's too sad."

Something in Pender's voice made Annette look over at him. He was staring wistfully at the lake, arms crossed, not moving. Like the personification of a sad poem. She walked to him, put an arm around his waist, and squeezed. He kept staring at the lake. She could feel sadness radiating from him and put both arms around him. He buried his face in the warm place between her shoulder and her neck. His tears warmed her skin like sad kisses.

"I've got nothing," he said.

When the moment passed, she took his hand, and they waded in the shallows. She turned them slowly in a circle, taking in the pristine lake and its forested shores the way the devout might experience the Sistine Chapel. "You have this," she said.

Pender was nodding when Chaos ended their reverie, crashing out from the forest. He ran to them in the shallows, stopped to drink, and then shook himself vigorously, coating them with water.

Pender bent to pet him and clap his hand on his ribs. He straightened and smelled his hand. "Your dog has found a friend, I think."

Annette looked at them, first Chaos, then Pender, a confused expression on her face. "What kind of friend?"

"Well, I'd guess this comes from an herbivore. It has that earthy, mild aroma that makes horse shit so pleasant. I'd expect a carnivore's stool to have a sharper, nose-curdling odor. But I'll defer to your judgment."

"He's been rolling in shit?"

"It's a favorite of many canines," said Pender.

"He can't come in the tent like that," said Annette, finally catching a whiff of him.

"I'll wash him out when we get back to camp. What the heck. I need a bath too."

"Okay. Let's clean up this campsite and dismantle that shelter."

————————

Annette cooked dinner, instructing Pender on the fine art
of the Canadian-guide-style shore lunch: a single-pan meal of
chunked fish, chunked potatoes and onions, vegetables, and
proprietary seasonings, heavy on pepper. After a long day
outdoors, it was, Pender told her, better than any restaurant
meal he'd ever had.

When the after-dinner chores were done, Pender poured
the wine, and they spread a poncho on the edge of the overlook and watched the light disappear in the western sky.
There would be no light show in the sky tonight thanks to
the overcast, but the loons began their mournful calls soon
after dark, and they stayed to listen. Chaos wedged himself
between them, providing warmth and humor to their repose.

"Gabe," she said quietly, trying not to disturb the spell
that hung over the lake.

"Mmm," he replied.

"Can I say something? About you?"

"When did you ever need my permission to say something
about me?" He laughed a little when he said it.

"I've seen a fair amount of sadness lately—my daughter
coming home from a broken marriage, my sometimes lover
trying to deal with his wife dying every day by inches, friends
dealing with cancer. But I don't think I've ever known anyone
as sad as you are. Do you know that? I think you're grieving."

"Over my divorce?" Pender was skeptical.

"No. Everything. Your country, your marriage, your job.
Everything you believe in has crumbled. You're grieving."

Pender considered this for a while. "Okay. So?"

Annette shrugged. "So recognize it. Deal with it. And try
not to kill anyone before it passes."

"Good idea," said Pender.

They were silent for several minutes.

"I need to head back pretty soon," she said.

"Yeah, I know."

"I need to go back tomorrow."

Pender nodded.

"You're welcome to come with me."

He sighed.

"What?" asked Annette.

"I don't think that would work."

She was visibly shocked. "What? Why? I thought we had something here."

"I feel disconnected when I'm with people. Like an alien."

"With me?"

"Not here, but in town, yeah," said Pender. "Around your daughter, your friends, people on the street. I mean, I know how to fit in. I know how to act so everyone is okay with me. But it's not me. It's me pretending to be someone other people like."

She wanted to ask him something but she couldn't think what.

"I'm just lost," said Pender. "I have trouble sleeping because all my dreams are nightmares where I can't touch what I see. Anything I want is just beyond reach. I just kind of float, and everything else is a distant planet."

"Me too?" Annette asked.

Pender nodded his head yes.

"You were faking it all this time?"

"No. We connected. I can't get enough of you. But it wouldn't work back in civilization. I need space. I have to work through things. It's better if I stay out here."

Annette pursed her lips and looked away.

"Think about it," he said. "It would be hard for your daughter, you coming out of the wilderness with some crazy old man in tow, trying to adjust to someone who has trouble talking."

"You underestimate Christy."

"Anyone would feel invaded. And I'm not in a place where I can deal with being anyone's burden."

Annette was quiet for a long while. "What are you going to do?"

"What I started out to do. Maybe go back to Kahshahpiwi Creek and enjoy it this time. Maybe go from there over to Kawnipi, then to McKenzie and do those crazy portages through Cache and Baptism to French Lake. That's supposed to be the toughest trip in the park. I'll never be in better shape for a trek like that."

"So you end up at French Lake. My front door."

"Worried?"

"I'd like you to come. Now or then."

"You sure?"

"Of course. We've exchanged body fluids. Just call the office when you get in and I'll come pick you up."

"I'd like to, but only if I get my head on straight. No promises, okay?"

Annette shrugged mutely. The time for voicing her thoughts had passed. They sat in silence in the thick blackness of an overcast night. When the chill set in, they retired to the tent. Pender's hand found hers as they walked. She thought it was the offering of a wounded man, an apology, a statement of caring. She accepted his hand and squeezed back. In the tent, she put her arms around him and held him close, their cheeks and torsos flush, offering him her warmth as if he were a wounded bird.

21

Gus and Bill came back to the island after they scored a couple of fat walleye, Bill relieved because they were out of food. This trip had gone way past crazy. It had started out as a challenge for Bill: find a solo canoeist with a half day's head start in a labyrinthine wilderness and put the fear of God in him, let him know not to mess with people. It would have made a great war story. But it was personal with Gus, and after the guy damn near broke his leg, it got more personal than that.

Bill took the fish to the fire ring and started the meal preparations while Gus limped along the shoreline, stopping every few steps to scan the creek with his binoculars.

After their encounter with the crazy old man, they made their way back through the creek system to the big lake and camped at the mouth of the creek so Gus's wounds could heal. He still limped a little when he walked and he had an ugly bruise on his shin, but he could have paddled home yesterday. They stayed, even with their food supplies gone, even though they were overdue at home, because Gus wanted payback. He figured the crazy old man who took a hatchet

to his shin would be coming back this way, and he wanted
to greet the man when he did.

When Bill called him to dinner, Gus put down the binoculars and trudged over to the campfire.

"I'm heading back tomorrow, no matter what," Bill told
him. "I'm going back. Period."

Gus argued for one more day. Bill refused. Their families
would be concerned. Gus's obsession was just as crazy as the
old tripper.

"Okay," Gus finally conceded. "But we don't take off 'til
nine. Just in case."

"Then what, Gus? What are you going to do?"

"We'll catch him in open water and capsize him," Gus said.

"You want to drown him? Are you crazy?"

"He knows what he's doing. He can get to shore with his
boat and a paddle. He'll lose some gear, but he should. He
deserves to suffer."

"What if he drowns?"

"Well, fuck him."

Bill shook his head. "I'm not in it for murder."

"Okay, we'll hang around to make sure he makes shore.
With a boat and a paddle."

They argued off and on until dark and turned in without
resolving anything.

———————

Dawn came soft and dim to Quetico, high clouds sifting the
sunlight, the air deathly still, the water as flat as a mirror. It
was quiet and eerie. And sad.

Annette stood on her promontory, letting the serenity of
the lake and the forest soak into her senses, ignoring the chill

of the morning dew. She felt forlorn and wistful. Sleep had come hard last night. Her dreams were filled with visions of Pender, from now and from long ago. The visions were a slide show of contrasts, the fierce young Pender arguing about a literary interpretation in their Modern American Authors class, the gentle young Pender embracing her in arms as warm as a womb, the predator Pender who crippled a canoe tripper with a hatchet, the broken man weeping over a lost country and a lost life.

She should have invited him to her home with more enthusiasm, she thought. He feels so unwanted already. Why would he accept such a tentative offer? Now he wasn't going to come, even after his trip. She was sure of it. She could see him just moving on, catching a bus or train to somewhere, a boat or a plane to somewhere else. The reality of it brought tears to her eyes.

Pender glanced up from his fire-starting work and saw her dab at her eyes with a shirt sleeve. Smoke curled off the damp twigs as flames from the pine needles and dry tinder spread to larger pieces. He moved clear of the smoke, watched to make sure the bigger pieces caught fire. He shifted to the table structure and blended pancake mix with water, put the last of his maple syrup on the fireplace to warm, and readied the coffee-making operation.

After he put the water on to boil, he joined Annette. Chaos leaped to his feet and shadowed him.

"You have a new best friend, I see," said Annette, her voice a little hoarse at first, nodding at Chaos, who sat at Pender's side, looking up at both of them, canine smile on his face.

"It's my reward for feeding and bathing him."

Annette looked back to the lake.

"You seem upset," Pender said.

Annette's chin trembled slightly. She dabbed away a tear and composed herself, determined not to play the broken-hearted woman role.

"I'm upset that we're leaving today. And I'm upset that it doesn't mean anything to you, but to me it feels like college all over again—us going our own ways, facing another forty years of emptiness. Except I don't have forty years, and neither do you."

She waited for him to respond, but he didn't.

"Why are we doing this? We already know how this works out. You're the one. I always knew it. I knew it when we were together and I knew it when you left and I knew it all the years I was married because I never stopped wondering what it would have been like with you. Even at the best times in my life, I was thinking about you. When my kids were born. When my business turned the corner. When the girls graduated. You were always there in my thoughts. Why couldn't it be you sharing this moment with me?"

She stepped in front of him, made him look her in the eye. "And you feel the same way about me. You said so. You never stopped thinking of me. You remembered that horrible breakup line. Why are we doing this?"

"You said you had to get home," said Pender.

"You know what I mean." She fought back tears. "We're splitting up again. You aren't going to call me when you get to French Lake. You're just going to leave. Catch a train to the coast, go to Europe or something—isn't that what you said?"

"I said that before. We didn't even know if we'd like each other back then. Yesterday I told you I'd call when I got out. I'm going to." He said it with resolution, even though he had spent the night wondering if he should call her when he got to French Lake, if he should even go to French Lake.

He could take out at Lerome Lake and walk into Atikokan, swap his canoe for a ride to Fort Frances or Thunder Bay, maybe head for Montreal or Prince Edward Island or maybe Stockholm and spend the winter there.

"Besides," he said, "you didn't sound all that sure about wanting me to stop in."

"I wasn't," Annette admitted. "It's hard. It's taking a chance. Maybe Christy won't like you, or maybe you won't like her. Maybe it blows up in our faces. But if we don't try, it fails for sure. We don't get to do this again. Let's get it right this time."

"I absolutely promise I'll call from French Lake. And I keep my word."

"That's not enough. We need to go home together or something will go wrong. You'll break a leg on a portage or I'll be out when you call or something. We need to paddle out of here together."

Pender was quiet for a long time. "Jesus, I have such a bad feeling about that."

"I have a worse one about you not coming now."

He thought for a while. "Let's compromise. I'll paddle with you today. We'll camp tonight and talk about it while we finish my wine. You'll be able to make French Lake tomorrow, and I can get to Kawnipi if I don't go with you. I need to think about it. I had some things I set out to do, things I may never get another chance at. I didn't expect us to love each other like this, you know?"

Annette nodded. She put her arms around him and pulled herself to him with arms made of water. She laid her head on his shoulder and closed her eyes, trying to conjure colors into her visions of gray.

They lingered around the dying fire, talking quietly, sipping coffee. She asked him about his most memorable trips in Quetico. He remembered his first one with the same clarity he remembered the first time he and she embraced. He talked about a trip during the blistering heat wave of the late nineties, the one that created a blackout across eastern Canada and the U.S., him bushwhacking into no-name lakes in hundred-degree heat. He talked about long trips and short ones, rain and sun, wind and stillness. But, he said, this would be the trip he'd most remember. What the heck, he said, it was forty years in the making. Then he asked her the same question, saying no fair using this trip as the winner.

Annette smiled. There had been so many, especially with the girls when they were young, and her first canoe trip, and her first solo. "But in terms of purely enjoying the park and coming away a different person for it," she said, "I think it might be my first guiding job. Canadian Shield Outfitters hired me to take a group of women on an all-girls trip. We flew into Clay Lake and came out through the Falls Route. They were from the Twin Cities and didn't have much experience. They practiced paddling before they came up here, thank goodness, but it was still an adventure coming through the rivers. Especially Greenwood. The water was high and a little fast, there were blowdowns to negotiate, and Greenwood is so twisty that even a skilled canoeist has trouble doing the turns without crashing into the banks."

Pender nodded appreciatively. You never forgot Greenwood Creek, so serpentine that you could have compass headings of north, east, south and west every kilometer.

"Our group did a lot of banging into river banks, and when we got into the water to pull the canoes over downed trees, we were standing in cold, dark water up to our chests. None of them had never experienced anything remotely like that. They were asking if there were snakes in the water or biting fish. I'm thinking the whole time, what courage they have to be doing this. You know? Their normal lives were air-conditioned offices and shopping malls and going to dinner in nice restaurants, but here they were, up to their necks in bog water.

"We had such a great time on that trip. They thought I was the queen of the wilderness. They called me Daniela Boone. We all had nicknames by the time we got out of the rivers into Kawnipi. And they were dead tired. That's a tough first day for anyone. We came into Kawnipi with the afternoon winds blowing up a surf, and even though we had paddled twenty hard miles already, we had to dig like crazy to get to a campsite. Those ladies did it without a whimper. We laughed and told jokes and traded stories as we set up camp and made our meal. The rest of the trip was easy. We had good weather, no crowds, and the falls were gorgeous because the water was high."

She stopped and glanced at Pender to see if he was bored. He was staring at her, his eyes warm and happy.

"I learned so much from those ladies. About courage, about trying new things, about what women could do if they put their minds to it. I've thought about them and that trip many times over the years. I think it helped me become who I am."

Pender nodded. "I'll bet those ladies still remember you and learned something from you too."

"If this trip is so great, why aren't you more eager to come calling?" Annette asked.

"I told you why."

"It feels like you just can't get that interested in an old woman."

He blinked. "I don't think of you as an old woman. I don't see an old woman when I look at you. You're the first woman I've been interested in sexually in . . ." He paused. "It's been a long time."

"I find that hard to believe," she said. "I saw the pictures. There were gorgeous women everywhere you went. There's no way you'd prefer an older woman to one of them."

"I can't help you conceive something you can't see," he answered. "I'm sixty years old, for Christ's sake. I have a thing for you and that's it. You're still the beautiful woman I was in love with all those years ago, but stronger and tougher and smarter."

"God, Pender, you say all the right things. Except for, you know . . ." A small, ironic grin played at her lips. "So you're going alone into the wilderness, like Jesus."

He laughed. "I'm no rabbi."

Bill took down the tent, stuffed the sleeping bags in their sacks, rolled the sleep pads until all the air was out, and secured them. He packed the packs and loaded the canoe, all the while eyeing the western sky nervously. It was too quiet. Even though there was no tell-tale sign in the sky, he could sense it. Weather was coming.

"How about it, Gus. Let's get a move on before the storm hits."

"What storm?" Gus yelled back. He was on the western point of the island, scanning the water for signs of the guy who had ruined their trip. He had been there since they rolled out of the tent.

Gus looked at his watch. "Fifteen minutes," he yelled. "A deal's a deal."

Bill shook his head and muttered to himself. His boyhood friend and lifelong fishing buddy had completely obsessed on that nut. They were already three days overdue at home, and there was going to be hell to pay for that—from his wife and his boss.

Bill sat on a rock near the canoe to wait the eternity the next fifteen minutes would take. Followed by Gus wanting to stay just fifteen minutes more. Jesus, like taking your kid to an amusement park, except this was way past fun.

"It feels like a storm is coming," Pender said as they paddled side by side back to the creek system that would take them out to the big lake.

"Maybe." Annette looked to the west and southwest. The sky was hard to read. Overcast but not unusually so. The clouds were high and indistinct. The southern sky was the same. So was the eastern sky. The north was behind them, invisible until they turned, but it had been just as nondescript when they launched. Quetico was as still as a cemetery.

They portaged out of Annette's lake and headed for the creek. Pender broke the silence. "Want to try for Blueberry Island today?"

It would be a full day's paddle. She gave a silent, noncommittal shrug. She was pushing the pace, even though she made it look easy. They were making time.

He was surprised she didn't shoot down Blueberry Island, figured she must be very distracted, needing her space. The island was way too popular. This late in the season it would be littered and maybe in use. Worse, the island's blueberry patch would be ripe now, calling to Quetico's bears like a candy store to children.

By himself, Pender would never stay on Blueberry in August unless there was no other choice. But with Chaos it might be fun. With Pender and Annette banging pots and pans and Chaos barking like a maniac, it would be interesting to see how long a bear would stick around. Of course, Chaos might just turn tail and run, but Pender figured him to stay and make a lot of noise.

The short creek portages came up quickly, and they swept through each one in a hurry, hustling on the trails, digging hard on the water.

It was still morning when they arrived at the delta at the south end of the big lake, passing the island where Gus and Bill had camped. The fishermen had already left, heading south for the Maligne River and on to Minnesota. Annette and Pender swung northeast.

22

As Pender and Annette traversed the creek system and Gus and Bill prepared to leave for the Boundary Waters, multiple storm cells formed fifty miles southwest of them. The cells formed quickly, like summer storms often do, blowing up from a collision between competing weather systems. But these storms were different. They merged together to form a single violent system, much larger and more terrifying than the average summer storm on the northern prairie. Its fast-breeding cells multiplied like a supersonic cancer as it merged into a single terrifying front. It began moving northeast in a line twenty miles long, expanding and becoming more violent by the minute.

Minutes later, people in Ely, Minnesota, saw black clouds coming their way from the southwest. The clouds came fast, and they got darker, denser, and lower. It was as if a nightmare was rolling across the prairie, black and angry, like a wall of doom. The U.S. Weather Service posted a severe-weather warning, but the storm raced across northern Minnesota so fast there was little time for people to react. Those who looked at the southern sky didn't need a government warning, though. They ran for cover and made sure their loved ones did the same.

As it passed over Ely, the front of the system drenched the area in rain and pounded it with the highest winds in memory.

Between Ely and the Ontario border, the storm expanded to a fifty-mile width and became a full-fledged derecho, its winds building to hurricane levels, the rain falling in horizontal currents. It traveled fifty miles in its first hour of life, flattening forests like matchsticks, whipping the waters of lakes and rivers into frothing seas, creating a trail of terror and destruction no one in the northwoods had ever seen or imagined.

Annette and Pender were oblivious to the storm. Their view to the southwest was obstructed by land as they paddled the creek system, and when they swung northeast onto the big lake, the storm was behind them, in their blind spot. They could feel a gathering wind out of the southwest, but that seemed like good news. It would push them on their way, the wilderness tripper's fondest dream. They paused to quench their thirst, reload water jugs, and down a snack. As their canoes drifted, they gradually turned sideways to the prevailing wind, giving them their first good view of the southwestern sky. Pender was chewing a mouthful of trail food when he saw the black curtain filling the horizon as far as he could see.

"Jesus Christ!" The dread in his voice caused Annette to look up, first at him, then following his gaze to the southwest. "Here comes Mr. Death."

He knew they should be fleeing for cover, but he was mesmerized by the wall of doom coming to swallow them like a voracious predator.

"Oh my God!" Annette gasped. She focused on the near shore, looking for a safe place. "Let's go!" she commanded, turning her canoe toward a fingerlike point jutting into the lake a kilometer or two away. Pender heard her paddle slap the water. It shook him from his trance. He followed, stroking fast and hard, thinking they might as well try to escape—what else would you do with the last fifteen minutes of your life?

They sprinted flat out, machine gun cadence, Pender drafting behind Annette, admiring her perfect form and speed, hoping she survived this. They were moving at lightning speed for canoeists, but they were racing a wall of disaster that was closing on them so rapidly it felt like they were hardly moving.

He could see where she was going, wished the little peninsula was longer and taller and closer because he figured the black wall was going to eat them just about the time they reached the tip. It would piss him off, to come that close and fail, thinking it was like a short-timer in Vietnam getting zapped with a week to go in his tour.

Annette stayed focused on the peninsula, planning what to do when they got there, if they got there, aware of the specter closing in on them. Her arms and shoulders burned from the breakneck paddling but she kept whipping her paddle back and forth without slowing down, as if fighting back a sea filled with snakes.

Chaos sensed the tension and started to stand from his perch on the pack, but Annette shrieked at him to get down and he did, saving her the need to miss a stroke to crown him. Every stroke counted. The wind was building. They could smell the moisture in the air. They could see sheets of rain in front of the black wall, a terrible waterfall followed by a black void that seemed to engulf the land it passed over, hills and forests disappearing into the gaping maw of a ravenous beast.

The first huge raindrops hit them like ice-cold water balloons, hard and fat, the peninsula still a dream and a prayer away. The pellets of rain sounded like gunshots when they hit the packs and hulls of the canoes, and they savaged the surface of the lake as if sprayed from a monstrous shotgun, slamming into the lake like rocks, sending drops of water exploding into the air, creating an epidemic of spray as far as Pender and Annette could see. The raindrops became a torrent, and the canoes started taking water. Then the wind lashed them, and Pender wondered if the wind would capsize them before the rain made the canoes impossible to handle.

The wind rose to howling velocity as they reached the tip of the peninsula, a low, muddy projection that gave them little shelter. They leaned into the gusts to stay upright and kept paddling, trying to make the hundred yards or so to higher land before their world ended, hoping to God there would be a place to take out and some place to sit out the wrath of the heavens.

The elevation of the peninsula increased as they paddled. Pender thought Annette would stop when it got to a six-foot elevation, but she kept going, even though they were fighting crazy waves and stiff winds and could capsize any second. He admired her courage, wondered if he'd ever get to tell her so, thinking if he went over, she wouldn't know it until she got wherever she was going because he was in her blind spot and the wind and rain made too much noise for anyone to hear the muffled splash of a canoe going over.

The lake was boiling with whitecaps when Annette broke for a small rocky beach where they could land the boats.

The land rose steeply from the narrow landing, leading to a vertical rock wall about five feet high. Above the wall, the land rose again to a forest maybe twenty feet above the lake.

Annette pulled her canoe ashore, snatched one of the packs and all the loose items in it and scrambled up the slope to the rock wall. Pender followed her lead. The ripping wind and pounding rain swallowed their words, but he understood what she was doing. They dropped their gear at the base of the wall and slid back to the canoes, water pouring down the slope and soaking their bodies and clothes. Annette gestured for Pender to hold his canoe so it wouldn't blow away as she shouldered his second pack, and then went to her canoe. She pointed to him, then to the canoe, and mouthed the word "Okay?" He nodded. He'd take care of the canoes. She slung the second pack from her boat over her other shoulder and headed for the cliff with both bundles.

Pender dragged the two canoes up the slope. He slipped on wet rocks and soft soil but got to a crevice at the foot of a large boulder halfway up the slope. He stashed the canoes in the crevice and tied them to a tree, wondering if the tree, the canoes, or anything would still be there when this was over, because it was still getting worse and this seemed headed for some kind of biblical cataclysm. The trees up above the wall were bent at impossible angles by a wind that had surged to a demonic pitch, blowing rain and detritus in a jet stream over his head and into the void.

He crouched low, like someone ducking under a helicopter rotor, and made his way to the wall where Annette was preparing a shelter. A tree snapped in half nearby, the sound so much like a gunshot that Pender dove for the ground. As he righted himself, he looked up above the wall where the sound came from. Jack pines, he thought. There was a stand of jack pines right above their wall. Trees with the most superficial root structure he'd ever seen, in the craziest winds he'd ever seen. Trees that had no chance of surviving this gale. Trees that would start coming down any moment.

The bitch of it was, the wall was the safest place they were going to find. In the forest, they'd surely get crushed. Here, if the trees coming over the cliff fell at an angle, they might survive in the nook between the wall and the ground.

Annette positioned the packs to mark off two sides of a shelter, with the cliff forming the third side. She pulled the tarp from her pack to fashion shelter from the rain, trying to secure the sides under the packs. Even in their protected nook, the swirling winds ripped the tarp loose. She had to anchor it with her back, feet and arms. When Pender was done stashing the canoes, he slid under the tarp with her, wet and cold, and helped her hold it down. They took deep breaths, trying to relax, like they'd done all they could. Then Annette startled and yelled in Pender's ear, "Where's Chaos?"

"I thought he was with you," he yelled back.

He bolted from the shelter, back into the driving wind and icy rain, staying low and casting about for Chaos. The big yellow dog was thirty feet away, disoriented, panic-stricken, swirling in circles, barely able to stand in the severe wind. Pender half crawled toward him. Another tree cracked and fell, sending waves of fear through Pender's mind, but he kept moving. When he drew near, the dog saw him and tried to leap and run around him in ecstasy, but the wind knocked him off balance. Pender just turned and crawled back to the shelter, Chaos following him like a shadow.

They positioned the dog between them under the tarp and pulled the sides closed, forming a claustrophobic tent. It shed the rain and trapped their body heat but lent no sense of security. The tarp flapped and shook in the rising wind, and they could hear trees snapping like firecrackers on the mesa above them.

Annette tried to say something to Pender, but he couldn't hear her. She pushed Chaos toward their feet and pulled Pender to her side, merging their bodies into one soggy mass. She leaned her face to Pender's ear. "We have to keep each other warm!" she said. "Hypothermia!"

Pender nodded. Yes, he understood. He started to kiss her on the cheek, but she turned and they locked in a full embrace powered by adrenaline and fear.

Outside their fragile hovel, the air was filled with the sounds of tree roots giving way and trunks snapping, two, three, four at a time, like bullets shot from automatic weapons. They huddled blindly in a chorus of demons for what seemed like an eternity, unable to speak, trying to keep their shelter together, trying to stay warm, dreading the moment a towering jack pine crashed to earth and crushed them where they sat.

The violent din eventually ebbed enough for them to shout back and forth to each other.

"Have you seen anything like this before?" Pender yelled to Annette. He glimpsed her face as he spoke. Her expression was taut.

"No," she yelled back, her lips inches from his ear. "I've heard stories . . . I can't remember what they call these things, but they're like hurricanes."

As she spoke, a crack as loud as a thunderbolt exploded above them. They ducked reflexively. Chaos barked, then whined. They heard more cracking, the sound of a large tree trunk splitting. They knew it was right above them, knew it was coming down on them. They hugged their knees to their chests and pushed into the wall with all their strength.

The tree fell directly over them, its lower branches snapping and cracking as the base of the trunk hit the ground above them, a precarious moment of silence as the rest of its length teetered on the edge of the wall, then the final crash as the top of the tree touched down just below their feet. Branches brushed against Pender's head and legs. He felt the press of the boughs and had a fleeting mental image of the three of them being spiked to death by the limbs of falling trees. Chaos felt branches push against him and slithered back between them.

"How long will this last?" Pender yelled in Annette's ear.

She shook her head, buried her face in his shoulder. They clung to each other and Chaos as more trees fell around and over them. The first tree that fell over them acted as a shield, flexing and quivering as each new blowdown piled on. With each close call, Pender swore loudly. It was a reflex he couldn't control. Annette tried to choke back short, fearful yelps, with no more success.

It seemed impossible that they would survive the onslaught.

After twenty minutes of bombardment, the gale tapered off to merely powerful winds, maybe thirty miles per hour, Pender thought. The deluge ebbed to a heavy rain. The sound of trees cracking and falling stopped. Their tarp leaked where the wind shredded it and tree branches punctured it. Cold water seeped into their dark niche, making them wetter and more miserable. The air temperature was dropping, too, and between the cold and the wet, they began shivering even though they clung to each other.

"We're getting hypothermic," Annette said. "We have to get dry and get warm!"

"Okay." Pender replied. "But it's wet in here!"

"Right. We have to get a tent up, get the packs inside. Then us."

"That'll be a good trick in this wind." Pender was dubious. They didn't have to yell anymore, but the wind was still high enough to make pitching a tent a challenge.

"Don't wimp out on me now!" she said. "You hold down the tarp while I get my tent."

"I'll do the tent," he said.

Annette started to object, then nodded. Pender had told her about assembling his tent in the dark, as fast and sure as an Indy 500 pit crew. One more crazy thing about the guy, though this one was helpful.

Pender pulled his gear pack under the tarp and removed his tent bag from it. He yelled to her.

"I'm going up above," he gestured. "Give me five minutes, then come on up. I'll need help with the fly, then you get in and I'll shuttle the packs."

Annette stared at him in silence.

"This'll work," he said, locking eyes with her.

She nodded her agreement.

Pender slipped out from under the tarp and crawled through the tangle of trees and branches piled over them. He emerged into an apocalypse. Fallen trees littered the ground as far as he could see, vast forests destroyed as if felled by a giant scythe. Most of the ruined hulks of the trees pointed to the northeast.

He forced himself to focus on finding a place to pitch the tent. Clambering up the rock face, he found what had been a campsite near the top of the hill. All of the mature trees were flattened. Only a few saplings still stood. He found an open area among the carcasses just big enough for his tent.

He spread it on the ground and tried to stake it down before it blew away. The site had very little soil. He could sink only two stakes to full depth and two others about halfway. The fifth and sixth he skipped. He assembled the two long tent poles and plugged them into grommets in the tent's floor and roof, then erected the tent by snapping clips on the tent's roof to the poles. The hard rain pelted the tent, threatening to soak it before they could erect the rain fly.

Annette came up the rock face, trying to haul two packs with her. Pender scurried down to grab one of the packs, and they hustled back to the tent. He secured the upwind side of the fly while she kept it from ripping away in the wind. They secured the fly to the four stakes he had driven for the tent, not sufficient to get through the night, but maybe good enough for now, Pender thought.

Annette got inside and began arranging things. Pender retrieved the rest of their gear and threw it in the tent's vestibule. Chaos followed him everywhere, his spirits higher now that the wind had died down.

They raced against time, the rain and the cold stalking them like a hungry predator. Pender dashed around the area collecting ten-pound rocks to anchor the tent and fly in the places he couldn't secure stakes. He tied guy lines to the rocks from the tent and the fly to achieve structural integrity and to maintain air space between the rain fly and the walls and roof of the tent so the whole structure could breathe. Otherwise condensation would overpower the interior in a short time; it would be like a rain forest but colder, and they would be in danger again.

The cold and wet were overtaking Pender. His teeth chattered. His legs cramped badly when he crouched. Hypothermia was knocking on his door, but he had to finish his work or they would both die of hypothermia when their structure failed.

By the time he entered the tent, Annette had positioned Chaos against the far wall, their gear packs inside the door, their food packs in the vestibule. Their sleeping pads were laid out and inflated. The sleeping bags were stacked on one pad, towels and clothing on the other.

Pender tried to close the tent door behind him, but his fingers had stopped working. They were sickly white, his lips blue. Annette stopped him and began pulling off his wet clothes. She extracted his shirt and T-shirt and threw them on a pack in the vestibule, then closed the door herself. She told him to take off his pants and began drying his upper body with a towel. She had him dry his lower body while she pulled a fleece sweater over his head, then gave him fleece pants to put on. She opened his sleeping bag and told him to scoot his lower body in. She zipped it to his hips and then rubbed his arms and legs vigorously. She threw the other sleeping bag over him as she changed into dry clothes herself. She pushed the pads together, opened the top sleeping bag, and draped it over them both like a quilt.

She snuggled next to him, felt his icy hands, heard his teeth chatter, fought back the urge to panic. She tucked his hands under her armpits and rubbed his body as best she could. After a minute or two, she rose and knelt at the foot of his sleeping bag, rubbing his toes vigorously, then his legs and arms. He was still shivering, his lips a deathly blue. The rain outside was falling as if poured from buckets. She had to hope they wouldn't take water. Had to pray that they would stay dry, because she didn't think Pender would make it if they got wet again.

She lay with him once more, her body flush against his, his hands in her armpits. She rubbed him again, arms, hands, torso, legs, feet. She took a wet towel and dried off Chaos as best she could, then placed him beside Pender's feet and legs for warmth, using the towel and dirty clothes to keep him from getting the sleeping bags wet.

When Pender seemed to be recovering body heat, she found a water jug and her stove and made two cups of boiling-hot soup.

"Gabe," she said softly, "can you sit up? I have hot soup here."

His eyes opened. He was still shivering, but he knew where he was, who she was. Good signs.

"Sure," he said. He struggled to sit upright. The tent was on a slant, the ground below was as rough as a cob. One leg cramped horribly as he sat, forcing him to gasp. He lay down again and extended his leg, groaning in agony. It passed. He sat up again, tried to cross his legs Indian style, cramped again, lay down again, groaned some more. It passed. He started to sit up again. This time Annette positioned a pack behind him to act as a backrest.

"Thanks," he said, his relief palpable. His shivering stopped for a moment. She passed the hot soup to him. He cradled it in his hands, his fingers still pale from the cold.

When he finished the soup, she made more. They became aware of the rain pounding on the tent. "One of life's dilemmas," Pender smiled. "I need the soup, but the soup makes me need to pee. The rain makes me think of peeing. If I go outside to pee, I get soaked and we start all this over again."

"Fear not, Yankee." Annette pulled a quart bottle from a sleeve on her pack. "One Quetico porta potty coming right up.

Pender smiled. "Thank you. Now all I have to do is figure out how to get on my knees without cramping."

"Drink up," Annette said.

"Do you ever get tired of having the right answer?" he asked.

23

When Pender's body temperature normalized, they talked. The rain still pounded on the tent, and every so often a gust of wind flapped the rain fly, creating a noise as loud as thunder, reminding them that they were more lucky than safe, that nothing was over yet.

"Did you get a look around when we came up here?" Pender asked.

"Not a good one. I saw a lot of trees down."

"I caught a pretty good view," said Pender. "As far as I could see, every tree is down flat, like we'd been nuked or something. And they're pointing sort of northeast. What force of nature causes that?"

"It's a special kind of storm," said Annette, trying to remember the name. "Derecho. That's it, they call it a derecho. It's a group of thunderstorms that merge and develop severe downdrafts. We had a downburst in the park in ninety-nine, but it was just a kilometer wide. It wreaked havoc on a few portage trails, but only a few people actually witnessed it.

"The old timers said a really big derecho came through the border region back in the seventies. It missed Atikokan, but I heard people talk about it."

Pender thought about that for a minute. "This looked huge to me. I think we're going to have a hell of a time getting out of the park."

He found his day pack and pulled his map from it.

"So now you're thinking of getting out of the park?"

Pender studied the map. "I don't think many portage trails are going to be passable after this," he said. "I think the next month or so in this park is going to be about clearing trails and campsites."

Annette groaned. She realized how devastating it would be for the canoe outfitters, herself included. August was an important month in their trade. "That's really going to hurt us," she said.

"Maybe you can shift your canoe customers up to White Otter," suggested Pender, referencing the vast White Otter Wilderness Area north of Atikokan. Like National Forests in the U.S., the White Otter Wilderness Area was mostly pristine land owned and regulated by the government of Ontario, which leased commercial rights to private vendors. It covered thousands of square miles of Canadian Shield terrain, including large and small lakes, twisting rivers, and endless miles of forests.

"That's a thought," said Annette. "And Canadian Shield Outfitters can try to switch some to their fly-in cabins or their lodge. We might be able to keep our cabins full, too. That would help."

They huddled over Pender's map, discussing exit strategies, anticipating difficult portages, evaluating take-out areas. They wanted a take-out with close access to the main highway, and one with a phone. The answer kept coming up, French Lake, even though it wasn't the closest.

"For now, let's just hope this tent hangs together and we don't get washed away," said Annette.

"You're right. We've been lucky so far."

They got quiet again. "Or maybe we haven't been lucky," said Pender. "What if our canoes got crushed?"

"We'd be okay with one canoe. If they're both out of commission, we'll have to raft out. That could take forever."

"Well, we have lots of logs to choose from."

Annette smiled. "I don't know how much flotation fresh blowdowns have. Let's hope at least one canoe made it through the storm."

"I could go check."

"Don't bother. Whatever shape they're in, they'll be like that when the rain stops, too. No reason to get wet and cold again."

"Might help our state of mind."

"You worry too much, Pender. We'll be fine. We have plenty of food, we're strong, and we're smart. Relax. Let's take a nap. Maybe mess around a little?"

"All you Canadians think about is sex."

The rain and wind tapered off in the midafternoon and stopped completely by 4 PM. They tumbled out of the tent, stiff and cold, and into an eerie wasteland. They walked through the downed timber and surveyed a scalped land covered by destruction and mayhem.

It was still and cool and eerily sunny. There was no wind, not even a breeze. It was as if the scariest storm Pender had ever seen never happened. Except for the devastation that surrounded them.

Annette brought her hands to her face in horror as she looked about. Not a single tree was left standing in the campsite. Most of the jack pines had been uprooted, their rope-like root tentacles stretching skyward from horizontal trunks. Some had snapped, their trunks still upright, their bodies missing, like soldiers brutalized by cannon fire. She could see root systems from spruce and pines in the distance, sad, dead sentinels overseeing a fallen army.

"Who needs a devil when you've got a God like this?" said Pender.

Annette hit him in the shoulder with a small fist. "Stop it. This is no joke. This is my world."

He put his arms around her and murmured an apology.

"I didn't mean it as a joke," he said. "It's how we dealt with death in Vietnam. Don't let anything get to you. Be the meanest motherfucker in the valley."

Annette didn't respond to him, just surveyed the wasteland around them.

"Where did you put the canoes?" she asked, finally.

Pender slowly looked about the ruined hill, trying to find the boulder where he'd stashed the boats. It was draped in pine boughs. He walked to it, Annette following.

The ends of the canoes poked out from under a felled pine. Pender lifted the tree, and Annette pulled the canoes into a clear space. Miraculously, they were unharmed. Annette smiled at Pender, who exhaled with relief.

He looked down the slope. The small shelf where they came ashore was underwater. He scrambled down to see how deep the water cover was. He slid the last few feet, unable to stop until he was ankle-deep in water, standing on the shelf. He took a moment to scan the lake. It was already calm. It could be glassy by dinnertime, he thought. An island a half kilometer to the north looked ravaged, its heights mowed down to scrub and juvenile trees, some forest left on its lower reaches. It felt like they might be the last survivors of a world-ending calamity. Jesus.

Pender started to climb back up the slope when he sensed movement out on the lake. He looked south again. He saw a distant light flash, disappear, and then flash again. He could make out a dark spot on the water. A minute later, he could see it was a canoe. The flash was a paddle being lifted and lowered. It was headed toward him, Pender thought. As it inched closer, it looked like there was only one paddler. When it got still closer, he could make out two people in the boat. They weren't moving very fast. The cadence of the paddle stopped for long counts, then started again. They might be in trouble.

Pender climbed the slope and got his canoe. "Might be some people in trouble out there!" he yelled to Annette. She was setting up a kitchen area. He hoisted the canoe on one shoulder, grabbed a paddle with the other hand, and made his way back down to the water. Annette got there as he boarded his canoe. She threw him a flotation vest and a ball of nylon cord.

"Give me a wave if you need help," she said.

He nodded, pushed off, dug hard with the paddle. When he got close to the canoe, he could see the man in the bow was doing all the paddling and the guy in the stern was just trying to use his paddle as a keel to keep them straight. The guy in the bow was tired, paddling weakly, resting every six or eight strokes.

"Need help?" Pender yelled.

"Yes sir," came the answer from the bow. The man's shoulder slumped. "We gotta get to shore, get a tent up."

Twenty feet away Pender knew that the canoeists were the fat boys, one of them hurt. When he reached them, Pender swung his canoe 180 degrees and stopped alongside them, both boats pointing north. The two canoeists were wet and cold, their lips getting blue, their fingers a pale white.

The man in the bow established eye contact with Pender. It was the one called Gus. The one with a bad leg.

"Jesus fucking Christ," Gus muttered, shaking his head. "You just keep popping up." In the stern, Bill mumbled a few obscenities through clenched jaws. He looked to be in a lot of pain.

"Karma, baby," said Pender. "You guys want to come over for dinner or wait for a better offer?"

Gus pursed his lips. "Bill's hurt. We're out of food. Everything we have is wet. The hull's cracked. We're taking water. We're pretty much fucked."

"Can you make it another kilometer or so without bailing?" Pender couldn't see the bottom of their canoe.

"We'll be okay." Gus was too tired to bail, too exhausted to mess with anything. They must have had a hell of a time in the storm, Pender thought.

He rigged a towline from their canoe to his. "We have an extra tent and plenty of food," he said. "Paddle when you can, okay?" Gus nodded. Bill writhed in pain, holding a shoulder. He was shaking noticeably. Hypothermic or close to it, Pender thought. Gus was maintaining body temperature by paddling, but he wouldn't be far behind Bill. The fat boys were in real trouble.

As Pender headed for the campsite, he could see Annette standing at the shoreline, watching them, Chaos splashing beside her. The fifteen minutes it took to get to her seemed like a lifetime. He was thinking of his own hypothermic episode. They'd have to get these guys in the tent, get them some dry clothes, and try to find some burnable wood. Get the other tent up. Figure out how to get through the night.

"Everyone okay?" Annette called as they neared shore. Chaos barked and jumped until she told him to stop.

"The guy in back is hurt and maybe hypothermic," yelled Pender. "They need dry clothes and whatever. Take them from my gear bag."

Annette grabbed the big canoe and held it so the men could get out. Gus gawked, surprised to see a woman in camp, and then stepped out. She positioned the canoe for Bill. "Can you get out yourself? Use me as a brace?" she asked.

Bill grunted. "I think so." He placed a shaking hand on her shoulder and tried to stand while she held the canoe steady. Gus stepped over to help. Bill struggled out of the boat into a standing position on the submerged shelf. "Can you walk?" Annette asked Bill. He nodded. "Can you climb this slope?"

"I'll try," he gasped.

"Put your hand on my shoulder," Annette said, positioning herself on his good side. She pointed to Gus. "You stay behind us and brace him." Gus nodded. Annette crab-walked up the slope. Bill grunted and groaned with pain but stayed with her.

When they got to the tent, she opened the door. "You two get in there. Get your clothes off and toss them out here. You'll find a towel and dry clothes in the green pack. Get dry, get dressed, and then get in those sleeping bags and cuddle. I mean it. Don't wimp on me, gentlemen. It's not love, it's survival. Okay?"

They nodded and ducked in the tent.

Pender came up the slope with two packs, water streaming off them as he walked. "This stuff is in bad shape," he said dropping them near the tent. He returned to the water to fetch the canoes and paddles.

When he returned, Annette was heating water on a gas stove.

"We need to get my tent up before dark," she said.

Pender nodded. "Yeah. And we need to hang everything they've got to dry." He had the nylon tow cord in hand, wanting to rig it as a clothesline, but there were no trees left to tie it to.

"We can just lay things on branches for tonight," Annette instructed. "Shake the needles out now, and they'll be pretty dry in an hour or so. But we can do that in the dark if need be."

"If I round up some wood, think you can get a fire going?" Pender was thinking he wouldn't even try if it was just him, but she was a magician with campfires and if she could get one started, it sure would help everyone's spirits.

"See if you can find stuff that isn't soaked," she answered. "If we have enough dead wood that's just wet and needles that are only a little damp, we can probably make something happen. But when I'm ready for your help on the tent, come running."

Pender nodded again, moved off to look for wood, Chaos tagging along.

For the next hour, he combed over the peninsula collecting wood from long-dead trees, hacking branches from the underside of dead fall, looking for needles and twigs in small nooks and crannies protected from rain. He carried armfuls of fire material back to the campsite several times, helping Annette erect her tent on one of the stops, then dragged large branches and small trees back to the site to be cut up to campfire-sized lengths.

He hacked, sawed, or broke everything to size, stacked it on a foundation of logs and rocks to keep it above the wet ground, sorted into piles according to thickness like Annette had showed him.

Annette handed him a cup of hot cocoa and inspected the wood. "Good work," she said. "You might be worth keeping after all."

He grinned and sat on a log with a grunt. Annette had cleared a cooking area, leaving two blown-down trees in place, stripping the branches off them with a hatchet so they could be sat upon. The branches of the other downed trees were covered with the wet belongings of the fishermen—sleeping bags, clothing, and fishing gear. "How are our guests doing?" he asked.

"They're going to be okay. The injured one is still getting dressed. His name is Bill. As long as he doesn't get cold again, I think he's okay on the hypothermia. We'll take a look at that shoulder when he comes out. The other man is Gus. He's the one you tried to cripple, in case you didn't know. He's fine. I've been pouring soup and hot drinks down them, and they say they're feeling okay. They were heading for the Maligne when the storm hit. Didn't see it until just short of too late. They saw our boats off in the distance when they made for shore. They got to land but couldn't find much shelter. Tried to ride it out in rain gear. Bill got hurt by a falling tree, the same one that cracked their hull."

Annette paused, shook her head.

"Sometimes you're just snakebit," said Pender.

"Gus thought Bill's shoulder was broken, so they took off for the Maligne again when the winds started to taper off. Gus was having trouble handling the boat by himself, then the rains came and they started taking water. They got back

to shore, waited out the rain, and then came looking for help.
We were the only paddlers they saw on the lake before the
storm.

"Oh yeah, and they're out of food. Haven't eaten all day."

"Wow," said Pender. "Just goes to show, huh? Those guys
are very good. They know what they're doing out here. Shows
how lucky we were, right?"

"I guess," Annette said. "But give us credit for reacting the
right way when we saw the danger."

They got quiet, lost in thought. Rustling came from the
tent. The fishermen were coming out. Chaos ran joyously to
greet them.

"They're going to be ravenous," Annette said.

"Why should they be different," Pender answered. "I'm
ready to eat Chaos."

"We should probably hold our freeze-dried stuff for emer-
gencies. I think we should at least try to catch some fish."

"Okay," said Pender. "You're the guide. Any ideas?"

"The island due north of us has a deep drop-off on the
south shore. Might pick up a pike or bass there. Another
kilometer or two north of there is a river mouth. Might be
walleye sitting in there waiting for baitfish. Definitely some
northerns. Think you can take care of our guests without
attacking them for an hour or so? I'll go take a shot at some
fish."

"Very funny. You'd have a better chance of catching something if I paddled the boat, held it in position for you."

"Maybe you're right," she said.

The fishermen approached, Chaos dancing at their feet,
Bill wincing with every step. Pender nodded to both of them.
They nodded back, avoiding eye contact. An awkward silence
hung in the air as they gathered in a small space, Pender

and Annette sitting on a log, Bill and Gus standing in front of them.

"Thanks for the clothes," said Gus. His voice was much louder now, like when they faced off at the portage, the deep, husky macho voice of a football player, filled with energy and testosterone. "They might never fit you again." He laughed a jock laugh and opened the baggy rain parka to show a T-shirt and fleece stretched to bursting by his girth, the shirt falling an inch or two short of his waistline.

Pender smiled. "I washed everything out yesterday, so you probably won't get a disease." The fishermen nodded, Bill wincing again.

"You better sit down," said Pender, standing to offer his seat. Bill nodded and did so, groaning as the jolt from sitting set off nerves in his shoulder.

"Let me look at that," said Annette. She stood and worked her hands around his shoulder, then under his jacket and shirt, asking him if this hurt or that hurt. After a few minutes she straightened up and stared at him, deep in thought. "You might have a broken collarbone. The best we can do right now is stabilize it. I'll rig a sling and we can experiment with the best position for you."

Annette stepped back to address all of them. "We need a plan for tonight. Pender and I were going to try catching some fish before dark." She stopped abruptly. "Bill and Gus, this is Gabe Pender. Gabe, meet Bill and Gus, and try not to piss them off this time."

After a round of self-conscious chuckles, Annette was all business again. She looked at Gus. "Do you fish as well as you paddle?"

"I've been fishing these waters for twenty years. Caught everything there is to catch. Even—"

"Okay, I'm sold," Annette cut him off. "We need to work together. We might be in a survival situation here. It could be days before the portages are cleared, so we need to conserve our food." She nodded to Gus. "You and Pender have fishing detail. I've told him where to fish. He'll manage the boat. You cast. Fishing may be awful after the storm, but let's give it a go."

Gus and Bill stared at her.

"She's lived here for about as long as you've been on the planet," Pender explained. "She guides. She outfits. She's our best chance of getting out of here. Don't worry, she gives me all the scut work."

"While you two are catching dinner, I'll take care of Bill and get the fire ready. Okay?"

The three men nodded.

As Annette tended to Bill, Pender and Gus got ready to fish.

"How much do you weigh?" Pender asked.

"Two seventy," said Gus. "Maybe less right now."

"Okay. We can use my canoe. You'll have to paddle and cast from a kneeling position. Can you do that for an hour?"

"Li'l fella, I can stand on my head and fart 'Jingle Bells' for an hour," Gus said. "You just take care of your end of things."

"Get your gear. You still have fishing gear, right? You didn't lose it in the nasty storm, did you?" Pender gave Gus an eat-shit smile.

Minutes later, they pushed off from shore, two men in a solo canoe, each perched awkwardly on his knees in the small boat. It sat dangerously deep in the water. "I think we're going to have to cut it off at fifty pounds of fish," said Pender.

"Funny," said Gus. "You're a real funny guy for a little fella."

"Just remember that I'm the little fella that chose not to kill you, Fat Man."

"I think we both know that wouldn't happen again. You wouldn't have a chance in a rematch. Not a chance."

"Don't push your luck. We already have one guy to carry out. I'm not sure I can get two of you out of here."

Their conversation was cut short by the twitchiness of the overloaded canoe. Every movement they made caused it to wobble. The canoe was also badly out of trim since Gus outweighed Pender by eighty pounds. But they were skilled canoeists, and they stabilized the vessel by keeping their body weight centered and paddling rapidly in perfect tandem, each man's blade pull perfectly countering the other's. They were sitting off the island in a few minutes. Pender explained Annette's scouting report. Gus had rigged two poles, one with a chartreuse plastic grub, the other with a floating minnow crank bait.

He cast the plastic grub first, eight, ten times, without a hit. He reeled it in and reached for the other pole.

"You think anything's going to hit a surface lure after this storm?" Pender asked.

"Probably not," said Gus as he produced two lead weights from the soft-sided pack that held his tackle. "I like the action the floaters have in the water. When I want to get deep, I just add weight to the line." He squeezed the weights onto the line a couple feet above the lure, then cast it toward the island. After a dozen casts with no action, they headed for the mouth of the river.

On his fourth cast, Gus got a fish. As he swung it into the boat, both of them exclaimed at once. It was a whitefish, a rare catch because they spend their summers at great depths in the deepest lakes.

"Storm must have turned the lake over," said Gus as he cast again. Pender had been thinking the same thing. The only other time he had caught a whitefish in fifteen feet of water was after a storm that disrupted fishing patterns for a couple of days. Gus, however, was not deterred. He kept pitching the line out and retrieving it. Every six to ten casts, they'd move a little. It took an hour, but they added a couple of bass and a middling northern pike.

"We're going to eat tonight," said Gus with relish after they boated the pike. They stopped at a rocky point and skinned and filleted the fish. Gus tended to the whitefish and northern pike. They were difficult to fillet, but he prepared them with the smoothness of a sushi chef and then turned to watch Pender work on the bass.

"I know. I suck at this," said Pender, feeling the attention. "But I have other strengths, such as dry clothes."

Gus acknowledged the humor with a facial grimace and silence. They paddled briskly back to camp, Pender sending Gus up with the catch while he took care of the canoe.

24

The fire crackled and smoked, filling the air with warmth and the enchanting scent of pine. It brought the survivors of the storm together as the light of day faded. They were tattered and wrinkled but happy to be warm and dry. Bill's arm was bound in a sling that held it in a V hard against his chest. It was enough to reduce the pain to a dull ache that only hurt when he moved his upper body.

Conversation started slowly as Pender and Annette prepared the meal, Pender tending to the fish, Annette the hash browns, corn, and fire. The questions and answers came stiff and awkward at first, but they were bound together by the heat of the fire and the tribulations of the day, and the group loosened up quickly.

Gus and Bill praised Annette's fire-making skills. Neither of them thought they could get a good fire going with damp wood, not without using petrochemicals. They even complimented Pender on the aromas coming from his skillet. Annette told them that he was a restaurant authority, knew all the great chefs, and what they were smelling was his own personal blend of spices and herbs. The fishermen nodded politely to

Pender, then looked away. There was plenty of tension to go with the warmth.

Bill and Gus were from a Minnesota mining town in the Mesabi Range. The Iron Range they called it. Bill managed a fleet of huge mining trucks and loaders, machines with engine compartments the size of an office, tires taller than a basketball player. Gus was the lead diesel mechanic for the company that kept the machines running, twenty hours a day, six or seven days a week. In better times, anyway. In the wake of the financial collapse, work in the mines had dropped off a cliff. Gus could get as much time off as he wanted; there were lots of good mechanics hungry for work. Bill was still full time, but business was so slow an extra few days of vacation was no big deal.

They talked about the halcyon days of the bubble economy. Machines running flat out, 22/7 some weeks. Changing out a behemoth 2,500-horsepower engine overnight, a feat more remarkable than an Indy pit stop.

Gus dominated the conversation with his booming voice and endless bravado.

They had been coming to the Boundary Waters to canoe and fish since they were kids. The two of them with their dads back then. Then in high school, the two of them and the other two guys, the ones who went home instead of chasing Pender all over Quetico.

"You must have been really pissed," said Pender, squinting at Gus through the smoke of the fire, talking about them chasing him, a small smile playing at his face.

"Yeah. Definitely. We try to help you and you do that to us? What the f—." He stopped himself before the obscenity came out. "Sorry," he said to Annette.

"Oh, don't worry," she smiled. "I heard all three of you say that one, and lots more, too."

"You were there?" Bill asked incredulously.

She nodded. "Yes, I could hear you from the other lake almost. I thought there was a murder going on."

"We didn't see you," said Gus.

"I thought it might be smart to stay out of sight until I could figure out which 'motherfucker' was the bad one." She smiled again, enjoying their discomfort.

"Were you two traveling together?" Bill asked. The two fishermen were confused.

"Not then," said Annette. "We were meeting nearby. Sort of a date. Pender was a day late. Surprised?"

"I'm surprised you were meeting him at all. He doesn't make a great first impression, if you know what I mean." Bill shrugged, like he was kidding, but with a little edge.

"Well, before he became an ax murderer, he was a pretty special guy." Annette looked at Pender as she said it. "Actually, he still is, but we try to keep sharp objects out of his hands."

Annette flashed a saccharin smile at Pender,

"That does it," said Pender. He moved his skillet to the side of the fire grating and walked to his food pack. He returned with his last bottle of wine, a Washington red in a collapsible plastic bladder. "Rinse out your cups, everyone. This elegant beverage is going to be the last good thing that happens to us for a while."

Minutes later, as the four sat down to a sumptuous feast, Pender poured the wine and made a short speech. "Gentlemen, please join me in saluting the woman who saved my life today and maybe yours, too." The three raised their glasses to Annette. She blushed.

As the night chill set in and the fire glowed low, the conversation turned serious.

"We'll try to patch your boat," said Annette. "But even if the patch works, you'll have trouble getting down the Maligne with one paddler. You might do better to travel with us. We're heading north tomorrow. There are only two portages to get from here to French Lake. There will be vehicles there and a phone if we need it. It's a twenty-minute drive to Atikokan, and there's a hospital in town."

Gus and Bill talked about it for a few minutes, wishing there was a more direct way home but realizing they had no chance alone. "We're with you," said Gus.

They talked logistics for a while. In the morning, Annette and Gus would patch the crack in the big canoe. Pender would get a fire going and make breakfast. Bill would check their wet gear and try to get the tent ready for packing.

"We'll have to dry your gear as we travel tomorrow," Annette said. "It'll still be wet in the morning. Tonight you two can share a pad and sleeping bag, and Pender and I will do the same."

"If you two lay off the kinky sex tonight, I might make pancakes for breakfast and some genuine Starbucks coffee," said Pender.

Gus twirled a finger in the air in sarcastic celebration. Bill grunted, becoming more uncomfortable with each passing hour. Annette stared off into space.

"You look far, far away, ma'am," Gus said.

"It's Annette, okay?"

He nodded.

"I'm just thinking that tomorrow will be a day of tests for us. We'll leave this lake and take a creek through a bog. It could be fouled with blowdowns. Then we'll see if the portage into the next lake is passable. That's the lake we want to camp on."

After a long silence, Bill asked Pender about his experience in the bush. "We know Gus and I have been coming up here for thirty years, and we know Annette is a guide and master woodsman. What about you?"

"Me? Oh, hell. I'm just a tenderfoot. I can read a map and a compass and catch a fish now and then."

Annette laughed. "Don't fall for his crap. He's been soloing up here for twenty years, and he was a soldier in Vietnam."

"Don't think your Vietnam experience is going to be much good up here," said Gus.

"Came in handy a few days ago," Pender replied.

"Easy, boys," said Annette. "We've got a long way to go, and we need to do it together."

The fishermen nodded to her. Pender smiled

Pender spent a fitful night of not-quite-sleeplessness, dozing for short periods, his sleep so shallow he was roused by the slightest noises, the call of a loon, a deep sigh from Annette, Chaos stirring. He moved frequently, from his side to his back to his other side, to try to ward off a backache. Sometimes he pulled his legs up into a prenatal curl. Sometimes he straightened out. Sometime in the middle of the night, Chaos gave up trying to cuddle against him and moved to the other side of the tent.

He didn't dream when he dozed, but he did during his waking minutes. His dreams were short vignettes flipping through his consciousness like a pulsating strobe light. Trees snapping in the wind. Kissing Annette. Patrick O'Quinn on his deathbed. Paddling on a mirror-smooth lake as if in a dream, the sky reflected in the water like a photograph, the Canadian Shield silent and still, a moment so perfect it was like seeing life begin. Evelyn's face, twisted and cruel. Gus charging him, red-faced with anger. Pender now wishing maybe he hadn't taken their boats. Group vice president Charles Jamison Blue doubled over, holding his gut, his aura of arrogance crushed by a single blow.

He marveled briefly that nary a single slide in his succession of images was about Peg. Thirty years and not a single memory for the sleepless-night hit parade. He was just as sure she never thought about him either. He could barely remember what she looked like, could just barely conjure an image of her walking toward him in the morning as she went to work. He could see her silhouette, her brisk steps, her tasteful clothes, but her face was just a shape, undefined. Jesus, what a waste of a lifetime.

It was a damp, chilly night, the humidity hanging on them like a wet cloth. At 4:00 Pender could feel his nose plugging up as if he had a cold. At 5:00 he gave up, dressed, and went outside, suppressing grunts as he forced his aching back and cramping legs to work.

He crawled into a wilderness encased in a dense fog. He could see maybe five feet in front of him. Then the world faded to nothing. His flashlight was useless, converting the wet air to a single blinding reflection of light as opaque as a brick wall. The fog was so disorienting he used his compass to reach the fire ring. Chaos followed him, full of energy but slowed by the fog and the tangle of downed timber.

Pender boiled water on a gas stove, waiting to start the wood fire until the others got up. He lay on the ground and went through his stretching exercises, trying to get ease of motion back in his body. He sat on a log when he was done. Chaos sat in front of him and put his chin on Pender's knee. Pender smiled, put both hands on the dog's head, scratching behind both ears. Chaos erupted in a canine smile of pure ecstasy.

"You're a good guy," Pender whispered to the dog. Then he bent over and hugged him.

In the tent, Annette woke and dressed. She had felt Pender leave, had sensed his discomfort all through the night. As she oozed in and out of slumber, she dreamed of Christy and her granddaughter, dreamed of her oldest daughter, Anne, so far away, dreamed against her will of her own death in the derecho and her loved ones learning to live without her. She dreamed of seeing them again, of scaling mountains of downed timber to get to them. She dreamed of Pender and her as college kids, wondered what he saw in her, then and now. She dreamed of Gus getting into it with Pender, Pender beating him to a pulp, her having to testify against him.

As she dressed, the image of Pender and Gus squaring off came back to her. Gus wore his resentment on his sleeve, but Pender's was subtler, a streak of anger bubbling just beneath a crust of ironic humor. He was a man of deep passions, trying to deny them, a complex organism of many disparate parts, all boiling within him, their steam erupting now and then to relieve the pressure inside. Could he ever find peace? she wondered.

Annette crawled into the dim fog. She could hear Gus and Bill dressing in the other tent and Pender snapping twigs for the fire. She made her way slowly to the fire ring. They exchanged a warm kiss.

"You had an awful night. I'm sorry," she said.

"Ah. Sleep is overrated. The only thing I worried about was having this back of mine act up again."

"How is it?"

"Not bad. Do you think this fog will last long?

"It'll probably burn off by nine or ten," said Annette.

Pender nodded. "I had fog like this once, and it was on this lake. I had to dead reckon it all the way to the north end. Lucky for me, the fog was lifting by the time I got in the bog. I always have a hell of a time finding the watercourse in there."

Annette squeezed his hand. "We'll probably start out just following a compass bearing today, too," she said.

Pender served coffee and pancakes for breakfast. Annette and Gus finished patching the damaged canoe and struck camp. They launched before eight, the fog still dense, the air almost viscous enough to drink. Pender and Gus paddled the big tandem canoe, towing Bill in Pender's solo boat. Annette paddled her own canoe, carrying fishing poles, ready to cast when the opportunity arose. Chaos rode with Gus and Pender so Annette could travel light. The extra speed would let her stop and cast and still catch up. The fishermen's damp clothes and sleeping gear were draped over the packs in all of the canoes, giving their small armada a ragtag look.

They paddled east-northeast all morning, the fog dissipating gradually at ground level, enough for them to see islands and reefs and the shores of the big lake, but a heavy haze still hung above them, low in the sky like a gelatinous cloud with no beginning and no end.

They made good time. Gus controlled the big canoe from the stern, calling out "Hup!" every eight to ten strokes to signal Pender to paddle on the other side. He adjusted easily to Pender's paddling style, and they kept up with Annette's tripping pace even with another boat in tow. They paddled in silence most of the morning, the swish of their paddles and Gus's "Hup" commands the only sounds, the air around them eerily still.

"This isn't good," Annette said, gesturing skyward. "No visibility for rescue planes. I haven't heard an engine all morning."

"Maybe this afternoon," Gus offered.

"Maybe. But it would help if we had some kind of breeze. Everything is just sitting there."

At the narrows where both Annette and Pender had camped earlier in the week, Annette paused at a few places to cast, then sprinted to catch up. At the next narrows, a four-kilometer stretch where the lake shrank to a river-like width, Annette trolled a crank-bait, working structures in the channel. She caught a walleye and two chunky northerns. Bill and Gus cheered.

"Why would a great woman like that settle for an asshole like you?" Gus called to Pender. Teasing in a guy-humor sort of way.

"Because assholes like you make me look pretty good," Pender returned.

Gus grimaced, then recovered. "Good one," he said. Pender nodded, thinking he probably should have taken the ribbing in silence. It was just a joke.

The improving visibility gave the paddlers a dramatic view of the devastation left by the derecho. Every shore was strewn with tangles of prone trees. All of the high points looked like they'd been buzz-cut by a scythe-wielding deity. Trees remained on a few slopes facing the east or northeast, in the lee of the winds, but these were small pockets of sanity in a landscape dominated by psychotic madness.

Annette's eyes were damp when she called for a short lunch break. An hour or two of high winds, and everything she held dear was in ruins. She was used to fires taking out forests. That was part of the natural force of change in Quetico, just like ice heaves and water erosion and heavy snows. But the fires affected only small parts of the park in any given year. A hillside here, a hilltop there. Once in a while, an entire ridge. But not everything. Not like this. Forestry companies didn't create devastation on this scale, she thought.

She tried to calculate the recovery time. After a burn-off, thick covers of seedlings cropped up in two or three years, and they grew like weeds, especially jack pines, so in ten years there would be a forest of immature trees in place. In twenty years you wouldn't know it from an old-growth forest. She wondered if she'd live to see it recover. She was sixty. And this wasn't a burn-off. The new growth would have to get past the downed trees. It would take them years to rot away. She might be eighty by the time this lake was lined by a juvenile forest. Eighty! She'd be sitting in a rocking chair somewhere waiting to die.

Their respite was brief and quiet. Annette distributed granola bars and her homemade gorp to each person. "Might not fill you up," she said, "but there are plenty of calories here. Just make sure you drink lots of water and everyone pee before we leave."

"Okay, Mom," said Pender.

When they prepared to leave, he stepped into the water to brace Annette's canoe as she boarded it. "You don't need to do that," she said.

"I know."

She looked at him, her face a question mark.

"It's a way a man respects a woman. Like opening a door. Everyone knows she can open it herself, but the man doing it for her says something about how he feels about her."

She blinked, nodded, and paddled away, still trying to figure out who Pender actually was.

25

They covered the final few miles of the big lake in a moody silence, sobered by the devastation around them and by the growing reality of their peril.

At the northern terminus of the big lake, its clear, blue waters gave way to a marsh filled with reeds and sedge grass and other bog plants. It was a river in the technical sense, but for paddlers, it was a bog that stretched two kilometers long and a kilometer wide and had a narrow channel that was navigable during periods of normal rainfall. In low-water conditions, it was a brutal trudge. At its average depth, the channel gave adventurers an intimate view of the beauty of a northwoods bog, but even then the passage came with the price of a good workout. It was littered with beaver houses and logjams that had to be scrambled over and low spots that had to be waded. Each time canoeists dropped into the water, they had to deal with the channel's silt, an oozing, dark, sticky goo that was knee-deep in places and sucked at a tripper's feet like an evil alien force. Pender had once lost a sandal in the primordial slime.

The channel was invisible from the lake. It was just a few feet wide in places and snaked to and fro around the vegetation with no discernable current. Annette led them directly to the waterway easily, a feat that wasn't lost on Gus.

"Could you find this channel?" he asked Pender, admiration in his voice.

"It usually takes me twenty or thirty minutes," said Pender. He left out the part about swearing like a mule skinner as he slogged through the muck, pulling his canoe, looking for the goddamn channel in a sea of silt and plants just tall enough to block your vision.

"Kind of a tenderfoot, aren't you," said Gus. It was a statement, not a question.

"I'm the tenderfoot that kicked your fat ass, bitch."

"Stop it, you two!" Annette ordered. She pulled alongside them. "Try to act like normal human beings. We need to work together, remember?"

The first logjam took twenty minutes to negotiate, Bill spending most of the time in agony. There were four more along the way. Gus and Pender spent much of their time in the water and silt, loading and unloading canoes, pulling them over partly submerged tree branches. Their exertions helped counter the cold water and cool air temperatures.

Annette called for a shore break when they reached the next lake. They were tired and grimy in sweat-soaked shirts and silt-spattered pants as they scrambled ashore. Annette boiled water for soup and distributed high-energy snacks. Gus tried to get Bill in a comfortable position. Pender sprawled on his back and closed his eyes.

"Looks like the old guy's plumb tuckered out," said Gus. Pender smiled.

"I didn't think you'd make it over those last two jams. Did you see me? I hauled the heaviest packs and didn't slip once. Like a high-wire act in the circus!"

"More like a dancing hippopotamus," murmured Pender, eyes still closed.

"For the last time, just stop it," Annette interceded. "When we get back to civilization, you can be as juvenile as you want to be."

When the water was high, the lake they entered was a single smallish lake with two wings connected by a short, narrow channel not much wider or longer than a canoe. It was a memorable spot in Pender's travels because the small waters were surrounded by towering shores. In some places, it was like paddling in a canyon. On overcast days, it could feel like a haunted canyon, especially early and late in the day when forested heights blocked direct sunlight and made the water look inky black.

"This place feels like hell to me," Pender told Annette as they paddled alongside each other.

"Seriously?"

"Edgar Allan Poe would have camped here."

"We have quite a few clients who would like to stop here," said Annette, "but there's only one site right now and it's hard to get to."

"I hope we don't need it." They were all worried about the state of the next portage. Annette scanned the forests around them. "We might be lucky. There's a lot less damage here than where we were."

Pender surveyed the shores, nodding. "The lee sides are completely intact," he said.

"And not so much damage even on the exposed sides."

"So it wasn't just the hills?" asked Pender.

"Derechos don't have constant wind velocity across the front of the system. We had hurricane winds where we were, but maybe here they were only thirty or forty miles per hour."

"And maybe it was sunny and calm on the portage trail," Pender cracked.

"We can hope," said Annette as she slowed her canoe to pull alongside Gus, then Bill.

They reached the portage with Annette wondering what Pender was thinking. They hadn't talked much since the derecho, not about themselves, where they were in their lives. So much they hadn't covered. She wanted to know when he had thought about her over the years and why and what he thought. He'd probably just issue the classic male shrug, a don't-know, don't-care expression, which would be humiliating because she was very aware of when and how she thought about Pender.

Annette stopped them a couple hundred feet from the portage to fill water bottles with fresh water. There was no telling how difficult the next leg of their journey would be.

Pender and Gus unloaded the canoes and tended to Bill while Annette reconnoitered the portage trail, which wound through a notch in the hills. The mouth of the trail was littered with flattened trees, but she was able to move over or around the blowdowns. The middle portion of the trail was almost untouched by the winds, but the last third was strewn with tree hulks, including one massive stack that had to be climbed. It was hard work, but she was able to navigate the mess. She hurried back to the portage area with the news.

They started their first carry with the sun arcing into the western sky at the three o'clock position. Pender and Gus toiled to clear a trail Bill could negotiate. It was a knuckle-scraping process filled with curses and sweat, and although they did what they could to help Bill across the larger logs, nothing could eliminate the pain he endured with each awkward crossing.

Two hundred yards from their objective, they came upon the barrier Annette had described.

"Motherfucker!" Gus exclaimed as he stopped in front of it. The tangle of trees was seven or eight feet high and blocked the narrow trail completely.

Bill drew alongside his friend and shook his head somberly.

"What do you think?" Annette asked Bill.

He swore softly, anticipating the pain. "I don't know. I'll give it a go."

They put him on a line. Pender scrambled to the top of the brush, anchored himself like a belayer in mountain climbing, and wrapped the cord around his waist once. The other end looped around Bill's upper chest, under his arms. If Bill fell, it would save his life, though the pain from his collar-bone and burns from the cord might be worse than dying. Gus climbed with his friend, staying just below him to give him boosts now and then.

When Bill topped the brush, they did the same thing to lower him on the other side. Pender told them to rest while he and Annette got the rest of the gear over.

They were dragging again by the time they finished the first trip. Gus kept up a brave front, but even he was fading. They were a glassy-eyed, rubber-legged crew.

Gus helped Bill find a good place to rest while they hauled the rest of the gear. Annette plucked two jackets from the packs for him to use as blankets, then hustled back for another load. Pender slaked his thirst from a water jug and followed her.

"I'll be along in a minute, li'l fella," Gus called after him. "Leave the heavy stuff to me."

When Pender returned to the other lake, Annette was talking to a slightly built, silver-haired woman. The woman's husband stared out at Twin Lakes, his back to them. Annette looked up the trail as Pender burst out of the brush.

Annette introduced him to Emily and Joe. Emily responded with a warm smile, and Joe never stopped staring out at the lake.

"Emily and Joe are celebrating their fiftieth wedding anniversary this week," explained Annette.

Pender regarded the two of them curiously. She was a tiny woman, not much over five feet tall, maybe not even a hundred pounds. But not frail. Wiry strong. Like Vietnamese soldiers. She had fine, handsome features, a beautiful older woman. Seventies. He nodded and glanced at the man, then at their canoe, a graceful sixteen-footer with two packs neatly stowed aboard.

"Joe has Alzheimer's," Emily said. "He comes and goes from this world. But he's still a good paddler, and he loves it out here. He doesn't talk anymore, so don't be offended."

Pender nodded. "You sure picked a hell of a week to celebrate."

"Oh, we've been paddling in these waters for fifty years. We spent our honeymoon in these lakes. Come back every year, just about. Different times, but this is our favorite time. I guess this is probably our last trip, though." She sighed.

"They were wondering if we could help them through this portage," Annette said.

"It's just too much for me to get Joe through the timber," Emily explained. There was a note of apology in her voice.

"Sure," said Pender. "We have a crew of strong backs."

He retrieved the stringer of half-dead fish, wrapped them in a plastic bag, and stuffed them under the flap of his pack. As he wrestled the pack on his back, Gus emerged from the forest into the portage area. He did a double take when he saw Emily and Joe.

"You leave the tandem for me," he said as he passed by Pender to join Annette and Emily.

Annette was making introductions when Pender left the area, his canoe overhead, and a pack on his back. Seeing how neatly turned out the elderly couple was made him aware of how rough he looked. His clothes dripped with sweat, he reeked, and he hadn't bathed or shaved in several days. His hands and wrists were laced with scrapes and scratches. He was seriously tired, and the day was getting late. Doing one, maybe two more trips on this portage to help Emily and Joe was not going to be fun, and it meant they would be looking for a campsite at dusk.

No good deed goes unpunished.

Pender fought the good fight on his second carry, warding off fatigue as he stepped up and over downfalls, scrambled through forests at the edge of blowdowns, strained to climb slopes, recoiled when the canoe hit an unseen tree branch.

He was making good time until he came to the tall pile of downed wood.

He tried to lean his canoe on end against the brush so he could climb to the top and pull it over, but the canoe slid away as he climbed. He was just setting up for the third attempt when Gus came down the trail.

"Tough one for you, li'l fella?" he boomed. "Don't you worry. Big Gus is here to bail your weenie ass out. You hop on up there and I'll pass things up."

As they worked, Pender thought about what an asshole Gus was. But a very strong one. He had spotted Pender a good ten minutes and still caught up to him. Impressive. He was a motormouth and a mindless idiot, but the guy could paddle and portage. They finished the portage and headed back for a third trip.

Gus caught his second wind. He kept up a steady stream of commentary as they made their way back for their last load, his voice loud and constant. His wilderness adventures. His feats of strength. What a hot babe Emily must have been back when.

"We're gonna have to carry the old guy over that big pile," Gus said. "Maybe the old lady, too. You might be able to handle her. She can't weigh more than a food pack or so. But if you can't, I can carry them both over, no problem." He droned on about his exploits of strength and endurance.

"Hey, Gus," Pender said, finally, "don't you ever shut up? Breathe for a while, okay?"

"You got a big mouth for a little old man. First thing when we get out of here, I'm going to beat the shit out of you."

"If you stop running your mouth for five minutes, I just might let you. Seriously, Gus, you carry on like an old brood hen. Give it a rest."

Gus muttered epithets under his breath but was otherwise silent until they got back to the other lake.

"He gonna be able to climb over all those blowdowns?" Gus asked Emily, nodding toward her husband.

"He'll need help on the big pile," Annette interjected.

"I'd be happy to carry everything if you'd keep that yapping son of a bitch a lake or two away from me," Pender told Annette in a private moment before they started the final trek. "Jesus Christ, the man never shuts up! I mean never! If he ever takes another shot at me, I'm going to bury that hatchet in his mouth."

Annette smiled and patted Pender's hand indulgently. "Be brave, li'l fella.

26

The ragtag group finished portaging shortly after 6 PM, Gus carrying Joe on his back like a father carrying a child in play. His bravado made Pender feel like kicking his ass, but it was all Pender could do to carry a pack and the elderly couple's canoe.

"I'm half man, half bear and meaner than a mountain lion," Gus yelled at the top of his lungs as he reached the beach. "My mama was a wolf and my daddy was a rattle snake, and I can outrun, outfight, outdrink, and outcuss any sorry son of a bitch on this here green earth!"

Gus had been practicing his imitation of the old fur trappers' braggadocio for the whole carry, making Pender fantasize that he was carrying an M-16 on his back and he'd be able to shoot the fucker as soon as they got to the beach. Pender figured the hot air was how Gus summoned energy when fatigue set in, but it was still annoying as hell. Even Annette wore an expression of resignation as the big man cupped his hands and hurled the final words of his monologue across the lake. Emily regarded the man quizzically while her husband, now standing on the ground, seemed completely oblivious, as he had been for the whole portage.

Bill struggled to his feet and joined them for introductions.

Annette, Emily, and Pender had all camped on the lake before, and they huddled together with their maps to plot a strategy for finding a campsite for the night. They expected to find several canoe parties on the lake because they were getting close to the perimeter of the park where most people camped and fished. They broke up and headed for the canoes just as Gus was screaming to the lake that he was hungry enough to eat a bear.

"And I'm tired enough to feed you to one," said Pender.

They checked the campsites on the south half of the lake first. One was littered with downed trees and occupied by two fishermen who had miraculously escaped harm. The second was occupied by four fishermen. One of their tents had been crushed by a falling tree, leaving one man with a bad head injury, the other with just scrapes and bruises. The second tent and the men in it were unharmed but shaken. The group was low on food and scared.

"None of us are getting out of here, not for a long time," their leader told Annette. "You can't get a hundred yards on the portage into Pickerel."

"Don't you worry," Gus yelled to the man. "We'll get you out of here tomorrow. Ain't no trail in the world that can hold us back!"

Annette cut him off with a hand gesture, polite but pointed, and spoke to the man. "With a little luck, visibility will be better tomorrow and we'll see some aircraft, maybe a medevac, maybe some people dropped in to clear trails." She sounded more convincing than she felt. The man nodded appreciatively.

"We're going to find a campsite," Annette told them, "Then I'll come back with some ibuprofen and anything else we have that might help your injured party. If we bring you some fish, can you cook them?"

The leader of the group nodded.

"Let's give them the fish we've got with us," Pender said to Annette. "I know this lake pretty well. We can camp on the other side of this point and pick up bass on the north end of the lake. I bet my fat-ass fishing buddy back there"—he gestured to Gus in the stern—"can catch four or five in a half hour or so."

Annette compromised. She gave the campers the big pike, and they checked the other two campsites near the portage trail to Pickerel Lake. They were occupied by trippers who had been heading south into the park when the derecho hit. The sites were devastated, but the trippers suffered only minor damage to their gear and planned to head south in the morning, undaunted by their experiences in the storm.

It was a smallish lake, about three kilometers long north to south. Its north shore was a featureless bay with a rocky rubble bottom and acres of shallow water. It faced south, so it caught a full day of southern sun in the spring, which, combined with the rubble bottom, made it a magnet for spawning bass in May and early June. The lake's south bay contained most of the established campsites and the trail to Pickerel Lake, the last trail they would have to portage to get to French Lake.

As they paddled into the north bay, Pender hoped his fishing luck would hold and that his old campsite was still intact.

And he hoped they would have a night of rest. They were a tired and aching group, even motormouth Gus. Even Annette.

The derecho had been capricious in its distribution of wreckage. The surrounding forest had been mangled by the winds, but Pender's primitive campsite had been spared by a matter of ten yards or so. Still, it didn't look like much. The beach below the site was overgrown with reeds and brush. Grass and woody plants littered the shoreline, and knee-high grass and brush covered much of the campsite. Rocks that had once formed the fire ring were strewn like rubble throughout the area. It was a dreary-looking place for a tired band at the end of a long day, but Annette let no one dwell on it. She put the able-bodied to work immediately, rebuilding the fire ring, unloading boats, and setting up camp.

When others began erecting tents, Pender and Gus went out to fish. As they launched the canoe, Chaos leaped into the middle of the boat and lay down, tongue out, face smiling. Pender started to order him out, then thought the better of it.

"If that crazy bastard snarfs down a fish, I'm going to kill him right then and there," said Gus, like he was half kidding.

"If you let him snarf down a fish, I'll hammer your fat ass flat," said Pender. He forced a small smile to take the edge off. Sort of.

It was twilight when they returned to camp with three more bass, filleted and skinned. The group was ravenous and exhausted, but there was still more work to be done. Annette and Gus took medicine to the injured campers. By the time they returned, Pender and Emily had a savory soup heating on the fire, fish filets ready for sautéing, and enough firewood to take the chill off the night and the next morning.

"Bill says you're a fabulous chef," Emily said as Pender worked the filets. "Big Gus, too."

"Really? Gus said something nice about me? Stop the presses, Lord!" Even Bill, sitting nearby, smiled.

Annette and Gus returned just as herb-laced aromas from Pender's frying pan filled the air like a Christmas promise. Chaos walked to the fireplace and stood, drooling. Gradually, the other paddlers made their way to the campfire area, drawn by the fragrance emanating from Pender's skillet.

Gus and Annette joined the group, everyone sitting on rocks and logs near the fire, watching Pender cook. To fill the hungry silence, Emily reminisced about how she and Joe drove the thousand miles to Quetico on their honeymoon fifty years ago, over a newly completed road, going to a place they knew nothing about, finding a wilderness paradise.

"It was like a dream," said Emily. "So we kept coming back every summer because there just wasn't any other place on earth we wanted to see more."

"I know how that goes," said Annette in a gentle voice.

"Usually we'd make it a two-week vacation and drive three or four days each way so we could see some of the other parts of Ontario. It's such a big province, you know. Toronto is more than a thousand miles from Quetico . . ."

Her voice trailed off, Emily lost in a flood of images from a half century of warm memories. Pender could feel what she was feeling, could taste the bittersweet moment, so much to be glad for, so much to miss in a life that might never come back to this place again.

Their reverie ended when the filets and chowder were ready to serve.

Dinner had a festive air despite the trials and tribulations of the day and the ones that lay ahead. The campfire chatter died when the meal was served, then revived a few minutes later as people finished eating.

"Li'l fella, I gotta hand it to you," said Gus. "You sure can cook."

"Hungry as we were—" Pender stopped himself from making a joke. "Thanks," he said.

After they finished the meal cleanup, Annette gathered the group again and shared the bad news, bit by bit.

"Gus and I visited the other two camps, and the news isn't good," she said. "The man with the head injury . . . it's a serious injury. He can barely walk to the latrine, and he's in great pain. He's going to have to be carried over the portage, which is supposedly impassible even for healthy people.

"The people in the other campsite are okay except for some bruises and scrapes, but their canoe is completely demolished, which means tomorrow we're going to try to portage out to Pickerel with ten people, two solo canoes and three tandems, and God knows how many packs."

Gus started to say something, but Annette raised her hand for a moment more of silence.

"There's more. We're low on food. The people over by the portage trail were scheduled to go out today, so they only have scraps left. We have maybe two days' supply for six people, starvation rations for ten. We won't get fishing time tomorrow. And we don't know if we can get through to Pickerel."

Gus could stay silent no longer. "We'll get through, if I have to carry every canoe, every pack, and every person myself," he bellowed. "I promise you, we'll make it. I don't care how high those trees are stacked . . ." he droned on, an adrenaline-hopped jock back in the halftime locker room of his high school glory.

When Gus finally shut up, Pender stood. "Let's start the day with a group of able-bodied people breaking trail, just carrying packs and saws and hatchets. We need to keep one canoe on this lake where an aircraft can see it. Maybe we'll get lucky and get a medevac for Bill and the guy at the other campsite."

"Good thinking," said Annette. "If we can get through to the other side with packs, we can figure out how we're going to handle the canoes and we can start sending other people with packs. Maybe the paddlers here can catch a fish or two while they watch for planes."

There were nods and oral consents all around the campfire.

"By the way," said Annette, "the people Gus and I visited said there's one more camp on this lake, so we might be joined by some more people in the morning."

"And don't expect them to be helpful," said Gus. "They didn't bother helping anyone all day. They were out fishing and sightseeing and checked out the portage, but they didn't even wave at the people in the camps."

Gradually, quiet overtook them—six people huddled around a crackling fire, not quite ready to retire to their tents, too tired to carry on a long conversation. Pender leaned against Annette, one arm around her waist pulling their bodies close together, enjoying the warmth.

"This is nice," said Annette. "Even after all we've been through and everything we will certainly face tomorrow, this is really nice."

Pender murmured his agreement. "If only we had another bottle of that Cab left, it would be perfect."

Gus snickered at Pender. "Wine is a pussy drink. I bet you pack cute little wineglasses and go, 'Oh what a lovely bouquet!' If you were any kind of man, you'd drink beer. Wine is for liberal wimps. Beer's a man's drink!"

"All the beer drinkers I knew were big, fat, draft-dodging cowards."

"Fuck you, Pender."

"Actually, I drink beer," Annette interjected. "My daughter and I split one every couple of nights. It tastes good after a long day, looking out at the lake and the stars. I like wine, too, but it's really expensive here."

Emily nodded. "We used to have wine regularly. I loved it, the different flavors and varieties. We bought wines from British Columbia, California, Chile, France, Australia. It was like being an armchair traveler. Sometimes we'd talk about the region the wine came from. Joe read a lot. He liked to research things. But we cut out alcohol when he was diagnosed."

They talked about wine and beer and perfect meals and beverages until fatigue overtook them all. They doused the fire and retired to their tents.

Annette and Pender pushed their sleeping pads together and slept under the same sleeping bag, their bodies spooned.

"Emily and Joe are something, aren't they?" Annette murmured.

"Mmm," Pender mumbled. "She reminds me of you."

Annette was thinking the same thing, except that Emily had always had someone. She fell into a deep sleep, dreaming worried dreams. Seeing the injured man in the other camp, his face contorted in pain. Feeling the dull, aching pain in his head, seeing him die on the portage to Pickerel, seeing the grief-stricken faces of his wife and children. She dreamed that people blamed her for his death and her business failed in the echoes of the tragedy. She was left trying to find a way to make a living, starting over at sixty years old. Christy having to move to Toronto, or maybe join her father in the States, her granddaughter gradually forgetting who her grandmother was.

Pender couldn't sleep. His back pain screamed through his body and mind, worse when he moved, awful when he didn't. Still, he spooned with Annette for more than an hour because the pleasure of her body against his outweighed the pain. He felt a deep bond with her. In a world built on quicksand and moving geological plates, Annette was warm and solid and true. He would mourn their lost love for as long as he had left. What might have been if only he had been a more mature twenty-one-year-old.

When the discomfort became unbearable, he rolled onto his back, still snug against her, and let his mind wander back to other painful times in his life, moments of anguish flashing into his memory like a slide show on fast-forward. Until he got to the all-night fire fight near Cu Chi. He hadn't thought of it in years.

It was a rare moment in the shadow war when a company-size NVA force was caught in open terrain, nowhere to run, no cover, fighting like demons. An endless night of muzzle flashes and the murderous zipping sound of bullets in the air, of streaking tracers, of nightmare screams, of thumping noises and dirt flying as bullets burrowed into the earth around him and rocket-propelled grenades exploded and flashed all over the battlefield. Then the relays of Cobra gunships rushing overhead like fire-breathing insects, their rotors throbbing like cannon fire, showering the desperate NVA soldiers below in a torrent of bullets, firing rockets that exploded with such violence Pender could feel vibrations in his chest as if he'd been hit by a powerful boxer. Firing his M-16 all night, aiming at muzzle flashes, rolling below cover, reloading, waiting for the responding fire to end, then repeating the cycle. Getting resupplied time after time. Shooting all night, until the first glimmer of morning light brought proof that every single NVA soldier was dead, many of them shot multiple times.

Flying back to base tired and filthy, numb from the carnage. He had never seen so many dead bodies, so many ugly deaths. Had never been so physically and spiritually exhausted. All he wanted was to take a shower and go to bed, but after the shower he decided to have a quick breakfast. Walking to the mess hall, hearing a faint shout, he turned and saw a small man in bright green fatigues yelling and waving at him. He waved back, continued on his way. Suddenly confronted by an angry man huffing from running to catch up, his face as red as a Santa suit, his fatigues as green as a Christmas tree. Bright green fatigues, the mark of a new arrival. Just off the jet and fully in command. A first lieutenant, Pender noted dimly, a first lieutenant who was screaming.

"Did you hear me?" the man yelled in his best command voice. Pender shook his head no.

"You're walking on my track!" The man screamed it as though Pender were walking on the bodies of women and children.

Pender looked about himself in disbelief. Track? Had he stumbled into some new reality? Was he in a dream? All he could see was the same dusty, featureless rock surface that had been there since the area had been deforested in clouds of Agent Orange.

"What track?" he asked.

"My track, Sergeant Pender!" the little man thundered, staring at the name on Pender's shirt. He gestured to the empty area again and Pender finally saw four traffic cones marking the corners of a square track of maybe a quarter mile.

"Right," said Pender. He took a last look at the man, figuring it all out. He was new in-country, right out of OCS, full of the autocratic superiority the army pounded into its junior officers. Assigned to some kind of cushy role that involved making a track out of poisoned ground so that people could play games in the middle of a fucking, goddamn war zone. Thinking that this was beyond insane, especially because this newbie lieutenant was absolutely dead fucking serious. The thought of it sapped all Pender's strength. He could not reply, so he just turned and walked toward the mess hall again.

"Goddammit, soldier!" the lieutenant screamed. "You don't just walk away from a superior officer!"

Pender turned, alarm bells ringing somewhere deep in his mind that he could get in real trouble with this asshole. "What do I do?"

The lieutenant sputtered for a moment, realizing he hadn't ordered Pender to do anything but knowing he was being dis-respected.

"You salute your superior officer!" he said finally.

"Oh, right," said Pender, flashing a sloppy, limp-handed salute, then turning and heading for the mess hall.

The lieutenant got in his face again, livid, demanding to know Pender's unit and his commanding officer, promising to make that officer aware of his disrespectful conduct, threatening Pender that if he ever walked on this track again, he'd be arrested. Pender shook his head in disbelief and started to walk again, half turning to flash another insulting salute. His captain said later that he wanted to punch the little bastard himself when he listened to the lieutenant's story, that this whole fucking war was a bad dream being stage-managed by morons and cowards but that we all had to keep our wits and walk out of this thing alive. The captain was a no-bullshit good guy. Got zapped a month later *by a sniper during a patrol. And that sniveling little basecamp louie probably went home with a medal for track building and a hundred bullshit stories of battlefield heroics.*

Annette stirred and twitched, then her body jerked and she breathed deeply, sighed a painful sigh, then sat bolt upright, twisting her torso from left to right trying to coax light from the inky blackness of her world, trying to discover where she was. She reached out with her hands, finding the wall of the tent on one side, Pender and Chaos on the other.

"Name's Pender," Pender joked.

Annette exhaled in relief. "Bad dreams." She said it and lay back down as though nothing had happened.

"Do you want to talk about them?"

"No. I'd like to talk about us sometime. But not in the middle of the night."

"Okay, but give me a hint. How would that start?"

"Huh?"

"What would we be talking about when we talk about us?"

"I just want to know if we've got a future together or if this is it. A fun week in the park and goodbye, see you in the next life."

"Am I still invited to stop by when we get to French Lake?"

"Of course, but I'm not begging you. I just want to know if you're interested."

"Yes. I am. Scared shitless, but interested."

"What are you afraid of?"

"What your daughter will think of me. Meeting your old boyfriend, your friends and neighbors. People have found reasons to dislike me all my life, and, generally, I don't care. But if the people around you don't like me, that puts us both in a tough position."

"Deep down inside, Big Chief Warmonger has the heart of a hummingbird. Take a chance, li'l fella."

"Very funny. Plus, what if everything else is great but I just can't hack living in a small town that spends four months a year in the dark with below-zero temperatures and the best theater is the annual high school play?"

"We don't have an annual high school play. Jesus, our sports teams have to travel hundreds of miles to get to games. The nearest movie theater is 150 kilometers away. Our television stinks, too. You make it through the winter by being busy and talking to people."

"Can we get away with necking in the Fort Frances movie theater?"

"Cute. Let's shut up and get some sleep now, okay?"

Pender shifted his body against hers, put a hand on her hip, and nuzzled the back of her neck with his lips. Much better than sleeping, he thought. Though he hadn't slept well in so long he wasn't sure what that was like.

27

Heavy footsteps outside the tent startled Pender from his shallow half sleep.

"Pender!" Gus called in a stage whisper, trying to be loud and soft at the same time. "C'mon!"

"Just a sec," Pender whispered back. He threw his clothes out of the tent, then crawled out and began dressing. "What's up?"

"Let's go fishing. Maybe we can nail something for breakfast."

Pender groaned. "Jesus Christ." But when he thought about it, he had to concede it was a good idea.

They fished the structure off the steep drops west of the peninsula they occupied, then the shores of an island across the bay. For once, Gus was quiet. As the gray essence of predawn crept over the horizon, the only sounds Pender could hear were the drops from his paddle drizzling into the water and the line unwinding from Gus's reel as he cast. It was enchanting.

Ten minutes after Pender would have given up, Gus caught a chunky northern pike. They filleted it on the rocks of the western shore and paddled back to camp as the hidden sun crept over the horizon and gave birth to a dim, gray morning.

"Are you two going steady now?" Annette teased as they returned.

Pender smiled and placed the foil-wrapped pike filet in her hands. "It was love at first bite," he said.

Annette and Emily had taken down the tents, rolled the sleeping pads, and stuffed the sleeping bags in their sacks. Everything was ready to throw into packs and go. They were boiling water for coffee and oatmeal. Emily took the filets and promised to have a Quetico breakfast ready in twenty minutes. Her announcement drew murmurs of approval around the camp.

They discussed portage tactics as they ate. Emily and Joe would stay out on the lake to flag any rescue planes that might come by while Annette, Pender and Gus, and the able-bodied base campers would try to carve a trail to Pickerel Lake.

Gus had no doubt they'd make it. "I don't care how many trees are down or how high they're stacked, we're going through. Right, li'l fella?" He playfully poked Pender with his elbow.

"Yay rah, big dude," Pender responded dryly.

The paddlers from the other two camps were waiting for them at the portage. The injured man sat against an incline like a man in an easy chair, his pain debilitating. Ibuprofen helped a little, but they were saving it for the nights.

"He needs to keep cold compresses on it," said Pender. "We need to keep the swelling down, and that's the only thing we can do to help."

"Can he walk?" Annette asked.

"Not really," said his paddling partner. "The pain gets worse, and he has problems with balance."

"We're going to have to carry him out of here," Annette said. She instructed the man on how to gather poles for a travois while the first party of able-bodied trippers tried to make the portage to Pickerel Lake.

Pender gestured to the darkening western sky. "Good news," he said sarcastically. "Looks like we're going to get wet today."

In normal times, the trail to Pickerel was as close to a walk in the park as any trail in Quetico. It was short, wide, and well trodden, one of the most heavily used trails in the park. Though it lacked wilderness solitude, it was a bucolic hike with its green, laid-back ambience and a soft pine scent that hung in the air.

But these were not normal times.

A few steps into the tree line revealed a savaged landscape. Fallen trees crisscrossed the trail like giant railroad ties. In the distance, Pender could see a virtual wall of downed timber. It wasn't a trail so much as a nightmare.

"This won't be like any other portage I've been on," Pender mumbled.

Annette nodded and stared ahead. Only Gus was unfazed. "Think positive," he rumbled.

Pender groaned.

"Aw, c'mon, Pender," said Gus. "We got this! You and me. Let's get to it!"

Gus moved confidently to the first blowdown and hacked away branches for a step-over. Pender followed and trimmed the next log, the others taking their turns as the party moved on. They made slow, steady progress until they got to the first great wall, a tangle of tree hulks rising six feet high, crossing the trail like a dam. Gus and the two campers looked for ways around it while Pender scaled it, dropped his pack on the other side, and climbed back.

Twenty minutes later, they knew that the only way past the pile was over it, Pender warning that the pile itself wasn't especially solid. Gus started scrambling up the pile to test it, Annette demanding that he take his time, test each log before putting his weight on it, admonishing him that if he broke a leg, the party was doomed.

"I believe she'd kick my ass if I objected," Gus said when they got to the other side.

"Bet on it, big dude," Pender answered. "And I couldn't help you. She's too tough for me."

"Hey, I thought you were a big brave war hero."

"Not me."

"Annette said you won a bunch of medals in 'Nam." The two men followed Annette through the carnage on the trail, Pender trying not to grunt with each step.

"Everybody got medals," said Pender. "It was just politics."

They reached another barrier of downed trees. Pender scaled it and offered Gus a hand up, but the big man scrambled up the pile with the agility of a gymnast. Pender was impressed, even if he didn't want to be.

"So what did you get? Medals, I mean." Gus kept talking as they descended the other side.

"It was all bullshit."

"Did you kill anyone?"

"I tried to."

"You didn't keep notches on your rifle or make marks on your helmet or something?"

"Everything happened at night. I never saw anybody I shot at."

"I never served," Gus said. "I feel like I missed something."

"All you missed was a circle jerk."

"Don't you feel kind of proud that you served? In a war?"

"The smart guys stayed home. Those people who died there or came home junkies? Their lives were wasted. And no one back here gave a shit except maybe their families."

"Made you tough, though. Right? How many guys your age go solo up here?"

"Yeah, it made me a mean motherfucker."

As they moved over, around, and under the fallen trees of a shattered forest, a light rain started. The sky was dark and low.

"No planes today," Annette muttered. "We better put on rain gear. We won't have time to get a fire going if we get wet."

It took them an hour to get to Pickerel Lake, stopping every few steps to clear branches from downed trees or mark a trail around them. The three-hundred-yard portage doubled in length from the twists and turns, and its physical demands skyrocketed with the constant climbing and scrambling. When they got to Pickerel, they were wet and tired.

Pender's shoulders felt like they were being sliced from his body by the straps of his pack. His lower back became more painful with each passing hour. Carrying the heaviest packs on the first crossing might not have been the best idea, since they spent a lot of time standing and waiting for the trail to be cleared, multiplying the amount of time everyone had to carry the heaviest packs they had.

Pender tried not to think about the fact that they were going to be doing this all day, that carrying the canoes was

going to be a pure bitch and carrying the injured trippers
was going to be worse. If he thought about it, he would
have wondered how he could possibly make it, since he was
seeing stars already. He wondered if he'd still be welcome at
Annette's place if he were seriously injured, unable to help
out with things. What would her daughter think of an old
crippled guy barely able to get out of bed?

All things considered, it would be a lot easier if one of
these trees fell on him, he thought.

———————

Annette surveyed the portaging crew as they took a break
before heading back for the next load. The base campers
were bushed but kind of impressed with themselves. They
were middle-aged, overweight men who came here to fish and
enjoy kumbaya evenings around a campfire. They had just
completed a daunting portage, far more arduous than anything
they had tried before. They had acquitted themselves well,
and they had a right to feel good about it. But pretty soon
they'd realize that they would need to do it again and again
and again. Their shoulders would ache, their neck muscles
would want to spasm, and their legs would turn to jelly. And
with every shaky step they took, they would know that they
would somehow have to do it again.

Gus was Gus. Talking constantly, always ready to break
trail, haul the heaviest pack. He'd be happy to make this
portage five times just to test himself and get some bragging
rights. Pender called him fat, but really the man was big.
There was a difference. Gus was big and strong. As in very,
very strong. Like an ox that could climb. And talk. The man
could talk.

Annette watched Gus talking to Pender, the two of them looking out on the bay, Gus gesturing and pointing. She thought it was probably a good thing that Pender had used his hatchet when Gus charged him. It would have been a massacre otherwise. It was also a good thing Pender didn't cripple the big man, because their only chance of completing this portage today with their injured people depended on Gus.

She worried about Pender. He was quieter than usual, and his eyes looked deeply fatigued. On the trail, the liquid ease of his movement had given way to plodding steps, his left leg dragging a little. He still scrambled over debris piles, but his agility had declined.

Annette herself was somewhere between Gus and Pender on the physical readiness scale. She was in good shape, but she was sixty years old and her body responded to heavy loads much differently than it did when she was thirty or forty. Her legs were burning, and her shoulders were sore. No matter. She would do this portage as many times as she had to. Her worry was time. She wanted to get everyone to Pickerel by early afternoon so they could make a run for French Lake and get the injured people to the hospital.

As they headed back for the next load, the rain stopped, the clouds passed, and the sun emerged. The clear skies brought heat and humidity. The hikers shed their rain gear, then long-sleeved outer layers as they trekked. When they reached the other lake, humid air hung thick and heavy over the lakes and forests. The distant drone of a single-engine airplane made everyone forget the monotony of the morning. Necks craned skyward, eager hands grasped paddles and articles of clothing to wave, but the plane never came into view, passing far to the east on its way south.

Annette tried to ignore her disappointment. It would have been a huge relief to get their injured people evacuated. She made herself focus on their immediate circumstance. Chaos blasted into her deliberations, charging toward the water, barking crazily, jumping up and down. A canoe carrying two paddlers approached the portage. The woman in the bow stopped paddling and stared in horror at the dog's wild celebration. Pender moved stiffly to the water's edge and corralled Chaos with a string of curses, followed by a command to sit. Chaos sat sheepishly but couldn't suppress the urge to wag his tail. His tongue lolled out of one side of his mouth, and his body trembled as the canoeists came to shore.

The woman disembarked with regal dignity, a day pack slung over one arm like a purse. People on the beach stopped what they were doing to watch her. She wore an all-khaki outfit as crisp and clean and perfectly matched as if she were stepping off a page of the L.L. Bean catalog. She was medium height, fortyish, slender, with shapely brown legs shown off nicely by her form-fitting shorts. Tufts of blonde-highlighted hair spiked out just so from under the brim of her khaki hat, which she wore stylishly pushed back from her forehead. She wore hiking boots so sparkling clean they could pass for new. Her hiking socks were folded over neatly. Her khaki blouse looked as though it had just been picked up from the cleaners, every button buttoned, not a wrinkle in sight, not a drop of sweat anywhere.

Annette watched the woman move up the beach while her husband plunged into thigh-deep water to pull the canoe ashore and begin unpacking it. The trippers and campers on the beach stared in stunned silence as the woman headed for the portage trail, carrying nothing, leaving the packs and canoe to her husband. As the woman passed near, Annette

was jolted by the realization that the woman's shorts actually had a crease in them, like dress pants. Annette scanned
the rest of the group, each person in soiled, sweat-soaked
clothes, the product of days in the bush and hard work in
a survival situation. Sweet Jesus! she thought. Has anyone
ever worn dress khakis in Quetico before? She wasn't sure
she'd ever seen anyone in town wearing dress khakis with a
crease in them.

She became aware that Pender had turned to watch the
woman, and it pissed her off. It was her nightmare coming
true, the male conquest urge being aroused by a city woman
with nice clothes, nice hair, and the strut of a fashion model.
But before she could get really worked up, Chaos gave in to
his baser instincts and bolted from Pender's side like a rogue
missile, bounding for the khaki woman, barking as if a pack
of bears had invaded the beach.

The lady froze, and Pender hustled up the slope to restrain
the dog. First he tried to just tell the dog to cool it, but that
didn't work. Finally he screamed "Goddamnit!" Chaos stopped
barking and sat nervously, his head moving back and forth
from Pender to the woman, tail wagging feverishly.

"He's really friendly." Pender said it with an apologetic
tone that made Annette cringe. Men were so indulgent of
pretentious divas like the khaki woman, she thought.

"I'm sure." The woman had a voice like ice water. She continued on her way without giving Pender or the dog another
thought, passed by Annette as if she weren't there, and disappeared into the trail. The people on the beach slowly resumed
their activities.

"Jesus Christ, Pender, why didn't you just pucker up and
kiss her ass?" said Annette.

Pender blinked. "What?"

"You know 'what.' You ogled that woman like she was doing a striptease or something. Don't you have any pride?"

"I kept my mouth shut because I didn't want to make trouble for you. This park has a leash law, and Chaos isn't on a leash. The least you could do is get off my fucking back."

Annette's fury evaporated in a flash. Pender had seen what she saw, had been as transfixed by the improbability of it as she had been. Her shoulders slumped.

She moved to the gear. Gus and Pender were sorting the packs by weight and bulk, deciding what to carry with each canoe. They had two tandem canoes to portage and the two solo boats belonging to Annette and Pender. Emily and Joe had the third tandem out in the lake on airplane patrol; it would portage on the last trip.

Like the solo boats, Gus and Bill's tandem was an ultra-lightweight Kevlar model and relatively easy to carry. The base campers' tandem would be a challenge; it was a back-breaking seventy-pounder crafted from composite materials—great for paddling in rocks, backbreaking on portages.

"I'm going to haul this beast and a pack," Gus told Annette. "Pender's gonna haul a pack and my boat, and these guys"—he gestured to the three healthy campers—"will haul packs and the two solo boats, and they'll just trade off on the boat carries."

Annette nodded. She wasn't sure Pender was going to make it all the way with pack and boat, but they had an extra man for rotations. As a team, they'd make it. The group would still have a few small packs and paddles to carry on a third trip, and Emily and Joe's canoe, but they should be able to complete the portage in three trips. A minor miracle.

She told Pender and Gus to take charge of the next portage while she constructed the stretchers for the wounded.

"You go right ahead, ma'am," said Gus. "We got this under control."

Annette glanced at Pender, hoping to see some sort of approval, but he turned, took a long slug of water, and then shouldered his load and headed down the trail. She couldn't blame him, but it would have been nice to be forgiven.

———————

Pender was deep in conversation with himself as he felt the dead, aching weight of the pack cutting into his shoulders. Remembered he was already seeing stars on the last portage. Hoisted the forty-five-pound canoe onto his shoulders and thought he'd pass out then and there but didn't.

He cursed Gus and his gung ho bullshit under his breath. He was old enough to be Gus's father, for Christ's sake. He thought about all the times they'd have to stop and relay the canoes over piles of fallen timber. He couldn't imagine handling a third trip with a load. Refused to think about it. Refused to give Gus something to rag him about. He'd go until he couldn't go anymore. Then he'd just curl up and die and be done with it.

"Yo, Pender." Gus's voice echoed through the fog in Pender's mind. "What was that with the scout lady, anyway?"

Pender shrugged. "Guess she doesn't like dogs."

"Probably afraid she's gonna get her cute outfit dirty. Jesus Christ, can you imagine being married to that piece of work?"

Pender followed Gus's gaze back to the beach where the khaki lady's husband was finishing up. He threw on a pack and hoisted their canoe on his shoulders and set out for the trail.

Gus and Pender exchanged glances again. "That's confidence, baby," said Gus. "Doesn't even have to recon the worst trail I've seen in twenty-five years of tripping. Just hit it running with a full load. Hot damn!"

"My money's on stupidity," Pender answered, loading the canoe. "I don't think those two have any idea what they're in for, especially not that poor bastard doing all the work."

"Maybe she's really good in bed."

"No one's that good in bed."

"Spoken like an old man who's over the hill," Gus chuckled.

They fanned out along the trail, struggling with their respective loads, Gus chatting happily the whole way, the others quietly enduring the pain and suffering. Pender focused his mind on things away from his body so he wouldn't think about the ache, wouldn't worry about failing. He thought about Annette, wondered what set her off with the khaki lady. He thought she might have been jealous but couldn't really imagine her being jealous. Thought about how he had never understood women and never would. Thought maybe that's the most knowledge about women he'd ever have.

He thought about the khaki woman, tried to figure where she was coming from. She seemed more like someone who would go bird-watching in Central Park. He could picture her with a butterfly net, standing on the edge of one of the clearings, yelling to her old man, who was shagging butterflies for her, her standing there with a $500 net bought from maybe the Smithsonian catalog or something. What the hell were they doing here? Maybe getting a war story for the next Sierra Club tea party?

Those thoughts got him to the first big pile. Gus arrived a moment later, and the two of them teamed with the base campers to move the canoes over.

28

Gus hollered for everyone to take five and for Pender to come forward.

Pender wove his way through the bodies and canoes to the obstacle. Gus and one of the campers were waiting.

"Thought we'd give you a little break," Gus explained. "Go ahead and take off your pack. I'll pass it up to you in a minute. First, I want to tell you a funny story, because I know you like funny stories, right?"

Pender shrugged, too tired to get into it with Gus.

"So I come hauling ass up here, and, lo and behold, Mr. Yuppie Dude is standing here trying to get his canoe over the pile. Asks if I'd help him because he scratched it up on the last pile doing it himself. So John here"—he pointed to the camper up on top of the brush pile—"and I, we say, 'Sure, we'll give you a hand.' And John goes up there and we send Mr. Yuppie Dude up and over, and then we pass his canoe over to him. He tells John to be careful because the hull's getting scratched. John does his best, the guy takes the canoe, puts it on his shoulders, and walks on down the

trail. Not a word of thanks. No offer to help us. Not a fuckin'
word. Just gets on his horse and leaves.

"Most unthankful person I've met in, what, four or five
days. This guy a relative of yours?"

Pender smiled and shook his head wearily. "Just don't chase
this one around the park for a week, huh?"

"That canoe was near immaculate. You notice that?" Gus
asked.

Pender shook his head no. "But their packs and paddles had
that first-use look. You don't suppose they bought a whole
rig for this trip instead of using an outfitter?"

"I sure as hell wouldn't use my own gear the first time
up here," said Gus. "Not unless I knew what I was doing."

When they got to the next pile, the last one, the tallest of
them, the husband of the khaki lady was nowhere to be seen.

"Pretty good work, him getting over this by himself,"
Pender commented to Gus.

"Deserves a deep-throat blow job, I'd say."

"He'll be lucky to get his owie kissed." Pender grinned.

He knew they were close to Pickerel when Chaos's wild
barks raised him from an imagined conversation he was having
with Annette about why she dressed him down for staring at
the khaki lady and how that would never happen with him,
how it had been Annette from the first time they kissed. And
besides, he was sixty years old, and, like Gus said, he was
way over the hill for girl-watching.

When he reached the beach, he saw Chaos jumping up
and down with that big dog grin on his face, trying to impress
the khaki princess. She was as rigid as a statue, not scared
but very pissed, her face looking like she had a mouthful of
lemon. Pender gritted his teeth. What was it with high-energy
dogs picking dog-hating people to roust?

Her husband was trying to shoo Chaos away, but it wasn't doing any good. You had to scare him or scream like a banshee. The guy didn't have it in him.

Pender put the canoe down and marched toward Chaos, cursing loudly. The dog dropped into a submissive posture like he'd been beaten with a bullwhip, then sat beside Pender, looked him in the eye, and wagged his tail hesitantly. Pender had to stifle a laugh. Chaos read his body language, let his tongue roll out the side of his mouth, and grinned at him.

The woman approached them and stood directly in front of Pender. "We have a very important meeting in the Twin Cities tomorrow. And the day after that, we have a wedding rehearsal to attend. And the day after that, we have a wedding. And two days after that, we have to be in Chicago for a conservation summit. And the week after that—"

"You lead a rich and full life," interrupted Pender. "And I have miles to go before I sleep." He started to move past her, but she stepped into his path.

"My point is," she said, "I have a very full calendar of obligations, and if your wild dog caused me to break a leg or incur a head injury like the poor man back there"—she gestured toward the lake—"it would make me very mad."

"No kidding?"

"Mad enough to take legal action."

Gus had stayed quiet for several minutes, a record that couldn't last. "Lady," he said, "this place is home to wolves and bears. If a friendly dog is going to ruin your life, you really should stick to dude ranches. Whatever you do, don't piss this guy off. He took an ax to me."

"It's true," said Pender. "And if you think I'm bad, I hit him with the ax and he's still walking and talking. Pretty much nonstop."

The woman turned and departed. Gus laughed. "I think she likes the dog a little better now."

They took slugs of water. Pender nodded toward the khaki woman, who was making lunch: peanut butter and jelly sandwiches, some kind of gorp, and red-colored water. He eyed the half loaf of bread sitting on a pack. "You suppose they'll be asking us over for lunch?"

"I think we blew our chance," said Gus.

One of the campers strode over to the couple, said in a conversational tone that it would be nice if they offered to share, given the circumstances and all.

"If we knew we were getting out of here today, we'd be glad to share," the woman replied, loud enough for everyone to hear. "But we really can't be sure of that. Sorry."

Her husband glared at her. She made a face and then offered the camper the bag of gorp.

"Let's get out of here before I shove that food pack up her ass," said Gus.

As they neared the lake, the distinct sound of an airplane engine droned into earshot. It was coming from in front of them, flying south. They caught a glimpse of it just for a moment and knew it was passing over the lake.

Hopes soared for a moment as they listened for evidence it was coming back to evacuate their injured people. But the engine sound droned ever fainter to the south and then was gone.

"Son of a bitch," Gus cursed. "You think Emily and Joe signaled them?"

Pender shrugged. "Who knows? Emily's pretty sharp, but you've only got a minute or so from the time you hear the goddam thing to the time it's gone. If they came in for a bathroom break or had a fish on line or something . . ." he shrugged again.

"You're a cheerful son of a bitch."

"I could have said they crashed."

When they got to the beach, the news was mixed. Emily and Joe had signaled, and the plane had dipped a wing in acknowledgment but had continued south. It had places to go.

There was a brief discussion about whether they should keep going or stay in place and wait for an evacuation.

"I think we have to go for it," said Pender. "We don't know if anyone is coming back today or what the weather will be. If we portage now, we'll have enough time to head for French Lake, and we'll be easy to see on Pickerel. We'll only be out of sight for thirty or forty minutes while we portage."

"He's right," said Gus. "We need to make time. We don't know about the weather. They may not be able to fly in an hour or two. Let's get this done."

Though some still had reservations, the group reached a consensus to make the portage. Annette made two stretchers, one for the injured camper, the other to lift Joe and Bill over the taller piles and carry whichever one needed it most. She assigned three people to each stretcher so one person could rest while two carried. "Gus and Pender and I will take Bill, and you three"—she pointed to the able-bodied campers— "can take John. Emily will haul their canoe."

With that, the ten members of the Quetico Survivors Club, as they were calling themselves, got silently to work. Bill was going to try to walk to the first pile that required scaling. They would lift him over and see how he felt.

They negotiated the first climb, the injured camper going first, then Bill getting on the second stretcher and being lifted up and over by Pender and Gus, then Joe. It looked easier than it was for Pender. When he lifted his end of the stretcher, his vision exploded with stars. Pain fired from his lower back as if he'd been shot. His legs felt watery. Bill's weight felt like a boulder the size of a house. Only the distant, muted rumble of Gus's voice kept him trying. Gus was spitting out a constant flow of that stupid gung ho locker room bullshit that pissed Pender off but also made him want to get the job done so he could tell the stupid jock motherfucker to just for once shut his mouth.

Pender stabilized the stretcher on top of the pile while Gus clambered over to the other side. As he lowered the stretcher to Gus, Pender summoned extra strength by holding his breath. It sent the hydraulic pressure in his circulatory system skyrocketing, which increased his strength for a moment and caused capillaries in his nasal passages to burst, sending trickles of blood dripping down his face. Gus paused as he grasped the bottom end of the stretcher, caught Pender's eye, motioned with one hand across his face for Pender to wipe away the blood. "Remember to breathe," said Gus. One weightlifter to another.

It was a weary group that straggled onto the beach in the early afternoon. Pender and Gus got right to loading the canoes.

"Stop, guys," Annette called to them. "Let's take a twenty-minute break. We need it."

"Time's wasting," said Gus.

"Why twenty minutes?" asked Pender. They both acted a little surly, in a fatigued way.

"Because it's more than fifteen and less than thirty, okay?" They looked at her, confused.

"We need a break," she said. "We're too tired to just start paddling. Twenty minutes is a good recovery time. And twenty minutes one way or the other isn't going to matter. So sit down and drink up."

The two sat against a long, low rock formation, grunting as they squatted down.

"Too bad you assholes squandered those beers you hauled in," said Pender. "Even that awful piss you drink would taste pretty good about now."

"Yeah, but some crazy motherfucker tried to steal that beer. We had to send it home for safekeeping."

Annette listened to their macho man talk, a glib mix of obscenities and insults, which for some insane reason seemed to bond them. This was a side of Pender she had never seen, could not have imagined. She wondered if Rob was like this when he was with just the guys. Of course, Rob was never with just the guys.

She watched Gus and Pender chuckling at each other's inane remarks, realized they were bonding like long-lost brothers. Realized she felt left out. Lonely, actually. A wilderness granny with the weight of the world on her shoulders, responsible for getting all these people out safely, all these people who were friends with each other but not with her.

She knew she was feeling sorry for herself, but it felt right. Her life was a path that led to a dead end.

Pender asked her to join them. He sat himself up straight and moved to one side to make room for her. It hurt him to do so. He winced and tried to swallow it so she wouldn't see, but she saw. How could she say no to that? She sat beside him. He took her hand in his and leaned his head to touch against hers. A breeze sent ripples scattering over the surface of the bay in front of them, followed by another small gust, followed by a continuing breeze, cool and free. It was frosting on a Quetico cake kind of moment—sun, blue skies, placid waters.

The conditions were hypnotic, and the two dozed off, only to be wakened ten minutes later by Gus's voice.

"Yo, sports fans, this is your official weather bulletin. Conditions are changing here in the great northwoods."

Pender noticed the wind first. The stillness of just a minute ago was gone. The breeze was building, enough to cool his wet shirt and bring a chill on a still-pleasant day. He and Annette got to their feet and turned upwind. Low clouds were coming over the ridges west of them.

"What do you think?" Gus asked Annette.

"Impossible to say, but it doesn't look terrible. I'm a little worried about the wind. It's picking up. I think we should go for it, have everyone keep their rain gear handy. If it gets bad, there are a million places to camp on Pickerel, so we should be okay."

Gus nodded. "Be nice to have this wind at our backs, too."

Amen, Pender thought. They had maybe thirty kilometers of paddling ahead of them, with two people who couldn't paddle and two who were close to eighty years old and three others who had already pushed themselves to the max. Pender made the calculations. Thirty kilometers, eighteen miles. Six hours? Five or less if it was just him and Annette and Gus. Yeah, a tailwind would be nice. Hell, one of those derecho blasts would be okay.

The base campers wanted to make for Stanton Bay. "It's much closer," said their leader. "We can be there in two or three hours."

"It's closer," Annette agreed. "But there's no phone there, the trail is going to be as bad as this one was, and the service road to the highway might not be passable for days."

"We could at least check it out. It's only a few miles out of our way."

"It's five or six miles out of our way," Annette corrected the man. "It's three miles in and three miles out, not counting the time to hike up to the parking lot, check the road, then come back down. You're talking three or four hours out of our way."

"What makes you think it's not open?" the camper continued.

"We'd see people out here if it was open. There would be a crew working on this portage right now. It's a busy portage and a main evacuation route. We can make French Lake by nightfall. There's a phone there. We can call for help. If the roads aren't open, we can call for a medevac."

Gus was getting impatient. "We're going to French Lake," he said. "That's it. If you want to go to Stanton, get to it. We're going to French Lake, and we're leaving now."

The campers looked to Pender for help. He shrugged. "When the beauty and the beast say French Lake, it's French Lake."

They put into Pickerel Lake a little after two o'clock.

29

They paddled through the portage bay and then through a spectacular narrows. Annette put Pender in the lead, followed by the campers and Emily and Joe. She and Gus brought up the rear, watching the paddlers in front of them for signs of faltering.

Massive Emerald Island greeted the band at the end of the narrows. Its shores rose like green walls, its towering forests now a tangle of broken and fallen trees on the windward side, but mostly intact on the leeward side.

Pender led the group east, across the south end of Emerald Island, took them slowly through the reef connecting Emerald to another island a hundred yards off its coast. He was tempted to continue due east into one of Pickerel's sprawling archipelagos. They could save a kilometer or so by going through the mass of islands, reefs, and jagged points, but it was easy to become disoriented in the archipelagos, and they would lose more time than they gained if that happened.

Also, the wind was picking up and blowing constantly east-northeast. The long route would get them in the jet stream faster. With the wind at their backs, they would gain a lot of hull speed. Even an additional one or two miles per hour in a canoe made a huge difference—the difference between pulling into French Lake in the late afternoon or in the dark.

Pender took the group due north into the lee of Emerald Island. He wanted to stay in sheltered waters until they could run with the wind. There was already a choppy surf, and the advancing clouds warned that the wind and surf could get worse.

A half kilometer from the island's north end, Pender pivoted his canoe to get a look back at the little flotilla, mainly to see if Annette wanted him to wait. He could see some whitecaps beyond the protection of Emerald Island, and he knew that this could be a fast ride home or a disaster. He wasn't sure if Annette would want them to bunch up for the run or stay spread out.

There was no signal from Annette or Gus. Pender took a long pull of water, checked his map and compass to set his course, and began paddling east-northeast to his first landmark, Lookout Island. When he got to Lookout Island, he'd sight the next visual cue, a low island lying another four kilometers east-northeast, and keep leapfrogging landmarks until they got to French Lake. Another twelve miles, give or take, Pender thought, as he entered the full wind and rough water zone just beyond the shadow of Emerald Island.

Annette watched Pender with growing respect. He was a strong paddler, revived from the ardors of portaging. He made good decisions. She was surprised when he headed north along Emerald Island. Most tired paddlers would have taken their chances with the archipelago. She would have taken Pender's course, especially with the wind building. Running with the wind might actually be faster than trying to quarter it coming out of the archipelago, and it was surely safer for their tired crew.

It was strange, she thought, that he was so reckless and violent in some ways and yet patient and considerate in others. Taking all that crap from the khaki woman so Annette wouldn't get any blowback—this from a guy who punched out his boss and took on Gus. Bonding with that crazy dog. Buddying up with Gus. It was very hard to put those pieces into the same picture.

The base campers were tired but game. Every few minutes, a paddle hitting a gunnel sounded a notice that they were getting heavy-armed, but they stayed with it. Emily and Joe paddled like a well-oiled machine, slow, perfect paddle strokes, perfectly synchronized, their power balanced so the canoe required almost no course correction. Their efficiency let them keep pace with the flotilla without seeming to try. She worried that they might not have the strength to deal with rough weather. They looked so frail.

When Pender paused before going east, she thought about signaling him to wait so she could give everyone a short rest and maybe set towlines. But she didn't want to coddle the group. It could make them dependent and vulnerable if things got bad. Plus, if she were tethered to another boat, she would be very limited in her ability to help anyone else. Better to run for Lookout Island, take a break there, see how everyone was doing, see how the weather was.

When Pender reached Lookout Island, the wind was blowing steady and strong. Pickerel Lake was a waterscape of swelling waves with deep troughs, serious but not yet perilous.

This was the kind of water that kept canoeists sober and focused, Pender thought. It was fairly easy to stay aligned with the waves and to float down the deep swells, like a surfer. But the threat was there. Lose your concentration for a few seconds, and you're swimming.

Pender shivered at the thought. You'd be in the middle of a cold, bottomless lake in stiff winds, your gear sinking to the depths, you trying to self-rescue in water you couldn't handle before your boat filled up with water. Good luck. And even if you somehow got upright, what do you do? It's windy and cold and you're trying to make shore in a boat half filled with water. Maybe the others would rescue you, but that's no panacea either. One more person would overload any of the boats, and so would Chaos.

At the southern end of the island, Pender neatly slid along the waves into the lee waters of its east shore, then turned his canoe west so he could see how the others were coming.

They were fanned out over a few hundred meters, Gus keeping his tandem just behind Emily and Joe, who were paddling calmly in the big water as if they had done it all their lives. Annette was a few yards behind the base campers, who were thrashing a bit but keeping their boat on the right line. Pender decided to wait for them to gather in the lee water.

He waved his paddle in a wide, overhead arc to signal Annette and the others to watch him, and then slipped back into the lee of Lookout Island to wait for them. He took a long drink of water, let Chaos lean over the gunnel and drink from the lake, and then lifted his legs above the gunnels so he could lie back on the pack behind him. It was uncomfortable, but it let him stretch his back for a minute, relieving taut muscles and aching vertebrae.

As the other boats drew near, the drone of an airplane engine came over the north horizon. Pender positioned his boat so he could scan the sky. Out in the big water, Annette was screaming at the base campers to keep paddling.

The floatplane came over the ridges behind them, riding low and slow. They could hear that it was close. They could hear it coming toward them, even though they couldn't see it until it got in front of them.

Pender saw the plane come over the ridgeline. The pilot spotted them and did a slow turn, coming east, a loud, lumbering beast floating on the air currents. The bow paddler in Gus's boat waved his paddle madly at the aircraft as it passed overhead. Pender waved his arms widely as the plane approached his position. It flew a few kilometers farther east, then made a wide, slow circle and came back into the wind to land.

Annette stifled a cheer when the plane dropped softly onto the churning surface of Pickerel Lake. She urged the group to keep paddling hard. There was still plenty of opportunity to capsize. But her sense of relief was like a giddy high. Her injured people would be taken to a hospital. The rest of them could make the run to French Lake in, what, three hours? Maybe less in this wind. Home free!

The pilot stood on one pontoon and opened the door to the seats and storage area as they approached. The aircraft was a de Havilland Beaver, nearly as old as Pender but the Mercedes-Benz of bush planes in canoe country. As the canoes converged on the plane, the wind and surf picked up more intensity. The seaplane pitched and rocked. Sprays of water droplets erupted into the air like monsoon rains. The base campers arrived first, their canoe banging hard against a pontoon, then rubbing and screeching as the plane and canoe rose and fell in the waves. The pilot held the canoe while the base campers helped their injured comrade into the plane. The pilot was yelling to the campers and they were yelling back, but Annette couldn't hear them in the din of the waves and the wind.

The pilot gestured to Gus to raft up, then Annette. She could barely hear him in the wind even though he was shouting.

". . . bad weather . . . wind . . ." She could only catch pieces of what he was saying. She cupped a hand to her ear. He stepped into the first canoe, kneeling, cupped his hands over his mouth like a megaphone.

"This is my last trip. Bad wind, low cloud cover. I can take eight people. No gear. No dogs."

Annette waved Pender to the plane. He had been treading water downwind from the plane. She yelled for the base campers to get on the plane with their comrade.

"Gus, get Bill on board, then help us steady these boats while we get everyone else on board."

"Okay," yelled Gus, "But I'm going to paddle out of here with the li'l fella."

"No!" yelled Annette. "You look after Bill and make sure they send someone to French Lake to pick us up."

"How about you and I paddle out?"

"No. Pender and I are on a date, remember?" She was thinking, this is the roller-coaster part.

Gus nodded, disappointment etched in his face.

As Gus loaded the others onto the plane, Annette, Chaos, and Pender moved into Gus's canoe and tethered the two solo canoes behind it. They threw all the gear in the three canoes and turned the others loose to float in the wind and surf. There would be plenty of time to go searching for the abandoned boats in the days to come.

Annette stationed Pender in the bow and Chaos on a pack in front of her. The waves banged the tethered boats into them and one careened onto the other side of the plane's pontoon, fouling its line. Gus signaled them to sit tight as he freed the line. The pilot finished seating the other passengers and then crouched by Gus on the pontoon, the two of them holding Annette and Pender's canoe steady.

"Run for shore," the pilot yelled. "This is going to get worse!"

Annette and Pender locked eyes. Her raised eyebrows asked him what he wanted to do. He pointed south, toward French Lake. "Why hide when you can fly?" he shouted into the wind. She couldn't hear him, but she knew what he was saying. She felt the same way.

Gus reached out a meaty hand to shake hands with Annette, then moved to the bow and shook hands with Pender. "You're a mean old bastard," he yelled. "I want to be just like you when I grow up." He punched Pender softly in the shoulder and then boarded the plane. The pilot pushed them off and waited for the line of canoes to pass behind the aircraft. Seconds later, the Beaver's engine fired to life, and the pilot slowly moved into the wind and took off.

As the Beaver droned into the ether, Pender was left with the same eerie feeling he had felt the first time a floatplane dropped him in the wilderness. It was a sense of dread mixed with a sense of excitement. The difference was, before he had also felt alone. This time he was with Annette and Chaos, and he felt a bond with both of them.

He hoped he wasn't getting them killed.

Annette was feeling guilty. A good guide would have insisted on paddling for safety, sitting this one out, rolling in tomorrow morning. But the thrill ride into French was too much to resist. How often did you get the chance to run like a bat out of hell in high winds and big surf? This was it. She was sixty years old and life had given her another chance to act like a kid. She just hoped she didn't get Pender and Chaos killed with her exuberance.

30

There was a jolt when they reached the end of the towline and the trailing canoes snapped into line, slowing their momentum. They strained at their paddles to get the line of boats moving faster than the waves, and Annette had a brief, passing doubt that this was going to work. It was one thing to run with the wind in a canoe. It was quite another to do it towing other canoes. How would that work? She checked the short-bladed knife clipped to her flotation vest to make sure it was at the ready. If things got bad, she'd cut the towlines.

Pender was on an adrenaline high. Sitting in the bow, his only job was to supply power and to switch sides when Annette told him to. It would be a mute crossing—he could hear her if she screamed; she wouldn't hear him until they got out of the wind. Ten miles with a howling tailwind. It would be a wilderness thrill ride, the ultimate last outing in Quetico.

Though they had never paddled a tandem canoe together, they found a paddling rhythm quickly and they were very fast. They focused on the navigation landmarks, the direction of the wind, the direction of the waves, the thickening clouds slowly covering them in dim light.

Halfway to their next landmark, Pender glimpsed movement in the corner of his vision. He looked north and sighted
a canoe, light colored, two paddlers hugging the shoreline,
coming out of Stanton Bay, on a southeasterly heading.

"It's the khaki people!" Annette shrieked from the stern.

Pender nodded in agreement. The white canoe, the smallish
figure in the bow seat, the slow hull speed, the bow paddler
stroking daintily, the stern paddler working hard. Had to be
the khaki princess and her loyal subject. They must have gone
for the Stanton Bay take-out, figuring it was much closer than
French Lake, only to find it closed off from the outside world,
just like Annette had predicted.

Annette and Pender watched the canoe with growing
horror. The khaki people were hugging the shoreline, probably feeling safer there, but they were catching the wind
and waves almost broadside and they were getting turbulence
from waves breaking onshore and echoing back. The roiling,
confused water was like being in a drunken boat, unsteady,
unsure of where it's going, unlikely to stay upright.

"They're going to capsize!" Annette yelled.

Pender nodded his agreement again. It was just a question
of when and where.

The white canoe made its way to the tip of the landmass, catching even harsher wind and wave conditions as they
entered the open water of Pickerel Lake. Both paddlers were
digging on the left side of the boat to keep the vessel upright,
and even the bow paddler had picked up the tempo. At the
tip of the landmass, they had a choice to make. They could
shoot over a reef to the lee side of an island, which would
protect them from the waves while they changed their course
to east-northeast—that's what Pender would have done—or
they could paddle across the windward tip of the island with

the wind and waves hitting them at a right angle and execute a hard left turn to the east when they cleared the island. The suicide option, Pender thought.

They chose the suicide option. As they came past the island, the khaki princess was nearly blown over from the force of the wind. Her paddle flew into the air, and she scrabbled wildly for something to grab.

"Go!" screamed Annette. And Pender dug as if he was in a race for his life.

They were a hundred yards from the canoeists and they covered the water with amazing speed, but it was still like watching a train wreck in slow motion. The white canoe floundered out of control. The stern paddler stopped paddling and tried to calm his spouse. She was screaming, her face upright, her hands clinging to the gunnels of the canoe, her body frozen in terror. The current seized the white canoe and rammed it sideways into open water.

The man tried to crawl across the packs to reach his wife, raising the boat's center of gravity into the danger zone. Wind and current rocked the canoe far beyond its point of initial stability, then beyond its secondary stability. The man fell into the water as the canoe lurched, then rolled over, the woman still clinging to the gunnels, wailing.

Annette thought the woman might drown just like that, too terrified to let go, too disoriented to find her way to the surface. She and her husband would both be dealing with the shock of a sudden immersion in icy-cold water, a shock that leaves you unable to breathe for several seconds. You think you're going to die—and if you panic, you probably will.

In the minutes it took for Annette and Pender to reach them, the man surfaced, looked about frantically for his wife, gasped for air, and dove back under. The man surfaced again, ten feet behind the drifting boat, not sure where to look for his wife. Annette steered their canoe to his side, motioned for him to grab the towline, and paddled to the overturned canoe. They pulled alongside, and Pender reached down with one hand to follow the gunnel. He stopped about halfway to the bow, pointed down, and screamed to Annette, "She's underneath. In the air pocket."

Annette nodded her understanding and fought to control their canoe.

The husband caught enough of the exchange to understand his wife was under the boat. He let go of the towline and swam in slogging strokes to the capsized canoe. When he was abreast of Pender, he dived again. Pender could feel the capsized hull roll and shimmy. The woman was resisting her husband's attempts to pull her to safety. The man surfaced again, took a deep breath, dived again. Pender stripped off his flotation vest and looked to Annette, his face questioning.

She knew what he was asking and shook her head no. It was too dangerous. They were in rough seas and hypothermic weather conditions, and they were going to need two able-bodied paddlers to make it out of here.

The man surfaced again, took a breath, then another, dived weakly into the chill. Pender knew the man wasn't going to make it, knew he was going to die trying to save his horrible wife. Pender looked back to Annette apologetically, then rolled over the side of the canoe. The shock of the cold water drove the air from his lungs and made his vision flutter like he was going to pass out. He forced himself to remain calm, waiting for the shock to pass. When he could make his chest work again, he took a lungful of air and dove.

Under the boat, the woman clung to a thwart, her neck arched so her nose was against the hull of the canoe, sucking

trapped air. Her husband was limp behind her, floating in sus-
pension, his arms moving weakly, a man about to die. Pender
grabbed the man's shirt, pulled him clear of the boat and
pushed him toward Annette. Then he grabbed the woman's
nearest hand and wrenched it from the thwart with all his
anger and contempt. She thrashed in panic. He held her free
hand away from anything it could grab and grasped her other
hand, tugging, tugging again, lacking the leverage to break her
death grip. He wanted to leave her there to die, but it wasn't
in him. He kicked his feet up above his head, walked them
up the hull of the canoe until he was upside down, and then
pushed up with all his might. The canoe and the woman's
hand separated in a single violent movement. Pender shot
into the depths headfirst, disoriented, not sure which way was
up. A wave of panic engulfed him. His lungs were exploding.
He choked down the panic and waited for his body to float.
He thought this might be how he was going to die, here and
now. Thought this was not how he wanted to die, so dark
and cold. So dehumanizing.

He started to float, got himself oriented, head up, feet down,
kicked up toward the surface, lunged for the air. Couldn't
hold his breath. He inhaled a moment before breaking the
surface, getting more water than air into his tortured lungs.
Coughed and gasped madly, opposing actions, one reflex to
get water out of his lungs, the other to bring air in. Hacked
and gasped repeatedly, sank into the water, kicked up, hacked
and gasped. Felt light-headed. He sighted Annette struggling
to keep the canoe perpendicular to the waves and keep the
khaki princess from pulling the boat over as she clutched at
the gunnel. The woman's husband was a few yards from the
boat, floating on his back, his arms flopping weakly in an
attempt to reach the canoe. Alive after all, Pender thought.

Pender willed himself to swim to the canoe. He held the gunnel for a moment, coughing and breathing until he had himself under control. Then he pulled the husband to the canoe, asked if he could hold the gunnel for a minute. The man looked at him with unfocused eyes but nodded yes. Pender went to the stern and reeled in the solo canoes. He positioned the first one by the woman, holding it with one hand and extending the other to her.

"Come on!" he yelled. The effort made him cough. He gestured for her to get in the solo canoe. She wouldn't let go of the tandem.

Chaos could stand it no longer. He dived into the water, splashing Pender and the woman. Pender saw it, figured Chaos was going to die out there and there wasn't a goddamn thing he could do about it. He wanted to hit the khaki woman as hard as he could just for putting everyone's life at risk and for being an asshole to boot, but that was just a panic reaction and he swallowed it. He grabbed her nearest hand and pried her fingers from the gunnel, transferred the hand to the gunnel of the solo boat.

"Other hand!" he ordered. But the woman's eyes stared blankly to the heavens, and her knuckles turned white, one hand frozen to one canoe, the other, to the second canoe.

"Motherfucker!" Pender swore. Another coughing fit followed. He reached for the other hand, pried it free, and guided it to the solo boat. She gripped it like a vice, body rigid.

Pender tried to push her up and over the gunnel, into the boat, but she resisted and he could hardly budge her. "Come on, lady!" he yelled, barely able to finish the sentence before the coughing started. She glanced at him for a moment, then heavenward again. "Come on, pull up!"

She gave a tentative tug on the gunnel, hardly rising in the water. Pathetic. But at least she wasn't resisting. Her husband saw what Pender was trying to do, swung weakly to her side and spoke directly into her ear. He nodded to Pender. They both braced with one hand on the gunnel, the other on her butt and pushed her up. She balanced precariously on the gunnel, half in, half out, the canoe rolling radically on its side, inches from capsizing. Pender summoned one final surge of energy and pushed again. It worked. She tumbled into the canoe. She screamed in pain as her body came to rest awkwardly, her feet and legs atop the pack in the forward section of the canoe, her head and shoulders thumping into the seat and the thwart just behind it.

Pender kicked himself higher in the water to look over the gunnel. She was struggling weakly and moving her mouth, not serious about changing her situation. He didn't have the strength to fight her anymore. She'd make it or she wouldn't.

The khaki woman's husband was done, so weak he lost his grip on the canoe and drifted away, thrashing for a moment, finally getting onto his back, floating, waiting for death. Pender and Annette exchanged grimaces, knowing they were deep in the danger zone. He paused beside her, yelling, "If that bitch manages to capsize the boat, cut it loose and don't look back."

Annette stared at him. He was right, of course. There was no saving her if the boat went over. If she tried to tow a capsized boat, her own canoe would capsize. Still, could she just paddle away and let someone drown?

Pender slogged to the husband, grabbed his collar, pulled him back to the tandem canoe. He didn't think about it, just focused on doing what had to be done. He flailed until they were alongside Annette. Chaos bobbed happily at his side, enjoying the swim.

Annette struggled to keep the boat aligned to the waves and in front of the towed boats as Pender pushed the man onto the side of the canoe, then, somehow over the gunnel into the boat, Annette bracing desperately to keep the canoe from rolling over. When the man tumbled into the canoe, Pender used the last of his strength to try to center the man's weight, but he was pinned between a pack and the side of the boat and Pender couldn't budge him. The canoe listed badly to the heavy side, staying up only because of Annette's powerful bracing strokes.

Pender didn't think there was any way to get in the canoe himself. He would have to get to the other side of the canoe and then pull himself in. It seemed as impossible as running a marathon. He let go of the canoe and tried to swim. He sank, his arms unable to respond. He struggled to the surface, put a hand on the gunnel, and looked at Annette, his face apologizing for leaving her like this. He started to let go again, get it over with.

"Try!" Annette screamed at him. It was like she could read his mind. He could see the desperation in her face, and he knew that she loved him and it would be hard for her. He'd give it one last shot.

Slowly, Pender pulled himself hand over hand along the gunnel to the bow, kicking just enough to keep from pulling the canoe over. When he got to the bow, he swung quickly to the other side of the canoe and worked his way to the seat. He looked back at Annette. She nodded, understanding he was going to pull himself up and in. Or try. She counted silently to three, forming the words for the numbers with exaggerated lip movements so he could see the count. On three, she braced hard on the left, and he pulled and kicked himself as high in the air as he could and pulled the boat under himself, landing his upper body on the pack behind the bow seat.

As Pender wriggled the rest of the way on board, the canoe's center of gravity shifted again, and Annette braced to keep them upright. Pender struggled to center the khaki man's weight, finally throwing a pack overboard to make space, his mind registering a sad farewell to the last of their food and the gear that had served him faithfully and well for many years.

The canoe was still badly out of balance. Pender crawled to the second pack, heaved it over the side, and then tried to center the khaki man, a limp, helpless form huddled against one side of the canoe, his feet and legs hanging on the gunnel. Pender moved him into the middle of the canoe and pushed him several feet toward Annette. He crawled back to the bow, looking around for Chaos, hoping to pull the dog in before he got in the confined space of the bow seat, where it would be too dangerous to deal with a sixty-pound dog. The dog was swimming gaily in a wide arc around the boat, a hundred feet away, oblivious to the crisis and to the fact that they were a good kilometer from any kind of land.

Tears streamed down Annette's face. "Paddle!" she screamed. Pender nodded. She couldn't hold their position anymore. They had to paddle or die. They would have to let Chaos fend for himself. It was a miracle she had kept them upright this long. It had been a bad trade, the surly yuppies for a great dog.

Pender tottered into the bow seat, his body not working right, every movement stiff and slow. He picked up his paddle. His hands cramped. He fought the pain, coughed, flexed his hands, made himself grip and stroke. His teeth chattered, his back ached, his arms felt like lead weights hanging from his old wrinkled body. His vision was wavy and narrowing, the

edges of his sight turning to black curtains. His body was shut-
ting down. In a minute, Annette was going to be on her own.
Motherfucker, Pender swore to himself. All for the sake of
two worthless, self-centered yuppie motherfuckers who should
have been shot. Pender paddled. He would go until he passed
out. That was the best he could do for Annette. He stroked
once, twice, a third time. Saw something at the edge of his
tunnel vision, turned, saw Chaos swimming alongside like a
big yellow otter, a grin on his face, a good-faith expression
that his canoe buddy would bring him aboard. Pender stopped
paddling, reached over the side, grabbed the nape of Chaos's
neck. His hand cramped but he squeezed anyway, pulled as
hard as he could, keeping his weight centered on the seat.

It was a horrible effort, weak as a baby. He barely got
Chaos's head to lap level and the dog's weight was pulling
him back into the lake. Pender was powerless to prevent it,
and he knew his next effort would be even less. Motherfucker.

But Chaos wanted back on board. His front paws clawed at
Pender's thigh, and he paddled with his rear feet and scratched
and scrambled with his front ones until he sat on Pender's
lap. It would have been a hilarious moment if the situation
weren't so dire, the big yellow dog sitting on the lap of the
bow paddler in the middle of a roiling sea, people fighting
for their lives. But Pender didn't get the humor of it at all,
just the menace of an imminent capsize.

He leaned to one side, kept his butt centered on the seat,
and threw Chaos backward on the other side. The dog flew
ass-first onto the feet and legs of the khaki man, who was
oblivious. Chaos scrambled to his feet, looked around, saw
Annette swearing at him, shook water from his coat, and lay
down between the yuppie man's calves.

Pender could hardly lift his paddle, but his vision was wider. The struggle had gotten his heart pumping. The sense of cold came back. His teeth chattered and he figured his body would lock up pretty soon, but he thought maybe he could stay conscious long enough to get them to Pickerel River, the narrow waterway that wound through the bog separating Pickerel from French Lake. After that, it would be okay if he died. Annette could make the last few kilometers on her own.

He hoped she got home safely.

31

Pender could no longer keep a steady paddling cadence. He could barely lift the paddle from the water at the end of the stroke. He labored to bring the blade forward and splashed it into the water on his fore-stroke, like a beaver tail slapping the water.

Annette thought about having him stop, but the effort was keeping him warm, and as anemic as his paddling strokes were, they helped a little.

She tried to make time. She paddled at a driving pace, switching sides when the wind and waves dictated it—three or four strokes on the right, correcting stroke on the left, two or three more left strokes, correcting stroke on the right.

Despite the loss of paddling power, they were flying across Pickerel Lake, pushed by a strong wind with occasional shirt-flapping gusts. Annette figured their speed for something around six miles per hour. Compared to maybe three or four with two healthy paddlers in still winds and seas. Yet their progress seemed agonizingly slow and, the slower she felt, the faster her mind raced. Should she run for shore? Minutes after they started paddling again, they passed the low island

Pender had sighted for a landmark. It was the last place on Pickerel that Annette knew had an easily accessible campsite. The khaki woman in the solo boat twenty feet behind her had stopped moaning, but she would be freezing cold now, or in shock, or both.

The woman's husband was sprawled in front of Annette, passed out, his body positioned under a thwart and the canoe yoke. He was in bad shape—blue lips, occasional shakes, passing in and out of consciousness. He was hypothermic or close to it. And Pender worked the paddle like a dying man, barely able to stay upright.

Should she get them to shore? Pitch a tent, pull out sleeping bags? Get a fire going?

She started to course-correct for the island and changed her mind. Did they even have a tent in any of the packs that were left? Did they have sleeping bags? Did they have food? Pender had jettisoned the only pack she knew had food in it and the gear pack that had their tents in it. Just getting these people warm might not save them. They needed calories, she thought.

They were seven miles from French Lake. Annette tried to calculate the travel time. At five miles per hour, an hour and a half. At six miles per hour, an hour and minutes. If she went for the island, it would take ten minutes to get there, ten more to get everyone on land, maybe twenty, another twenty minutes to off load the packs and find a tent and sleeping bags. If they had a tent and sleeping bags. Another ten minutes to erect the tent. Another ten to inflate pads—if they had pads. Twenty minutes to find wood and start a fire. About the same amount of time as continuing on to French Lake. Plus they'd probably be on the island without food.

She focused on French Lake. She prayed someone would be there to put the sick and ailing in warm vehicles, whisk them off to Atikokan General, put hot fluids in them, a hot meal. God help us if no one's there, she thought. She would have dead people on her conscience. She just didn't know which of them would die. Maybe they all would. How would she deal with that? How could she deal with losing Pender? Not now, she thought, not after all this. They had waited a lifetime.

Thirty minutes later, she could see the two arms of land hooking across the east end of Pickerel. The one from the north stretched like a long, narrow pincer, low and flat, almost to the opposite shore. The one from the south a short, blunt point, a landmark called The Pines. Almost home, she thought. She could see the narrow passage between the points into the east bay, could visualize the quick two-kilometer crossing to the bog that marked the path of the Pickerel River. She could visualize the placid, twisting waterway ending in French Lake.

She checked the khaki man again. He was still breathing, still moving a little now and then. He was still alive. Who knew for how long? Pender was on the edge. His paddling rate had descended into a weak pantomime, seconds elapsing between strokes, his pull on the blade so feeble it no longer affected the boat.

As Annette thought it, Pender slumped headfirst toward the prow, jolting to a stop when his waist could bend no further. The paddle slipped from his grasp, splashed into the lake, and floated into Annette's outstretched hand as the canoe overtook it. She wanted desperately to hold him and warm him and tell him how much she loved him. But there wasn't time. They had to get to the take-out, or people would start dying.

Pender pushed himself erect with an effort that sapped his last reservoir of strength. He tried to hold himself in a sitting position, but his body had shut down. His vision turned to blackness, and he lost all feeling in his body. He could not tell up from down, could no longer hear or think or will his body to do anything. He fell backward, over the thwart behind his seat, landing on Chaos, who yelped with surprise. His back seemed impossibly arched over the thwart, Annette fearing a fracture. Seconds later, he groaned loud enough for her to hear, a painful groan, and lifted his feet onto the seat. He pushed his torso backward in the boat until his head hit the yuppie man's body, his back flat on the bottom of the canoe, his calves resting on the thwart, his head between the yuppie man's legs. And he passed out.

Annette stifled an involuntary moan. He was dying. And there was nothing she could do. He would be dead before
The thought made her choke. He might be dead now. She cursed the khaki couple in a silent rage. She cursed them and all people who gave nothing and took all. Pender was right. They were everywhere. Self-absorbed morons entitled to whatever they wanted, when they wanted it. The warmongers in the U.S., the ruthless capitalist wannabes in Ontario with their contempt for wilderness, their obsession with strip-mining and clear-cutting and "monetizing" the people's assets.

Her rage fueled a furious paddling cadence. They were on the pinch point in minutes. She knifed through the pincers, cutting left around one point, then a circle turn ninety-degrees to head east-northeast again. It was a perilous turn. For a few seconds, they were broadside to the waves. The water lapped at the very top of the canoe. She feared her boat would take water, maybe enough to drown the two men, maybe just enough to send them into full hypothermia. She wondered if the waves and wind would somehow capsize the boat with the yuppie lady in it. If that happened, Annette knew she would leave the woman to her own fate. You were right, Gabe, she thought. Sometimes there's no right answer.

Minutes later, she entered the Pickerel River delta, a soggy, confusing lowland filled with reeds and marsh plants. It was a classic bog waterway, twisting and turning in every direction, its current almost invisible. From countless journeys through the marsh, she knew the river cut south from the opening, even though your eyes told you it had to be the body of water continuing north-northeast. Annette slowed her hull speed to make sure she had plenty of space for her train of canoes to negotiate the tight curves. Fifteen minutes later, the river opened to a pond, the southwest terminus of French Lake. Home at last!

Spirits buoyed, she searched the far shore for any sign of human help. She started to cut northeast toward the park pavilion, where there would a be telephone and maybe a ranger, then saw two human figures on the sand beach near Baptism Creek just a hundred yards or so to her right. There was a parking lot just above the beach. She tried not to hope one of the people was Christy, just hoped they had a car or a van and a willingness to help.

Annette glanced again at Pender and the yuppie man. They looked dead. Their faces were an unearthly white, their lips blue. She couldn't tell if they were breathing. She charged for the beach, hoping the figure there that looked like Christy was Christy.

Fifty yards away, she could see that it was Christy and she was yelling to someone back up the wooded trail behind her, a short trail that led to the parking lot. Chalk one up for a benign, interactive god, Pender, Annette thought. As

she hit the sandy shallows, Christy splashed into the water
to pull the canoe ashore, Chaos leaped out of the canoe and
ran mindlessly on the beach. Eric, Annette's CSO assistant,
burst onto the beach from the trail.

Annette fell into Christy's hug and then leaned on her
daughter to get out of the canoe.

"These people are dying," she said. "We have to get them
to the hospital."

Christy looked at the two men in the bottom of her mother's canoe. "They might be dead, Mom."

Annette felt Pender's wrist for a pulse. It was there. Faint,
very rapid. Not normal but not dead.

"Is that Gabe?" asked Christy.

Annette nodded, choked on a sob, moved to the yuppie
man and checked his pulse. It was faint but stronger than
Pender's. It figured.

Eric trotted to join them. He waded into the water, looked
at the bodies in the canoe, turned pale, ran up on the beach,
and vomited.

"They aren't dead, you idiot," Christy yelled at him. "Help
me get them up to the van."

Annette reeled in the solo boats, beached Pender's long,
slender vessel, bent to check the khaki woman's pulse, trying
not to think that if anyone deserved to die, it was her. When
Annette grasped the woman's wrist, her eyes opened, clear
and blue. She blinked a few times. "Where are we?" she asked.

"We're at French Lake. We're taking your husband and
my friend to the hospital. Can you walk?"

The woman struggled to a sitting position. "I'll try."

Annette helped her sit on the beach, then joined Christy
and Eric to carry Pender and the khaki woman's husband to
the van. She came back to help the woman negotiate the

trail to the van and gestured for her to sit on the seat where her husband lay.

Annette called Chaos, who jumped into the van and began investigating every nook and corner. She slid into the farthest seat, where Pender was lying, eyes closed, skin deathly white. The khaki woman was still standing in the open door frame, disoriented, reluctant to sit next to her husband, who looked dead. "We're leaving right now," Annette screamed. "Get in!"

The woman started to object.

"In or out! We're leaving!"

Eric watched the interplay with an open mouth. Christy slid behind the steering wheel, a grim smile on her face. "All aboard!"

The woman got in, fumbled with the door. Eric got out, closed it, and then got back in. Christy sped out in a cloud of rocks and dust, Eric grabbing for his seatbelt, the yuppie woman pitching against the seat.

Annette covered Pender's upper body with her torso and tried to rub his arms and legs with her hands. His breathing was shallow and weak. She thought he might stop breathing at any moment, thought about what she should do then. Artificial respiration? Strike his chest to stimulate the heart to beat again? She tried to visualize it. She was crying aloud. Couldn't stop. It was the only thing keeping her going.

Christy made the run from to Atikokan at 140 kilometers per hour on Kings Highway 11.

Atikokan General Hospital was a rural, forty-one-bed facility with a staff of a half dozen family-medicine doctors dispensing care to the several thousand residents of Atikokan and thousands more spread across hundreds of square miles of the Canadian Shield. The derecho had kept the staff hopping, though—miraculously—only a few Quetico canoeists had been seriously injured, none fatally.

Christy called ahead, so the on-call physician and two EMTs were waiting as they pulled in. They rushed Pender and the khaki man, still unconscious, into the ER on gurneys. The khaki woman entered in a wheelchair.

Thirty minutes later, the physician came out to the waiting area to speak with Annette and Christy. In a small town, Dr. Mary Bonet was their family doctor and a friend.

"They're alive, but it's going to be touch and go for a while," Bonet started. "They're both hypothermic. We have them on oxygen and IVs, and I've started them on antibiotics. We packed them in heated blankets to get their body temperatures back to normal. I'm especially worried about the older man. He has chest congestion and a fever, and his pulse is racing. He could be developing pneumonia."

"But he's going to be okay?" Annette asked.

"It's too soon to tell. He's in trouble. We'll have to monitor him closely for the next twenty-four to forty-eight hours."

Annette closed her eyes and pursed her lips. Good God, not now.

Bonet paused for a moment. "The woman's health is okay, but she is very agitated over the loss of their equipment and the fact that they are going to miss an important series of dates in various places. She may need to be sedated."

Annette shook her head.

"Are they customers of yours?" Bonet asked.

"No," said Annette. "The older man is a friend of mine from long ago. He was my college boyfriend. We ran into that couple on the portage into Pickerel and then fished them out of the water when they capsized. I don't know anything about them except the lady wore the most stylish clothes I've ever seen in the wilderness, and she acted more like royalty than a canoe-tripper."

Bonet's eyes widened. It wasn't like Annette to take such exception to anyone.

Annette hung her head and cried. Christy put her arms around her mother and held her. Bonet put one hand on Annette's back, her other on Christy's. "Don't give up hope," she said. "He's in good shape. He's got a chance."

"He risked his life to save those fools," Annette sobbed. "Can you believe that?"

When she recovered, she sat with the registration clerk. The information she had to share was sketchy. She presumed the khaki people's identification documents went down with their gear in Pickerel Lake, and she knew Pender's went down when he jettisoned the packs to save the yuppie man. It was surprising, really, how little she knew about Pender. She gave the clerk his name and his last known address, along with the certain knowledge that he didn't live there anymore. She didn't know where he was headed after his canoe trip, but she had invited him to stay at her place while he figured things out.

Annette asked about the other members of the Survivors Club. Bill had been treated and released for a broken collarbone. The camper with the head injury had been flown to a larger hospital with neurological specialists. The others just had minor bumps and bruises.

Afterward, Christy told Annette to go home, shower, change into clean clothes, and get something to eat. "I'll stay here, and I'll call you if anything changes," she promised.

For the first time in days, Annette took notice of herself. Her clothes were rumpled and smeared with tree sap and soil, her hair matted and hanging askew. She could see blisters forming on her toes where the sandal strap rubbed. Her hands were sore from gripping the paddle. Her arms and back ached from the hours of hard paddling. She was glad there was no mirror handy. Her face must look like a Halloween mask. She nodded to Christy and thanked her. "Ask them to set up a chair or a cot or something in Gabe's room if you get the chance, okay?"

32

Christy called Annette from the hospital parking lot before dawn the next morning. Annette checked Pender, who was still asleep, and then picked up two cups of coffee before joining her daughter. They sat in the van's open doorway, side by side, mother and daughter sipping coffee, gazing eastward, waiting for the first light to seep into their world while Christy's daughter, Rebecca, slumbered in the back seat.

"I still remember the first time we did this," Christy said.

Annette was mute.

"I was thirteen, and I hated it here. I kept telling you I wanted to go live with Dad and be a city girl. I wanted to wear makeup and dresses and go to parties in beautiful houses. One morning you came in and woke me up and hauled me out to the lake and made me sit beside you drinking hot cider in the dark, shivering, waiting for sunrise. I kept whining and moaning, and you told me to be quiet and listen. When I finally did, there wasn't a sound in the world. I thought you were crazy and I said so. And you said, 'Keep listening.' I did, because there wasn't anything else to do. Pretty soon a little breeze rustled through pines and I heard the needles swish. Then a loon called, and I could hear the mourning in its voice. A fish broke the surface of the water. I couldn't see it, but I could hear it.

"Then you pointed across the lake, and I could see some light on the far horizon. You said, 'Watch this. It's a miracle.'

"And you told me how the sunlight comes every morning, how it chases away the dark, how just before we see it, it lights up Crayfish Lake, then Deman and Stetham and Ridge and Huronian and Mackie and Rule and Windigoostigwan and Nydia, and by the time we see it on the edge of Eva, it has reached us and moved on like the dawn of life moving at the speed of light."

Christy leaned against her mother.

"You said, 'You can go live in the city if you really want to, but you should get in touch with this place first. Most people never experience this. You can't buy it. You can't save it. You can't store it in a closet. You can feel it and you can remember it, but only if you experience it.'"

Annette laced an arm under Christy's arm and smiled.

"I never forgot that," Christy added.

"How many sunrises did you get up for that summer?" Annette asked, laughing.

"None. But I made my boyfriend watch a lot of sunsets with me."

They smiled.

"I'm just trying to say I love you, Mom. I hope Gabe makes it."

Annette nodded, sipped her coffee, put an arm around Christy, and hugged her close. "I love you too, sweetie."

After a silence, Christy spoke. "I guess the two of you hit it off."

Annette nodded. "It sort of ebbed and flowed, but yes, by the time we started back, I invited him to stay with us for a while."

"That's great."

"He was thinking maybe he'd do another week or so in the park, then come by. We were going to paddle to French Lake together. Then he was going to go to McKenzie and come back through the Falls Route. The derecho changed everything."

"Going to McKenzie in August? Is he crazy?"

"More desperate, I think. It's probably hard for you to imagine with so much of your life ahead of you, but he's sixty years old and everything that consumed him in life is gone."

"But sixty isn't that old. He's got lots of years left."

"It's not about the future. He lost his history. He said once, 'Everything I ever did is gone now. It's like I never existed.'"

They watched the light peek over the horizon and flood toward them.

"Every sunrise erases the night before, and every sunset wipes out the day," Christy murmured. "Those days and those nights will never happen again. It's sad when you think about it."

"Is it?" asked Annette. "Or is it the real miracle of life? Every day is a new day. Every night is a new night. A constant flow of new beginnings."

They finished their coffees, looked in on Rebecca, who was still sleeping soundly. Then Christy walked into the hospital to continue the vigil at Pender's bedside while Annette took Rebecca to Canadian Shield Outfitters, where she would shower and change and tend to her granddaughter while she started picking up the pieces of their merged outfitting businesses.

As a sun-drenched morning blossomed outside the hospital window, Pender stirred again, mumbling nonsensical syllables. As she had before, Christy stood at his side, took one of his hands in hers, and talked to him in a quiet voice.

"Good morning, Gabe Pender. Welcome to a beautiful day in Atikokan, Ontario, Canada. I'm Christy. I'll be your guide this morning. Ask me anything you want about northwest Ontario, and if I don't know the answer, I'll make something up."

His eyes remained closed, but his fingers jerked slightly.

"Hello, Gabe Pender. Are you in there?" The morning-shift nurse had told her to encourage him to come to a conscious state.

She squeezed his fingers lightly and continued talking. Nothing. She sat down again, looked out the window, wondered what Rebecca was doing right now, how her mom was holding up. Pender stirred again. She went to the bedside. This time his eyes flickered open. He blinked several times, trying to focus.

"Do you know who I am?" she asked. He didn't look as if he was really conscious.

He murmured something so weakly she couldn't hear it. She bent lower, putting her ear near his lips.

"You are your mother." He said it in a raspy whisper followed by a cough that seemed to hurt him horribly.

"I'll call the nurse," she said.

"Why?" He smiled weakly. His eyes closed. He mumbled something but drifted off in the middle of it.

Christy paged the nurse. She stared at Pender. He looked dead. The nurse swept into the room and took his pulse without a word.

"Is he alive?" Christy asked when the nurse let go of his wrist.

"Yes. Did you say he opened his eyes?"

Christy nodded yes. "He talked, too."

"What did he say?"

"He told me I looked like my mother."

"That's a good sign," said the nurse. "About his health, I mean." She smiled at her humor. "His pulse is stronger, too. The doctor will see him shortly, but he may go in and out of sleep for some time."

"So the outlook is good?"

"It's better than it was last night."

When the nurse left the room, Christy called her mother.

"He woke up for a minute." Her voice was excited. "Well, for a few seconds actually. But he talked. The nurse said it was a good sign."

"He talked? What did he say?" Annette was elated and at the same time feeling guilty for not having been there. What if he was disoriented and looking for her? A stranger in a strange land.

"I asked him, 'Do you know who I am?' And he opened his eyes and he said, 'You are your mother.' I almost fainted. Then he went back to sleep."

Annette smiled. Pender had a way with words.

———

Mother and daughter sat down to lunch in Pender's room.

"Tell me about the dog," Christy said.

Annette told her about the Stuarts and finding the dog on her way to the island. Trying to boat-train him. The confrontation. Swapping their lost gear for the dog.

"Chaos is a great name for him," Christy marveled. "But he's really a sweet dog. Are we going to keep him?"

"Maybe. He follows Pender everywhere, and Pender just loves the guy. Maybe he'll want to take him when he goes, but maybe not. The places he was talking about traveling to aren't good dog places. Stockholm. Paris."

"He doesn't seem like the Euro type," said Christy.

"Well, he mentioned the Maritime Provinces, too. Can you see him in Nova Scotia?"

"Maybe, but Newfoundland seems more like the guy you've told me about."

Before Christy could ask another question, Gus and Bill knocked softly and entered.

"How's the li'l fella doing?" Gus whispered.

Annette almost laughed out loud, two huge men trying to be quiet and polite. "You can talk in a normal voice, guys," she said. "He woke up for a minute this morning. He told Christy she looked like me. We're trying to decide if she should be insulted." Annette smiled so they'd know it was a joke.

"This is your daughter?" asked Gus. "Oh yes, sure. I can see it. I don't like to agree with the li'l fella, but I see his point." He crossed to Christy and extended a hand in greeting. "Ma'am, I'm Gus, and this one-armed bandit is my best friend Bill. Your mom and this mean old man here probably saved our lives."

Bill waved with his good arm, the other one trussed tightly to his chest in a V shape, much like Annette had rigged it. "It's true," he said. "Your mom's the best canoe tripper we've ever seen."

"And we're pretty experienced ourselves," said Gus.

"My wife's here to take us home," said Bill. "We wanted to thank both of you for everything."

Annette waved a hand. "We thank you. I know Pender would if he was awake right now. And I certainly do. You were good company. And Gus, even Pender said you were the best portager he ever saw."

"The li'l fella said that? Really?"

Annette nodded in the affirmative.

"I'll bet those words came hard."

They laughed quietly. Annette told Bill it was good to see him when he wasn't in pain. He beamed.

"You can get your canoe over at the CSO building," she said. "The staff knows who you are. Check the gear, too. I'm not sure which packs made it. We had to toss ours overboard when we fished the khaki people out of Pickerel. Did you hear about that?"

Gus nodded. "It was the talk of the town this morning. Some reporter at the White Otter Inn was telling everyone about the rescue on Pickerel yesterday and how one lady had to get everyone to French Lake on her own. I knew that was you."

"Actually, it was Pender who dove in and saved them," said Annette. "That's how he got hypothermia and pneumonia." She glanced at him sadly.

"And it was those yuppie shits he saved?" Bill said it more than asked it. "What a waste."

"We saw them checking out of here when we came in," he added. "The guy looks like he's been in a train wreck, but the lady looks like she's going to the prom. They saw us and neither one of them said a thing. I bet they didn't stop in here either, right?"

"Right." Annette shook her head slowly in wonder. "Some people."

"No kidding," said Gus. After a long silence, Gus shook his head and smiled. "Pender damn near killed me, and I was trying to help him. Then he turns around and damn near kills himself to save two people who wouldn't lift a finger to help anyone. Go figure, huh?"

"Pender has a universal wisdom to cover that," said Annette.

"Okay, I'll bite," said Gus.

"Life can be a mind fuck."

Gus stared blankly at her. "I don't get it," he said.

"Would you have let them drown?"

"Hell yes!"

"No, you wouldn't," said Annette.

"Why would I want to save people like that?"

"Because it's not about people like that, not for people like you and Pender."

Gus glanced at Bill. Bill shrugged and said, "Maybe you two were related in a previous life."

"We were probably brothers," said Gus.

Gus and Bill scribbled their addresses and phone numbers on a piece of paper. "I'd like it if you'd let me know how Pender's doing," said Gus, handing the paper to Annette. "When he's up and about—and he will be up and about, I know it, he's way too mean to die—tell him I meant what I said at the plane."

"What did you say?"

"He'll tell you."

After the men left, Annette turned to Christy. "How do you suppose that reporter heard about the rescue yesterday?"

Christy blushed. "He may have been over at CSO when I hauled in the gear last night. There were a bunch of people there, and I did some braggin' on my mom."

"Why were so many people there?"

"Well, Eric and I went back to French Lake to get the canoes and the gear, and I called Dan to let us in at CSO. The word must have just spread. Someone called the *Progress*, and their intern and some other reporter came, maybe from Toronto?"

"What on earth did you tell them?"

"Pretty much what Gus said. I told them you had led a bunch of stranded canoeists out of the park after the storm. When no one else could get out, you got them out. And somewhere on Pickerel, you found this man and woman who had capsized, and you paddled into French Lake yourself with three half-dead people and two canoes in tow."

Annette nodded wearily. "It's been a hell of a week."

33

When Christy left, Annette positioned her chair next to Pender's bed and set to work on a laptop computer. Pender stirred frequently. Each time, she stopped what she was doing and held his hand.

The doctor came and went in the early afternoon. "Better," she said, "but no promises."

In midafternoon, with Pender's window enveloped in shadows, Annette set aside her work and walked to the vending machines to get a soft drink. She lingered on her way back to look at art hanging on the walls and to peer out the big window at Atikokan, the greatest town on earth. She wondered if Pender could ever love this place like she did, doubting it could possibly compare to Michigan Avenue and traveling to the great capitals of Europe. It didn't seem possible, except that it was a choice she had made. Years ago. And had never regretted.

She thought he'd recover and he would probably move on before winter. But maybe he would come back after a year of globe-trotting. He seemed to be looking for something, some kind of human connection. Maybe he'd find it in the

Maritimes, or maybe in Paris. Or go back to Chicago. Or not. Maybe there was no right answer for him anymore.

When she returned to his room, Pender's eyes were open. He was blinking and looking about, trying to get his bearings.

"Well, the prodigal awakes! Good afternoon, Gabe Pender. Do you know where you are?"

"A hospital?" his voice was just above a whisper. His words came slowly.

"Very good! You're in our very own Atikokan General Hospital. We're quite proud of it."

"Atikokan . . . a hospital? . . .. Didn't know that."

"We have lots of things you don't know about," Annette laughed. "How are you feeling?"

He smiled weakly and rasped, "I feel like Mike Tyson just beat the crap out of me." He coughed painfully, saw the tubes and wires attached to his wrist and hands. "What day is it?"

Annette thought for a moment. "I think it's Tuesday."

Pender coughed, winced, and tried to remember when he was last aware of the days of the week. He couldn't remember. "How long have I been here?"

"We got you here last night, around six. It's about three in the afternoon right now. Do you remember anything about yesterday?"

He thought for a moment. "I remember that portage . . . getting people on that floatplane." He thought some more. "I remember those khaki people capsizing . . . dumb bastards . . . jumping in the water to get them out." He paused, smiled weakly. "Boy, that was a cold motherfucker . . . nasty bitch fought me."

"Do you remember me telling you not to jump in after them?"

Pender closed his eyes and seemed to gather his strength to answer. "Yeah . . . should have listened."

It was quiet. Pender coughed weakly, closed his eyes and grimaced, fighting off pain. "Chaos . . . did he make it back? . . . I miss him."

"He made it. He came back to the canoe just in time. You pulled him in."

He couldn't recall it. "How about that . . . just remember getting back in . . . so cold . . . so cold . . . couldn't stop shivering . . . thought . . . going to die . . . forty years . . . world just went black."

"You don't remember meeting my daughter?"

He closed his eyes in thought. "Christy?"

Annette nodded. "You told her she looked just like me."

"I said that?"

"Yes. And we're both offended. You told a young woman she looks like her old mother. Good work, Pender."

"Shit." He groaned and closed his eyes.

"I was just kidding." She held his unwired hand in both of hers. The warmth felt good. He kept his eyes closed and smiled, focusing his senses on her touch.

"Christy thinks you're handsome."

"Don't bullshit a bullshitter."

"Okay, she didn't say that. But it's what I think, and I raised her. She knows what a good-looking man looks like."

The silence was longer this time. "Am I going to make it?"

"The doctor said you're doing better. You have pneumonia. They aren't making any promises, but no one told me to try to get into your will either. And your buddy Gus has already said you're too mean to die."

"Gus? . . .. Wouldn't know squat about pneumonia . . . he's a brain surgeon." He coughed and blanched in pain.

Annette bent over and kissed him softly on the cheek. His pain hurt her.

"By the way," he whispered, "you're in my will."

Annette scoffed.

"Really . . . just before the animal shelter . . . maybe just after."

"We hadn't even met. What if you hated me?"

A long silence, so long Annette thought he had passed out. He licked his lips, swallowed, whispered, "Not my problem . . . if I'm dead . . ." His voice trailed off. His eyes closed. He was as still and pale as death, his skin lined and sagging. This man so vibrant in her memories all these years now reduced to a gray corpse. Annette reeled. How could he be dead? She checked the monitor. The numbers that rotated through the screen looked similar to the numbers she had seen all afternoon. She called the duty nurse who came running.

She told Annette that Pender had just fallen asleep again. It was a good thing.

This time when the doctor came through on her rounds, Annette insisted on some answers.

"What is your relationship to Mr. Pender?" the doctor asked. It was a new doctor, a woman Annette didn't know.

"I have no legal standing, if that's what you mean," said Annette. "We were college friends, and we had a reunion in the park. He has an ex-wife and a daughter who he says he isn't close with. I think his parents are dead. I don't think he has any siblings."

"It might be time to get in touch with his daughter," said the doctor. "His pulse is slow, his temperature is high, and the congestion is bad. There's no guarantee he'll make it through the night."

Annette sat heavily. She had expected an all clear. "How can that be?" she asked. "How can that be? We just talked. We had a whole conversation. He was telling jokes."

"These things can be tricky. Maybe the conversation just tired him out and caused his vitals to dip temporarily. Or . . ." Her voice trailed off.

"Or maybe it was his last gasp?"

"Something like that," said the doctor.

Annette noticed the youth of the doctor for the first time. She was younger than Christy. Maybe just out of med school.

Later, a woman from hospital administration stopped in to speak with Annette, looking for contact information for Pender's next of kin, insurance, current address, and all the other blanks in his registration paperwork. Annette had no answers.

"Do you know anything about his family?" the woman asked.

Annette shared what little she knew.

"Can you help me reach the ex-wife? Maybe she can help."

"I think I have her name and the company where she works," said Annette. "I'll have to go through e-mails. I'll get that information to you when I find it."

When the administration woman left, Annette went through her e-mail history with Pender. She found the mention of Peg and the company she ran. An Internet search turned up the company's website, which listed Peg McLanahan as president. She dutifully jotted down the contact information. Before she closed her laptop, she clicked on a link that took her to Peg McLanahan's welcome letter. There was a crisp portrait of her in a dark navy-blue suit, white blouse with a ruffled collar, a beautiful amber pendant slung from a fine gold chain, pearl earrings peeking out from a flawless bob. She was smiling in a way that was both professional and personally engaging, and she was beautiful, as Pender had said. The picture made Annette feel dowdy.

She wondered what Peg McLanahan was like. Was McLanahan her professional name, or had she remarried? From what Pender said, Peg was the type to keep her own identity. Was she cold and cruel or just tired of Pender, or was there something Pender left out about their relationship? Did she hate him, or would she want to know he was fighting for his life?

Annette felt an overwhelming urge to call the woman just to hear how she responded to the news that her ex-husband was lying close to death in a distant place. She knew she shouldn't call. She had no standing to get involved. That was the hospital's job. But she might very well save time for the hospital administration people, she rationalized. She could share the news of Pender's condition and say she was trying to help the hospital locate a next of kin or someone with power of attorney.

She dialed the number. It was 4 PM in Illinois, a good time to catch management types at their desks.

An administrative assistant answered on the second ring. Annette stuttered for a moment. What to say? Where to start? "Oh, hello. May I speak with Ms. McLanahan please?"

"She's on another line. Can I tell her what it's about?"

"Yes. I'm calling from northwest Ontario—Canada—and I'm trying to get next of kin information for Gabe Pender, who is, I think, Ms. McLanahan's ex-husband."

"Is he dead?"

"He's ill."

The assistant put her on hold. Two minutes later, just as Annette was giving up hope, the line clicked and a pleasant, animated voice filled her ear. "Peg McLanahan. What's going on with Gabe?"

"Good afternoon, Ms. McLanahan. I'm sorry to bother you at work. I'm afraid he's in serious condition in our local hospital. I'm calling from Atikokan, Ontario, and we're trying to locate next of kin or anyone with power of attorney for him or anyone who can help the hospital contact his physician or his insurance company."

"My goodness! Poor Gabe!" There was something about her voice. Annette could feel it more than define it. She was skilled at these things. Sincere but not emotionally involved. It was as if she was hearing that a long-time customer was seriously ill. Interesting.

"What happened?"

"He rescued some people in Quetico Park, but he got hypothermia and developed pneumonia."

"Good God. I always told him those canoe trips were dangerous. How sad. Now, let me think for a minute. His next of kin would be my daughter, Margaret. His parents are dead, and he doesn't have any sibs. But he and Margaret aren't close. I would guess his financial advisor either has power of attorney or knows who does. If you hold for a moment, I'll get phone numbers for both of them."

Annette thanked her and waited, wondering who has the phone number of their ex-spouse's financial manager at their fingertips?

Seconds later, Peg clicked back on the line with phone numbers and e-mail addresses for Margaret and the financial manager. "We have the same financial manager," she explained. "He's fantastic, and it's not like we fought over money."

"Margaret might like to know that Gabe was keeping a journal for her," Annette said. "It was lost in a storm, but it might mean something to her that he was reaching out."

"I'll tell her," Peg said, her voice unemotional.

Annette thanked her again and started to say goodbye, but Peg interrupted her.

"So," she said, "who are you?"

Annette inhaled. Who indeed? "I'm an old friend of Gabe's. From college. He looked me up on the Internet last winter. I have a business up here. We decided to meet in the park and get caught up on old times. We've had some bad storms up here, and when we were coming out, we tried to help some people when their canoe capsized." Annette felt like she was babbling.

"What's your name?" Peg asked.

"Annette. Annette Blain."

"Were you the one who was in the antiwar movement?"

"Yes. He mentioned that?"

"Oh, yes. When we were younger, just starting out, you know, we talked about things like that . . . where we'd been, what had affected us emotionally. You made a big impression. He told me when you broke up, you told him you hoped he went to Vietnam and got killed. He never forgot that. I bet nothing ever touched him like that. Certainly nothing in our marriage."

Annette caught her breath. It was like a curse, those words said in anger so long ago, words that were the opposite of what she meant, but she said them and that might be the thought he took to the grave. Tears flowed freely.

"Thank you for telling me." Annette managed not to sob when she said it, then covered the mouthpiece of the phone and doubled over in pain.

"I'll let Margaret know. Is there a number she can call if she wants?"

Annette gave her the telephone number for the hospital and for her cell phone.

"How are the people he rescued?" asked Peg.

"They're fine. They left for home this morning."

"That figures. Poor Gabe. He always did have a misguided sense of social conscience. I hope the people he saved were worth it."

"I guess they were to him."

"I meant, like, the prime minister or an ambassador or something."

"No," said Annette, tears falling freely now. "Nothing like that." It wasn't about the people. It was about Pender. Who he needed to be.

They said goodbye, and Annette sat back, wiped her tears with a tissue, and thought about Peg McLanahan's calm reaction to the news about Pender. Annette wondered how would she react to the same news about Rob? She'd cry, she thought. She'd cry for him and for their daughters and for the lost possibilities of their lives together. Unless you hated someone, how could you not feel something at their passing?

How could Pender, of all people, end up with a wife like that?

Then again, how could she have ended up with Rob?

An hour later, Pender began groaning and writhing in bed. Annette rang for help. Dr. Bonet and a nurse answered the call.

"How long has this been going on?" Dr. Bonet asked as she checked his vital signs.

"Just the last few minutes."

"Is Mr. Pender an athlete?"

"Yes," said Annette. "He is a distance canoe racer, lifts weights, exercises a lot."

"I think this pulse is in his normal range," Dr. Bonet said. "I'll bet his normal resting pulse is around fifty. The congestion is still there, but the antibiotics are working. His lungs are starting to clear."

Annette exhaled with relief and leaned back in the chair.

"Well, let's hold the band and the fireworks," Dr. Bonet said. "We have no history on Mr. Pender, so we have to wait and see. But if I was a betting woman, I'd put my money on him feeling pretty chipper by morning." She looked at Annette. "Are you okay?"

Annette nodded, swallowed. "Yes. This is great news."

She began thanking Bonet for coming to see Pender personally. The doctor waved a hand in a dismissive fashion. "It took two minutes to drive here. It was faster than calling. Try that in Toronto, eh?"

Pender woke up an hour later, almost twenty-four hours after he had been admitted. Annette hovered over him, drawn by his indistinct mumbles and movement.

He opened his eyes, blinked, and slowly focused on Annette's face. He smiled dreamily. "Oh my, what a beautiful sight," he said. His voice was weak but strong enough for Annette to hear without bending low. He closed his eyes and rested a moment. "You can't imagine how many nights

that face was in my dreams," he murmured. "Am I alive, or
is this heaven?"

Annette kissed him. "Your prospects for heaven aren't that
good," she said. He smiled languidly.

"How do you feel?" she asked finally.

"Not too bad." He coughed a shallow cough. "It only hurts
when I cough."

Annette put her hand on his forehead. "You feel cooler."

"I'm hungry," he said. "Do they serve food here? Maybe a
moose-hump steak? Slow-roasted bear?"

Annette rang for the nurse. An hour later, Pender sat up
for the first time and enjoyed a meal of broth, crackers, and
dry toast.

"That looks pretty awful compared to the gourmet fare
you were serving up in the park," Annette said.

"I'm so hungry it doesn't matter." He took a few more
mouthfuls. "I guess my herbs and spices are rolling around
the bottom of Pickerel Lake now, eh?"

"You're talking like a Canadian already, eh? It's a sign!"

Pender laughed lightly, coughed.

"Yes," said Annette. "You threw our packs overboard to
get the khaki man in the boat. Do you remember that?"

Pender nodded that he did. "How are the khaki people?"

"They're fine. They left this morning. Not a scratch on
them, not even a runny nose."

"What were their names?"

Annette shrugged. "No one knows. They left without saying a word to anyone."

"No kidding? They didn't even thank you?"

Annette shook her head no. "They didn't even thank you.
Or ask if you were living or dead."

"I guess we were idiots to save them, huh."

"Like you always say, it wasn't about them."

"I guess."

After a silence, Annette smiled. "Pender?"

"Yes."

"Actually, it was you who saved them. You jumped in the water. It was you. So according to the old Japanese belief, you're now responsible for their lives."

"What a disgusting thought."

"Why do you suppose the Japanese have that belief?"

"Because you messed with karma. Those people were supposed to die, but you kept them in this world, so the rest of their lives are your responsibility."

"Oh. I never thought of it that way. So how does it feel having two stepchildren like them?"

"Makes me feel better about my daughter. She'd have said thanks." Pender thought for a moment. "You know, you're the one who saved my life."

"Don't get maudlin on me."

"I'm not. I just want you to recognize your responsibilities here."

"I'm not Japanese. That doesn't apply to me."

"It doesn't matter who said it. It's a universal truth. You have to change my diapers when I get senile."

34

Two days later, Pender served lunch for Christy and Rebecca at a picnic table in their backyard. The sun brightened and dimmed as patches of clouds flowed in a liquid stream overhead. Beams of light sifted through the leaves of a birch tree and covered the table in a dappled pattern that fluttered and waved with each puff of breeze.

Rebecca crawled on Pender's lap as they sat down. He hugged her and kissed her temple. They had been bonding all day. Chaos had shadowed his every movement and sat next to him at the table, putting his head on Pender's knee.

"My daughter is quite taken with you, Gabe," said Christy. She was squinting in the sunlight and smiling. She had her mother's smile. She had her mother's everything.

"She won my heart right away. I was thinking how nice it would be to try raising a child again. Right up until she crapped in her nappies."

They conversed quietly as they ate, Christy raving about the meal, Pender admitting he was trying to show off, Rebecca grabbing Pender's attention when it strayed from her too long.

"You know, she's not like this with everyone," Christy said. "This is really special."

"Maybe she senses that I wish I was her grandfather."

"Maybe she feels like you are her grandfather."

Pender hugged the little girl, smiled.

"Did you tell my mother you wished I was your daughter?"

"Yes."

"But you didn't even know me."

"No." He shrugged.

"I feel a bond with you," Christy said. "My mom has talked about you so much I feel like I know you. Now, seeing you with Rebecca, I see how you are with her. You just sort of fit together. I have this eerie feeling you were supposed to be my dad. And I shouldn't be saying this."

Pender stared at her.

"Really, I'm sorry. I was way off base." Christy blushed.

"No," said Pender. "It's not like that. I've felt a connection, too. Think your mom has linked us in some kind of mystical way?"

"It doesn't make sense, but it feels like that."

"Makes more sense than a god who works in mysterious ways."

Christy smiled. "Mom told me you were an atheist."

"Hah," he waved a hand. "We're all atheists. Some say so, some hedge their bets, and a lot of people use religion to codify their hatreds. We're all connected."

———————

Pender helped Annette and Christy get their businesses ready for the Labor Day surge, laundering sleeping bags and linens, cleaning tents and cook kits, mopping floors, scouring toilets.

When he was off antibiotics and feeling good, he went into the park with a crew to clear portage trails, taking Chaos with him. He learned to handle a chainsaw and how to pack logs into corduroy walkways across wet terrain. He helped place rocks to bolster washed-out paths and move the carcasses of fallen trees so that new growth could prosper.

He camped with other people for only the second time in his life—the first having been his outing with Annette and, eventually, the Survivors Club.

He fished every night with other members of the crew, took his turn at cleanup, graciously accepting his appointment as permanent dinner chef. He lay in the tent one night listening to wolves howl, Chaos's body rigid next to his. Later, he woke to loon calls, then fell back asleep.

When they returned to Atikokan, he had seven new friends. After another week, seeing his new friends at a church social, a softball game, and a couple of different restaurants, he had more friends. He recognized people wherever he went, though he couldn't remember everyone's name.

The bond with Rebecca and Christy grew stronger despite how exhausting Pender found the frequency of contact and conversation to be.

Annette asked him how it felt to see the area like a local sees it. He said it was like the difference between living in New York and visiting there. He used to just see it. Now he was experiencing everything—the town, the people, the nooks and crannies. "There's a personality emerging," he said.

"Is that a good thing?"

"Sure. People are nice here. Cars stop in the middle of the block to let you cross the street. You folks look after each other better than any place I've been. But not everything I see is storybook stuff. The town has its share of alcoholics and someone at the hospital told me the area needs a methadone clinic. Jesus, there's just no escaping that shit, you know?"

They were quiet for a while.

"Have you made plans for the fall and winter yet?" Annette asked.

Pender shrugged. "I'd like to stay . . ."

"But . . .?" Annette could feel a second thought coming.

"But it's a risk. We both need to understand that."

Annette felt a sense of dread creeping over her body. "What are we risking?"

"I'm starting to take you for granted already. There are some whole days where even though I look at you and talk to you and I like being near you, I don't actually see you."

Annette's face puckered into a questioning grimace.

"I look at you, but I don't notice what you're wearing or the color of your hair or how beautiful your eyes are."

"Everyone does that."

"Yeah, but for forty years I remembered you as a goddess. I could visualize your face in perfect focus, the way you smiled, how you looked in a sweatshirt. I remembered how your hand felt to hold, your eyes, how you walked."

"So?"

"So if I stay, you become human."

"I am human."

"I know. But if you become human in my mind, everything changes. Pretty soon, we're like every old couple anywhere. We plod along in a routine, birthdays, Christmases, barbeques, watch the news on television. We keep doing that until one of us dies. So it's like, if I stay, I die. This is it. This is all there is."

Annette shook her head. "You are so full of shit, Pender. Do you think if you move on, your life will be better?"

"No. But if I stay, it could be the end of something."

"What?"

"The adventure."

"You lost me."

"Finding you, after all these years. It feels like the end of an adventure. Like an explorer who's been out in the wilderness for forty years, searching and fighting, adapting, making it work, finally finding the lost treasure. In the middle of dancing and celebrating, it hits him: this is the end of the adventure. That the best part of his life was the search, not the treasure."

"You sure know how to flatter a girl."

After a silence, he looked at her. "We both know I'm staying. I couldn't live with myself if I left you now. But I have to be honest. I'm not sure I really belong here. I don't feel like I belong anywhere."

When he said the words, Annette knew this was the truth about Pender. Not the only truth, but the truth that brought him to this place and this time.

"You do belong here. You've always belonged here. It just took you sixty years to get here. Typical."

"I wish I felt as sure as you do. I'm not even sure I can hack the winter. The only day we experienced thirty below, it hurt to breathe. I stayed in and read a book until it got back up to minus ten. What am I going to do when it stays minus thirty for a week?"

"We have books," she said. "You can read to your heart's content."

"What will you be doing?" he asked.

"Cross-country skiing. Ice fishing. Getting the cabins ready. Life goes on."

"You're one tough woman," Pender marveled.

"No. I just got here before you did."

"Funny you'd say that. The first time I came up here, I kept thinking, Damn, if I'd seen this place before I finished college, I might never have gone into the army."

"You would have served," said Annette. "You were meant to. But, you were meant to be here, too. This place exists for people like you. And me."

Pender was mute, his face a question mark.

"This is the Canadian Shield, and Quetico is the heartbeat of the Shield," said Annette. "It's not for everyone."

"That's for sure," Pender laughed.

"It's for people who need more than wealth and ease. The hard winters keep the place pristine. Like a biblical flood that washes out the heathens. The people who live here are like the animals who live here—either they *want* to live here, *just* here . . . or they can't survive anywhere else."

"Which am I?" Pender asked.

"You tell me."

"Maybe both," he said.

Annette nodded. "I agree. We just have to get you acclimatized. For the holidays this year, I'll take you on our Christmas picnic. The girls and I have been doing it since they were children. We'll eat Christmas sandwiches and sip Christmas cider and sing Christmas carols in one of our special places. Are you game?"

"What if it's minus twenty? Can't we stay in and watch a football game? I can't enjoy the holidays if someone isn't getting their bones broken."

"No football game. We just layer up and get out there. It's fun, you'll see. We get a great view of a frozen lake that's five hundred feet deep and a forest that stretches to the horizon, and we'll be sitting on a boulder bigger than a house that's more than a million years old. How would that make you feel?"

"Young," said Pender, just to make her smile. She did, and it was just like his dreams, gentle and warm, except he could touch her and put his arms around her and feel her soft breath on his skin.

Acknowledgments

The road from magazine journalism to long-form fiction is filled with potholes and mind-numbing doubts and perilous missteps. For mortals like me, the journey can only be completed through the help of others. Here are just a few of the people and institutions who helped me shape the final draft of *Alone on the Shield*.

My brother, Scott Landers, and my wife, Taffy, had the courage to read the first draft of this book in its dreary entirety. Scott wrote a detailed and actionable critique of it, and Taffy's comments helped me shape the characters of Pender and Annette. To appreciate their sacrifices, it's important to know that I offered the first draft to the Department of Homeland Security, suggesting it could be read to the detainees at Guantanamo Bay in lieu of waterboarding, but they felt waterboarding was more humane.

Several writer groups provided immense help: the Chicago Writers Association (especially founder Randy Richardson), the Off-Campus Writers Workshop (especially my Critique Group colleagues), and the Novel-in-Progress Bookcamp in Wisconsin.

Four beta-readers risked their sanity to review the next-to-final draft of this book, wading through an avalanche of typos, misspellings, and fragments of old drafts floating like space debris through the current draft . . . and helping me fix flaws in plot and characters: Larry Green, my friend and colleague of forty years or so, is a man of letters, and his spirit of independence and rebellion against ill-informed authority inspired part of Gabe Pender's character.

Andy Marein and Rhonda McDonnell are veterans of the Novel-in-Progress Bookcamp and accomplished writers who bring intellect, empathy, and integrity to everything they do, including the analysis of a colleague's work.

Geoff Coulson's day job is warning preparedness meteorologist for the Meteorological Service of Canada. Geoff took the time to educate me about extreme weather events in the northern plains and prairies of North America. There aren't many, and a derecho of the magnitude described in this book hasn't been observed in the Canadian Shield, but it lingers on the edge of possibility.

My special thanks to two editors: Chris Nelson gave me early encouragement and direction, and Richard Thomas (of Darkhouse Press) provided the comprehensive critique that shaped the final draft. All writers should have the benefit of editors like these, and more important, all writers should appreciate the unique value they bring to our work.

And finally, my thanks to Al Hembd, a veteran of the shooting war in Vietnam and a friend who took the time to share his thoughts about this book, and especially about Gabe Pender.

About the Author

Kirk Landers launched his professional writing career in the US Army, later entering the special-interest and trade magazine worlds. His magazines won more than a hundred awards for journalistic excellence, and he is a member of the Construction Writers Hall of Fame. He lives in the suburbs of Chicago.